# Under and Over

D1333817

# Under & Over

## Rachel Rigby

Copyright © 2022 by Rachel Rigby.

ISBN:          Softcover              978-1-6641-1830-0
               eBook                 978-1-6641-1829-4

All rights reserved. No part of this book may be reproduced or transmitted in any form or by any means, electronic or mechanical, including photocopying, recording, or by any information storage and retrieval system, without permission in writing from the copyright owner.

This is a work of fiction. Names, characters, places and incidents either are the product of the author's imagination or are used fictitiously, and any resemblance to any actual persons, living or dead, events, or locales is entirely coincidental.

Any people depicted in stock imagery provided by Getty Images are models, and such images are being used for illustrative purposes only.
Certain stock imagery © Getty Images.

Print information available on the last page.

Rev. date: 02/14/2023

**To order additional copies of this book, contact:**
Xlibris
UK TFN: 0800 0148620 (Toll Free inside the UK)
UK Local: (02) 0369 56328 (+44 20 3695 6328 from outside the UK)
www.Xlibrispublishing.co.uk
Orders@Xlibrispublishing.co.uk
840335

# Contents

# Chapter 1

# Mexico

Eleanor awakens face down in a sand dune. The sea looks blurry in the distance. Her eyes are burning and her mouth is filled with the bitter taste of blood and salt. She's still drunk from the night before. She tries to get up but collapses in a heap, swept away in a flurry of sand to the bottom of the dune.

She groggily brushes herself down, limbs exposed in a thong bikini and a flimsy, torn cover up. Her bikini top has come untied and she can see it fluttering in the sand nearby.

Her red hair is matted and stuck to her head; wet with salt water, sweat, and what feels like blood. Eleanor lifts her hand to shield her eyes from the harsh sun and flinches at the sight of her naked ring finger, marked with a tan line where her wedding band used to be.

Reality cuts through the haze of alcohol and her heart sinks when she remembers the sorry state of her life, and the domestic mess she's been running away from.

She can't even bring herself to care what happened the previous night. Things couldn't get much worse. *"Bring it on, keep the shit coming,"* she croaks into the harsh blue sky above her.

Blinking in the sun, she spots a rusty white caravan within crawling distance. It's pitched on an island of green grass, like a shabby oasis among the dunes. She retrieves her bikini top and manages to slip it on, wincing with every movement.

Dragging herself up the caravan's crumbling steps, she leans on the cracked chrome door handle and the door falls open easily. *There's a sink*. Gratefully, she swallows water straight from the tap, then sinks down onto a brown fake leather sofa in the otherwise-bare living room. She's longing for the alcohol to take her away again, but its numbing effects are wearing off.

A man appears at the doorway of the caravan, anger written all over his weather-beaten face.

"Who the hell are you?" He shouts in a Texan accent.

"My name's Eleanor…sorry, I can't remember much. I just woke up this morning on the sand dunes…" Eleanor struggles to find words that make sense. "I've got no bag, no nothing. I saw your place. I've been attacked. Can you take me to hospital?"

Eleanor starts to lean toward him but immediately slumps back on the sofa.

"Do I have a choice?" The man is older than she is, maybe in his fifties, with silver sideburns and a deeply-creased face.

"Fine, don't help me then," Eleanor says, trying to get up.

"I'll take you to a private clinic, but that's it. And you need some clothes on." Her reluctant rescuer reaches out a grimy hand and helps Eleanor to her feet. He leaves for a minute and comes back with a T-shirt for her to throw on. In silence, they leave the caravan and walk the few steps to his red pick-up truck. Her head throbs and her whole body is starting to ache.

Wincing, she lets him help her into the passenger seat. He drives fast once they hit the dirt track. Sand and grit spew out behind the noisy engine, and she flinches at every bone-rattling bump in the road.

"Are you really taking me to the hospital?" Eleanor is slowly sobering up and becoming suspicious of this unshaven stranger. Maybe he was the one who attacked her last night?

She's suddenly convinced of it. And equally convinced that she doesn't even care if he's a serial killer.

"Put me out of my misery, kill me if you want," she says, looking at his dirty cowboy hat and his grubby hands at the wheel.

"Girl, you're crazy. You're the one that broke into my caravan. If I wanted to hurt you I wouldn't be driving, would I?" His eyes stay fixed on the road and he clenches his jaw.

"I'm all on my own and I think I really am going crazy." Eleanor's voice is cracked, her throat still dry. Everything hurts.

"Mexico is no place to come alone. It's no place to drink alone either." He takes his gaze off the road long enough to give Eleanor the side eye.

She knows she must still reek of last night's tequila and feels the judgement in his glance.

They hit another bump in the road and pain shoots through her face, but it's followed by a wave of relief when she realises they're pulling into the car park of the emergency room.

Speaking in Spanish, the American gruffly hands Eleanor over to the doctor and hops back in his van. She feels abandoned when he pulls away in a cloud of dust and exhaust fumes. The doctor takes her to a private room and asks her to lie down on a clinical metal bed.

"You were drinking last night?" The doctor's words sound more like a statement than a question, but Eleanor is so happy to hear him speak English that she doesn't take offence.

"There's no need to be embarrassed, I just need to know so we can make the right tests. I assume you don't remember anything that happened?"

"What do you mean?"

"I mean, do you remember how you ended up robbed, beaten and on the sand dunes near Mike's place?"

"No, sorry. I don't." Eleanor says sheepishly. She is aware that her behaviour might be more appropriate for a teenage girl than a woman in her thirties.

So, her caravan friend is Mike.

"I'm going to test your blood for Rohypnol", the doctor is matter of fact. "We've had a few cases of spiked drinks recently."

She's still processing his words when he asks her which hotel she's staying at.

"It's the Oaxaca, but I have no money. Everything's gone, even my phone." Eleanor realises she's crying.

"Do you have travel insurance?" Apparently unmoved, the doctor is efficiently cleaning her right eye even as tears drop slowly down her cheeks. She nods in between his cotton wool dabs. Slipping an antibiotic drip into her arm, he says: "we are also going to have to do some vaginal tests, to see if you were sexually assaulted. How about HIV or STDs, you got anything we should know about?"

"No." Eleanor smarts at the bluntness of his words. She hadn't thought about the possibility of an STD. But she doesn't feel any pain to suggest she's been sexually violated. Perhaps she should think herself lucky.

The doctor tells her he will have to report the incident to local police.

He's so blase about the process, it makes Eleanor wonder just how many tourist victims come through these worn hospital doors. But she doesn't have time to dwell on it: the drip releasing little drops of vital fluids into her vein soon lulls her into sleep.

Two Mexican policemen abruptly disrupt her weird dreams. They are standing over her, dressed as though they are part of the royal guard. They look absurd to her sleep-hazy mind, and she fails to stifle a giggle.

But they aren't laughing. "Madam, we want to ask you about last night," says the taller, darker of the pair in a thick Mexican accent.

"I took a tour that went to the Mitla tree, you know that giant huge tree...and finished with a tequila tasting. I did that, I remember because I was drinking Mescal at the tequila factory, thinking it was a lot better than the tequila I used to drink in college. Then the guide took me to some club... with his friends." She's rambling, and talking more to herself than to the policemen, trying to get things straight in her own head.

"Do you remember the name of the tour group, or the guide?"

"No, not really. It was Miras Travel or something...does that sound right? The guide was older. He knows reiki." As soon as she said it, she internally chastised her brain for bringing up this apparently random fact.

"Sounds like Pedro at Miras," the smaller policeman, whose moustache makes him look like somebody playing the role of a Mexican cop in a film, seems to have jumped on the reiki connection. But he's already moving on: "We brought a claim form, so you can keep these documents for your travel insurance. Please tell us what was stolen."

"My iPhone, my money...I think it was about 400 pesos...my credit cards and my camera."

*My life, basically…* She thinks to herself.

The policemen take the rest of her details and leave just as the doctor comes back in.

"I'm keeping you overnight for observation. Tomorrow you can return to your hotel. I have asked the police to let reception know you are here."

"Ok." Eleanor can see the doctor is in a rush, with no time for small talk

"Do you want to make a phone call to your family to let them know you are OK?" He asks.

Eleanor knows that if her mother knew she was in hospital she would fly straight over and that would be the end of her trip, when it was only just getting started.

"No, I don't need to call anyone."

The doctor leaves, and Eleanor hauls herself up to survey the damage in the mirror. Her right eye is deep purple to the cheekbone. A long, red scratch runs down her right cheek to her chin.

Looking at this wreck of a face is like looking at a stranger. She can't see any emotion in those blackened eyes. She finds it hard to believe she ever felt loved, safe, and secure. But she did, once. She would do anything to be back there in that happy place again.

# Chapter 2

# *Modern Romance*

The warmth of the roaring fire in the pub enveloped Eleanor as she elbowed open the door of the Pitcher & Piano on Fleet Street.

Her eagle eye almost immediately swooped in on a good-looking man standing in front of her at the long wooden bar. He was struggling to catch the bartender's attention, but he didn't have to try to catch hers. She'd already given him the once over and approved of his woollen sweater and the blue jeans whose loose fit didn't disguise the pertness of his backside.

Single for longer than she cared to remember, Eleanor was on a mission to rectify the situation and instinctively gave every half-decent looking guy the once over as soon as she clapped eyes on them.

She was blatant about it, filled with the breezy confidence that came with knowing she was eye-catching herself. Her long red hair, Pilates-toned physique and designer wardrobe usually drew admiring glances from the well-to-do types she was attracted to. Which made it all the more frustrating that she was still single.

A financial journalist with a sense of humour as sharp as her sense of style, Eleanor outwardly laughed about her on-the-shelf status, but deep down it gnawed at her. She was all too aware that her youthful looks would not last too much longer.

It seemed like all her friends were married. Some more happily than others, but married all the same. Her own parents - still living in wedded bliss - had surprised everybody by upping sticks and retiring to Florida when Eleanor was in her early 20s, fresh from university and still feeling her way around the world of adulthood.

She was already working and happily house-sharing at the time, but it had still felt like they were abandoning her. But she never let this sting of abandonment show. She had plastered on a smile and carried on being the good-time girl, the career woman who worked hard and played hard.

A decade later, she thought of herself as a modern, self-sufficient woman. She didn't like to fail at anything. And so far, she had been failing at love. The *Project Husband* idea had seemed funny when she first coined the term over a second bottle of wine with her workmates. As she had tipsily railed against the lack of suitable men, they had all promised to help her snare the man of her dreams and achieve her dream of cosy domesticity.

Friends said it seemed a little unlikely that this fast-tempered, headstrong woman would be content with evenings flicking through Netflix channels and Boden catalogues, but she insisted it was what she wanted. She was hunting for a good husband and good genetic material. She wanted her children to be born into the type of real money and privilege that her own parents had never aspired to. Although there was a claim to genuine Scottish aristocracy on her father's side of the family, her dad had never been particularly interested in pursuing any of the family cash.

Her parents had been happy with a mid-range life, but Eleanor wanted to be top flight. She had seen how the very wealthy lived, and she wanted into that lifestyle.

And over time it had become real to her, this *Project Husband*. More real, in fact, than the extra work projects and the endless home improvement projects she would embark on to stave off the nagging loneliness.

She eyed up every potential suitor but was becoming tired of getting flirty looks in return, only to clock a telltale wedding ring or a pissed-off girlfriend glaring at her from a distance.

*Perhaps she should lower her exacting standards if she didn't want to find herself the drunken single aunt at every family gathering until her own funeral.*

Or perhaps not. The handsome man at the bar met her blue-eyed gaze with his own, while her friend John clapped him on the shoulder and introduced him as Ryan.

*Was this a set up?* She didn't really care if it was. He was her type.

"Nice to meet you Ryan, what brings you here tonight?" She asked, with a flip of her shiny red hair.

"More business than pleasure, I'm afraid. I'm in the City for some meetings with brokers, that type of thing," he feigned a yawn, then asked: "Can I get you a drink?"

Another box ticked – she liked a man who offered to get the first round. "A gin and tonic would be great," she replied, not missing a beat.

Ryan turned to the bar to put the order in, and she caught herself mentally marking him down for the slight bald patch at the back of his head.

She told herself to get over it. He was friendly and apparently successful. And handsome. Definitely *Project Husband* material.

She knew that she set the bar high when it came to the opposite sex, but she didn't do pity dates: she wanted a partner whose face she would be happy to see on the pillow next to her every morning for the rest of her life. And someone with the financial means to keep her in the lifestyle to which she very much hoped to become accustomed. And not a snorer, of course. That would be unthinkable.

She was the first to admit that she was a little high maintenance. She'd grown up in middle-of-the-road, middle-class suburbia, but she wanted more for herself than the one-foreign-holiday-a-year routine she had grown up with. At university she had felt drawn to the wealthy set and found she could easily tone down her own slightly northern accent and adapt her vowel sounds to match those of her well-spoken peers.

She might not have been born into money, but she wanted to marry into it, and wasn't ashamed to admit it. She always felt a thrill in the company of the very wealthy, and when she began working in the City as a financial journalist, she found herself socialising with the cream of the wealthy crop on a regular basis. Trying her best to look the part, she'd max out her credit card on the type of clothes she wanted to be able to afford, then sell everything online to help pay for new stuff.

*Fake it until you make it, baby.*

She often joked about her own high standards, but sometimes wished she could just relax a little and stop ditching potential partners before their relationship even got started: her friends still poked fun at her for dumping a tall, rich, good-looking medical surgeon because she had discovered a Facebook photograph of him wearing Crocs.

Thankfully, Ryan wasn't wearing plastic clogs, and she made a mental tick in the footwear box as he turned back to Eleanor in his casual, subtly expensive-looking Gucci loafers. He passed her the drink and then clinked her enormous goldfish bowl of a gin glass with his dinky whisky tumbler. John was looking on awkwardly, so Eleanor surmised that it wasn't a set up after all.

"What do you do for a living in the human sewer?" Ryan asked Eleanor in the kind of posh, London public schoolboy accent that she found impossible to resist.

"Ummm, what do you mean?" She was half-pretending to take offence, but he was on dodgy ground. She loved London and didn't take kindly to people criticising the city she called home.

"London is a sewer of course," Ryan said, giving her a gentle prod in the ribs with his elbow.

"I'm going to ignore that, I love living in London." Her tone was sharp, but she poked her tongue out at him, trying to ramp up the flirt factor.

Sewers were not a sexy subject.

"I'm a financial journalist. I like to investigate all the big movers and shakers. What kind of sexy stocks do you trade?" Eleanor was moving closer to him instinctively, like a predator closing in on its prey. She barely noticed John making excuses and joining friends at the other end of the bar.

"Financial journalism… interesting. I trade mining stocks. I split my time between London and Windsor…it's different there, much calmer." Ryan was stumbling over his words and seemed suddenly almost shy, shifting his feet and not looking her in the eye.

Never one to back down from a challenge, Eleanor fluttered her eyelids. "Naturally, when you live on the river, London must seem dismal by comparison." She made puppy dog eyes at him as she said, "I've never even been to Windsor."

Instead of picking up on the hint, he drained his glass and looked in the direction of the bar. Eleanor cringed inwardly.

Luckily, John reappeared in time to relieve the awkward silence. "You've lived in London for ten years and never made it to Windsor?" He was hovering behind her and making a show of incredulity.

"Ryan, you should take Eleanor that way sometime. She needs a bit of education, to see how the posh people live."

It was clearly a joke, and John playfully ruffled her hair as he said it, but Eleanor felt more irritated than she was letting on. John was making it clear that she didn't have access to the posh crowd she so wanted to be a part of.

"It would be my pleasure," Ryan said, still shifting from one foot to another. "My parents have a boat, so I can take you on the river if you fancy it. Another gin and tonic?"

A boat trip down the river with Richie Rich sounded damn appealing to Eleanor, as did a second gin and tonic. But why was he acting so coy all of a sudden?

When he still hadn't asked for her contact details at the end of the night, Eleanor decided to take the matter into her own hands. "We should swap emails so we can talk about mining shares. I need some insider quotes for an article I'm working on," she lied. The gin was telling her this harmless fib was a good idea.

Ryan didn't answer, and distractedly turned his gaze to a group of people talking in the corner of the room.

"Unless, of course, you don't want to talk shop." Accustomed to men falling at her feet, Eleanor was feeling an unfamiliar burn of humiliation and wanted to give Ryan a way out that didn't involve rejecting her advances. She reached for her coat.

"Oh, gosh, yes of course, it would be my pleasure to exchange emails."

She had Ryan's attention again, but she wondered where it had drifted to. He added her details to his phone contacts and gave her a warm wave as she set off into the cold November night, propping herself up a little on John's solid shoulder as they walked towards her waiting cab.

It was a week before an email from him pinged into her inbox. A week in which she both cursed herself for not getting his phone number for texting, and began to ask herself if she had unknowingly said or done something so embarrassing that he never wanted to see her again. Surely she hadn't drunk that much gin?

When it did arrive, the email was far from flirty. "Hey, I have been looking at Xstrata shares recently, what do you think?" Not even a kissy sign off. Had her entry into her mid-thirties really made her so much less desirable than she once was?

After a quick bit of research on Google, she responded to his dull shop talk with shameless flirtation.

"Oh yes that's the big one, the biggest ever, I am all over the big ones."

He still wasn't biting, and after some tedious back and forth emails she began to grow tired of feigning interest in mining shares.

Frustrated, Eleanor called John for advice.

"John, I don't get it, Ryan said we should keep in touch, but he never suggests we meet up, even though we email each other all the time. What's his story? I need a husband, not a pen pal."

John laughed, "You women always complicate things, why don't you just ask him out? He's definitely very eligible. But you can't just force someone to be your husband, Eleanor."

She gave an exaggerated sigh and said in mock despair: "It's just that men who expect women to make the first move for everything are so very tiring."

After conducting some more tedious research into mining stocks and sending Ryan some insider trading tips, Eleanor decided John was right: a more direct approach was needed.

She poured herself a glass of wine and, riding the wave of Dutch courage, texted Ryan:

"Was wondering if you would like a drink sometime? X"

Within minutes, the ping of a text message put Eleanor out of her misery. "How about we go for drinks and dinner next Friday?"

Eleanor sighed with relief. Project Husband was back on track. He must have just been too intimidated to ask, she reassured herself.

When the big night arrived, Eleanor felt uncharacteristically anxious. She wasn't sure why, but she had a deep conviction that she and Ryan were going to be in it for the long haul. She knew it sounded like a cliché, but really felt like this was the first night of the rest of her life.

# Chapter 3

# No Prescription Necessary

Eleanor gratefully accepts the offer of a little cash from a sympathetic nurse at the hospital who wanted to make sure she had enough money to get back to her hotel. Without this act of kindness, she would have been totally screwed. Noting the nurse's name - Rita - and promising to repay her the minute she has access to cash again, Eleanor leaves the hospital in Oaxaca clutching an eye-watering medical bill that she hopes her insurance will stump up for.

She heads straight to a shabby-looking internet cafe (*a loose term,* she thinks to herself, since the place doesn't do coffee or food…) across the road.

Eleanor knows she looks more than a little shabby herself and tries to ignore the curious glances from gaming teenagers gathered around one of the screens. *Needs must.* And she needs to get online and sort out her lack of bank cards and phone.

The young man at the reception desk glances at her scratched hands and bruised arms as she hands over a couple of coins, but says nothing. He nods in the direction of computer four.

*Password incorrect.* Eleanor swears out loud at the email login page, but after several failed attempts at trying to remember her own password, she finally gets it right on the sixth attempt.

Her heart breaks a fraction more when she scans her email inbox. Nothing from Ryan, of course.

She desperately needs to see a friendly face and knows that Vanessa, her best friend, wants to join her. Eleanor drops her an email which she hopes will give the impression that *yes, things have gone a bit wrong but it's all under control. Everything's fine!*

"I got drunk and was beaten up and robbed. I'm OK and it's good to know I don't have any STDs LOL. Sorting out the credit cards right now and as soon as they've arrived, I'm going to get myself on a tour heading your way, I don't want to travel alone anymore. There's a group going from Cancun to Guatemala and then I am getting into Panama a day or so after you arrive there. No phone yet but will sort ASAP xxxx."

On re-reading it, she strongly suspects that her situation sounds like one holy hot mess of a shit storm, but her internet access time is down to its last few minutes, so she sends it anyway.

Back at the hotel, she manages to convince the reception staff to let her use the lobby phone and calls her bank to cancel all her cards and get emergency replacements sent out. For the next 24 hours she concentrates on emptying the contents of the hotel mini bar while soaking in the bath, flicking through the channels, and sleeping. Anything to numb the feelings and the throbbing pain in her head.

She sleepwalks through the process of getting her new cards, booking her tickets, packing her bags, and jumping on the flight to Cancun. She wants more booze, more numbness, until she can distract herself with human company again.

It's a relief to check into the hotel Xbalamque in Cancun. She's opted for a shared room on the group tour: unable to face nights alone with only the TV and the minibar for company. The place isn't high end, but it has a pool and a spa and a lobby with a bar, and the rooms are comfy enough, so she's taking it as a win considering it costs a fraction of the price of the last place. She's here for the company and the camaraderie more than the Instagram appeal, anyway.

The tour group gathers in the lobby, sipping ice cold beers and zesty mojitos, excitedly making plans for their trip. Eleanor's roommate, Barbara, is a chatty German who works as a travel agent. *Do free trips come as a perk of the job?* Eleanor finds herself wondering, but suspects it might be rude to ask. At 35-years-old, Barbara is the same age as Eleanor and has the kind of fresh-faced, freckled, blonde looks that scream 'wholesome outdoor type'.

Eleanor suspects that her own complexion probably screams 'accident-prone drinker', but she's grateful for the fact that she doesn't have any visible bruises or anything else that would hint at her very recent trauma. She really doesn't want to keep explaining what happened, especially when she can barely remember.

It's easy to be distracted in Paradise. On the first day, the 10-strong group, led by tour guide Flavio, heads out on bikes to see the famous ruins of Tulum and, after a spot of chin-stroking admiration, peddles onwards to jump into the sapphire waters of a nearby *cenote*.

Eleanor had heard about these natural wonders before: sinkholes dropping into the clearest of clear underground pools and flowing out to underground chambers. Flavio explains that there are thousands of these in the region, and that this one is considered sacred. Eleanor can see why: in the sticky tropical heat, the pool looks little short of miraculous. The water glitters like a jewel beneath the surface and is surrounded by the sort of giant-fronded vegetation and swaying palms that have always made her heart sing.

It's a sheer drop: a leap of faith into these sacred waters. One of the youngest in the group, an American called Robert, is the first to take the plunge, and he yells with adrenaline-spiked happiness when he hits the cooling water. Eleanor's not far behind: stripped to her swimwear and taking a running jump before leaping in feet-first. She loves the sense of free-falling before she hits the water's surface: a short sharp shock that has her feeling truly alive for the first time in weeks. For a few minutes she barely registers the lingering pain that throbs day and night.

The day is a blissful distraction. She and Barbara are the eldest in the group by several years, and Eleanor enjoys being surrounded by these young, fun-loving free spirits who never seem to worry about anything more serious than booking their next hostel or a broken strap on their Havaianas. Eleanor revels in their youthful exuberance, and tries her best not to wince whenever she feels a sharp, shooting pain. Her designer one-piece was designed to flatter her shapely midriff, but now she's just grateful it hides her still-bruised stomach.

They pile themselves and their bikes onto a bus heading back to Cancun, and when they alight, Eleanor's eyes stop at a flickering pharmacy sign: *'No Prescription Necessary'*.

*What's she got to lose?* While the others are getting ready for dinner, Eleanor scurries back to the pharmacy and brazenly asks for Prozac and Valium. A month's supply of each. She can't believe how easy it is. She's never taken either before, and she doesn't even realise it takes weeks for Prozac to take effect. She just wants a quick happiness fix.

When she gets back to the hotel, Barbara is sitting on her bed in their shared room. Her face is equal parts concerned and pissed-off. "Where have you been, girl? They all went for dinner. I've been waiting for you, I didn't know where you'd gone."

"Sorry...I went to that clothes store in town, but I didn't see anything I liked." Eleanor lies, because admitting that she snuck off to buy tranquillisers and antidepressants would mean having to explain a whole lot of other stuff.

Barbara and Eleanor walk to the restaurant. When they arrive, the others in the group have already ordered and are steadily getting through the wine. Eleanor goes to the toilet and pulls out her haul. She squints at the label, unable to understand the tiny Spanish words. She swallows two Prozac pills and one Valium. Back at the table, she picks at her dinner but feels weird and woozy, and when the others head off for a night of drinking and dancing, she makes her excuses and winds back through the noisy streets to the relative calm of the hotel. The group is leaving for Belize early the next morning, travelling by boat, but she's already feeling seasick.

After a fractured night's sleep, and fueled by several cups of strong coffee, Eleanor joins the others as they leave for the port. Her racing heart jolts when she sees armed guards stopping each passenger and rifling through their belongings - clearly looking for drugs.

Panicked, she pulls Barbara to one side and says in a frightened half-whisper: "God, this is going to sound weird, but I bought two bottles of Prozac and two of Valium yesterday in town. Are they illegal?" Even if they're above board, Eleanor's terrified that the guards will mistake them for something else.

Barbara almost snorts with laughter. "Pull yourself together girl, this isn't Bangkok Hilton. Get back in line, that stuff isn't even banned."

A stern policeman looks briefly in Eleanor's bag and then nods her away, either oblivious to, or uninterested in, the stash of pills right there in her hand luggage. The surge of sweaty panic begins to ease as she boards the bus.

"Belize, here we come!" She hugs Barbara with relief once they've settled into their seats. Barbara looks less than elated. "I've heard this is a rough crossing," she says. After a loaded pause, she adds: "By the way, I want the story on those pills later."

It's a two-hour crossing to the island of Caye Caulker in Belize, and Eleanor soon realises that 'rough ride' is an understatement. Several people throw up over the side before the boat is even out of the harbour. Eleanor closes her eyes and tries to sleep, but the waves crashing over the sides of the boat are doing nothing to calm her fraught nerves.

When the boat finally docks, Eleanor notices Flavio, their guide, helping everybody disembark on their wobbly sea legs. He has a kind word with every seasick member of the group. He's so good looking and considerate that Eleanor can't help but wonder what he'd be like as a lover. *Stop it,* she tells her frisky brain.

"Can I help you get your bag to your room, Eleanor?" Flavio asks, helping her off the boat.

"Ok, thanks," She can't help wondering why he's offered this favour to her and nobody else. Walking along with the rest of the group, Flavio hauls Eleanor's heavy bag to her hotel room.

Barbara shuts the door behind them. "So, what's the story with the Prozac?" She demands.

"I'm having a really bad time with my husband…" it's the first time Eleanor's really talked about her personal life since it began to totally unravel, and her voice cracks. Tears start dribbling down her nose and chin.

She's shocked when Barbara moves across the room and hugs her. She hadn't seemed the hugging type.

"Wipe those tears girl, no man is worth it," Barbara says. "You're coming out tonight, no more of this shit."

Eleanor's spirits lift. She tells herself to get a grip and enjoy herself, after all, she's in paradise isn't she? After dinner, she feels lively enough to go to a nightclub with the rest of the group.

It's a downstairs joint, thick with the smell of cigarette smoke and sweat. Working their way through the thick throng to the bar, she and

Barbara decide their best bet is to sink a couple of tequila shots before braving the dance floor.

The men are relentless in their attempts to make headway with the fresh-off-the-boat gringas.

Eleanor clings to Barbara and recoils from the wandering hands of a man who mutters "I will fuck the fat right off you," *Is that supposed to be some kind of chat up line?*

"They must have had some luck with other tourists, but I can't imagine how," she says to Barbara.

"I know, Jesus, I can't take this place, let's get out of here." Barbara links her arm and marches her off the packed dance floor and towards the stairs. They're happy to get outside to fresh air and respite from the groping arms and lecherous looks.

As they walk back to the hotel, dizzy with tequila and the muggy heat of the night, Barbara addresses the elephant in the room.

"So, what's the story? Have you run away from a Mexican drug lord?" She jokes.

"That might be less embarrassing. My husband has basically ignored me for two years, and he won't give me a baby. My ticking biological clock is keeping me awake at night and I thought the valium might help with that, and if I could get a few happy pills, all the better. Anyway, what about your love life, any boyfriend back in Germany?"

"Stop trying to turn the conversation back to me!" says Barbara with a laugh. "And that's a strange logic about the pills, I think you should just chuck them."

Eleanor looks unconvinced. She hopes Barbara will talk about her own demons for a while. "There's no man in my life in Germany or anywhere else. I've had my fair share of man trouble too…I just remind myself that I was born alone, I'll die alone, so anything that comes in between is just a bonus."

Eleanor manages a laugh, oddly reassured to know that she's not the only one with a disastrous love life. All her friends back home seem to make it look so easy.

The hotel bar is still open when they get back, but there's not a customer to be seen, and the bored-looking bartender grins when they come in. "Can I get you girls a margarita?" They exchange glances and nod in unison.

The pair sip their drinks at the bar while the bartender gives them some tips on the best and worst nightclubs in the area: the bar they had just left is top of his list of places to avoid. "Full of gringo-hunting girls and sleazy men, and the music's just cheesy pop shit." "Now you tell us!" Eleanor says with a laugh. The pair decline a second drink, give him a wave good night, and make their way back to their room.

Woozy with booze and the warm fuzz of new friendship, Eleanor sleeps soundly for the first time in as long as she can remember.

The next day, Eleanor wakes up feeling smug that they turned down that second margarita. She and Barbara are up for breakfast before the rest of the group, and pick the best spot to enjoy the fresh fruit and pastries laid out on a long table in the hotel's gardens. The others won't be able to sleep off their hangovers for too long, as they're due to travel by bus to Belize City later that morning. Sipping coffee under the shade of a mango tree, Eleanor feels a stab of traveller's remorse. She didn't get much chance to explore this lively island, with its colourful riverfront shacks and its dusty streets. She suspects the terrible nightclub they visited doesn't represent the best of the place, or its inhabitants.

Belize City doesn't sound overly appealing: she's heard it's a fairly rundown place where you have to keep your wits about you, but it's a necessary stopover on the way to their next destination - the ancient Mayan city of Tikal, in Guatemala.

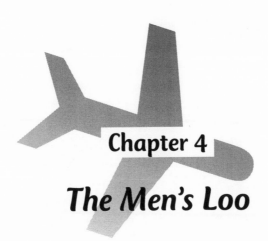

# Chapter 4

# *The Men's Loo*

Eleanor watched Ryan's hands repeatedly straighten his fork and knife next to the dinner plate in front of him. He moved his napkin from the table to his lap, and then back again, before casting his eye around the restaurant for the twentieth time. Eleanor inwardly smiled at his apparent nervousness. She found his social awkwardness oddly endearing compared to the cocky banking types she usually met.

"Like to keep your hands busy?" She joked, adding to his awkwardness by rubbing her foot against his leg under the table. They were at a rustic-chic restaurant in Covent Garden, and Eleanor glanced hungrily at other diners' plates. They'd been waiting ages for their own tasting menu of local cheeses and artfully arranged small plates to arrive. And their drinks - where the hell was the bottle of British fizz they'd ordered about half an hour ago?

After several attempts at getting the waiter's attention, Ryan finally managed to catch his eye and remind him that they were still waiting for their food and drink. The harassed-looking young man dashed off in a flurry of apologies before reappearing with their drinks and some marinated olives *"on the house sir, so sorry for your wait."*

They drank their bubbly and Ryan relaxed a little. They made light work of the very small plates, and Eleanor did her best to keep the conversation away from mining shares. *"Let's not talk shop...tell me about you!"*

When the waiter arrived with the bill, Ryan deftly picked it up before Eleanor could so much as take a glance, and it was settled up with a quick swipe of his Gold Card. Ryan asked Eleanor if she'd like to go on somewhere, and his jaw dropped to the floor when she replied, "How about The Men's Loo?"

"You should see your face!" she said with a laugh. "Don't you know anything about the hipster scene around here? Hipsters are all about the Men's Loo."

"They are? I must have missed that..." Ryan looked genuinely baffled. Eleanor explained that *The Men's Loo* was a trendy cocktail bar in a converted public toilet along the Strand.

The tiny space was absolutely packed when they arrived, and they were crammed into a cubby hole next to the bar while they tried to sip their Dirty Martinis.

A combination of enforced proximity and strong alcohol prompted Ryan to lean forward and take a strand of Eleanor's glossy red hair in his hand, his amorous expression turning to shock when his fingers became stuck at the roots and Eleanor shouted out in dismayed surprise.

"They're extensions!" She almost sprayed her drink into his face in an eruption of amusement and horror. "Please get your hands out of there right now!"

"Oh God, how embarrassing!" Eleanor giggled and she shook her red mane back, attempting to brazen it out.

"So, you're not a natural redhead then? This is not the way I expected to find out." Ryan's eyes were twinkling and she playfully punched his arm. She explained that yes, she was a natural redhead but just needed a little help with the length.

"Not something you have a problem with yourself, I imagine?" She turned the flirt dial up to the maximum, feeling the warm rush of alcohol and the suddenly intimate turn that the conversation had taken.

"Indeed not," he gave her a wink as he turned to the bar to try and order more drinks. By way of a drinks order, she had just said "surprise me."

*Why is he so useless at getting bartenders' attention?* She thought for a split second, before immediately chastising herself for her critical nature.

When he eventually turned back to her with two Negroni cocktails, she complimented him on his choice of drink. She did like a Negroni, but added that she'd have to leave shortly. "Otherwise, I'll turn into a pumpkin," she joked. The reality was that she was pleased with the flirty turn the evening had taken and wanted to leave it on a high note before she had too many cocktails and started letting her decorum – and her immaculate makeup – slip.

After they had finished their drinks and pushed their way through the crowd and into the chill of the evening, Ryan called a cab for her and gave her a soft, brief kiss on the lips before she jumped in the back. Eleanor was feeling giddy with that first rush of romance and, although she felt a twinge of embarrassment at the way he had discovered her hair extensions, she felt she'd worked it to her advantage. At least her fake eyelashes had not come off, she laughed to herself.

She was barely through the front door of her flat when he texted her to check if she had got home safely. She smiled to herself, and after a half-hearted attempt at removing her makeup, fell asleep feeling more optimistic than she had in months.

A week later, they met again for a date at a comedy club, and this time Eleanor did not hold back on the drinks. Everything was hazy after the first act - a mildly amusing Australian comic poking fun at his own attempts to navigate British social etiquette - during which Ryan had plied her with one double gin and tonic after another.

Heading to work the next day, Eleanor nursed a sore head and a burning sense of shame. She was trying to fill in the blanks, but her mind just kept flashing back to an image of herself strutting around the living room, naked except for a pair of high heels, slurring: "Ooooh yes sir, I am all that and a bit more. I am an IT girl," before Ryan attempted to cover her up and put her into bed. Alone. *Oh God.*

Clutching a double espresso and groggily making her way along Oxford Road, she called her best friend, Vanessa. "I'm soooo mortified! I got totally smashed and all I remember is that I was prancing around naked, but Ryan just tucked me into bed by myself. Isn't that weird?"

Vanessa audibly found this funnier than Eleanor did. Through stifled giggles, she told Eleanor that it was a good thing, and that Ryan was probably just being a gentleman.

"It's a good sign if he respected you too much to take advantage," she said, but Eleanor was not buying it. "He must have put me to bed and left. Oh god, where's my dignity? He hasn't even texted. There goes Project Husband!"

Eleanor was laughing, but she was dogged by remorse. *Never drinking again.* But even beneath the drinkers' regret, there was something else. She remembered Ryan looking almost embarrassed at the sight of her naked body, and that was not the reaction she usually got from men.

Eleanor struggled to maintain a professional front during a morning editorial briefing. She found herself glancing at her watch and wondering when she could get out of there and burrow down into a pile of paperwork. She was extremely grateful that she didn't have any important interviews or pressing deadlines that day.

*"Any other suggestions for this week's breaking news?"* Eleanor shook her head to the editor's question and gathered her papers together before slipping out of his office with a barely-disguised sigh of relief.

Her hangover was beginning to ease up slightly by the time she was back at her desk, sipping a diet coke at her desk and stealing a glance at her phone. A text from Ryan. God. Her blood ran cold during the few seconds it took for the message to open. *Morning gorgeous. How's the head? xxx*

She felt a flood of relief. Maybe she hadn't ruined everything, after all. *Got caffeine, am surviving, sorry for being a shameless drunk xxx*

She fired off the text and then muted the conversation, wondering if it was too late to play hard to get.

Perhaps it worked, because Ryan's texts came thick and fast once she unmuted him at the end of the day. Eleanor suggested that their next date should be a dry one, and they met up a few days later at a Leicester Square cinema to catch a horror film. Despite not being the jumpy or squeamish type, Eleanor relished the idea of clinging onto those strong biceps for 'comfort'.

Sure enough, his arm worked its way around her shoulder during the creepy opening scenes, and clutched on to his other hand while masked baddies stalked hapless teenagers through the woods on the big screen. She felt like a teenager.

As they left the cinema, he hailed just the one cab for both of them, and Eleanor felt a knot of anticipation in her stomach when he asked her if she wanted to come back to his place.

Their first time was not earth-shaking, but at least it was mutually satisfying, and sober. A rarity in Eleanor's social circle. She felt respected and even loved, although neither of them used the L word. He took his time, used protection, called out the right name and held her tight afterwards. *Oh yes, Project Husband is going nicely,* she thought to herself as she fell asleep watching the rise and fall of his broad chest beneath the softest of cotton sheets.

Eleanor drifted along in a cloud of romance for the next few days and weeks, feeling the thrill of a new relationship and a deep sensation that she really had met The One. He would surprise her with flowers sent to her workplace, and she couldn't help feeling smug as she placed them on her desk. *This one's a keeper,* she told her colleagues with a smile.

One Saturday morning, she sat soaking in the deep bubble bath he had run for her, and Ryan sat at the edge of the tub scrolling through some images on his phone. "What do you think of this house?" He asked, handing the phone to her so that she could take a look. It was a Georgian town house in Kensington, and she immediately felt the familiar twang of property envy. Her own rented apartment was nice enough, but this was another level entirely.

"It's gorgeous. Whose is it?"

"It's mine." Eleanor's jaw almost dropped right into the fragrant bubbles.

*Wait, what?* He had mentioned he had a few property investments, but this must be worth millions.

"I rent it out, but the current tenants' contract is coming to an end so I'm thinking of moving back in there. Lots of space for both of us." He smiled at her and took the phone back. "Something to think about, anyway," he said, and left her alone with the suds, the radio, and her own racing thoughts.

Was he really suggesting they should move in together? They'd only been properly dating for three weeks, and while she was giving herself a mental pat on the back for making such solid progress with Project Husband, she couldn't help thinking it was moving a little fast, even by her standards. When he didn't mention it again that day, or the next, she began to think he'd thought better of it anyway.

He still hadn't broached the subject when, a few weeks later, he asked if she would like to come out to the family home in Windsor. *Time to meet the parents* was the subtext. He still hadn't met hers and, while she was by no means ashamed of them, she was slightly relieved that they were in Florida - she wasn't in any huge rush to brag about the semi-detached cottage in Rickmansworth in which she'd grown up.

She had never tried to hide her middle class background from her upper-class friends, but she rarely talked about it unless pressed. By now, she'd spent so long socialising with the very wealthy that she'd assumed so many of their mannerisms and social quirks. She could almost pass as super-posh herself.

The next weekend being Easter, they decided it would be a good time to make the trip to Ryan's family home. Eleanor put on her best parent-pleasing dress (a knee-skimmer with a cinched waist and very respectable neckline) and they climbed into his BMW, leaving the choked traffic lanes and congestion charges of Central London for the wide lanes of the Royal Borough.

By now, she'd become accustomed to the fact that she was dealing with some Serious Money, but she still blinked in disbelief when she clapped eyes on his family home. It was a huge, rambling estate sitting pretty on a tiny island in the middle of the Thames. She smoothed down her dress and took a deep breath, stepping daintily out the car in case Jane and Ted were peeping out the enormous windows.

Perhaps they were, because Ryan's parents appeared at the door before Ryan could ring the bell. They were all smiles and friendly hugs and exclamations of how *absolutely wonderful* it was to meet Eleanor.

If Eleanor had any nerves about meeting the parents in such grand surroundings, they were quickly assuaged by Jane's effusive friendliness. A petite woman, Jane was smartly dressed in tailored black trousers and a silk shirt, with pearls around her neck and green gems sparkling at her ears. She was wearing black ballet flats, and Eleanor towered over her when they embraced.

Ted looked almost like a caricature of an elegant country gentleman - fitted waistcoat and all - and seemed the quieter of the pair, but his beaming smile suggested he was genuinely delighted to have their company.

Jane led Eleanor through to the living room and the two women sank down into the Chesterfield sofa, between two bronze statues of horses and beneath a framed painting of the house and its gardens. Ted poured them each a glass of tawny port from a crystal decanter.

Jane asked Eleanor a string of questions about her home, family and work, but it felt less like small talk than genuine interest. Crucially, Eleanor didn't detect any snootiness when they asked about where she went to school and what her parents did for a living. "I'm a self-made woman!" Eleanor joked, and there was no edge to Jane's voice when she replied: "Which is exactly as it should be, in this day and age!"

Eleanor secretly suspected that her relentless pursuit of a rich husband to fund her lifestyle didn't fully fit with this depiction of herself as an independent career woman, but she kept that to herself. Maybe it was because she had worked so hard to this point that she wanted someone else to take over and give her a rest.

Jane had prepared a roast with all the trimmings, and the champagne flowed as they ate at a long dining table set with fine silverware and a white linen tablecloth so spotless that Eleanor found herself wondering if it had ever been used before. *Maybe they have a new tablecloth for every meal?* She couldn't help comparing the elegant scene with her own upbringing: their Sunday dinners usually involved gravy granules, and everybody crammed around the extending table in what passed for a dining room. Her family had never been hard up, things had always been comfortable, but this was another level entirely. Rather than feeling intimidated, she felt oddly at home.

After lunch, they all headed out for a walk across the fields to a country pub, Jane taking the lead, with the family's two golden retrievers tagging her heels. The dogs, Pippa and Elsie, sporadically made a dash for the stick Jane threw for them, always obediently returning and dropping the stick at her feet, tails wagging. The air was crisp and fresh, and Eleanor felt wholesome and vibrantly alive as she strode through the long, wet grass in borrowed Hunter wellies.

It was about an hour's walk to the whitewashed, thatch-roofed pub, and when they arrived, the dogs raced ahead of them through the narrow entrance to curl up in front of the glowing fire. The bar staff greeted the family like old friends, and the handful of other patrons all gave a friendly wave in their direction as they took a seat in the snug to enjoy a sherry. *Somehow these posh country folks make Sunday day drinking seem like a wholesome pursuit,* Eleanor thought to herself, approvingly.

Driving duties meant Ryan was abstaining from the booze, but Eleanor noticed that he seemed much more relaxed and at ease than he did on their evenings out in London. His cheeks were flushed from the fire and the country air, and he looked totally at home nursing a glass of orange juice from the comfort of his deep armchair.

She felt a pang of sadness when the time came for them to leave, but was buoyed by Jane and Ted's apparently sincere and enthusiastic insistence that they should *come back soon, and stay for the weekend next time.*

Ryan was somewhat subdued on the drive back, and when they hit the traffic of the city again, Eleanor started to see what he had meant when he called London 'the Human Sewer': everything looked a little grimy and polluted after the fresh air of the countryside.

But Eleanor had always been a fan of London's own green spaces, and a few weeks later it was warm and dry enough for them to head out for a picnic in Hyde Park. They were sitting on a blanket she had found in Ryan's garage, and she picked at its frayed edges between nibbles of store bought hummus and vegetable sticks. *Sometimes simple things really are nicer than super-fancy* she thought out loud, grinning at Ryan as he lay basking in the spring sunshine. After months of winter, the sun on her own face felt wonderful, and she was in a carefree, happy mood: literally full of the joys of spring.

Ryan sat up to pour her a glass of elderflower juice and smiled at her. "I love your cheeriness," he said.

She chuckled at the compliment, but was almost speechless when he lay back down and murmured, "We should definitely get married and have kids." She was never entirely sure how serious he was when he said these things, but she could feel her scepticism melting away by the day. *Had she really done it? Had she found her Prince Charming to rescue her from a life of lonely nights and dubious online dating decisions?*

She almost had to pinch herself when he added: "My parents would insist on paying their tuition fees, I imagine. I'm not sure if you have any socialist objections to the public school system?" Once again, she had no idea whether he was joking or not, and merely replied with a laugh: "none whatsoever! Only the best for our kids!" He wasn't really listening, anyway, he was almost drifting off to sleep in the warm sun.

# Chapter 5

# *Monkeys and Ruins*

Eleanor wakes up feeling a buzz of excitement even before she's had her morning caffeine fix. She can't believe she is travelling to Tikal today. This pre-Columbian city buried deep in the rainforest in Guatemala has been on her bucket list since she first read about it five years ago in a copy of *National Geographic* she had idly picked up in the waiting room at her Botox doctor's surgery. As she waited to be injected with wrinkle-erasing toxins, she had felt stirrings of wanderlust.

And now she is finally getting to see Tikal for herself, although it's no easy place to reach. Flavio explains that, for their own safety, they'll need to enter Tikal National Park with a military convoy. To Eleanor, this sounds both thrilling - *all those men in uniform* - and terrifying. In his rather formal tour-guide English, Flavio says: "There have been a series of violent robberies on tourists in the region lately. The police were asked to step in and protect the tourists. Attacks became even more frequent and it was discovered that the police were being bribed by the robbers. The situation has become so bad that the government has removed the police and brought in the army to keep us safe." For Eleanor, this adds an extra frisson of drama to the expedition, and the sight of the convoy sets her nerves tingling.

Feeling like a badass Lara Croft type, she picks her way through thick jungle flanked by the group's armed, serious-faced companions. For the first time in ages, Eleanor is fully immersed in the moment. Her problems vanish from her mind like the capuchin monkeys that skitter into the treetops at the sound of the visitors' marching footsteps through the jungle.

They reach a clearing in the forest and suddenly there they are: the grand white temples of Tikal towering above them. A series of giant, pyramid-style towers rises to the heavens, matched for size and spectacle only by the giant trees that surround them.

*And perhaps by Flavio.* Eleanor finds her attention drifting away from the towers and onto his tanned face as he reels off the facts she already knows.

"These ruins of Tikal reflect the pre-Columbian Mayan civilisation and date back more than 1,000 years," he's explaining, but Eleanor's focus is more on his thick, sensual lips than on the words he's saying.

Eleanor loves the fact that Flavio is from Costa Rica. It makes him look so exotic to her suburban British eyes, with his green eyes, long dark hair, tanned skin and those gorgeous lips. Despite all the emotional baggage she's brought with her on this trip, she finds herself longing to kiss him. It's out of the question though - she knows the guides aren't allowed to get involved with the people on their tours. She tries to cast aside the many stories she's heard about guides playing fast and loose with these rules.

The visitors aren't alone: more and more monkeys appear as though guarding their territory: running up, down and over the abandoned city that has become their playground.

Eleanor follows Flavio around, firing questions at him about the site and its history. It's partly genuine curiosity, and partly an excuse to accompany him.

At the top of one temple, Eleanor grabs Flavio's hand. "It feels like we've been through some magic portal back in time!" She shrieks, with heartfelt enthusiasm. She's never seen anything like it.

As they stand and survey the view from the tallest of the towers, she almost feels compelled to lean in for a kiss, but he turns away at the crucial moment and she loses her footing, almost tumbling into him.

"Watch your step, it's dangerous up here!" he says, with a sideways glance at her Prada trainers: clearly designed for posing, not for clambering up Mayan ruins. He grips her hand to steady her and she gingerly descends the steep, uneven steps back to the jungle floor.

The rest of the group are all in hiking boots: a fact Eleanor only notices now that they are all gathering to leave before night falls.

They make their way through the jungle back to their minivan and, as the light dims, an orchestra of chittering and hooting sounds echoes from the treetops and the undergrowth, increasing in volume with every step they take.

It's near-darkness as they drive out of the national park – their military escorts jumping out at the exit – and continue to a town called Rio Dulce ('*Sweet River*'). Their accommodation for the night is a hotel built on stilts above the river, and Eleanor feels a kind of giddy excitement, like a child given permission to spend the night in a treehouse.

The next morning, Eleanor wakes up later than the rest of the groups, and staff at the hotel tell her the others have already walked down to a nearby lake to take a swim. She grabs a coffee and puts on her swimsuit, throws a loose vest and tiny shorts over the top, and walks down to join them.

The clear blue lake beneath the trees is about as picturesque as it gets, but Eleanor's eyes are immediately drawn to Flavio in his swimming shorts. He's floating on his back in the water, but swims to shore when he sees her approaching. He looks like something from a men's fragrance advert when he emerges, dripping, from the water.

"Hey, you slept late, all ok?" He asks, with real concern written on his face. Not for the first time, Eleanor wonders if he feels pity for her. She baulks at the thought and she manages to pull her gaze away from his taut stomach to look him in the eye and assures him that *yes, everything is great, I just needed the sleep.*

Their next destination is the town of Zacapa, and when they arrive after a hot, bumpy bus ride, Flavio leads them into the main square, where locals sipping beers outside a hole-in-the-wall bar shoot curious glances in their direction.

Eleanor is looking around for anything resembling a hotel when Flavio tells them that they'll be in home stays for the night. There are no hotels here. Which means the group will need to split up. He gestures at an unassuming nearby building and asks: "Who's going to stay with me in this family home right here?"

Many of the others are already in couples, and as everybody knows Eleanor has a thing for Flavio, nobody rushes to take him up on the offer. Eleanor stays silent and enjoys the tumbleweed moment for a minute before she says: "Go on then, if nobody else can put up with you, I suppose I'll do it."

The other home-stays are all just a couple of minutes' away and, after they have walked everybody to their doors and introduced them to their hosts, Eleanor and Flavio head to their own base for the night. It's a simple family home in the centre of the village, and the six children in the family have all decamped to the living room to free up their bedrooms.

Her room is painted green and, with no windows in its concrete walls, is stifling. A small courtyard outside the room connects it to Flavio's: a fact that does not escape her attention. Nor does the free-standing outdoor shower. *At least the toilet has a door,* she thinks to herself when one of the children gestures at the small wooden outhouse next to the shower.

They meet up with the rest of the group again a little while later, aiming to climb uphill to a local beauty spot to catch the sunset. When they get to the top, Eleanor sits down to admire the view: the lights of the town are beginning to twinkle sweetly into life beneath them. Barbara sidles over to join her, and hands her the bottle of Mexican beer she is drinking from. She whispers: "Tonight's the night, lover girl! You should totally make your move at the guesthouse."

"Oh my god. Our rooms are connected, I can sneak over and look at him while he's sleeping." Eleanor feigns a swoon.

"You want to be doing more than looking at him," Barbara says, and Eleanor pokes out her tongue in response. "You reckon?"

Any attempts at seduction seem thwarted later that night when they sit down to eat. The host family has prepared a meal over a wood fire, and the smoke makes Eleanor's eyes itch like crazy. Blinking furiously and aware that her eyes are probably turning an attractive shade of pink, Eleanor accepts a plate of what looks like chicken stew and finds herself awkwardly picking out bits of gristle from her teeth. She doesn't even normally eat meat if she can help it except in situations like this, where there's no other food alternative. She attempts to make small talk in her limited Spanish, and Flavio, sitting next to her, steps in to help out whenever she struggles.

She doesn't need a translator when the grandmother of the house asks, *estas casada?'* Are you married? Eleanor automatically nods her head, and sees Flavio's eyebrows shoot up in surprise.

Seeing an opportunity to open up, she turns to him and says in a low voice: "I just left him, but please don't translate that for a complete stranger."

"Oh wow," he replies. "Bride on the run, eh? But seriously, let me know if I can do anything."

Eleanor blushes just thinking about what she would really like him to do for her, and stands up with an offer to do the dishes: a ruse so she can surreptitiously pour her soup away.

Before she can escape to the sink, the elderly lady asks her something else, and this time she doesn't understand, so Flavio steps in: "*Oma* wants to know if you have children."

"No." Eleanor says, turning towards the sink.

The grandmother of the house gives her a pitying look, and Eleanor quickly shifts the topic away from herself by enlisting Flavio's help to translate a little small talk questions for Oma, asking about her grandchildren's ages and schooling, before adding: "please tell her we are so happy to be staying in her lovely home."

She hopes she managed to sound sincere. Looking around at the smoke-filled living room with its broken chairs and splodges of black tropical mould on the walls, she's secretly relieved that they are only staying two nights.

She's even more relieved when she sees Flavio shifting in his chair and thanking *Oma* for dinner. He's saying something in Spanish that she hopes is 'we're going out now', and can't hide the beam on her face when he turns to her and says: "Come on, let's join the others at the bar down the road."

Walking across dirt tracks to the bar, he tells her that he used to work as an artist before becoming a tour guide, and travelled the world on a tiny budget before deciding he needed to earn some decent money while he travelled. He still painted, but there was no real money in it.

They reach the bar, which doubles as a grocery store, and find the others sitting on plastic chairs and drinking from plastic cups. There's a half-empty bottle of rum on the table. "Luckily we don't need a huge salary to drink at places like this," Flavio grins as he pulls out a chair for her.

Eleanor had been enjoying their one-on-one chat, but joins in the group camaraderie, contributing some of her own misadventures to the travellers' tales shared over strong rum and cokes. When the bottle runs dry, a young Swedish guy motions for another. Flavio yawns and announces that he's tired and going to head back. He asks Eleanor if she's coming too, but she still has a full glass and is trying her best to play it cool, so she shakes her head and tells him she'll be a little while yet. *Maybe he'll still be awake when I get back,* she thinks.

Half an hour later, she makes her excuses and leaves the others in the bar, walking back across the square accompanied by moonlight and the sound of chirruping cicadas. Entering a back door onto their shared courtyard, she can hear the sound of snoring coming from his room as she lets herself into her own stuffy bedroom. She feels the sting of disappointment and kicks herself for drinking Coca Cola at midnight as she lies awake in the muggy darkness, unable to sleep and feeling foolish for thinking that Flavio might see her as anything more than just another clueless tourist. She feels bereft. *This was her last chance*: she'll be travelling with the group to Antigua the next day, before flying out to meet her friend in Panama.

Lying down, she remembers why she usually avoids caffeine as a mixer late at night. Her mind and pulse are racing, and she's filled with a mix of longing and self-recrimination. Eventually, tiredness and strong rum send her into a fitful sleep.

She awakens to eye-stinging, throat-clogging smoke drifting under her door. Breakfast has never smelled less appetising. Eleanor dresses in her standard *tropical heat* outfit of denim shorts, designer cotton vest and flip flops, and splashes her sleep-deprived face with cold water from the outdoor shower before heading into the kitchen-living quarters. Flavio is already sitting at the table, looking a lot fresher than she feels and seemingly unaffected by that itchy smoke. She sees that the children have been sleeping on the floor in the living room and feels even more uncomfortable about being there and taking their bedroom.

"*Buenos dias!*" He greets her cheerily: "How much longer did you stay out after me?" Not much longer," she replies, "but I shouldn't have drunk all that caffeine, it was really hard to sleep."

He looks at her with real concern and says: "I was thinking about what you said about leaving your husband...I don't want to pry but I'm here if you need to talk about anything."

She's both touched and embarrassed. "Your eyes sometimes look red, I thought maybe you'd been crying?" Eleanor gives an awkward laugh and blames it on the smoke. "Ok", he says, looking unconvinced, "well like I said before, if you need anything..." he tails off as he passes her a plate of fried eggs covered in some kind of thick brown sauce that seems to be made of beans and possibly meat. Its smell, mixed with the smoke, is making her feel sick but she doesn't want to look rude, so she does her best to clear her plate.

Minutes later, the whole thing comes back up again just as they are bidding goodbye to their host family. *Oh good God,* she thinks to herself in horror when she vomits eggs and putrid beans onto Flavio's new-looking canvas shoes. He looks both disgusted and pissed off even as he tells her not to worry about it. She's mortified, and suddenly glad they only have one more day together.

He fumbles around to get his flip flops out of his backpack and puts the vomit soaked shoes in a plastic bag, in a side pocket of his backpack. The family are still standing there and look disappointed, probably because she just wasted food they could have eaten that morning. Eleanor attempts an apology in Spanish before Flavio reminds her she must head to the bus.

Barbara gives her a knowing look as they climb onto the bus and jumps into the seat next to her. *So...what happened?* Eleanor merely shakes her head, *nothing, nothing happened.* She knows her friend would find the shoe-puking funny, but right now she doesn't even want to think about it. She manages to avoid Flavio until everyone parts ways. She's thankful he doesn't mention it when the tour is over and gives him a large tip for his kindness. It's also to cover the price of new shoes but she doesn't say anything to him about that, or about the feelings she has for him. Even if she wanted to talk, there's no time. She has to rush to the airport.

# Chapter 6

# *The Engagement*

The South Dakota sunlight peeked through stained Travelodge curtains and wrenched Eleanor from a dreamless sleep. She nudged Ryan awake, telling him to *get a move on, lazybones.* She was anxious to get out of there and get on the road to Mount Rushmore.

Ryan furrowed his brow and grimaced into the sunlight for a second, then kissed her cheek, swung his legs over the side of the bed and stumbled to the adjoining bathroom for a noisy morning pee. It wasn't the type of hotel that encouraged long, languorous mornings. Eleanor would not have booked this kind of hotel if she had known Ryan would be joining her.

Eleanor was dressed in record time, and they rushed their room service breakfast of stale croissants and watery coffee: in 20 minutes flat they'd settled their bill and were buckling themselves into the car.

They were both excited, and the mood in the car was lively as they made the hour-long drive, Eleanor enjoying feeling like a road movie cliche as they sang along to cheesy rock songs on the only radio station they could tune into.

Even though she knew where they were heading, it still came as a shock as they turned a corner and the enormous heads of former presidents loomed into view. *Larger than life and even more ugly,* Ryan deadpanned as Eleanor let out a little yelp of glee.

Although they had flown together from London to get here, Eleanor was well aware that it was really *her* trip. It had taken a while to persuade him to come at all: only a month ago, just as she was about to make the booking, he had told her he was happy for her to go alone. He had told her he knew she'd been dreaming of it for years, but he wouldn't be joining her, as he hated flying.

Eleanor had been disappointed on a number of levels. For starters, what kind of successful businessman hates air travel? And as somebody who had always loved exploring far-flung places, she was genuinely saddened that he didn't share her wanderlust. She'd been planning the trip long before she met him, and assumed she'd be able to convince him to come along. When he said no, she went ahead and booked her flight.

At the last minute he changed his mind, and she had wondered if it was a sudden flash of jealous insecurity. Either way, she didn't mind, and she was glad they had been able to sit together on the flight. A couple of stiff whiskeys for Dutch courage had melted his fear of flying before they even boarded the plane.

And now he was here, with his beautiful bright blue eyes and his slender, tall body. His gentle hands. Her Adonis. It seemed to her a huge step, his coming here with her, and she thought that maybe now they really were on the same page, ready for a life of sharing adventures together.

They spent the first day walking around and just goggling at the incredible landscape of the Black Hills, climbing right up to touch those huge faces. They posed for countless selfies that never quite came out right and had Eleanor in snorts of laughter at the unflattering angles and windswept hair before a fellow tourist stepped forward and offered to take a proper photo for them.

They strolled back down the mountain, stopping at the main entrance for burgers and Coca Cola. The usually health-conscious Ryan said *"when in Rome!"* as he raised his giant paper cup, and Eleanor was pleased to see him cutting himself a little slack.

While they recharged their batteries, the afternoon sun grew hot and fierce, and by the time they were walking again Eleanor was regretting her decision to wear jeans instead of something cooler.

They climbed up little trails leading to who knows where, and stood surrounded by wildflowers and butterflies as they gazed down over wide valleys. Eleanor was trying to savour the moment, but something in Ryan's mood had shifted since lunch. He barely said a word as they walked, and when she asked if he was OK, he just nodded in reply. His phone rang a couple of times but he looked at the screen and didn't pick up, sticking it back in his pocket without comment and leaving Eleanor wondering what was going on.

After a couple more hours of walking, Ryan was looking uncomfortably red and sweaty. Eleanor passed him the Factor 50 she carried in her bag, and he smeared it inexpertly around his face.

She didn't tell him he had bright white sun cream eyebrows, so he walked around like that for the rest of the day, which she found both endearing and amusing. Knowing how image conscious he was made it all the funnier, and at the back of her mind she thought: *serves him right for being silent and secretive.*

Her redhead colouring meant that she wasn't a natural in the heat but had long since learned how to keep her pale skin from burning while still allowing freckles to peep through. She'd had the sense to get rid of the heavy extensions before the trip, and her shoulder-length hair was up in a ponytail, loose strands sticking to her cheeks. As the sun began to set they made their way down to their car, turning their backs on the great presidents of America.

Back at the motel, Ryan and Eleanor lay on the bed, looking into each other's eyes as they kissed. The kissing began to take on more urgency and Eleanor's hands travelled down to his trousers. They came to an abrupt halt when they found a hard lump – not where she was hoping to find it, but in his shorts pocket. "What's this?" She asked, thrown off her stride and watching the lust drain out of his face.

He sat up, straightened his clothes, and regained his exposure as he said: "let's go outside," and virtually pulled her out the door. His face was serious.

She felt as though she were sleepwalking. He led her past the motel's hot tub, which faced a freshwater creek complete with tumbledown wooden pier. An overweight man in late middle age sat in the tub, staring at this bemused redhead being pulled along by a sunburned Englishman.

Ryan's face was shiny with perspiration and Eleanor watched a single bead of sweat make its way to the tip of his nose before trickling off and plopping silently by her bare feet. The scene felt surreal to her: the majestic Mount Rushmore dominating the skyline to her left, while to the right sat another three overweight men sitting on picnic coolers and fishing in the creek. One of them was so enormous Eleanor was surprised the cooler could take his weight.

It was far from a romantic setting, which made it all the more startling when Ryan dropped onto one knee. Any faint shred of romance was killed by the tinny ringing of his phone. He ignored it, and was about to open his mouth to speak when Eleanor said: "Aren't you going to get that?"

Ignoring her question and seemingly oblivious to the fact that they were being watched by a fat man in a hot tub, he asked "Eleanor, will you spend the rest of your life with me?" He pulled a small box out of his pocket and nimbly flipped it open to reveal a simple silver ring topped with a large, glistening diamond. He had tears in his eyes.

Eleanor felt almost numb. She could see the fat man in the tub still staring at them, jaw dropping. This was the moment she had waited for her whole life. And yet…and yet it didn't feel right. The moment was too special for such drab surroundings. Instead of feeling a rush of joy, she couldn't help asking herself why he'd left it until now instead of asking the question at the top of Mount Rushmore. Or one of the beautiful viewpoints they had visited.

It felt like the right question at the wrong time. Almost on autopilot, she found herself taking his hand and pulling him to his feet. "Yes, yes I will marry you."

Wrapping her arms tightly around him, she could see over his shoulder that the three large fishing men had now joined the watch party.

One of them raised a beer can aloft and caught her eye. They all looked amused and astonished at the scene they had just witnessed, and Eleanor felt something like a tug of shame that her special moment had been reduced to a few minutes' amusement for some bored fishermen and a red-faced fat man looking like he was about to be boiled alive in the hot tub.

But she had always known that, for all his style and poise, Ryan could be extremely awkward at times. This glitch in his armour, this vulnerability, was part of what made him so special to him. She took a deep breath and whispered: "Let's go indoors and celebrate." The fat man in the hot tub mumbled his congratulations as they passed.

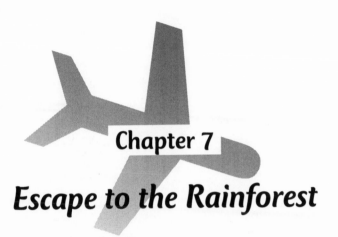

# Chapter 7

## *Escape to the Rainforest*

Eleanor has often said she can take any crap life has to throw at her as long as she has sunshine, booze, and pretty views. She might say it as a joke, but as the plane bumps down on a rain-soaked runway at Panama airport she's painfully aware of how much her mood is affected by weather and surroundings.

Looking out at the forlorn-looking palm trees and scurrying airline workers dashing to the safety of the terminal, she wishes she could stay on the plane and head straight back to sunny Guatemala. Dragging her suitcase through passport control and into a taxi, she casts a critical eye over the grey tower blocks and thinks *Panama City is bloody ugly in the rain.*

Feeding her foul mood is a gnawing sense of regret at the way she left, without saying goodbye to Flavio. Her initial embarrassment at the shoe-vomiting has now dissipated, leaving in its place a real disappointment at the way they left things.

But Panama means Vanessa. And sure enough, when she's checked into the hotel and wanders into the lobby, her best friend is already there: sitting on a stool by the bar with a drink in her hand and a beaming smile on her face. Eleanor drops her bags and launches herself towards her friend, mascara running down her face in a flood of happiness, sadness and relief felt all at once.

Forever the ice queen to Eleanor's drama queen, Vanessa pulls away and says: "you need a drink, love. Come on, don't get all emotional on me." She expertly catches the bartender's eye, taps her Martini glass in a 'one more like this' gesture, then turns around to check out the men at the bar.

They have so much to catch up on that nobody knows where to start. Carrying their drinks over to a corner booth, they keep talking over each other, laughing and saying 'no, you carry on!' over and over. Vanessa launches into a story about how when she arrived from London two days before, she had met military men from the jungle and got lost on local buses. Eleanor's dying to talk about Ryan, but she doesn't want to bring the mood down, so she just makes a flippant reference to 'the twatty husband' and puts the topic on the back burner.

On a drab, rainy night, Panama City doesn't seem to have much by the way of nightlife. The best the barman can suggest is the casino. 'Feeling lucky?' he asks, with a wink in Vanessa's direction. Used to being the object of admiring male glances herself, Eleanor feels like she has become invisible next to her glamorous friend. She makes a quick change into a dress and heels, but still feels frumpy. She misses her long extensions.

Once they're out on the rain-slicked streets she jokes that her lovely long locks would have been wasted on this place anyway. Neither of them is impressed by the city, but they stumble tipsily along the streets hoping to find something to make them change their minds. Instead, they see the bright lights of Hard Rock Cafe.

They head inside and stifle laughter at the po-faced rich South Americans sipping overpriced Long Island Ice Teas beneath walls full of Michael Jackson memorabilia. Eleanor almost spills her own ridiculously priced drink - an attempt at a Margarita - when they try to strike a serious pose for a selfie beneath the framed Jackson jacket. "I have never done anything so cheesy," she splutters, and a leather-jacketed man with a dark beard shoots a glare in her direction. He must think Hard Rock is a bastion of high society, she laughs to herself. Once they've drained their drinks, Vanessa mumbles that it's no fun being the youngest and drunkest people in the place, and they decide to call it a night.

It's still pouring with rain a day later.

"Let's get the hell out of here," Vanessa says, pacing the small hotel room as Eleanor lies on the bed flipping through channels.

"What's the deal with the ferry to Cartagena?" She asks. Christmas is fast approaching and neither of them wants to spend the festive season holed up in a high-rise hotel. They want sun, sea, and sexy guys.

The Colombian city sounded appealing, and although there were no road links from Panama ("Panama's government wants to keep it as jungle to stop people trafficking drugs through the Darien Strait" was the hotel bartender's explanation) Eleanor could swear she'd seen a post somewhere in a Facebook travel group about a direct ferry from Panama City. She'd found no further information online, though. "I asked at the hotel reception, but they knew nothing about it," she shrugs. Her channel-flipping lands on Frasier. In English. It feels like a small win.

"Eleanor, we need a travel agent, not the hotel receptionist." Vanessa says, looking annoyed and starts using her phone to Google local travel agencies. Having found a number, she gets through on the first ring only to be told: "Madam, the schedule on the internet is wrong: the ferry never arrived from Greece. There is a plane, or a slow boat." Vanessa asks the price of a one-way plane ticket and physically winces at the reply: "$750 one way madam." "What? That's insane!" says Vanessa, as the disinterested-sounding travel agent informs her that prices are high because of the Christmas holidays. She adds that there is a Turkish-owned boat going to Cartagena via the San Blas Islands. "The trip takes three days," she says, "and the price is $500."

"What are you doing?" Vanessa asks.

"Oh hon, I'm just booking the last seat on the only flight out of here," Eleanor says, deadpan.

"Are you serious? You're not going to leave me here, are you?" Vanessa looks at Eleanor's iPad to make sure she's joking.

"Come on, you know I wouldn't spend that much on a one-hour flight, even though it is tempting to leave you behind…" They look at one another and burst out laughing. It feels so good to laugh. *Thank God Vanessa is here.*

The pair do some more Googling and discover there's a three-day boat trip that would take them to their final destination, Cartagena, the famously beautiful Colombian city on the Caribbean coast. It's a third of the price of the airfare, and they reason that they'd also save on three nights' accommodation. "It goes via the San Blas islands," Vanessa comments. "I've always wanted to see them…but then again it's three days on a ship, and I've not got that much time left before I fly back to the UK…"

Eleanor can see her friend is conflicted. "It'll be an adventure!" She says, not sure whether she's trying to convince herself or Vanessa.

"But what if the boat's grim, and everybody stinks?" Vanessa screws up her nose. "We'd be stuck with them for days."

"And what if it's full of hot Colombian sailors? I say we just go for it, the online reviews are OK…"

"Go on then, book it now before I change my mind!" Vanessa covers her own eyes with her hands, dramatically.

Eleanor doesn't want to give either of them time to overthink it and chicken out, so she books them onto the next departure, leaving in two days' time.

The boat leaves from a port several hours' drive away, on the edge of the Darien Strait. Not sure how rough the boat trip will be, they decide to treat themselves to a stopover at a fancy-looking jungle lodge on the way to the port.

The lodge offers a trip on a private boat. Together with a handful of other guests, Vanessa and Eleanor clamber aboard a small fishing schooner for the hour's boat ride. Gently floating downriver, Eleanor loves the sensation of leaving the city behind and becoming immersed in wild nature. Sloths hang from trees over the river's edge, and howler monkeys race each other through the underbrush, hooting and whooping. Low hanging branches dangle like arms dragging into the river.

"Oh my God, what's that?" Vanessa cries, gawping at a sloth dangling above them. "I never really believed these creatures actually existed!!" Her obvious delight makes Eleanor smile.

It's Eleanor's turn to be taken aback when they pull into the lodge's river pier and climb down onto dry land. The resort's manager is heading out to greet them, cutting a path through a pack of what looks like pig-sized rats. Eleanor stops and grabs Vanessa's arm. "What the hell are those?"

The manager laughs. "These are capybara," he tells her. "The largest rodents in the world - they're native to South America."

"Do they attack humans?" Vanessa asks nervously, and the manager laughs again.

"Don't worry, they're harmless. They're pretty shy, and they only eat grass and seeds." Eleanor lets go of her grip on Vanessa's arm and they stop to peer at these gentle giants, grazing happily on the grass. Up close, they look more like giant guinea pigs than rats. "Shall I show you to your room?" asks the manager, wafting mosquitoes away from his face. Judging by the buzzing and humming sounds in the air, Eleanor assumes the setting sun has brought all manner of flying beasties out to play.

Their room has a balcony overlooking an enormous pool surrounded by palm trees, and they crack open a bottle of Panamanian bubbly to take in the view. Nightfall has brought little relief from the muggy heat, and the turquoise waters look so inviting, they can't understand why the pool is totally empty. "God, we should totally get in," says Vanessa. Eleanor doesn't take much convincing to change into her bikini and sarong.

They grab the bottle and two glasses, and head straight out the door. The pool is warm and delicious to the skin as they slide down the rails and jump in.

"This is the life..." Eleanor begins, seconds before something large and black swoops directly at her face. "What the fuck is that?" she screams, dropping her glass of bubbly into the pool. Vanessa is hysterical with laughter. Bats. They swoop low into the water, right over Eleanor and Vanessa's heads.

"Well this explains why the pool's empty!" Vanessa giggles as they clamber out of the water.

They finish their bubbly in the safety of their air-conditioned suite, windows firmly closed to stop any bats or other nocturnal beasts from disturbing them in their sleep. The crisp, clean sheets feel like a real luxury, and Eleanor feels oddly comforted by the insect and animal sounds of the rainforest at night. She slips into the deepest sleep she's had in ages, and the 4 am wake-up call feels like a physical wrench. It's time for them to board the jeep that will drive them through the rainforest to the ferry port and the boat bound for Cartagena.

# Chapter 8

## South Dakota

Flushed with the excitement of their engagement, Eleanor and Ryan headed down to the small town below their hotel, in search of somewhere to grab a celebratory meal and a bottle of bubbly to mark the occasion. But no sooner had they reached the outskirts of the town than the heavens opened - dramatic torrents of rain accompanied by jagged bolts of lighting and the loudest cracks of thunder Eleanor had ever heard. It was all very different from the polite drizzle of London.

Drenched within seconds, the newly-engaged pair ran into the first place they came to - a distinctly uninspiring diner. "Well, it's kind of romantic, escaping from the rain..." Eleanor insisted, shaking the drips from her soaking wet hair. One glance at the peeling wood laminate floor and plastic chairs was enough to tell her they were unlikely to find real French Champagne here. "Take a seat, madam," said Ryan, pulling out a stainless chair.

"We just got engaged!" Eleanor announced to the surly looking waitress arriving at their table.

"Oh, is it your first time?" asked the waitress, with no suggestion of irony, as she placed two large laminated menus on the table. Burgers, chicken wings, and large glasses of Coke seemed to feature heavily. "I don't suppose you have any Champagne?" Eleanor asked, without much hope.

The closest thing available was a litre bottle of sweet fizz with a screw top. It tasted terrible on the first glass, but became bearable by the second.

Ryan's phone rang for the umpteenth time that day, and he hurriedly declined the call before putting it on silent and shoving it into the laptop bag he carried everywhere with him. Before Eleanor could quiz him about who the call was from, he struck up a conversation with the hovering waitress. "Hello, how are you today? Would you mind terribly suggesting which steak dish to get? A pretty thing like you – you must know about the finer things in life."

He was suddenly all Hugh Grant, letting his floppy hair fall over his brow. The surly waitress broke into a wide smile, responding like a moth to light.

Eleanor felt a pang of jealousy. She sometimes hated the fact that Ryan could elicit the same feelings from other women that he did from her. And his shameless flirting was annoying, especially when they'd just got engaged. She looked at this woman with her bleached hair, false eyelashes, and prominent cleavage. Surely this wasn't Ryan's type?

"So, honey, how long y'all gonna be here?" The waitress directed her question squarely at Ryan, ignoring his new fiancée.

"Just one week, I'm afraid," Ryan was unnecessarily apologetic. A typical English gent.

"Aww, that's too bad, you should definitely stay a bit longer – and, my God, your accent! It is soooo cute!" The waitress flicked her long, blonde extensions forward across her shoulder.

Eleanor knew the waitress had a fair point - Ryan's charming upper-class English accent was one of the first things that attracted her to him.

"Oh – why, thank you, that's very kind." He flushed pink from his face to his neck, looking like a schoolboy with a crush. Eleanor felt a flash of anger. Why was he flirting so blatantly, and on their engagement night?

"Excuse me," Eleanor piped up, interrupting the cosy conversation, "I think I need more of this deliciously refreshing, sparkling wine. And I need it now, thank you." The waitress looked irritated, but scuttled to the back to get more booze.

"You're drinking a bit quickly tonight," Ryan observed, with one eyebrow cocked

"The occasion warrants it, doesn't it?" Eleanor's brain was getting cloudy now, and she was beginning to feel seriously put-upon. Wasn't it bad enough that they got engaged out the back of a cheap motel, without having to watch some random woman hit it off with her new fiancé?

The waitress returned with the second bottle, and was wearing freshly applied lipstick. Eleanor immediately asked about the status of the steak and omelette they had ordered. She'd lost her appetite, but wanted the woman to go to the kitchen and leave them alone. When she did bring their plates of food, she placed them on the table with a smile for Ryan and a scowl for Eleanor.

They were still finishing their food when the waitress reappeared. "How will you be paying, cash or cheque? We'll be closing up soon." She addressed the question to Ryan.

"In all the fuss I left my wallet back in the motel." Ryan leaned towards Eleanor, looking flustered. Eleanor was pretty drunk by now, and annoyed that she was going to end up with the bill. He was the rich one, but she frequently had to pay for their nights out due to his apparent forgetfulness.

She took her irritation out on the waitress: "I'm paying. What makes you think he's the one with the money?"

The waitress shot Eleanor a condescending look, as though pitying this woman who had to pay for her own engagement dinner in an empty diner. Ryan pushed his knife and fork together, made his excuses, and headed for the bathroom. He left his bag on the table, and the waitress disappeared to get the bill.

Eleanor swiftly dived into the phone pocket. His mobile had been ringing all day and he'd not picked up. Her heart ran cold when she saw the list of missed calls - each and every one was from Susan Everton, his ex-girlfriend. She stuffed the phone back in his bag. She felt sick, and wasn't sure if it was the greasy food, the cheap sweet wine, the flirty waitress or the fact that Ryan's ex had tried to call him 23 times that day. "Can you call us a cab, please?" She handed the waitress a wad of notes to settle up.

# Chapter 9

# San Blas Islands

Neither Eleanor nor Vanessa were morning people, and the pair have to drag themselves, bleary-eyed and still clutching cups of coffee from their hotel rooms, onto the jeep waiting in the darkness in front of the jungle lodge.

The young driver doesn't look much more awake than Eleanor feels. Any hopes of getting a bit more sleep on the journey are dashed early on - they soon have to hold tight to avoid being bounced out of the Jeep and onto the rough dirt tracks through the jungle. It seems an eternity before the driver turns to his shaken passengers and asks if they want to pull over for coffee.

"I'd love some, but listen - how much longer is this drive? Is it going to be this uncomfortable the whole way?" Vanessa yells into the darkness.

The driver shrugs and fills plastic espresso cups from a flask. "It's a couple more hours. There are no proper roads because the Panamanian authorities don't want to make things easy for traffickers." The silence hangs heavy in the air. *Traffickers?*

"I picked you up so early because it's more dangerous to drive through here later on," he says, reassuring nobody. "It's scary for me too, sometimes."

"Great, so what you are saying is that being uncomfortable is the least of our worries?" Vanessa's sarcasm goes right over the driver's head.

"Yes. It's possible a trafficker stops us. it's also possible that someone asks you to deliver some goods. If you are asked, please politely refuse, because it's not going to be anything legal," he advises in the same flat tone, putting the coffee away and starting the engine up again. Eleanor's not sure if it's the caffeine or the situation that's making her jittery.

Light gradually begins to filter through the trees, until they're bouncing along in broad daylight. The jeep slows down, and Eleanor shoots Vanessa a worried look. There's a checkpoint up ahead, manned by cops with gold teeth, huge shades and enormous guns slung over their shoulders. Eleanor can't help thinking they look more like movie versions of South American drug lords than real police. Two of the men step forward, asking to check the passengers' documents, and for a second Eleanor worries she'll never see her passport again. But the officers merely check the documents and resume their position of lounging beneath the trees before waving their jeep onwards.

By the time they reach the tiny port and clamber down from the vehicle, Eleanor's nerves are shot and her limbs feel battered and bruised. Vanessa's stretching her own long legs by the side of the jeep. "God, my arse is killing me!" The only ships at the port are tiny fishing schooners, and numerous shifty-looking characters are eyeing the tourists with silent curiosity. There is a small hut with a tin roof that passes as a waiting area.

"Think of it like a movie," Eleanor tries to feign enthusiasm, all too aware this was all her own idea. "It's going to be an amazing adventure." She's not sure whether she's trying to convince Vanessa or herself.

Any hopes of hopping straight on the boat for Cartagena are dashed when a bare-chested man smoking a cigarette arrives in the hut and starts gesturing at his tiny fishing vessel. "Please God, don't tell me that's our boat," Eleanor's voice is high with panic. "This boat take you to big boat. Twenty dollars each," the man says in broken english.

Their jeep driver, last seen snoozing in his car since they all got out, arrives to explain that they need to take a small boat down to the main port, where they will catch their long-haul vessel, The Dolphin. "Thanks mate, you probably could have explained that earlier," Eleanor grumbles.

Vanessa is having a heated conversation in Spanish with the shirtless boat owner, eventually turning to Eleanor to inform her that she's knocked the price down to 10 dollars apiece. They hand over the cash and haul their backpacks onto the wobbling boat. Eleanor's just glad to be out of the stifling hot tin hut that passes for a waiting room.

The boat glides out of the small harbour and past countless tiny islands, each of which houses a handful of wood and tin huts. Canoes sit on miniature beaches, some strewn with litter, and women dressed in colourful jewellery and ankle-length gowns linger in doorways, gazing at the tourists floating by with what looks like mild disdain. Detaching strands of sweaty hair from her forehead, Eleanor can't help but admire their cool, perfectly put-together appearance in the midst of wild jungle and brutal humidity.

Around an hour later, the schooner pitches up at a shabby wooden pier surrounded by bobbing sail boats. The Dolphin is among them, its name emblazoned in peeling paint on the side. It doesn't look big or sturdy enough to carry more than a few people, but there's a queue of people with hefty bags waiting to board. Warily, they haul their bags on to the main deck and Eleanor notices Vanessa has a face like thunder. It only gets worse when their captain - an elderly Turkish man - greets his passengers with the news that they might not make it to Cartagena by December 24 as planned. "Oh God," Eleanor whispers to Vanessa, "this boat is grim. Imagine being stuck on here over Christmas. But we can't go all the way back now…"

"I guess we have to stay with this then. I for one am not getting my arse back into that jeep," Vanessa looks like she's either going to burst into tears or punch somebody. "Apparently it's only four hours from here to the San Blas islands," Eleanor offers this fact up like a peace offering.

"I might just steal some rum and stay there," Vanessa retorts, her engagingly crooked smile lighting up her face for the first time that day.

By sunset, they're gazing at the type of idyllic Caribbean islands that look like they're straight from a travel brochure - spits of white sand, covered in swaying coconut palms and washed by the clearest turquoise waters Eleanor has ever seen. Vanessa's mood has noticeably picked up, despite her very vocal disapproval at the extremely basic cabin she's going to be crammed into with Vanessa.

With the boat docked at an apparently uninhabited island, a sturdy Turkish woman emerges from below deck and introduces herself as Shiloh, captain Yaddish's wife. She looks a lot younger than her husband, and Eleanor catches herself wondering whether Shiloh fell for Yaddish or his boat. She chastises herself for her own suspicions later that evening, when Shiloh shares her life story in between chopping vegetables and taking slugs of rum from the bottle. She's already poured generous draughts for everybody who happened to be nearby when she cracked the bottle open.

"I used to be a city trader in Istanbul, but I fell in love with the sea," Shiloh tells Eleanor. "I was always on boats. I met Yaddish in Panama and that was it. True love," she says, pointing in the captain's direction with her wooden spoon.

There's a mixed bag of passengers on board - Panamanians, Colombians, and a good-looking Aussie couple called Nick and Kara. The whole group gathers on the top deck to enjoy Shiloh's spicy tomato pasta, which she's spooned onto tin plates. When her second bottle of rum runs dry, Kara produces another one from their backpack and cracks it open. "Cheers!" says Eleanor, lifting her refilled cup. Sipping rum against a picture perfect island backdrop, even Vanessa looks content.

Buoyed by Panamanian rum, Eleanor tells Vanessa she can have their cabin to herself. "I'm going to sleep on deck and look at the stars," she explains. Shiloh looks vaguely amused, but produces a mattress for Eleanor to sleep on and says she'll take it to the best spot on the ship for stargazing.

They're standing by the ship's mast, looking at the crystal clear constellations in the deep black sky, when Shiloh suddenly dives in and kisses Eleanor full on the lips. Taken aback, she pulls away and mumbles that she needs to go to sleep. Shiloh squeezes her arm and leaves her to lie down on her mattress under the stars, and Eleanor is asleep within seconds.

She wakes in the middle of the night to a warm breeze, and drips of water falling gently onto her face. It takes her a while to work out that she's on the deck of a ship, and that it's raining. The raindrops and gentle rocking of the boat are soothing, as is the realisation that she has no ties, and no timeline to stick to. She quickly drifts back to sleep, feeling like a true adventurer.

# Chapter 10

## Hot Tub

Eleanor woke up in the same clothes she had been wearing the night before. Her head was spinning and the taste of sweet sticky wine lingered in her mouth. She was glad they hadn't planned any energetic hikes for the day.

Ryan's side of the bed was empty, and through the thin curtains she could see him having an animated conversation on his phone. The memory of all those missed calls from Susan hit her like a punch to the stomach. She didn't have the energy for a fight, all she wanted was caffeine. Coffee and a soak in the hot tub would make everything better. Eleanor dragged herself out of bed and towards the kettle and packets of cheap instant coffee.

"Are you coming to the hot tub?"

Ryan almost jumped out of his skin at the sudden appearance of his bikini-clad wife-to-be on their tiny patio. With one hand over the phone, he told her in a low voice that he'd be along in a minute.

Eleanor grabbed her towel and headed to the hot tub in her swimwear. She realised too late that the fat guy who had witnessed Ryan's proposal was already up to his hefty man boobs in hot tub water. She felt suddenly self-conscious about her own prominent chest in her skimpy bikini. She was steps away from the hot tub, and it seemed too awkward to turn back.

With a weak smile, she dropped her towel and slipped into the warm water.

"You were here last night with that guy who got down on one knee?"

"Yes, that was me," she confirmed, wondering where the hell Ryan was. She had a banging head, and the last thing she wanted to do was make small talk with a random guy while wearing a tiny bikini. "I actually thought we were the only guests here."

"I work nearby. This is on my way home. Kinda friends with the receptionist here, if you know what I mean?"

Eleanor wasn't sure how to respond, and some kind of hollow laugh spluttered forward. "Never seen a proposal here before," the man was still talking, but also hoisting himself out of the water and onto the wooden side deck. It wasn't a graceful exit, and Eleanor struggled not to stare.

"You can relax now, there's more space," he said, spreading his bulk across a towel on the decking.

Suddenly the hangover, the heat, the bubbles, and the close proximity to this man mountain were too much. Eleanor leaned over the side of the hot tub and vomited down the side of the hot tub, narrowly missing the man's bare feet.

Eleanor was mortified, but the man burst out laughing. "So that's why you got engaged in this place," he chuckled, like it suddenly all made sense.

"You got a little one on the way and gonna have a shotgun wedding."

He laughed and reached for a hotel towel to gently wipe the vomit from her face, then wiped down the side of the hot tub and threw the dirty towel in a nearby basket. The sudden act of kindness took Eleanor by surprise, and she wondered if he'd have been so thoughtful if he knew she wasn't pregnant, just hungover.

"It's not the first time there's been a shotgun wedding, I am sure it ain't gonna be the last," the man said. "I'm sure it's all gonna work out." Eleanor didn't have the heart to tell him the truth that she was just hungover from terrible "champagne" the night before.

Ryan appeared clutching a towel, and she felt suddenly awkward.

The stranger stood up, patted Ryan on the shoulder and said, "Don't worry, I looked after your woman. Good luck with the wedding...and the little one." Before Ryan could respond, he'd grabbed his towel and headed to the motel door.

"What did he mean, good luck with the little one?" Ryan looked horrified.

"Oh I told him we were having a 'little' wedding." Eleanor knew it was a terrible cover story. But why the look of horror? Would it be so dreadful if she was pregnant? Didn't "Project Husband" naturally evolve then into "Project Procreation?" Hadn't Ryan mentioned he wanted to have children with her? It seemed now as if that conversation had never happened, but she didn't want to push the issue, especially since Project Husband was on track.

Ryan seemed to have bought her poor excuse, of a "little wedding" and slipped into the hot tub beside her. "Happy, darling?" He asked, and she looked out over the dirty, crooked creek behind the Travel Lodge. "Yes, of course," she nodded, hoping that if she said she was happy, it might come true.

# Chapter 11

# *Living with the Kuna Tribe*

The rising sun wakes Eleanor before anybody else on the boat has surfaced, and she feels surprisingly fresh considering the rum and the curious goings on of the previous night. She cringes inwardly at the memory of Shiloh swooping in for a kiss, hoping it's not going to make things awkward on the trip. Propping herself up on her elbows, Eleanor looks out over the water, taking in the almost surreal beauty of the surroundings. There's a tiny speck of an island within easy swimming distance, and it looks inhabited. She earmarks it for discovery after some strong coffee.

Shiloh emerges with a coffee jug moments later. If she has any memory of the previous night, she's not letting on. Shrouded in an enormous towelling dressing gown despite the already-warm temperature on the deck, she pours Eleanor a metal beaker of the thick, sweet brew and bids her good morning before busying herself making various concoctions with eggs.

Vanessa appears, already in her tiny bikini. "Buenos dias chica!" She says, clearly a whole lot happier than she had been the previous day. "Ready for some swimming?"

Eleanor points out the island, and they make a plan to spend the day exploring.

Captain Yaddish joins them for breakfast on the deck, swiftly followed by Nick and Kara - or 'the touchy-feely Aussie couple,' as Eleanor and Vanessa have dubbed them. Eleanor enjoys their company, but can't shake off a twang of envy for their young, apparently stress-free, love. Nick is enthusiastic about exploring the island - especially when the captain tells them there's a sunken ship close by - and Eleanor feels an odd sense of relief when Kara says she'd prefer to take it easy on the boat. "No worries," says Nick, and Eleanor's secretly pleased that they won't be surrounded by love's young dream for the whole day.

With their cash in waterproof belts, Eleanor, Vanessa and Nick dive into the crystal clear water and splash their way towards the island.

"It's paradise!" Nick shouts, running ahead of them through thick tropical foliage in the direction of what Yaddish has told them is a tiny village. It turns out to consist of a few straw huts and one metal shack with yellow plastic tables and chairs. "I found the bar," says Nick with a grin.

It takes them less than five minutes to discover that it sells rum, coca-cola, red wine in a carton, water in small plastic bags, stale crisps, and not much else. They order a bit of everything, and settle down on the yellow plastic chairs to consume their drinks and snacks in the late morning sunshine.

The island's colourfully-dressed inhabitants take little notice of these noisy, sunburned interlopers, and Eleanor assumes they're the latest in a long line of foreigners to have 'discovered' their island. Their guidebook tells them the Kuna tribes people have been living here for centuries, closely guarding their language and customs. Shiloh has told them that, far from being a closed-off community, they are proud to show off their way of life to visitors, and it's often possible to stay in their huts overnight.

Although the locals barely cast a glance at these salty-haired sun seekers, Eleanor finds it hard not to stare at them.

The indigenous Kuna women and girls are so beautifully dressed in colourful fabrics, their limbs covered in numerous strings of bracelets, and their heads swathed in elegant headscarves. She wonders aloud what they must make of the backpacker uniform of shorts, swimwear, and flip-flops. "They probably think we're a right bunch of scruffy bastards," says Nick, between mouthfuls of rum and Coke.

"I need a pee," says Vanessa. "I don't suppose this bar has a toilet?" A quick conversation with the young woman serving them reveals that there is in fact just one toilet and one shower for the whole island. It's a 10-minute walk away.

They set off on their toilet mission, and Nick points out that they've covered most of the island already, it's so tiny. "I don't think there's much else to see," he says with a shrug. "Shall we see if we can borrow some masks and snorkels? Maybe we can find this sunken ship the captain talked about."

Asking around at the bar the goods turn up, courtesy of a couple of local fishermen who ask for a can of Coke each in exchange.

They happily splash off into the warm Caribbean waters, but Eleanor's hopes of finding the wreck are dashed within seconds - her snorkel mask is so scratched she can barely see. When it starts filling with water, she decides it's mission impossible, and splashes back to dry land with her mask and snorkel perched on top of her head.

The others are already lounging on the sand, having come to the same conclusion. "I tried to catch a lobster but he was a slippery bugger," says Nick. "And these masks are useless. Any ideas on what to do for the rest of the day?"

A teenage boy rows past them in his canoe, his oars shining in the afternoon sun.

"I can think of something that might liven things up," Vanessa says with a sly grin. She beckons the boy over, and Eleanor wonders what her friend is plotting. The boy begins rowing in their direction and Vanessa splashes through the water to meet him, shouting something in Spanish. He nods, and Vanessa swims back to the beach with a huge smile plastered on her face.

"What on earth are you doing?" Eleanor is genuinely baffled. "I thought I'd see if we could get some coke to go with our rum," Vanessa's still grinning. Nick looks blank for a second, before the penny drops. "Oh, well I guess we ought to try the local specialities while we're here," he agrees. Eleanor shakes her head in mock despair. "How much? You know there's no cash point here, right?" Vanessa's grin gets even wider. "Four dollars for a gram."

Moments later, a group of disconcertingly young boys zoom up on bikes. The smallest one, who looks about 10, holds out a bag of white powder. "Four dollars."

"Too expensive. We'll pay three dollars," Eleanor says, expecting the boy to laugh in her face. To everybody's surprise, he nods in agreement and holds out his hand for the cash.

Vanessa pulls two dollars from her belt, and Nick pitches in with two 50 cent coins.

"That's a bargain, mate," Nick says, and wanders off in the direction of the trees with the tiny plastic bag clutched in his fist. Vanessa and Eleanor thank the kids and head off to join him in sampling the stuff.

"Wow, it's good," says Nick. Eleanor's only previous experience of coke has been in London, when her friends have paid upwards of 50 quid a gram for a vague high that makes everybody bleat self-congratulatory nonsense for hours at a time. This is a different experience altogether. Her nerves are tingling, and she feels an instant rush of excitement and positivity.

They head back to the bar, giving the lingering kids a thumbs up. "Can we get more for later?" asks Vanessa, and another three-dollar deal is done. They spend the afternoon sipping rum and taking sneaky, but not very subtle, trips out to the trees. The thought of heading back to the boat and making polite conversation over another of Shiloh's hearty meals fills Eleanor with dread. "Do you reckon we can get a hammock in a hut here?" She asks Vanessa, after Nick has swum back to the boat, to "face the music" with Kara, as he puts it.

They're sitting cross-legged on the sand, a box of red wine between them. Vanessa gets up giddily and goes to ask at the bar about accommodation. "We can get a hammock in the chief's hut for five dollars each," she says on her return. "It's that one right there." She gestures to the largest hut on the island, sitting just metres away from where they're perched. "Apparently lots of women live in the hut, too. I reckon we'll be safe enough." "Come on, then, let's get set up," says Eleanor, getting unsteadily to her feet.

They pay the chief directly and he points them towards two empty hammocks, swinging near the entrance to the hut. Eleanor's head is fuzzy with strong coke and cheap red wine.

"I've been avoiding the topic but why haven't you come back to sort things out with Ryan yet?" Vanessa asks a little while later, swinging gently in her hammock.

"I want to be Ryan's *Zahir*, like the author Paulo Coelho talks of..." Eleanor says dreamily. "Ryan will be tortured day and night, thinking of me and wondering where I've gone and whether I'll come back."

"That is not the answer I expected," Vanessa interrupts, giggling.

But Eleanor's on a roll: "He'll be confused and in pain and be forced for the first time, to wonder why his wife vanished, why she went away so often, and what he can do to get her back. He will become obsessed and realise he loves me more than himself and in this moment, conquer his fear and follow his heart and find me."

Vanessa stops giggling and falls silent for a second, then: "Ryan is not Paulo Coelho, whoever that is. Ryan will not come and find you. I'm sorry to say this but you are not his Zahir or whatever romantic rubbish you've dreamed up, and Ryan is just not a deep enough person to delve into his soul the way you want him to."

A voice booms out from the chief's hammock: "Goodnight!"

Eleanor tries to keep her voice down, but she's shocked by Vanessa's blunt opinion. "Well, I don't want to come back until he apologises for the way he's treated me the last two years. All it would take is an email asking me to come back to be honest."

"Goodnight!" their host says again, louder this time.

"I didn't know this dude spoke English, I think he's trying to tell us to shut up and go to sleep," Vanessa says with a laugh.

"Maybe this should be about your journey and not Ryan's? Just enjoy your time away. You deserve it, it's not often you get time to travel the world the way you are. Sleep well honey."

"Goodnight," the tribesman says again and they lie still, both trying to silently stifle giggles.

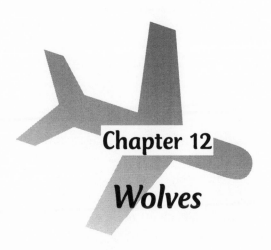

# Chapter 12

## *Wolves*

For years, Eleanor's mother, Mary, had been badgering Eleanor about getting married and settling down. Pretty much every boyfriend Eleanor had ever brought home had been assessed for suitability as a potential husband. So when she called her mother to share the news of her engagement, she envisioned her mother breaking down in happy tears on the other end.

But Mary didn't react with the unbridled joy that Eleanor had anticipated. She sounded surprised, and politely enthusiastic, but not a lot more. With Ryan sitting right beside her, Eleanor didn't feel she could press her mother on the issue, but she felt oddly shaken when she hung up the phone

Eleanor was torn from her ruminations by the all-too-familiar sound of Ryan's phone ringing. Before he could switch it off, Eleanor told him to "just answer the bloody thing!" She knew who it would be.

"Oh hi, Susan," Ryan sounded even more flustered than normal. "Yes, I am well, yes – thanks. No, sorry, I can't tomorrow... yes, yes – next week would be fine. Bye for now."

Ryan looked at his mobile and put it back in his pocket. Eleanor barely tried to hide her irritation - she knew Ryan was still on good terms with his ex, but why was she blowing up his phone the whole time, and why didn't he mention the engagement?

"Right, shall we get some air before the day is over? There's a short hike near here I was told about – and it's getting late," she said, pulling on her trainers and yanking the laces in one angry movement.

According to the route map they picked up at reception, they could take a pleasant six-mile stroll on trails that wound prettily along the mountainside before looping back towards the hotel.

The walk started off so well that Eleanor almost forgot to be annoyed with Ryan. The trail was filled with brightly-coloured wildflowers, and they'd only been walking a few minutes when Eleanor stopped dead in her tracks: a herd of buffalo was passing by, just metres away from where they were standing.

"Oh my God, Ryan…" she gripped his arm. The magnificent horned beasts were close enough to make out every detail of their shaggy coats and enormous horns, but thankfully not close enough to be startled by Eleanor and Ryan's presence. Any closer, and Eleanor would have been terrified. She and Ryan stood gazing at the herd of slow-moving animals, before they eventually disappeared from view.

The walk was exactly what Eleanor needed to lift her spirits. "Isn't this heavenly?" she said, stepping through the tree-dappled light into a clearing with views for miles. Ryan nodded in agreement, and Eleanor could tell he was enjoying himself a lot more than he had on the hike up Mount Rushmore. The shade meant he was less hot and bothered, for one thing, and this time he didn't have the pressing matter of a proposal to worry about.

They meandered along the ridge of the mountain for what seemed like miles, not another soul in sight. The calm, the gorgeous views, and the twittering birds overhead felt almost too good to be true. Eleanor's enthusiasm began to turn to a nagging anxiety that they might have taken a wrong turn. Shouldn't there be other hikers out on these trails? She stopped to look at the map, and in the silence heard the tell-tale ping of a text message on Ryan's phone. "At least you've got a signal out here."

Eleanor felt genuine relief at getting a phone signal, mixed with her anger at Susan's constant contact. She couldn't face an argument in the middle of a fast-darkening forest, so decided to bite her tongue, at least until they were back to safety.

"Ryan, I don't know how much longer this will take. We ought to have looped back on ourselves ages ago, but I don't recognise anything. And it looks like the sun's already setting."

"Yeah, if it gets dark in here we're screwed, it's hard enough to navigate in the daylight."

"It's mostly downhill from here – and I can see the Travelodge through the trees." Eleanor said, peering along the forest track. She picked up her pace until she was almost running, feet snagging on tree roots. The darkness was descending at an alarming rate.

Within minutes, it was almost pitch black. They seemed no closer to the edge of the forest. In fact, the trees seemed even thicker and they could no longer make out the reassuring gleam of the Travelodge sign. Eleanor was in full panic mode, and she stumbled on rocks in her haste to at least get out of the trees and into the moonlight. Ryan was breathing heavily, saying nothing.

A wolf howled somewhere in the distance and sent a chill down Eleanor's spine. It dawned on her that this was not the same as spending the night in the English woodland. It wasn't a matter of a few moles and badgers snuffling around - there could be coyotes, wolves, venomous snakes and spiders...even bears.

In her panic, she caught her foot on a thick root and almost turned her ankle. An injury right now would take things from bad to worse. She had an idea: "How's your phone charge? We can use the light to see where the hell we're going."

Ryan passed her the phone in silence. The phone's torch shed a faint glow on the trail. Despite her panic, Eleanor still clocked the unread text message on the screen:

"Looking forward to catching up next week. Have a lot of updates to tell you xx."

She wasn't about to start an argument about Ryan's ex while they were still trying to get out of the woods alive. But then the phone began to ring, flashing up Susan's name. Eleanor's patience snapped. She stabbed at the green button to answer, before Ryan could stop her.

"Susan, it's Eleanor, Ryan's fiancée. We just got engaged and we are trying to enjoy our vacation in America." She skipped the part about stumbling along a perilous mountain path in the pitch dark. "I would appreciate it if you could respect our privacy and stop calling and texting Ryan constantly!"

Ryan grabbed the phone out of Eleanor's hands. "Sorry, Susan... yes, yes, we are engaged – why, yes, thanks. I was going to tell you in person when I got back. Oh, ok – I am glad Charles is comfortable. Yes, yes, of course. I will pass on your apologies and congratulations to Eleanor. Yes, Susan. Have a lovely night. Sorry about the confusion, Eleanor doesn't mean it. Thank you for everything. You're a star."

Ryan hung up the phone. Although Eleanor couldn't see his face in the pitch black, she could feel his silent anger. He pointed the phone's torch towards the ground and stomped loudly ahead, breaking branches and bushes as he went.

They stumbled along in mutual silent fury until his voice suddenly boomed out, breaking the silence. His loud voice sounded odd in the stillness of the forest, echoing through the trees.

"What the hell were you doing, talking to Susan like that?"

Eleanor felt bad, but not that bad. What did he expect her to do?

"This whole trip, that woman has been calling you. How do you think that makes me feel? Are you here with me or there with her?"

"Right, let's keep walking." Ryan stormed ahead with his dim phone light.

"I refuse to walk any further until you explain," Eleanor called after him. "And by the way, how many of those calls were from Susan? Your phone has been ringing this whole bloody trip."

"Fine!" he snapped, coming to a halt.

"Only a couple of those calls were from Susan. The rest were work-related. My godfather is dying. Susan is a close relation of his and she's been looking after him. I asked her to give me regular updates on his health."

Barely stopping to draw breath, he cut Eleanor short when she tried to interject. "I decided not to tell her our good news as this is neither the time nor the place for it," he continues in a flat, dead sort of voice. "And I decided not to tell you about my godfather because I wanted to introduce you to him as my fiancée when we get back. That's assuming he even makes it until then."

Ailing godfather or not, Eleanor knew he was lying about the phone calls.

"Well, I'm sorry," she snapped. "You've never mentioned your godfather before. How was I supposed to know what was going on? What do you think I would assume when another woman keeps calling and texting you on our engagement holiday?"

Eleanor was so wound up, she almost forgot how scared she was, lost in the forest in the dark.

She turned to stride down the dark path, but Ryan put his hand on her shoulder and turned her around to face him. Two people staring at each other in the pitch black. "I can't believe at this stage of our relationship, when we are just engaged, you are already doubting me." He was almost yelling. "Maybe we should end our engagement. You do nothing but criticise me all the time."

He charged ahead, leaving Eleanor stumbling along in the darkness behind him. She suddenly felt very alone.

"Ryan, I'm sorry. Please, let's make up, I'm really sorry."

Eleanor was unsure what she was even apologising for. She just felt a sudden, desperate fear of abandonment.

When she looked back on this moment, she would see it as the beginning of the end. The beginning of apologising for things that she knew weren't really her fault. The beginning of losing her sense of self, and self-worth.

But in that dark moment, filled with fear, she followed Ryan through a break in the trees and into a clearing made almost magical by the gleaming lights of the Travelodge.

# Chapter 13

# *White Christmas*

Eleanor wakes up early and, blinking in the morning sun, gradually becomes aware that a group of Kuna women are standing over her hammock. She can't quite work out what they're doing, but they seem to be using a long pole to hook colourful rolls of cloth from a space just over her head. She realises they're pulling down their outfits for the day, and sleepily wonders why the women store their belongings there in the mens' hut. From her vantage point in the hammock, she can see reams and reams of fabrics in vibrant colours, stored high in the roof space of the hut.

Eleanor sits up in her hammock and, seeing the head tribesman still asleep, creeps past his bed and out of the narrow thatch doorway which opens onto the beach.

Sand in between her toes, she watches the sunrise and thinks about Vanessa's words from the night before. She realises Vanessa is right, it's time to stop worrying about Ryan and what might be happening back home, and start embracing this amazing opportunity to see the world.

She takes deep breaths and tells herself to seize the day, to live in the moment, and to have more belief in her abilities to deal with all the crap life has to throw at her.

Her new positivity is put to the test almost immediately: at breakfast, the ship's captain tells the group that the sea is too rough for them to set off that day as planned.

Eleanor takes a deep breath and shrugs it off as he breaks the news: "The trip from San Blas takes over 30 hours on the open sea, so when a storm comes in it can be brutal. There's no way I can risk leaving today."

Vanessa and the rest of the group groan at the idea of another day stuck on the tiny island, but Eleanor points out that it's a pretty attractive place to be stranded.

Her point is proved when, after a morning's walking and swimming around the island, she and Vanessa head to the bar and are nursing their first drink of the day when two gorgeous men appear, dripping, from the sea.

It's like a scene from a James Bond movie, but twice as good, says Eleanor as she and Vanessa stare in disbelief at the two six-packs walking their way.

"What brings you gentlemen to this out-of-the-way place?" Vanessa asks, fluttering her eyelashes as the hotties approach the shack. Suddenly self-conscious, Eleanor tries to smooth her own salty, matted hair. The most ludicrously handsome of the pair says: "We both have yachts, and every year we sail around the world from Italy, west to east."

"Wow, lucky you," says Eleanor. Hopeful that the men will take a hint, she adds, "We're on a tiny boat, way too crowded. I'd love to be on a boat with fewer people."

"Yeah," Vanessa chimes in, "it's so uncomfortable we slept in one of the huts here last night."

"That's too bad," the hottest hottie replies and walks towards the bar. The two men order a coke apiece and crack the drinks open as they start walking back towards the sea.

"I don't suppose there's any room for us little ladies on your yachts?" Vanessa asks, putting on her best damsel in distress face and halting the men in their tracks. in their tracks. "We're trying to get to Cartagena," she tells them, her blue eyes wide.

"Sorry, ladies, we're headed to Panama and the sea is far too rough for us to go back to Cartagena," the hottie tells them, looking a little regretful. After finishing his can of soda, he tells Vanessa she looks just like his girlfriend back home, and the men disappear back into the sea and onto their boats. The girls' hopes of rescue dashed, they steel themselves for another night on the boat with the increasingly bad-tempered Captain.

That evening when they go back to the boat for dinner, the captain is in a foul mood. He says the toilet was blocked and it must have been a passenger who did not respect the 'no toilet' paper rule. During dinner, Eleanor spots a green towel hanging behind Vanessa's head, covered in shit stains gently blowing in the breeze. She quietly puts her plate back by the sink and tells everyone she will be spending another night with the Kuna tribe.

Vanessa hasn't seen the cloth above her and sighs, "I'm skint. I have to stay on the boat tonight. But first, we should all return for a night on the town at the shack. Thankfully, the Kuna haven't run out of the red wine cartons and dirt cheap rum, so let's go!" She rounds up the others and they all jump off the boat and swim to shore.

After drinks, Eleanor goes into the hut on her own. The night is pitch black, the wind is howling and she swings alone in the hammock, feeling vulnerable. Her mind goes back to Ryan and she hopes somehow he can feel her loneliness, and that she misses and loves him. She sees his face in the darkness and wonders what he would think if he knew she was stuck here with no internet, no phone and no way of getting home.

She drinks the remains of the box of red wine, hoping it will lull her to sleep amidst the storm which rages on through the night. At some point, she stumbles into the pitch darkness with her flashlight to the toilet hut, on the outskirts of the village. It is raining and the wind is strong and her little point of light barely penetrates the dark bushes that surround the village. She returns to the Chief's hut, grateful that she is not on the boat tonight, being tossed around on the angry sea. Finally, Eleanor falls asleep with the howling of the wind in her ears.

She wakes to a calm sunny day and crosses her fingers that they will finally be able to leave the island as it looks like the storm has passed. Eleanor sees the captain and his wife heading towards her at the entrance of the hut. Shiloh stops in the clearing in front of them and waves.

"Good morning?" Eleanor tilts her head, wondering why Shiloh is just standing still a few metres away.

"Morning!" calls Shiloh. "I was telling Vanessa about a scary thing that happened here, right here where you are. Get your things, get out of your hut and come join us."

Before Eleanor can say a word, Shiloh continues: "We were friends with this Spanish guy who had been camping for months on the very spot where we're standing. His boat had sunk, but strangely enough, he hadn't done much to save it. We later found out that he'd stolen the boat from a couple in Bermuda that he had murdered. He'd run off and sailed to these San Blas islands to sink the evidence.

Eleanor's eyes widen and despite the tropical heat, she feels a chill run over her body as Shiloh continues: "He parked himself here on a quiet corner, waiting to see who he could murder next. This is before the Kuna henchman built his hut over there, where you stayed last night."

"Oh God, is that why the ladies keep their clothes there?" Eleanor asks, but Shiloh isn't listening. She's too involved in telling the story.

"We didn't know this, of course. One night he came up to our boat in the night to see us. He offered us rum and asked to come aboard."

"If it hadn't been for Shiloh he would have killed us," the captain says, putting his arm around his wife. It's the first time Eleanor has seen any affection between them. "She insisted that we shouldn't let him on the boat even though he was offering rum. The next day another skipper and friend of ours was missing, along with his boat. Eventually, it was discovered that our friend had been murdered and his boat stolen. The killer had left on his boat to other waters that very same night. That could have been us. Every time I walk in this spot I think to myself *we could have been killed here.*"

"I find it hard to believe you turned down rum," says Eleanor, half-joking. "I guess this island is not as small and peaceful as it appears." As chilling as the story is, she's more concerned about the couple's sudden friendliness than about the fact that a serial killer was once on the island. *What are they playing at?* She wonders, but just asks: "Will we be leaving today? It sounded like the storm blew itself out last night. I'm starting to get island fever!" The captain and his wife look nonplussed, so she adds: "I want to get to Cartagena by Christmas so we can meet our friends there."

The captain just shrugs and says: "We'll set sail tomorrow morning if the conditions seem good enough," the captain says. "But you'll have to sleep on board tonight as it will be an early start." We might arrive in Cartagena on Christmas day if we are lucky and the sea lets us," he adds, looking unconvinced.

Eleanor's not ecstatic about the idea of another day on the island and a night on the stinky ship, but she remembers her vow to be more positive and tries not to listen to Vanessa's grumbles as they spend another day swimming, sunbathing and drinking boxed red wine.

The night passes without incident, but the group's relief is palpable when they finally set sail early the next morning. The mood is cheerful onboard as they sail past the San Blas islands, which shelter them from the full force of the ocean winds.

But then they become aware of the previously elusive ship's cat, which suddenly decides to make its presence known. "She's gone a bit crazy and only likes being out at sea," Shiloh says with a laugh as the cat begins to prowl around and demand attention from each of the passengers. Eleanor's happy to give the animal attention until it scratches her thighs while sitting on her knee, and she can't help notice that the litter tray is full and stinking.

The tray is not far from where Eleanor and Vanessa are sleeping, and at night Eleanor can barely breathe with the smell. She wonders how Vanessa can sleep so soundly, and gets out of bed to go and sleep on the wooden deck. She steps on the cat's tail by accident and he promptly sinks his teeth into her big toe. *Ouch, you bastard,* she thinks as she tries to sleep through the throbbing pain. The next day her toe is swollen and looks septic, so she asks the captain for help. He gives her the first aid box.

"You hurt my baby. I have no kids, this cat is like a child to me. Never step on him again, you understand?" He glares at her, and she wishes she could just jump off the boat and swim away.

At one of the island stop-offs, the captain brings a Spanish skipper, Juan, onboard to help with the sails. The boat is already crowded, so no one is happy to have another person aboard. Even Shiloh looks irritated. The man always seems to be on the toilet when everyone needs it. Eleanor comments to Vanessa that he doesn't appear to do much work on board to justify his free ride.

As they round the last island, wild dolphins appear, and everybody oohs and aahs with excitement. Eleanor can reach out and touch them from her starboard seat. But it is only a temporary moment of joy: the dolphins retreat into the distance as soon as the boat hits the rough open sea.

Vanessa reveals the stash of prescription-strength sleeping pills she carries "just in case," but Eleanor's too nervous to take any after her experience with the antidepressants. Vanessa takes a couple and sleeps and sleeps through the lurching and crashing, while Eleanor stays awake and nauseous. At night, she escapes the litter tray smell again and sleeps on deck. The waves are high so she hangs onto the mast and gulps in the fresh air, trying to move as little as possible. At one point she feels herself rolling across the deck. She grabs the rail and crawls back to the mast, wrapping herself tightly around it. Sleep seems impossible.

She can feel the waves splashing over her face, the saltwater spraying her eyelids as she hangs on through the night. When she briefly opens her eyes, she sees the captain steering the wheel as if piloting the boat of the living dead. He stares ahead into the darkness slumped over the wheel. She looks at the moon instead and tries to keep her face covered and away from the spray.

Sometime in the middle of the night she sees the captain surrender the wheel to Juan and understands why the Spaniard was brought on board. Juan has settled into his position, a shadow in the night, when Eleanor hears somebody calling her name over and over in the darkness.

She starts to fear she's going mad. "Maybe I'm dreaming," she thinks to herself as she blinks her eyes open and can see nobody but Juan, silent at the wheel.

Soaking wet, with salt stinging her eyes, she lies down and prays for the dawn to come quickly.

The next morning, Eleanor wakes up to the sunlight warming her cold wet body. Her stiff arms are still clasping the mast. Vanessa is standing on the deck prodding her.

"Hey, what happened?" Vanessa is demanding. "I woke up in the night and came looking for you on deck. I shouted for you loads of times but there was no answer and I couldn't see you."

"I thought I was hearing voices or having a bad dream," Eleanor's head is still swimming when she peels herself from the mast and stands up.

It's midday before Vanessa and Eleanor realise that it's Christmas Day. Eleanor looks at the date on her watch and bursts out laughing at the ridiculousness of their situation. "What a way to spend Christmas!"

The captain announces he will be able to get them to Capugarna, a Colombian island a long way down the coast from Cartagena.

Vanessa snaps at the captain: "We've already missed our non-refundable nights in our five-star hotel. Now it looks like we won't reach Cartagena until when? We're, what, three days behind schedule?"

Eleanor hears the wobble in her friend's as Vanessa says: "You promised us we'd make it there by Christmas. I've had enough of this shitty boat."

The captain merely shrugs and walks away.

That afternoon, they pull into the dry, dusty, car-free Caribbean town of Capurgana, and Vanessa begins to relax a little as the sun beats down on them and they soak up the tropical Christmas vibes. There's drinking and dancing on the streets as people celebrate outdoors in cafes and restaurants.

With the palm trees and blue water, it doesn't feel much like a 'real' Christmas, but Eleanor knows her family will be gathered at home by the fireside in their festive jumpers and that her parents and grandparents will be distressed if she doesn't get in touch on Christmas day.

She manages to convince the receptionist at a small hotel to allow her to make an international call and gives her a few notes to cover the cost. She calls her family back in the UK and tells her brother about her recent escapades.

He laughs and says: "So you've been having a white Christmas." Her grandmother takes the phone.

"Hello dear, what's this I hear about you having a white Christmas in Colombia? I didn't know it snowed over there," she says.

"No, Gram," Eleanor replies with a laugh. It's not snowing here, he was trying to be funny because it's so hot."

# Chapter 14

## *Burning Down the House*

Eleanor always found it hard coming back to her desk after she'd been away on holiday.

The rows of desks in the open-plan office on the Strand aimed for minimalist chic, but in her post-break state, they just looked soul-destroying and drab: row upon row of hunched figures sitting in black swivel chairs, facing each other but saying nothing, staring at their screens and tapping away at their keyboards.

Even though Eleanor felt vaguely depressed at the sight of that worn, always slightly dirty, cream office carpet and the little grey metal desks, at least her return was more triumphant than usual.

She was walking back into the office an engaged woman, with the flashy diamond ring to prove it.

Having spent so much time listening to updates on Project Husband, Eleanor's workmates were collectively thrilled to hear about her engagement: even Belinda, her perpetually stressed and grumpy editor, rushed over to offer her congratulations and admire the ring.

As Eleanor extended her freshly-manicured hand to flash the engagement band, she felt a thrill of pride that Ryan had chosen such an extravagant symbol of their engagement. She knew it must have cost a fortune: a huge two-carat princess-cut diamond sitting pretty on a white gold band, surrounded by a shimmering cluster of diamond chips.

Eleanor was sure she caught a couple of the married women in the office glancing down at their own, much more modest, engagement bands, while one of her single colleagues, Jane, shouted "fiancé goals!" as she held Eleanor's hand aloft.

Once the excitement had died down enough for her to settle back in at her desk, Eleanor fired up her computer and immediately emailed Ryan: "A wedding makes some women go ever so slightly mad. In the office, there's much more interest in my wedding ring right now than there is in, say, starving children in Africa, wildfires in the Amazon or the polar ice caps melting..." She was still keen to present herself as archly witty, and not at all shallow, even though they both knew she was, a bit.

After the confusion surrounding the proposal itself, Eleanor was pleased that Ryan appeared to be wholeheartedly embracing his role as husband-to-be. So, when he set about arranging house viewings at a breakneck speed she was happy to go along for the ride. She didn't put up much of an argument when he batted away any talk of merging their funds and insisted it was a husband's role to buy the family home.

Eleanor began to dream of the house he would buy for them. She drew up checklists whenever she had a quiet moment at work: child-friendly, light and airy, with a large garden. On her lunch breaks, she no longer went out for a stroll but instead ate at her desk, browsing property porn on the internet and imagining her future family enjoying life in these dream houses. She began to daydream of a little boy and a little girl racing around their garden, both of them dark-haired, with blue eyes and pale skin, long limbs and freckled faces. Happily racing around their large, unusually sunny garden.

The first house Ryan took them to didn't tick a single one of Eleanor's boxes. Its pokey rooms were spread over four floors, with the living room inexplicably located at the top, and a concrete patch at the top masqueraded as a garden by sprouting weeds through the many cracks. Eleanor huffed. "I have no idea why you arranged for us to see this place." The estate agent's rigid smile began to fade as she added: "If we had a dinner party, I'd have to walk up four floors with all the plates. Not to mention when we have kids they could fall down all those stairs. And the garden – it's like a little concrete slab with no light, no plants. How could a child play out here?"

"I asked to see it because it was the best value per square footage compared to the other ones in the area." Ryan was digging his heels in. It was clear to Eleanor that he hadn't listened to a single thing she had said she wanted in a house.

After viewing several similar properties, all with multiple floors and no gardens, she was in a pretty bad mood. *Was it some kind of inherent male behaviour that made them see everything in terms of square footage, or did everything she said to Ryan just get misinterpreted somewhere between the ear canal and the brain? Or perhaps he just had no common sense.*

"I'm going to arrange the next set of viewings," she said firmly. "This is ridiculous, nothing we looked at today was in any way suitable for a family. I can't understand how value per square foot is as important as the actual structure and design of a house?"

Ryan groaned in response.

The following weekend, Eleanor tried to convince a grumbling Ryan to look at a large ground floor apartment in leafy Pimlico. It ticked all her boxes for style and layout and had a large leafy garden: a rarity in Central London. She even made sure it met Ryan's precious 'value per square metre' rules. Ryan turned up his nose at the mention of the neighbourhood and said he refused to live in a bad area. Eleanor almost laughed in his face: "My god, how snobby are you? It's right next to Belgravia! That's one of the poshest parts of London!"

"It's also right next to a social housing estate," Ryan countered as he zoomed in on Google Street View.

"And?" Eleanor was beginning to see the downside to Ryan's super upper-class background. "Bloody hell, even Tory ministers live in Pimlico, Ryan, you'd be right at home!"

"Alright, you win," he said, reluctantly tossing aside his copy of the Financial Times and grabbing his jacket. "Let's see how the povvos live." She laughed but bristled inside. She wasn't entirely sure he was joking.

Eleanor was determined to prove to Ryan that Pimlico was a perfectly respectable place to raise a family, but things didn't get off to a good start. As she stepped out of the car and walked ahead of him to view the apartment her eye was immediately drawn to a small police notice in front of the building. She was too startled to take in all the details, but it seemed to be a call for witnesses to a stabbing the night before.

Ryan was busy removing all valuables from the car, so Eleanor knew he hadn't seen the notice. She stood in front of it as he approached, blocking his view for the few minutes it took for the estate agent to arrive and usher them into the building.

*That kind of thing must be a rare occurrence, right?* She was half tempted to ask the estate agent, but didn't want Ryan to catch wind of what had happened. The flat itself was pretty perfect, in her eyes: large, open plan living spaces, floor to ceiling windows letting in lots of light, and a child-friendly garden complete with slides and a swing. It was a family home, and Eleanor's eyes lit up at the sight of two children's bedrooms: one filled with twinkling fairy lights and unicorn scatter cushions, the other a veritable museum of all things dinosaur-related. "The current owners have seven-year-old twins," said the estate agent with a smile.

Ryan looked unconvinced, and the estate agent decided to play the 'square footage' card. "As you can see, the apartment has amazing natural light – you won't find this amount of square footage so centrally very often," he said eagerly. When he tried to hasten them out the back door, Eleanor thought it was safe to assume the agent had also seen the police notice.

Ryan was halfway out the back door when he suddenly stopped.

"I need to see the parking place outside the front."

"Really, Ryan, it's just a parking spot, what's there to see?" Eleanor knew full well that if he spotted the notice, it would be game over.

"It's important because I want to see how exposed the space is," he insisted. Her heart sank as he stepped out the front door and immediately clocked the sign.

"I told you this was a waste of time." He glared at her, righteous indignation written all over his face. "I won't live in a dangerous neighbourhood."

The agent, clearly sensing a lost opportunity, put up a weak argument: "It only happens occasionally."

Ryan merely snorted and hurried back towards the car. Eleanor made the "I'll call you" sign to the estate agent and opened the door to the passenger seat.

That night, she felt deflated. It felt like she and Ryan were at polar opposites when it came to what they wanted in a house. *This is London, a crime like that could happen anywhere, we were just unlucky* she thought to herself but lacked the conviction to try to persuade him. She wanted to live in the home he had shown her when they first started dating, so why were they continuing to look when he already had a suitable home?

Ryan, on the other hand, was suddenly in a good mood. *Oh, how he loves to be right,* she thought, but her grumpiness lifted when he cooked dinner and then massaged her feet as they lay on the sofa to watch a film. *Perhaps we are compatible, after all,* she silently mused.

They hadn't even argued about which film to watch, for once. As she dozed off on Ryan's shoulder in front of a forgettable Jennifer Aniston rom-com, she mumbled partly to herself and partly to him.

"We'll get there in the end. Everything will work itself out…" She woke an hour or so later and realised she'd been drooling on his sleeve. Luckily, he was asleep too and hadn't noticed.

The following week at work, Eleanor was waiting for an update on a major business merger and using the downtime to continue her property hunt online. Her interest was piqued when she noticed a property had come up in The Cut: a hipster development in Waterloo. Properties at The Cut rarely came on the market, and this was not just a super-modern flat with a garden, but it included the coffee shop below.

Eleanor had no desire to manage a coffee shop, but she had long held a vague dream of one day opening a beauty salon. She didn't intend to work there, but she was convinced she had the style and business savvy to oversee a business offering upscale beauty treatments and hairdressing. She saw no reason why she couldn't work her media contacts to make it a huge success and eventually branch out into a chain.

But while this was something she'd often talked of over a few glasses of wine, she'd never taken any steps towards making it a reality. This property sparked a chain of thoughts about transforming the coffee shop into a trendy space catering to the beauty needs of the pretty young things that lived in the area.

They could live above the salon in their chic apartment until she was ready to expand the business.

She arranged a viewing and, riding a wave of excitement, called Ryan straight away.

"Darling, I've found the perfect redevelopment site! It's got a refurbished three-bedroom flat above and a shop below. I'm so excited, I booked for us to see it later today."

Ryan asked for the specs and told her he'd take a look at the property online and call her straight back.

"I don't know," he said, and her heart sank at his serious tone of voice. "It's extremely dangerous living above a shop, they often catch fire, and the lease on the shop is for another three years. You wouldn't be able to open your business for at least three years."

"Catch fire?" she spluttered. "Don't be such a drama queen. And think how handy it would be to go out for coffee until I open my business!"

She was shooting for humorous, but Ryan had his earnest businessman hat on.

"I'd have to charge the current owners rent and charge you the same for your business if you went ahead with it. You'd need to take it seriously."

Eleanor felt like he'd slapped her in the face. She had imagined them starting the business venture together and had hoped he'd be as excited as she was. Charging his wife rent? *Good God,* she thought, who was she about to marry? It wasn't like he needed the cash. "Charging me rent, are you serious?"

"Well dear..." he began but she quickly cut him off, softening her tone. "What about all my free facials, pedicures, and manicures? Imagine how good I'd look! And don't forget the constant stream of hot girls downstairs..." She knew her attempts at playfulness were falling flat.

Ryan said nothing, but she could picture him rolling his eyes. She had become accustomed to his disapproving silences. She felt her own patience snap.

"When have I ever even asked you to pay for anything for me? You offered to buy our family home but you just turn your nose up at everything. I could really make a go of this, and the flat looks perfect, but clearly my needs mean nothing to you!"

There was a long sigh from the other end of the line before he said, in a patronising tone: "Darling, living above a coffee shop, it's a fire hazard."

"For Christ's sake, stop going on about fire! Why would that even be a thing?" Please can we just look at it?"

"Ok ok, you win. What time?"

Eleanor was so excited, she could barely concentrate on her work for the next couple of hours. Wading through the details of two merging tyre manufacturers held little interest for her, and she slipped out the door as soon as lunch hour rolled around.

She jumped into a cab and arrived at the property a good 20 minutes before her viewing appointment.

She could barely believe what she was seeing.

*"Oh my God, is this a bloody joke?"* she asked nobody in particular, as she stepped out of the cab. The door to the property was swinging open, revealing the burned-out shell of a coffee shop.

For a split second, Eleanor almost suspected Ryan of organising the whole thing just to be proven right once again. But the estate agent, stepping out of her car with an apologetic look on her face, said: "Well, goodness me, it seems there was a fire in the coffee shop last night. The apartment wasn't damaged, but we won't be able to view it today, obviously."

"Will they be able to fix up the coffee shop?" asked Eleanor, and the estate agent replied that it was probably superficial damage. "I gather it looks worse than it actually is", she said, flashing straight white teeth. "I don't think there was any structural damage, can we arrange a new appointment in a few weeks?"

"I'm here now, I want to see the apartment," Eleanor insisted, trying to shoulder her way through the blackened doorway.

"Sorry madam, you can't go inside, it's not safe," the estate agent protested, placing an arm over the doorway.

And there was Ryan, striding towards them with a predictably smug look on his face. "Don't you dare say 'I told you so'" said

Eleanor, feeling on the verge of either punching him in the face or bursting into tears. Or both.

Instead, she bit her lip and handed her business card to the estate agent. "Please tell us the moment it's fit for viewing again."

The estate agent never called her and didn't pick up Eleanor's frequent calls. But Eleanor was not one to admit defeat, and left regular voicemail messages demanding an update

Her emails went unanswered, and when the estate agent finally did return her call, it was to say that the property had been sold. A quick dig online revealed that it had sold way below market value.

"Hah", she said to Ryan: "Clearly an insurance job and we never got a look in. I bet that smug estate agent was in on the whole thing."

Ryan just shrugged and said: "Well dear, it clearly wasn't to be." He appeared particularly distracted, and when he looked up from his laptop it was to tell her that Charles, his terminally ill godfather, had died.

*Christ.* Eleanor realised, with a deep sense of guilt, that she had barely given Charles a second thought since they returned from America. She had been so caught up in house hunting and wedding planning that she hadn't even asked Ryan about him, and Ryan hadn't mentioned it either.

"He was at his local, in his wheelchair, apparently," Ryan was still peering at his computer screen. "Drinking a pint. At least he will have died happy." He gave a little strangled laugh that sounded almost like a sob.

He wasn't the type to wear his emotions on his sleeve, but Eleanor instinctively rushed over and flung her arms around him. "I'm so sorry, Ryan…"

"I really wish you could have met him before he died," Ryan was reaching for the bottle of Scotch he kept on a shelf behind his work station, his hand shaking.

"Maybe it's for the best that I never met him," she said. "He sounds like he was a lovely man, and it would have been so hard to say goodbye to him before I could really get to know him." Ryan pulled her close to his chest as she rolled out the platitudes, wishing she could think of something more original to say.

"Don't worry, darling. He's in a better place now, he was so sick and now he won't be suffering anymore."

She had never seen him this vulnerable, he continued to hug her and she could feel his shoulders shaking. But even as she comforted him, she couldn't help wondering why he hadn't taken the time to introduce her to Charles, when he had made such a fuss about it in South Dakota. It felt churlish to bring it up now.

The following day, Eleanor found a printout of the funeral details. *Richmond church, 4 pm Thursday,* she made a note in her diary. It was a workday, but she told herself she could book the afternoon off if he really needed her there.

But Ryan didn't say a word about it. Thursday morning rolled around, and she sat sipping her coffee, idly gazing out of the window and pondering on what to do. Perhaps Ryan was just too proud to admit he needed her there? Surely he knew she would easily be able to get the time off work.

She contemplated just telling him she would go, but then wondered if that would seem odd, as she had never met the man.

*And of course, Susan Everton will be there,* she caught herself thinking.

She couldn't stop thinking about it as she brushed her teeth and went through her morning skincare routine. She dithered over the correct etiquette while she put on her makeup, and still couldn't shake the thoughts as she made her underground commute to the office.

Surely the most important thing was that she should be there, showing his support as Ryan's future wife? By the time she walked into the office, she'd already made her mind up and was preparing an excuse to leave her desk that afternoon.

"Oh, wow, the super wanker banker just said he's free for lunch this afternoon," She announced to her boss, midway through the morning. 'Super Wanker Banker' was the office nickname for an elusive and particularly high flying banking CEO, whose real name was Dennis Fossardes. He was, as the nickname suggested, a prize twat. But he was also an undeniably influential figure in the world of finance, and Eleanor's editor Belinda was constantly badgering her staff to try and schmooze him. Belinda looked up with suspicion. Eleanor had assumed this was a safe name to drop. She told herself she could just nip off to the funeral and then just say he hadn't given her anything to get her journalistic teeth into. She could tell Belinda the truth: that she needed to attend the funeral of somebody she'd never met.

"I suppose you'd better get going then," Belinda said through gritted teeth. "Oh, and Eleanor?"

"Yes?"

"Make sure you get his opinion on the huge wank bank deal he closed last week. I want to know where he's going with that."

Eleanor grinned, but her heart was sinking. *Shit.* She hadn't seen that one coming, and as she grabbed her bag and made for the exit, she realised she was going to have to speak to the banker wanker. How, though? He hated journalists. As she headed for the tube, she called every number she had for him: his office landline, his work mobile, his secretary and his intern, but it went to voicemail every time. She left messages but knew nobody would get back to her. On Eleanor's fourth attempt, the secretary picked up.

She wasn't happy.

"Eleanor, I'm going to have to report you for harassment if you call my landline one more time asking for my boss. He'll get back to you in his own time."

Eleanor was undaunted: as a breaking news reporter, it was something she had heard many times before. She ignored the threat and demanded to know when Mr Fossardes would be back in the office, silently congratulating herself for remembering not to call him the Super Wanker Banker to his staff.

"He should be back by four," said the secretary, "he'll call you. Don't call us." And she hung up.

*Balls.* This was not what Eleanor wanted to hear: the funeral began at four. But what could she do?

She fretted about it on the train ride to Richmond and anxiously clutched her phone as she arrived at the church, just in time to see a crowd of smartly-clad mourners heading through the gates. Seeing everybody dressed in black made her regret putting on a blue blouse that morning.

Ryan was nowhere to be seen, but Eleanor saw his parents heading through the church doors. It was almost four, so she found a secluded bench in the graveyard and pulled out her notepad and pen. She stared hard at her phone, willing it to ring, but was surprised when, at 4.02, it flashed up "super wanker landline."

"Hiiii there! Thank you so much for taking the time to call me back!" She put on her best sycophantic voice, and after a few minutes' dull banking chat she managed to get some quote-worthy info about the banking deal. She let him waffle on for a minute longer then said: "Oops! Going through a tunnel, I might get cut o…"

She switched her phone off.

The church was already full and the ceremony was in process, so Eleanor snuck in at the back and stayed standing up. An elderly woman in an ankle-length black gown and pillbox hat was delivering a eulogy.

"Charles was a wonderful man," the woman was saying. "Fit as a fiddle until the day he died. It was such a great shock to us all when we heard of his sudden heart attack."

*Wait, what?*

The pain and sadness of having him taken from us so abruptly are immense. His life was so full and he has always been so healthy, none of us could have seen this coming. He was a wonderful father and a dear husband, and we will miss him beyond words for the rest of our lives…"

The woman – Charles' widow, Eleanor assumed - was still speaking, but Eleanor was no longer taking in the words. She was struggling to breathe and clung onto the side of a pew to steady herself.

*If Charles hadn't been sick for a while, then everything that Charles had told her on the mountain top was a lie.*

Her head was swimming.

*Is he even here?* She had wanted to come here and show her support, but at that moment she didn't want him to see her. She scanned the rows of people in the packed church and eventually spotted Ryan with his parents in the front row. Beside him sat a tall woman with blonde hair. Susan, she presumed. Eleanor decided to sneak out of the church and head back to the office. Her grand plan of meeting Ryan after the service to cheer him up and show him she was there for him, had been well and truly dashed. She felt angry and embarrassed. *He didn't want me to come here today,* she thought, *maybe he doesn't want me at all.*

She tried her best to push the thought away, but it was clear to her that something was very wrong. She felt like she was on autopilot as she sat on the train. What could she do except get back to the office and act as nothing had happened?

Belinda was visibly surprised when Eleanor arrived at her desk at five-thirty and wrote up the story from Mr Super Wanker Banker. It felt good to concentrate on something other than Ryan, and Eleanor felt a hint of smugness. At least she had won some brownie points with Belinda.

She'd just filed the copy when Ryan called to say he would meet Eleanor outside her office at eight so they could go for some drinks before heading back to his place.

She was both surprised and confused: Ryan rarely swung by her office, and she had expected him to be at the wake.

Part of her was pleased, but a nagging voice at the back of her mind told her he was coming to break some terrible news. Like he was in love with Susan or something.

"I mean, let's face it, nothing has been going smoothly since we got engaged," said the paranoid devil on her shoulder. "None of the houses we look at is suitable, communication has gone right out of the window – I don't even know who Ryan is anymore, and given his house viewing choices, he doesn't seem to know a great deal about me, either."

When Ryan arrived, he was looking irritatingly dashing in his suit, his lovely blue eyes highlighted by the dark blue of his tie. They walked from her office to the Coal Hole, a dumpy traditional pub on the Strand. Ryan liked old man pubs and beer on draught, and the Coal Hole was strong in both categories. Even though she would have preferred to be sipping a cocktail somewhere a little fancier, it felt nice just to be out with him on a school night. Recently it had felt like all they ever did was work, eat, sleep and bicker over house viewings and seating plans for the wedding.

"How was the funeral?" She asked, trying to look innocent.

"It was fine," he mumbled, sipping his beer.

"You look kind of down. Who was there? I didn't think you'd be back so early."

"Susan got a strop on about something and won't talk to me anymore."

In the next breath, he looked almost embarrassed as he said: "Old Charles is safely buried. He left me something in his will. He didn't have any kids of his own, so it's quite substantial."

Eleanor was unsure what to say, and sat in silence for a few minutes, drawing circles in the condensation on the outside of her glass.

"Give me a hug, you poor thing." She pulled him tight into her chest and tried not to grimace when he began to snivel into her new Chloe blouse.

At least he seemed unaware that she had even been at the funeral. She began to relax a little, as it seemed that her fears that he had come to break up with her or demand an explanation for her short sojourn in the back pew, were unfounded.

"Hey, it's alright," she said. "It's nice that Charles left you something, you meant a lot to him."

"Yes," said Ryan, blowing his nose on a hankie he had pulled from his top pocket. "He even left me a 200-set encyclopaedia. It's a collector's item. I hope you don't mind, but I plan to keep it. I might have to make a special bookcase for them in the new home." His eyes were welling up again and he squeezed Eleanor's hand.

"Of course we'll take the set, darling, and make a special place for them."

"When we finally get our home, that is," She added, under her breath.

"Darling, I'll keep them at my place until we find our new place. And don't worry, I've set up more viewings for next weekend."

"I wanted to talk to you about that," Eleanor began, choosing her words carefully. "I think all the stress of house hunting and worrying about square footage is getting to us, especially on top of all the wedding planning."

Ryan raised his eyebrows as he sipped his pint, but said nothing. Eleanor took a deep breath and continued: "I keep thinking about the house you have in Kensington, you did say we could live there. Wouldn't that make sense?"

Ryan looked a little put-out, drained his pint and said: "We can wait, but as I told you, my house in Kensington is too small to be a family home."

They had visited the house in the summer, and Eleanor thought it was perfectly big enough for a family. *Why was he making excuses?*

"Please don't be pissed off, I just feel like we've got enough on our plates right now." Eleanor put her arms around him at the bar and rested her head on his shoulder.

Although she was supposed to be the one consoling him, she felt like it should be the other way round. She was feeling uncharacteristically deflated. Project Procreation was desperately behind, and she could feel her fertility dwindle with each passing month. Ryan didn't seem to feel the urgency around having a family, that she did.

In addition to that she didn't want to bring up the circumstances of Charles' death, not least because she didn't want to admit she had been at the funeral. But it nagged at her, that feeling of being lied to. She didn't know what to believe any more.

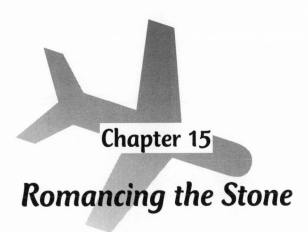

# Chapter 15

# *Romancing the Stone*

Down to their last few coins and festive spirit wilting in the heat, Eleanor and Vanessa are sweating in every sense.

The banks are all closed for the holidays, and the one ATM in the town is out of cash. To make matters worse, no shops or restaurants will take their cards.

"We can't even get a drink," grumbles Vanessa, as they sit on a sun-baked wooden bench by the water, weighing up their precious few options. Trying to work out how to get hold of some cash, Eleanor reasons that the boat captain owes them some compensation for not getting them to their destination, and Vanessa nods in weary agreement.

Neither of them fancies their chances of getting any money from the surly captain himself, but Shiloh seems a softer touch and, sure enough, after listening to the girls' sob story, she hands over $100 in a wad of crumpled bills.

Shiloh refuses to refund any of the other passengers, and Eleanor isn't sure whether she managed to get the cash because Shiloh has the hots for her, or because she feels sorry for her. She doesn't really care and just pockets the money with a deep sense of relief. She's so grateful that, in her tipsy state, she almost kisses the woman. Almost.

Instead, she links Vanessa's arm and they head straight to the ferry terminal's ticket office, in the company of the boat captain, who appears to be quite deep into his Christmas drinking. Miraculously, the ticket office is open, and they buy tickets to leave at 8 am the next day.

"Looks like we're having a lucky day!" says Vanessa.

"You shouldn't have tempted fate!" says Eleanor less than five minutes later, as they make a failed attempt to get their visa entry stamps for the country. "Lucky day, my arse."

The immigration office is open but unmanned. "The officer is drunk in the centre of town!" say the many inebriated locals who stop to laugh at the two stranded tourists. "He won't be back today."

The news does not go down well. They know they need their visa stamps if they don't want to face an expensive paperwork nightmare later on, and the captain appears equally anxious, saying that he'll get a fine if he brings people into Colombia without the relevant stamps. Vanessa's lower lip is trembling, and Eleanor's not sure if it's purely for show, but her tearful expression appears to melt the heart of the grumpy boat captain, who is clutching their passports in one hand, beer in the other. "I'll take you down here before the boat leaves in the morning," he says, somewhat unconvincingly given his woozy stagger. "We'll sort it out, don't worry."

Vanessa's tearfulness quickly gives way to anger, "I demand that you give us our passports back now so we can get on board tomorrow." She says sternly, looking directly into the captain's dark brown eyes.

"I brought you out of Panama and into Colombia. I'm responsible for your entrance into the country. I will be fined if I do not do this myself within the first 24 hours of us arriving here. I'm tired of you insisting so don't you dare ask for your passports again."

He scratches his chin and it's dark, bristly stubble. Shrugging his shoulders at Vanessa's high-pitched objections, he sways back to the boat, still clutching his sun-warmed beer.

That afternoon, Vanessa and Eleanor check into a grotty hotel by the docks. The power keeps cutting out, so with no TV or internet to keep them occupied, they climb into their stiff, uncomfortable beds for an early night. Loud music is blaring from crackly box speakers on the street outside, and even with her basic Spanish Eleanor can make out the slurred obscenities from every group of revellers that passes beneath their broken window. "Merry Christmas, hun." Eleanor attempts to make light of the situation.

"Do you mean "have yourself a merry, jolly, shitty Christmas?" Vanessa replies, grumpily.

The next morning they get up early, anxious to get their visas stamped and catch their ferry out of there. At 7 am, they sit on the edge of the pier, sipping takeaway coffee that's stiff with sugar. There's no sign of the captain or his boat. At 7:45 am, they're still scanning the horizon, nerves and tempers frayed.

Fifteen minutes later, Vanessa starts to cry as they watch the only ferry for three days slowly pull out of the harbour and out to sea. Eleanor doesn't even have the energy to cry. She just feels empty and exhausted, and one of them needs to keep it together. Penniless and fed up, they are in no mood to spend another three days in this hot, dusty town.

"I feel awful, it was my idea to get on the boat and we've wasted three weeks of your holiday. I'm so sorry," says Eleanor, pulling Vanessa into a hug as they watch the ferry disappear over the horizon.

The captain arrives shortly after the ferry has disappeared over the skyline. As he pulls up to the pier in his little dinghy, Vanessa hurls a torrent of abuse at him.

"You absolute bastard!" She yells. "Thanks to you, we've missed the only ferry out of here for the next three days. Give us our passports back now!"

Ignoring her, he climbs ashore and walks up to the immigration office. It's locked, which suggests the immigration officer is still out embracing the Christmas spirit. "See? You wouldn't have been able to leave anyway, not without a passport stamp," says the captain with a smug grin on his hungover-looking face.

When he once again refuses to hand over their passports, Eleanor's patience snaps and she storms towards a policeman sitting smoking a cigarette outside the closed immigration office. Her Spanish fails her, but she gesticulates towards the captain until Vanessa arrives and loudly explains the situation. The policeman walks up and begins questioning the captain, who shrugs and says: "No hablo Espanol." "He doesn't speak Spanish," says the policeman, stating the obvious. Then he sits down again to finish his cigarette.

"What you are doing is illegal," Vanessa yells, standing in the doorway of the crumbling immigration office, its dirty faded white walls and huge splats of black tropical mould making it look almost like a deserted building. Eleanor struggles to picture any vital immigration exchanges taking place inside.

The captain is sweating, greasy strands of long brown hair falling over his knitted eyebrows. "I explained the situation to you yesterday, now shut up," he says. Eleanor takes Vanessa aside before things escalate further. "Let's ask the policeman to go and find the customs officer, everybody knows everybody around here..."

Vanessa bats her eyelashes at the young officer and he marches off into the village. Half an hour later he returns with a sleepy, clearly hungover immigration officer who grudgingly opens the office. He motions to the captain and pulls open the metal door. Eventually, the captain emerges from the immigration office with their stamped passports.

Vanessa snatches them from the captain's grubby hand, and he almost yanks them back. Grudgingly letting go, he shouts at her: "Watch your manners! You give backpackers a bad name."

Vanessa bursts out laughing.

"Maybe that's because I'm not one of your bloody backpackers. Go back to your stinking boat."

They march off, not knowing where to go next. Vanessa starts crying again at the hopelessness of their situation. They have their stamped passports, but they have no money and no way off the island for another two days.

"Ness, I'm so sorry, hun, this is a horrible situation," Eleanor rubs her friend's shoulders. "It's so stressful, but let's put our thinking caps on. There has to be another way out of here."

Half-joking, she says "You have seen the film *Romancing the Stone,* right?"

Vanessa pulls a sceptical face and shakes her head no.

"It's my all-time favourite film, and it's based in Colombia. Michael Douglas and Kathleen Turner are stuck on a little island like this one, and they catch a tiny plane with a drug dealer to get out of there."

Vanessa raises an eyebrow. She doesn't look sold on either the film or the escape route.

"Know any drug dealers with planes around here?" Her voice is dripping with sarcasm and her fringe is dripping with sweat.

"Ok, it doesn't need to be a drug dealer," says Eleanor defensively, "but I have seen small planes flying pretty low, so maybe they land and take off here."

A hint of a mischievous grin is spreading over Vanessa's impish face. "That does sound like a pretty cool adventure," she says, "and it certainly beats staying in that crappy hotel with no money."

The same policeman who had tracked down the hungover customs officer is back in his usual spot outside the immigration office again, smoking another cigarette and idly looking in their direction.

Vanessa gives him a beaming smile and beckons him over. She doesn't have to ask him twice. Grinding his cigarette on the hot ground, he leans in close to hear what she says and gesticulates towards some fields behind them as he speaks in his rapid Spanish. Grinning, Vanessa translates for Eleanor. There is a landing strip on the island behind the village, and he's pretty sure there's a plane leaving for Medellin, a big city on the mainland, that same afternoon.

All four of them start to pull their suitcases down the dirt road until a young boy on a donkey-pulled cart offers to take their luggage to what he calls the 'airport' for a few dollars. They laugh as they follow the donkey past some trees and into a clearing where a concrete house sits overlooking a field with a makeshift landing strip. There are scales for luggage on the veranda of the house, and a group of young men in military uniform are leaning against the walls, rifles poking from holsters slung casually over their shoulders.

They barely pay the stranded tourists any attention, and Vanessa strides past them towards a back room, where a man appears to be issuing tickets. Vanessa quickly establishes that there are no flights to Cartagena, but there is indeed one to Medellin in two hours. They only take cards, no cash, the ticket vendor adds.

None of them has enough cash for the flight, so Vanessa ramps up the charm, flipping her hair to and fro with flirty abandon as she explains their predicament. There is a cashpoint at the other end, it transpires, and the enamoured salesman agrees to let them pay once they disembark.

They loll around on the fields swapping boat horror stories until a small propeller plane bumps down on the landing strip, and together with a group of partied-out looking passengers, they clamber aboard.

Vanessa and Eleanor have to sit separately because the flight is full, and Vanessa squeezes her shapely legs beside a handsome 'silver fox' type with blue eyes, leaving Eleanor to find a seat beside a matronly-looking woman with bulky great carrier bags full of what look to be thick blankets.

*Typical,* thinks Eleanor, as Vanessa strikes up a conversation with the hot guy.

The flight takes an hour, and Eleanor's bad mood lifts as the small plane circles Medellin, making a stunning descent into this sprawling city in the middle of the Andes mountains.

But Medellin is not on their agenda, and as soon as they arrive, Eleanor and Vanessa book themselves straight onto the next available flight to Cartagena, where their UK pals must be wondering where the hell they've got to. And then there's the small matter of their prepaid fancy hotel."I just can't wait for a proper hot shower!" says Vanessa, whose usually-perfect hair is pulled into a dishevelled ponytail, dry with dust. "I just really hope they refund the first nights," says Eleanor as they clutch their boarding cards and join the queue for the gate. She doesn't even want to think about her bank balance.

The smiling hotel receptionist expresses deep sympathy for their situation while refusing point-blank to refund even one of the three nights that they didn't use the room. Neither of them has the energy to argue about it, so Eleanor and Vanessa just take the key cards and let the porter carry their bags to their room. It's spotless, and Eleanor doesn't even wait for the porter to leave before flinging herself backwards onto the deeply soft bed. Vanessa tips the porter and immediately pulls two miniature bottles of Champagne from the mini-bar. "We can replace them later from the supermarket," she says with a wink before heading straight into the bathroom and letting out a deep sigh of happiness at the sight of the power shower and deep tub.

They take it in turns to get cleaned up, and Eleanor doesn't think she has ever felt so grateful for a decent shower and expensive hotel toiletries. Wrapped in the soft bathrobes they find hanging on the bathroom door, they sit on the balcony, sipping their overpriced bubbly and chinking their glasses "here's to making it off that boat alive!"

Their London friends, Eva and Dan, are both relieved and surprised when Eleanor calls. "We'd almost given up on you!" says

Eva, on speakerphone, with Dan's voice in the background repeatedly asking, "Is it them? Are they here?"

"Yes Dan, it's us, we're alive and getting a cab now."

Eleanor is giddy with excitement and relief at hearing a familiar voice so far from home, and the two of them throw on simple sundresses and flip flops before dashing down to reception and asking for a cab.

Eva and Dan's bed and breakfast is more 'rustic charm' than luxury, but Eleanor finds it even more appealing than their fancy five-star. "It's giving me Morocco vibes," says Vanessa, as they sit around a pool in a tiled courtyard that does indeed look for all the world like the Moroccan *riads* Eleanor has seen in style magazines.

Sitting by the pool, sipping more champagne and chatting with their good friends from home, they can finally laugh about their recent horror stories. "It sounds so funny now!" says Eleanor, giddy with bubbles and good vibes.

They sleep in later the next day, and venture only as far as the pool, lounging in their bikinis and keen to make the most of their pricey surroundings. The other guests are all immaculate-looking Colombians - ladies with ironed hair, shapely backsides and perfectly pert breasts; men with sharp suits and equally sharp facial hair.

"What do we think? Reggaeton stars? Footballers? Drug traffickers?" wonders Eleanor out loud, only half-joking. She looks down at her shorts and vest and says: "We need to get properly dressed up to go out tonight."

Vanessa glances around and says "We really fucking do." They have only one night in Cartagena, as they've found cheap flights back to Medellin the following day. "It looks like a cool city," Vanessa had reasoned as they booked the tickets.

Back in their room, they dig out the hair straighteners, eyelash curlers and statement jewellery that had been buried at the bottom of their suitcases for weeks. Pulling out a tiny dress, Vanessa says: "You know that rule about showing either legs or boobs, but not both at the same time? Well, sod that. Have you seen the competition?"

Eleanor grins in complicity. She smooths a tight-fitting dress over her curves and slips her feet into the first pair of heels she's worn in ages. "I'm putting flip flops in my bag in case I can't walk in these later. They feel weird now!"

Dressed to the nines, they grab a cab to the walled historic centre of the city. They've heard all the usual safety warnings, but Vanessa's more concerned with finding cocaine than anything else. It's not a hard task. Within seconds she's identified a likely-looking character loitering by the walls. She strides purposefully over, pulling Eleanor along in her wake, and with a brief exchange of Spanish, followed by an even briefer exchange of notes for a small plastic bag, the deal is done.

"Easy peasy," she says to Eleanor, as they make a beeline for the nearest bar. It turns out to be a gringo hangout, which is something of a relief to Eleanor, who's in the mood to pull but doesn't fancy trying out her stilted Spanish.

They've barely ordered their drinks when a couple of posh-looking English guys hone in their London accents. The two men live in Sloane Square, and it amuses Eleanor that they should come to Cartagena and end up chatting to guys from their neighbourhood."

Funny we should meet these hotties here when we lived near them for years," she says, and then feels a jab of pain at her use of the past tense.

"I suppose I still live there," she says… "my marriage might be over but all my stuff is in that house…it's still my home."

Shrugging off the sudden wave of sadness, she looks up at the taller of the two hotties, smiles at him and says, "you know, I live near Sloane Square too! How funny." She realises that flirting now feels almost as forced and unnatural as walking in heels after weeks in flip flops.

They make small talk for a while, and the men's repeated trips to the toilet suggest they have also done business with the chap lingering by the walls outside. Eleanor and Vanessa have already tucked into their own stash, and after a couple more drinks are itching to move. "See you in Sloane Square, gentlemen", says Eleanor with a slightly lopsided smile, and they head for the door and the still-sticky air of this tropical city.

They wobble slightly on their heels as they walk along the cobbled streets, swapping their heels for flip flops to climb the steep steps up to the ancient walls. Walking along, they stop to gaze at the view of twinkling lights to the Caribbean sea, before hearing the siren call of live South American music coming from a nearby bar. They walk in, and Eleanor almost has to pinch herself: it's wall-to-wall hotties.

Eleanor and Vanessa had quickly observed that Colombians tend to tip the scales towards 'ludicrously attractive', but this place has the added benefit of being a popular hangout for New Yorkers on weekend breaks. "It's only a four-hour flight from JFK," says a sculpted guy who clearly spends a lot of time in the gym. His repeated dry sniff suggests he is a 'work hard, play hard' type who likes to take advantage of the old Colombian marching powder. Eleanor feels too giddy to try and make a move, but shamelessly flirting feels good. Like she's moving on from her broken marriage. "We better head back if we're going to be up in time for checkout," she says, pulling a reluctant Vanessa away from another buff American she's talking to.

By the end of the night, Vanessa is hanging on the arm of a handsome Californian. They all go back to a fabulous apartment that he is renting. Eleanor crashes on the sofa while Vanessa disappears into the bedroom with her new paramour. A couple of hours later she wakes Eleanor up and they get a cab back to their five-star hotel.

Vanessa's trip is almost coming to an end, and she's told Eleanor she wants to have some Medellin adventures before heading back "to mundane reality" as she puts it. They both know that Medellin has a pretty gnarly history as the home turf of some of Colombia's biggest drug cartels. But their online travel guides assure them the city has cleaned up its act, and that tourists are unlikely to run into trouble as long as they keep their wits about them.

It's an early start, and both of them are feeling pretty groggy from the night before as they down coffee, settle their bill and climb into a taxi to the airport. It's only an hour's flight, and they both sleep the whole time.

They clamber into another cab at the other end, but Eleanor's unprepared for the steep descent from the airport to the city centre - she feels a plunging sensation in her gut, like being in a lift or on a rollercoaster ride, and only just manages to hold back being sick. Vanessa looks at her, noticing she's a grey colour.

"God, are you alright?"

"Yeah, but I need to get some fresh air," Eleanor gives the driver a feeble smile in the mirror. "Sorry about that...can we pull over?"

Once outside the car she gulps in the fresh air of the mountains, looking at the winding road ahead of them and appreciating the stunning view of the valley below her.

It's a relief to everybody when they pull up at their apartment hotel a half an hour later. "It's a bit pricey but we can save money by doing our own cooking," Vanessa had reasoned as she made the booking. Eleanor had never seen Vanessa cooking in her life, but she didn't like to point that out.

It's a smart little apartment, and the balcony's view over the Andes mountains lifts Eleanor's spirits. They get cleaned up and dressed in denim cutoffs and vests for the sticky heat of Colombia's second-largest city. They head straight for the famous squares in the centre of town and pose for photos alongside a series of increasingly large and ornate statues, sipping Diet Coke to help their flagging energy levels in the heat.

They're both fascinated by the story of Pablo Escobar and the Medellin Cartel, and Vanessa's read online about a tour of Escobar's house. "It has to be more interesting than bronze men on statues," she says and heads over to a group of tour guides idling by a fountain. The group of bored-looking men are all wearing T-shirts with Medellin Private Tours written on them, and Vanessa works her charm to convince one of them to take them up to Escobar's former residence for a reduced rate. "His brother still lives there!" Vanessa tells Eleanor in great excitement.

They laugh at the fact that they're feeling starstruck at the thought of meeting "cocaine royalty" as Eleanor puts it, and she points out that the Escobar brothers were responsible for a lot of brutal deaths. "I know, it's complicated, but I'm so curious," says Vanessa. In broken English, the driver tells them that Roberto Escobar is happy to receive visitors, but lost his eyesight years earlier when he opened a package addressed to him in jail, and it turned out to be packed with explosives. "The Medellin Cartel was serious shit!" says Vanessa.

They pull up at an enormous metal gate, which slowly opens when the driver says something into a speaker. Despite her misgivings about the morality of "narco tourism," Eleanor feels a shiver of nervous excitement. It's a surprisingly inauspicious looking home, rather than the sprawling mansion had envisioned, and Roberto himself opens the door, eyes closed, and invites them in.

Eleanor understands only a little of his Spanish, but Vanessa chats away with him in Spanish as he shows them around the notorious residence. "This car used to belong to Al Capone!" She translates for Eleanor. "He says Pablo paid a fortune to have it shipped over because he was a hero to the South American drug lords. Look at the bullet holes!"

Escobar takes them on a tour of the house and the garden, telling the hair-raising stories behind various escape vehicles and a picture of a racehorse that met a sticky end. They both know that Pablo himself met a sticky end too, eventually, at the hands of the police, but Eleanor is intrigued by the stories of life in the cartel. She knows that Escobar was a hero to some and a villain to others, and asks Vanessa to help her ask Roberto some questions about his feelings: "For many years I had nothing to do with Pablo and his drug deals," Roberto tells them. "I was an accountant and stayed out of the business, but the police and Pablo's enemies constantly accused me of working for my brother. When the government started accusing me as well, I just gave up and joined Pablo as his bookkeeper for all his deals. It made little difference since everyone thought I was involved anyway!"

He tells them about all the wild parties and the high living that came with the territory as one of the most powerful drug cartels in history. But he doesn't look especially happy as he recounts the memories, and Eleanor asks him if he would do it all again given the chance.

"I would have never been involved with drugs. I would have stopped Pablo if I could." He has a look of resigned sadness on his face.

The tour ends with a peek at the secret hiding place where the brothers retreated when police would raid the property: a small hole under the main stairway equipped with two oxygen tanks in case they got stuck down there too long.

Their guide is sitting outside waiting for them in the stifling afternoon heat. As they approach him, Vanessa nudges Eleanor and tells her that it's her turn to sort out their powdery entertainment for the evening.

Feigning innocent curiosity, Eleanor asks the guide how cocaine is made from the coca leaves that grow in Colombia. He gives her an explanation of the process, and she uses this as her cue to tell him that she's chewed coca leaves but is keen to try the end product "just once." He laughs and tells her that it's not a problem: he can meet them with the goods later that night in the same spot they had met earlier on. His name is Frederico, he tells them as they get out of the hot car and wave their goodbyes.

Back at their hotel, they change into dresses and strappy sandals and get ready to hit the town. Frederico has told them there's a performing arts festival in town that night, and they're keen to check it out. Their enthusiasm begins to fade when, after surreptitiously handing over a small bag of white powder in exchange for cash, he insists on accompanying them around the festival.

The noise and crowds feel stifling, and Eleanor's getting the impression that Frederico's taken a shine to her. He's about 20 years older than her and has no front teeth, and Eleanor whispers to Vanessa that they need to make their excuses. Vanessa makes a show of looking at her watch and says "Oh, we're late to meet friends, but thank you so much!"

She hails one of the many passing cabs, and almost shoves Eleanor inside, giggling as she does so. Eleanor's glad to be out of there, but can't help but feel a little sorry for Frederico as the cab pulls away leaving him waving despondently in the middle of the festivities.

They ask the driver to take them to the main nightlife area, and he drops them off a few minutes later in a street full of rather cheesy looking bars. Standing out from the row of neon-lit bars pumping salsa, reggaeton and pop music onto the streets is a slick-looking modern hotel, with what looks like an open-air roof bar on the top floor. "Do you reckon that place is only open to guests?" Vanessa asks, and they decide there's no harm in trying their luck. Slipping in through a doorway onto the street, they climb up floor after floor of steps, catching glimpses of minimalist chic corridors where tall and beautiful young people stand around in very expensive looking clothes. When they reach the top floor they order Mojitos at the bar and pretend not to wince at the price. There's an infinity pool at the edge of the roof, and they sit on poolside loungers, sipping their expensive drinks and trying to look like they belong. They're still not entirely sure if they've gatecrashed a private party or not.

They've already had a small sampler of Frederico's white goods, and judging by the queues for the toilet, they assume the entire crowd is partaking. Sure enough, a sweaty-browed man in a white Armani shirt sits down next to Eleanor, muttering something about being a doctor in town for a plastic surgery convention. He's sniffing repeatedly and struggling to string a coherent sentence together. He stands up, swaying slightly, and tells them he'll be back in a minute. He leaves his beer by the pool and staggers into the crowd. His beer is still sitting there half an hour later when Eleanor says they should go somewhere less expensive "and where the people are a bit less off their faces, maybe."

When they get back out onto the street, they clock the name of the hotel and instantly fall about laughing: emblazoned in tiny, elegant gold letters above the discreet doorway is the name Charlie Lifestyle Hotel. "Seriously? Only in Colombia!" Eleanor giggles.

They keep walking along the party street, but each of the bars seems to be packed with couples dancing salsa, and there's a distinct lack of solo men. After the fifth salsa bar in a row, they're seriously considering going home. "Do you have to be able to dance salsa to pull around here?" Eleanor is only half-joking as they stand surrounded by whirling couples. But the next bar they come to is a somewhat shabby-looking place pumping out reggae music to a predominantly male clientele. There's a group of good-looking gringo guys hanging out at the bar, and one of them pulls Eleanor onto the dance floor before she can even order a drink. Vanessa has already honed in on one particular blue-eyed Aussie Adonis, and before long they're all chatting like old friends. When the bar closes, everybody decides to take the party back to Eleanor and Vanessa's place. They all have flights to catch in a few hours - the guys are heading to Cartagena, the girls to Bogota - and a huge amount of local produce to use up before they go. They pile the stuff on the kitchen counter, and Eleanor jokes that it looks like some type of chemicals testing lab. The guys have to leave at 7am for their flight two hours later, and they're totally bug-eyed by the time they leave, but the blue-eyed Aussie still has enough of his wits about him to swoop in for a passionate kiss with Vanessa before they hit the road.

The next day, Eleanor scrapes the mountain of coke off the kitchen counter and into a bag. She is tempted to keep it but Vanessa insists it's not safe to take through the airport, so instead she disposes of it in an airport toilet bin "maybe a cleaner will get lucky," she says with a shrug as they board their plane, the pair of them still high as kites.

Eleanor's starting to feel the unpleasant stirrings of a coke comedown as their plane touches down, and her nerves are frayed by the time they drag their bags off the luggage conveyor belt and towards the cab rank. Vanessa's looking similarly strung out as their cab drives through a dark, industrial zone and into the city centre. They've had to downgrade their hotels as both of them are getting low on funds, but the grim-looking building still comes as a shock, with its bare concrete walls, 70s-decor and stench of cigarettes.

They'd both heard great things about Bogota being a fun party city, and it had seemed like a good place to spend New Year's Eve, less than 24 hours away. But the streets seem eerily quiet, and as they pick at an uninspired Italian meal in a near-empty restaurant, Vanessa laments the fact that they're not in Cartagena for the big night. The next day they walk to the historic centre of the city, which is less picturesque than other Colombian cities they have visited, and also seems oddly quiet. But they buy tickets for a New Year's Eve party at one of the city's most famous nightclubs, and hope for the best. The big night comes, so they buy tickets to a well recognised party venue. The place spans several floors and is totally packed. They wander from one room to another, looking for a place to sit, but end up ordering drinks and standing by the bar. Two pilots come to chat them up. It's hard to believe they are pilots, but it gives them a thrill, nonetheless.

Nursing hangovers the next day, they brave the cable car up to Monserrate - the highest point in the city. On their way back down they come face to face with a grass-chewing llama, and Vanessa's astonished expression makes Eleanor laugh so hard she struggles to catch her breath in the altitude. It is hard to accept that it's almost time for Vanessa to begin her long journey back to London. Eleanor feels tears welling up when she sees her friend packing her bags. It feels like a lot longer than three weeks since they met up in Panama. They hug tightly, and Vanessa says, "If we'd gone back to Cartagena I might never have got back on the plane to London, so maybe it's a good thing we chose Bogota as our last stop! Take care of yourself, darling," she says with a sad face, as she rolls her wheelie case out of the hotel door and hails a cab.

Eleanor has one day left in Bogota before she flies to Brazil. With her friend gone, it feels like there's a gaping hole in her life. That dreadful sense of loneliness has returned with a vengeance. She tries to keep busy, and half-heartedly joins a group walking trip to Cartagena's famous Gold Museum. But she can barely work up enthusiasm for small talk with the backpackers in the group, or for admiring the exhibits. Without Vanessa's company to distract her, thoughts of Ryan are sneaking back into Vanessa's mind.

She hasn't checked her emails for a few days, and there's a sinking sensation in the pit of her stomach at the thought of trying to get in touch with Ryan again. Eleanor can hardly bring herself to imagine him no longer being in her life, even though he's made so little effort to be a part of it.

# Chapter 16

# *Wedding Jitters*

Aside from their disagreements about property, Eleanor felt that her bond with Ryan was growing stronger by the day. They would spend long, lazy weekend mornings in bed, and in the evenings would just snuggle down on the sofa watching movies or comedy series - she took it as a good sign that Ryan shared her love of Frasier and Seinfeld. And he could really make her laugh. His humour was so dry that it wasn't always easy to know when he was joking, but his straight-faced observations on people and situations could have her chuckling for days afterwards. And she loved his small, but thoughtful, touches, like surprising her with breakfast in bed, or flowers at work when he knew she had a stressful day of meetings.

It wasn't all love and laughter, of course. He tended to deal with stress by becoming withdrawn and moody, and it was disconcerting to her that sometimes his phone would seem to be switched off for an entire day if they'd had a row the night before.

It wasn't perfect, but no relationship is, Eleanor would reassure herself, whenever they had a petty squabble over something like who left the milk out overnight. She knew any argument would blow over soon enough, and threw all her energy into organising the wedding - it was going to be spectacular, and Ryan had told her he was happy to get involved with the party planning. It grated on Eleanor slightly that he'd said it as though he was making a personal sacrifice, but she was willing to let it slide - none of the men she knew had made even the slightest effort to get involved with the planning for their own wedding days.

Eleanor approached it with the excitement of a kid planning their dream birthday party.

She had always been known for organising the most fabulous parties, and for her big day she had an extra fabulous card up her sleeve: she was going to get married in her family's very own castle.

It was a card she kept close to her chest, but Eleanor's Great Uncle Richard was a genuine Scottish aristocrat, and his rambling castle estate had actually been her birthplace. Her grandparents on her father's side had been titled gentry, with a fortune built on the back of generations of successful sheep farming. As the eldest son, Richard had inherited the lot, but he'd never had airs and graces, and Eleanor's parents had spent a lot of time on the estate during the early years of their marriage, visiting for extended holidays and helping to keep things in order.

Eleanor had even been baptised when she was two years old, in the estate's chapel, and now in the circle of life, she was going to get hitched in the same place in which she was baptised.

Ladedar Castle was carved out of the limestone cliffs in the remote Scottish Highlands, and Eleanor couldn't imagine a more romantic place for her wedding. It had earned her some major brownie points with Ryan's family, and American relatives on her mother's side were chomping at the bit to attend a wedding in a genuine Scottish castle.

Uncle Richard was more eccentric than intimidating, but his 18th-century castle was a real rough-hewn beauty, and the surrounding area had undergone some serious gentrification over the years - marinas, golf courses and luxury hotels cropping up among the heath and heather.

Sitting swathed in mist by the water, the castle was the subject of many local ghost stories, and Eleanor had loved to hear the chilling tales as a young girl visiting her outlandish uncle with her parents.

She had always dreamed of getting married there, and while her mother made disapproving noises - the words 'trying to impress Ryan's hoity toity family' were thrown around - Eleanor had convinced her parents to contact Uncle Richard on her behalf.

Eleanor had always struggled to understand a word he said, but that hadn't stopped her bonding with her great uncle as a child, and she was thrilled he'd given the go-ahead for her to hold her wedding at the castle. It wasn't often she got to compete with Ryan on the fanciness front, but he'd been genuinely impressed when she told him about "Lah-di-dah castle' as he called it. It was her one claim to aristocracy, and she was thrilled to be able to share it with her friends and family.

Uncle Richard had given Eleanor the number of his son, Cecil, Eleanor's second cousin. Or was it first cousin once removed? She'd never been entirely sure. He lived on the estate, helping his father keep the stately pile from falling victim to time and the elements. In order to keep funds coming in, Cecil occasionally rented out parts of the castle and its grounds for corporate events and weddings, so Eleanor felt confident she was in safe hands.

Eleanor and Ryan didn't have a firm date in mind for the wedding, so when Richard suggested they go for the afternoon of the June summer solstice, it made perfect sense: being so far north, the sun wouldn't fully set, and the sky would stay a deep blue all night. When she hung up the phone after a conversation with her great uncle, Eleanor excitedly texted Ryan: "We have our date, darling - June 19th. And for once I understood almost everything he said!"

Eleanor's boss Belinda (More commonly referred to by Eleanor as Morticia, or simply "The Witch") was away on holiday, so when Eleanor was back in the office on Monday, she seized the chance to make wedding-based calls on work time. She dialled Cecil's landline number, hands trembling with excitement. No answer. She tried again, and again, but the call just rang out each time. She tried the mobile number Uncle Richard had given her for his son, but it went straight to voicemail. She left a series of increasingly frantic messages, but there was no response. Uncle Richard had left the estate to embark on one of his regular overseas adventures, and he barely knew how to use his mobile.

When she'd still not managed to get through by Friday, Eleanor's excitement had turned to panic. Where was Cecil? Finally, during her Friday lunch break, he picked up on his mobile. Eleanor struggled to make herself heard over the sound of rustling paper - or was it crashing waves? - and cawing seagulls.

"Cecil, are you there? It's Eleanor! I need to talk about the wedding!"

"Aye, I thought a heard ma mobile ringin'," a cheery voice replied in a thick Highlands accent.

"I dinnae plan on bein' home in the afternoons, at the mo', princess. Shooting season you see." There was a pause, and further rustlings.

"I see, well, listen – there's some things we must talk about for the…"

"Aye, and, lassie, we got no mobile reception, so I dinnae hear yer call."

"Yes, but Cecil, did you get my voice messages on your home phone?" Eleanor was desperate to have an actual conversation while the signal held out.. "Uncle Richard told me we could have the wedding at your place – that you could organise it…"

She tried to decipher Cecil's words against what sounded like howling winds. "Aye, yes I think my dad told me somethin' 'bout a wedding."

There were various rustlings and mysterious crashing noises, followed by: "Well, no worries lassie. We'll have ten rooms for yer friends and I can cook a good Scottish breakfast! Got to get off the loch now, nice to talk to you, lassie."

"Wait – please, cousin Cecil!" Eleanor raised her voice in something approaching panic. Was this as far as his organisational input was going to go? "I really need your help in organising my wedding – can you at least give me an email address? Maybe we can communicate that way?"

There were more rustlings and crashing noises on the other end, and Cecil's voice was breaking up. Eleanor got up from her desk and paced the office in a vague attempt at improving the connection. "Lassie, I dinnae hear yeh – yeh got a get a crack of that in the Highlands. But yeh got a room, don't you worry – I dinnae use these new fangled emails!

"Yes, but Cecil – we need to plan the wedding!" Eleanor implored, but she was met with silence. The reception had gone. Eleanor sat staring blankly at her phone, suddenly aware of the scale of the task ahead of her.

She hadn't seen Cecil since she was an infant, and he didn't seem quite the debonair party planner she had envisioned. She picked up her phone again and texted Ryan: "We're going to need a wedding planner."

A quick Google later, and Eleanor had found the smart-looking website of Maggie, a wedding planner based near Glasgow. It was two hours south of the castle, but wedding planners didn't seem to exist any closer to the Highlands. Maybe the poor phone reception was off-putting.

Eleanor was relieved when Maggie picked up immediately, with a crystal clear reception. She gave a few details of the date and the location, and was surprised when Maggie replied with a laugh:

"Aye, we all know Cecil in these parts."

"Oh, good! Then you know what I'm dealing with!"

Maggie didn't seem daunted at the prospect, and the two women were able to discuss logistics for 100 guests, undisturbed by mysterious rustling and howling sounds. But when Eleanor opens her email to check the projected costs, her heart sank. Her dream wedding came with a lot of costs she hadn't budgeted for.

*£500 for the big bus to pick people up from their hotels and take them to the church on the day.*

*£600 per van to take people down the dirt track that runs from the church to the manor house.*

*£450 for a local ceilidh band.*

*£1000 for portaloo as Cecil's numerous toilets apparently ran into a Saniflo too small for a large number of guests.*

*£8000 for marquee hire - apparently only two companies in the whole of Scotland could bring a marquee to this area.*

*£7200 for the one and only chef that Cecil was willing to work with (or was it the other way around, Eleanor couldn't help wondering). Then there was the £2000 for Maggie's wedding planning services. And £500 for the use of the church, and the priest.*

And this was before the extra costs of drivers on the day, servers, alcohol, wedding insurance, accommodation and travel to Scotland. And what about the cost of her perfect wedding dress? What about the darling little dresses Eleanor had in mind for her bridesmaids?

Eleanor wanted to cry, and for a split second considered abandoning the whole idea. It was so much money for one day.

Only half-joking, she called Ryan and asked; "Are you sure we shouldn't just elope?"

Despite his family's wealth, Ryan had never been a big spender, and Eleanor expected a horrified reaction to the mounting costs. She was pleasantly surprised when he told her not to worry. "I know this venue means a lot to you," he reassured her, "and I'm sure my parents will help out with the costs, it's not like the old coffin dodgers are hard up." Eleanor burst into relieved laughter."Don't let them hear you calling them coffin dodgers or we won't get a penny!"

Ryan's breezy reassurance filled Eleanor with confidence that they were in this together, and the day was going to be every bit as fabulous as she imagined.

But her heart lurched in her chest the very next day, when she passed the open living room door and overheard him talking on the phone. "Honestly, Mummy...she's moaning constantly about the wedding plans. None of my friends ever had to even get involved when they were grooms, they just showed up on the day and had a good time...I know...she says I need to support her because her parents are in America and not here to help."

There was a pause, and Eleanor shifted uncomfortably at the door. She didn't want to hear, but felt rooted to the spot. "I've written contracts for the caterers and had hours of conversations about different meals, transport logistics, all the tiny details that someone else should be worrying about. It's not like I have nothing better to do!"

A further pause, then: "It just seems that we disagree on everything. Just yesterday, she put me in charge of ordering the wines. I want to make sure that we don't run out so I ordered five bottles of wine per person. Yes, five. Oh, not you too. I wanted to make sure we wouldn't run out. Anyway, next thing you know I have Eleanor on the phone, shouting that I am crazy to order so much, since it's non-returnable. When I explained I would rather have too much than risk running out of booze up there, she got the wedding planner, Maggie, to call me to "talk some sense into me" as Eleanor put it."

Eleanor felt furious and deeply sad at the same time.

"Mummy, it's just that this wedding lark is really starting to be a hassle. And we need another £10,000, it's extortionate the costs of getting married there in remote Scotland." Another pause.

"Ok ok, thanks mummy, speak soon."

Silence, then the sound of Ryan settling into his armchair with a deep sigh. Eleanor thought about biting her tongue, but instead burst into the room and whipped Ryan's Daily Telegraph from his hands.

"I heard your conversation. Why are you bad mouthing me to your mother? I thought you were happy to be involved?"

Ryan opened his mouth to reply, but Eleanor raised the newspaper angrily and continued: "Nobody drinks five bottles of wine. Maybe some people might drink two on a big occasion, but there will be people there that don't drink at all. Kids! And the older guests won't drink more than a couple of glasses. Five per person is insane, everybody would be rolling into the loch!"

Ryan rolled his eyes in response, and made to rise from his chair. "Eleanor, you're being hysterical..."

"Oh, am I? Well, I'm sorry you can't understand the stress this is putting on me. I've got loads of pressure at work. I have no private time to make calls during the day. You have three days a week working from home, and doing precious little as far as I can see! So what's the problem with helping me?" She was almost crying with frustration.

If Ryan felt any sympathy, he certainly wasn't showing it. "Thanks a lot for nosing in on my phone call. I think I have every right to complain about the bloody wedding hassle because this isn't the stuff a groom should have to do." He grabbed his newspaper from Eleanor's hand and stormed out, pausing in the doorway to angrily declare: "As for the wine order, I'll be keeping it exactly as it is."

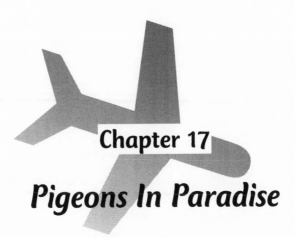

# Chapter 17

# *Pigeons In Paradise*

Waiting in the slow-moving queue to board her plane to Salvador da Bahia in northern Brazil, Eleanor does a quick Google search, and learns that the definition of 'squatter' is *'a person who settles on land or occupies property without title, right, or payment of rent'*.

Further Googling tells her that 10 percent of the world's population falls into this category, and she laughs a hollow laugh. She's become one of those people.

Eleanor had bought a beachfront apartment in the northeast of Brazil several years back, on the advice of a British-Brazilian couple who had assured her it was a guaranteed return on investment.

Almost on a whim, she had stuck a work bonus into buying the property, but had never received the title deeds. After wading through reams and reams of red tape, she had become an owner without any legal documents to prove it. She had put the project on the back-burner for years, but now, with nowhere else to go, has decided to squat in her own property.

Arriving in Salvador, groggy from the flight, she gets a cab straight to her property. She doesn't have the key, and hasn't been there for five years, so it's a relief that the security guard hasn't changed since the last time she was here. He remembers Eleanor and greets her with a wide smile and cheery *"Tudo bem querida?"* before giving her the key. "It maybe has changed lots" he says in broken English, his thick northeastern accent upbeat, but his words sounding ominous to Eleanor's travel-weary ears.

Whenever she had pictured coming back to her apartment, Eleanor had recalled the large rooms, high ceilings, dark beams and crisp white walls. And the balcony looking out over swaying palms to the white sand beaches and crashing Atlantic waves. When she bought the property, it seemed like she was buying herself a slice of Paradise.

But the apparent 'bargain' had become a major headache, stuck in legal limbo for the better part of a decade. When she finally manages to turn her key in the rusted front door, Eleanor's jaw drops in appalled surprise. Her piece of heaven now looks like something from an apocalyptic horror film.

The damp sea air has clearly eaten away at the plaster in the ceiling, and huge blocks of it have crashed into the living room, leaving gaping holes above. It's uninhabitable to humans, but clearly not to pigeons: the birds are everywhere, staring at Eleanor as though asking what the hell she is doing in their home.

Gobsmacked, Eleanor opens the doors onto the balcony, and the handle comes off in her hand. She stands there, taking in huge gulps of sea air as she tries to process the situation. From the balcony, she can see that the entire apartment complex has suffered a similar fate.

The 'luxury' flats had been sold to foreign investors at prices that had seemed incredible bargains at a time when Brazil was experiencing a real property boom.

But with the owners too far away to keep tabs on their properties, the shoddy workmanship has become painfully visible, and only a few of the numerous apartments are occupied. The rest are visibly dilapidated, and the whole place has a mournful look.

Sitting on the floor of the balcony looking out at the sea, Eleanor tries to figure out her next move. Even with the building in this sorry state, she can see how she was seduced by the place. The rolling waves, the pristine white sands and the jungle surroundings are as spectacular as ever. As she takes in the scene, she notices a blonde lady waving up at her from a ground floor patio. "Hiya!" the lady calls in an unmistakably British accent. Eleanor waves back as the woman shouts: "I'm Emma, the security guard told me another Englishwoman just arrived! Fancy a beer?"

Eleanor doesn't have to be asked twice. She grabs her key and, before she knows it, she's sitting on Emma's sofa, sipping an ice cold *cerveja* and sobbing her heart out.

Between sobs, she says: "This is all I have to show for my dream of living in Brazil and my one employment payout all those years ago... I just jumped into it like I always do...they told me it was a perfect investment, they said it was a safe location, and Brazil was having a boom, and where else in the world can you get beaches like this?"

Eleanor fears she's rambling. Everything is spilling out at once. But Emma is nodding sympathetically. "Well", she says: "Your friends were half-right. Properties in Brazil did go up in price, but not this place, not this wonderful freaking *Faulty Villas* complex." She laughs in a resigned fashion.

Eleanor takes a breath and continues her rant: "I met this British developer, David, and his Brazilian wife, when they were selling property plans back in the UK. I was suspicious, but I listened to my friends' advice more than my own gut, that's where I went wrong. And when I saw the place for myself I just fell in love with it. I didn't even get a lawyer. Big mistake. Did you get a lawyer?"

She doesn't wait for Emma to reply, but carries on her tale of property woe: "I have no title deeds, I don't even have a ceiling. But anyway, here I am." Eleanor begins to laugh a little hysterically at her own predicament. "So, Emma, do you live here in Faulty Villas?"

"I do, for my sins. You're very welcome to stay here tonight and drown your sorrows over a few more beers? Can't have you with no roof and a load of pigeons for company."

"Thanks so much, you're a real lifesaver. I'll take you up on that, and find somewhere to stay tomorrow while I call in the builders to make my place habitable for humans."

The next day, Eleanor books herself into a hostel in a beach village called Praia do Forte, which is close enough that she can come every day to meet the builders and keep an eye on repairs.

The hostel helps lift her spirits. It's low season, so she has the four-bed dorm to herself, and the bargain nightly rate includes the type of enormous buffet breakfast that Brazilian hostels and guesthouses do so well: colourful, fresh tropical fruit, excellent coffee, and cake. Eleanor is fully on board with the Brazilian fondness for cake at breakfast.

She quickly develops a routine: filling up on the huge breakfast in the morning and then lounging with her laptop in one of the poolside hammocks and firing off deceptively breezy responses to questions about her marriage.

Emma has put her in touch with a trustworthy local builder, and each morning Eleanor hops on the back of a moto taxi and clings on to the driver for dear life as he speeds over the bumpy roads to the apartment complex.

Once there, she checks up on the painfully slow progress and gossips with Emma about who's sleeping with who.

She also gets all the details of who is robbing who, and which of the local hotties are not to be trusted. Most of them, it seems. On the days when she's not at the apartment, Eleanor parks herself at her favourite spot on the beach, spreading out her sarong to lie down with a book until sunset. After an early dinner, she heads to the almost-empty hostel. For the first time in a long time, she's totally alone, but doesn't feel lonely.

Thinking about the apartment is a welcome distraction from worrying about the state of her marriage, and she's enjoying the sense of stability and routine.

Still, with all the gorgeous guys strolling around, wearing the standard Brazilian beach uniform of Bermuda shorts, Havaiana flip flops, and nothing else, she's also feeling damn horny.

One afternoon she arrives at the beach, lost in thought about whether her relationship with Ryan is truly past the point of no return. She's jolted away from her thoughts by the sight of a bronzed hottie occupying her usual spot on the beach. She plonks herself down a little farther along, but within minutes he's at her side and asking if she wants company. Good question... she isn't really sure what to say, but he seems polite enough. And hot. So very hot.

"I suppose we can talk if you want," She says, pretending to be engrossed in her book.

"So where are you from?" He asks her in English with an accent that sounds like he spent a lot of time watching American movies.

"I'm from England."

"I'm from Salvador," he says. "I work as an artist there but I come here to stay with friends sometimes." He asks her if she's married. She decides not to spare this man the details.

"I'm having a very horrible divorce." She gives him a shallow smile.

"What a foolish man!" He says through a smile that displays gleaming white teeth, and Eleanor almost believes him. "Your husband, he is a fool to lose someone as beautiful as you."

Eleanor's confidence is boosted by his flattery, but she's pretty sure he's just laying on the charm to get into her bikini bottoms.

"Don't worry about him," he flashes that pearly smile again. "You're in Bahia now."

He's wearing nothing but the tiny sunga swimming trunks that Brazilian men are so fond of. Just as the women like to flaunt their assets on the beach, so do the guys. Eleanor isn't complaining. She takes a good look at his body: he's all muscle, a dark tan suggesting some native Indian blood, dark brown, almost black, hair and eyes. He's definitely sexy enough to have some fun with, she thinks.

"So, what kind of artist are you? Oh, and what's your name?" She asks. He whips out a photo album from his backpack and shows her some of his artworks. She wonders why he has this with him on the beach, but doesn't ask.

"My name is Edilson. My ex-wife and daughter live in Salvador," he says. "But my daughter, she only calls when she wants money, and my wife, she won't speak to me. I don't see them a lot. I had a German girlfriend, but she was a bitch too and left me."

Eleanor wasn't expecting quite so much detail. And she's too absorbed in her own problems to hear about his, so she shrugs and says nothing.

"Where do you stay?" He asks her, but it doesn't seem wise to tell this stranger her address.

"Just down the beach from here," She gestures vaguely. He takes one look at her wristband, which she had forgotten had the hostel name on, and says, "Canazaro hostel, it's a very good one."

"Yes, it's really good – I should get back," Eleanor says, deciding this character seems a bit too smooth. She realises she has actually been enjoying the solitude of her evenings. She gets to her feet and he stands up too.

"Ahh okay, no problem. Can I meet you later for dinner tonight, maybe?" Edilson sounds hopeful.

"No thanks, I'm busy tonight. Nice to meet you though."

"I see you again," he calls after her. She rather hopes not. He's good looking, but there is something a little unnerving about him.

The next morning after breakfast, she finds Edilson sitting on a chair in the reception of the hostel, looking handsome in a crisp shirt and shorts, but with the same tatty backpack he evidently carries everywhere.

"Good morning!" He grins, getting up as Eleanor walks out of the hostel entrance. "I waited for you so we can go to the beach together." Eleanor feels taken aback by his forwardness. But how much can a bit of company hurt?

They go to the beach. It's quite a pleasant morning and he talks again about his 'psycho' former girlfriend. A lot.

Eleanor retaliates with chat about her psycho soon-to-be former husband, and in between dissing their crazy exes, they swim in the clear, cooling water. At lunchtime he takes her to a small hole-in-the-wall café that has such good traditional food for such a low price that Eleanor insists on paying for him. He doesn't put up much of a protest.

When she decides she's had enough sun and needs to do some work at the flat, she goes back to the hostel and tells him she'll meet him tomorrow. She realises she enjoyed his company a lot more than she expected. Although she's well aware it might just be her base urges kicking in. The next day, Edilson is waiting for her just like before and they do the whole day over again. By the fourth day, it's like they have done this their whole lives – just swim, eat and talk.

But then a switch is flipped. Eleanor has a lot of beer at lunch. They walk back to their usual spot and she has no builders to meet back at her flat that afternoon.

Eleanor is swimming in their usual spot when he comes into the water with her. He starts kissing her and it is smooth, salty and warm. She can feel he is massive and hard. No one is around.

She's dying to have him, but the nagging angel on one shoulder tells her she's technically still married, and that they can't use a condom like this in the water. She doesn't have one anyway. But her horniness takes over, and she lets him edge into her little by little, each time penetrating a tiny bit further until she realises he is completely inside. It feels fantastic. She starts to thrust against him, pushing him into her over and over. She hasn't felt this good for so long. She grabs his arms to steady herself.

People have started arriving onto the beach so they move deeper out, trying to hide what they're doing. She thrusts and grinds against him as he stands firm, and she rises up and down against him. The combination of the warm water lapping against her body and his hands caressing her is mind blowing, and neither of them are able to stop what they have started.

She clutches his hard arms while he thrusts and thrusts until she comes in a flood of physical relief. Her cries make him push harder, and when he's done he clings to her.

She desperately wants to get out of the water as she is sure they are being watched by now. After a few minutes of total abandonment, her sense of sanity is back. Having sex with him in the sea without a condom doesn't seem like such a good idea anymore.

They swim around for a while, feigning to onlookers that nothing just happened. Eleanor feels not just the physical pleasure, but also a pleasure at being wanted again. But it's tainted by sadness that this is just sex and they don't have anything else in common.

They walk back to the hostel holding hands and he asks her if they can go to dinner that night. He disappears off to wherever he goes, and she retreats to her room to shower and get changed. She chooses a nice restaurant that she has regularly visited alone. They order cocktails and food, it's a warm evening and she's feeling fairly happy.

The mood quickly evaporates when, out of nowhere, Edilson says, "You only love me with your body. You don't love me with your mind, you still love your husband, not me."

Eleanor wants to reach over and slap him for bringing it up. She is annoyed that he's spoiled her evening, so she blurts out.

"Yes I do. I do not love you, Edilson. I still love my husband. Is this going to be a problem?"

She's not even sure if she's addressing the question to Edilson, or to herself.

# Chapter 18

# *Nice Day for a White Wedding*

Eleanor wasn't finding the run up to the wedding anything like as much fun as she'd imagined. The six bridesmaids didn't seem to be putting themselves out to organise her hen night, and she wasn't sure they could be trusted to organise something that wasn't going to be ridiculously expensive.

With the phrase, "if you want something doing well, do it yourself," running through her mind, Eleanor found herself telling the bridesmaids that they needn't worry, she'd organise it all herself.

The bridesmaids - all close friends of Eleanor's who had managed to bag themselves six-figure salaries, loaded husbands, or both - collectively put up an unconvincing show of resistance. Despite their feeble protests, Eleanor could tell they were happy to hand over the reins to 'Bridezilla,' as one of the girls had jokingly called her. At least she hoped it was a joke - she was being pretty laid back about the whole thing, wasn't she? Eleanor had been on enough eye-wateringly expensive hen weekends to know that she wanted hers to be more about having a good time than bankrupting all her female friends and family.

Painfully aware that she was edging ever closer to her credit card limit, Eleanor decided to stump up for a 'booze cruise' bus to transport herself and 25 of her closest friends around the capital. And a stripper, of course - there had to be a stripper, and he had to be hot.

She'd heard worrying stories about grim-looking old guys shoving their saggy bits in brides' faces. Good job she was organising her own hen do, she thought, as she called the number for the stripper company she'd found online. The glowing reviews suggested the guys on the books would be young and hot rather than old and saggy.

Still, as she kept a nervous eye on her boss's office door while the phone rang and rang, Eleanor couldn't help wishing they had an out of hours contact number or an email contact. She knew her boss could emerge from her morning meeting at any moment. Finally, somebody picked up, and Eleanor tried to keep her voice down as she told them she wanted to book a stripper. She could barely work out what the bloke on the other end was saying, and it seemed he couldn't hear her either.

"I WANT TO BOOK A STRIPPER," Eleanor winced as every head in the office whipped around to look at her. The guy attending the Stripper Hotline didn't seem to understand anything except shouting. Ignoring the audible sniggers in the room, she brazened it out: "Yes, it's a hen party. The bride, yes. June 1...HOW much? Can I at least see a photo? No? Well I want your best man for the job, at that price. Yes, I'll pay by credit card."

Now that he was ready to take payment details, it seemed the guy on the phone could hear her loud and clear. As could everybody else in the office.

She gave her card details and tried to look nonchalant as she hung up the phone and returned to tapping away at her keyboard in what she hoped was a professional manner. In fact she was emailing her friend and chief bridesmaid: "I didn't even get to choose the stripper! It seems we just have to wait and see who's free on the night. And it's 250 quid for 20 minutes! At that price I should get a pre-inspection."

Belinda's door opened. Eleanor rapidly pressed send and opened up an Excel spreadsheet.

"Please keep private calls out of work hours," Belinda's voice was abrupt as she strode past Eleanor's desk with the managing director. She was out of earshot before Eleanor could even think of a reply.

Eleanor cast an angry eye around the room - clearly an office spy had reported her to Belinda. How petty. It was exactly this kind of thing that made Eleanor feel demotivated at work: she couldn't stand office politics. Even as she tried to muster enthusiasm for reading up on the morning's merger news, Eleanor found her thoughts straying to the prospect of nine months' paid maternity leave. Ryan had said they could start trying for a baby on honeymoon, so theoretically she could be out of there in less than a year.

Bring it on, she thought. Dirty nappies and sleep deprivation sounded far preferable to dealing with the Belinda minions in the office. Plus, a baby with Ryan was sure to be beautiful, she thought to herself with a smile.

Despite the dull days in the office, the weeks leading up to the hen party somehow flew by. Before she knew it, Eleanor was sitting on a booze bus, roaring with happy laughter as her grandmother drank shots from a penis-shaped glass.

She'd lost count of the number of hen nights she'd been tearfully drunk at, wondering if she'd ever be the bride. Now, finally, it was her turn to wear the cheesy L plates and a glittery wig. Telling herself that good taste and subtlety had no place at a hen party, she was fully embracing the cheesiness factor in a tiny dress that was virtually see-through. She was glad Ryan wasn't around to disapprove.

By the time the stripper made his way onto their garishly-coloured double decker bus, everybody was drunk dancing beneath a giant glitter ball. But the sight of a Jude Law look-alike in a high-vis workman's jacket and helmet was enough to halt the flailing limbs and hollered Britney lyrics.

Eleanor's eyes lit up. This guy didn't look like he'd have saggy balls - his body was as buff as you could get, and every woman on the bus was clamouring to get a better look. As he whipped off his trousers and gyrated in Eleanor's direction, she was almost elbowed in the face by her lusty mother and grandmother. Clearly a hen party full of lusty females was a force to be reckoned with.

When the stripper's 20 minutes were up, he escaped from the bus with his manhood and clothes just about intact. The older members of the party headed off not long after, leaving Eleanor and her friends to dance and drink the night away at a cheesy nightclub, screeching to each other over the sound of tunes they'd never listen to while sober. Somebody bundled a giggling Eleanor into a cab at 4am, and she felt woozily happy as she curled into bed next to Ryan. Yes, she had stumbled in drunk on countless Saturday nights, but this time was different. This was a celebration of her new life with her prince charming. "I love you," she mumbled before she fell into the depths of a drunken sleep.

After the flurry of planning and the haze of the hen night, the week before the wedding felt oddly calm. Eleanor returned to work, and with Ryan occupied elsewhere ("boring family stuff," he would say as he dashed out the door), spent her evenings packing and repacking her weekend bags. They were finally going to Scotland, and Eleanor could barely wait.

The prospect of the long drive north was exciting in itself - finally, Eleanor would have Ryan all to herself. Granted, she would have to divide his attention with the road, but her soon-to-be-in laws were treating them to a night at a luxury lodge in the Lake District, to break up the long journey in style.

As the miles ticked by, Eleanor felt calm and happy. She and Ryan talked about anything and everything, and the London tailbacks soon gave way to the kind of picturesque rolling countryside beloved of Sunday evening dramas on ITV. It was the first time they had spent quality time together in what felt like forever, and as Ryan uncorked a bottle of chilled white wine on a terrace overlooking Lake Windermere, Eleanor genuinely couldn't recall a time she had felt happier.

"Excited for the big day?" Eleanor's tone was inquisitive, but it was more of a statement than a question. "I am," Ryan replied, taking a seat next to her. "I can't wait to spend the rest of my life with you."

"I wish we could stay here a couple more nights, it's so tranquil," Eleanor replied.

As much as she hated to leave the cosy retreat, Eleanor was eager to get to the castle she had such fond memories of. She was nervous, too - in a few hours time friends and family from across the world would be arriving in the sleepy Scottish Highlands for her pre-wedding party.

It seemed a good omen when they awoke to clear, bright skies, and set off on their drive in good spirits after coffee, juice and fresh pastries on their terrace. Ryan's first glimpse of the castle saw it bathed in glorious sunlight, and he whistled with appreciation. Eleanor felt a mix of pride and relief - she realised she had been dreading the kind of eerie Highland mists that could make even Disneyland look foreboding. The dark stone castle stood proud against the bright blue sunny Scottish sky: Ladedar as solid and permanent as the rock it was built from, like it had always been always a part of the landscape. An impenetrable fortress.

Eleanor's great uncle Richard rushed out to greet them with open arms - and a crystal tumbler of Scotch whisky in each hand. "Welcome, welcome!". He set the glasses down next to a decanter on a carved wooden coffee table, and gestured for them to sit down on the faded, but deeply comfortable, leather sofa.

Eleanor sipped the single malt gratefully. In another generous gesture ("showy!" Eleanor's mother had tutted defensively), Ryan's parents had forked out for the entire top floor of the Canal Hotel - a nearby waterfront five-star beloved of the yachting set and - rumour had it - minor royals keen to party away from the public gaze. As she attempted to understand her great uncle's broad Scottish dialect, Eleanor drained her glass and stood up to leave. "We'll see you later!" She said, feeling the warmth of the drink bring a flush to her cheeks.

Eleanor couldn't hold back the tears when she walked into the drinks reception at the hotel. Friends and family - some of whom she hadn't seen in decades - were gathered beneath the twinkling lights, in front of picture windows framing her family's castle in the background. She barely knew which familiar face to beam at first. There were her godparents, who she hasn't seen since childhood; her uncles and aunts from America, and friends who had settled in all the four corners of the world. They were all here for her special day. and she felt flushed with pride that they would see her marry the wonderful man she loved.

Ryan himself was greeting his own friends and family in a separate room - and Eleanor couldn't help noticing that his own parents had arranged for him to have the smaller space - correctly assuming that he would have fewer guests present than she did. She'd squeezed his hand and given him a kiss as they'd headed off to their respective pre-wedding parties - "See you at the altar!" she said with a grin. In a nod to the tradition that dictated a groom shouldn't see the bride before the wedding, Ryan would stay at the hotel while she went back to the castle with her parents.

After a round of greetings, Eleanor was so overcome with emotions that she made her excuses and dashed to the toilets. She was shaking with the kind of sobs she knew would ruin her eye makeup. The rush of emotion she felt seemed to be tied as much to the location as to the occasion - it felt like her life had come full circle. She had been born at Ladedar castle and baptised in its chapel, and here she was preparing to take her vows in the same place. And begin a family of her own.

Hearing tipsy guests entering the bathroom, Eleanor checked her reflection in her pocket mirror, tidied up her mascara, and headed back to the throng.

Everybody was here to party with the happy couple, after all.

The evening went by in a blurry, boozy flash. Eleanor felt like she was in a dream, catching up with so many people all at once, in such a meaningful place, with her wonderful future husband by her side. It felt like she was just getting into the swing of things when her parents ushered her towards the door, telling her it was past midnight and they should all be getting back to the castle. "We've got a big day ahead, and an early start," said her ever-sensible mother. Eleanor felt like a real life Disney princess, being whisked away to her tower. "I have to leave before my car turns into a pumpkin!" She laughed as she hugged and kissed as many guests as could be found.

Back in the castle's ancient kitchen, Eleanor and Mary, her mother, were both a little tired and emotional in every sense. Mary held Eleaor's hand as they waited for the kettle to boil for sobering tea.

"I know I was critical of you getting married here," Mary's face was earnest as she looked into Eleanor's eyes.

"To be honest, I thought you were putting on airs and graces. I thought Ryan was a bit too snooty for you too."

Eleanor was about to protest, but her mother squeezed her hand tighter as she continued: "Now we're here, it really does feel right. You were born here, and now my baby's getting married here. It's like your life has come full circle in the best possible way. And Ryan seems like a nice enough man."

Eleanor used her free hand to wipe away a tear. "Yes, I felt the same thing. But I'm not married yet! Let's just hope I don't get ditched at the altar," she's joking, but Eleanor realises a tiny bit of her is terrified of being a jilted bride.

"It's a new beginning, my love," said Mary, with tears in her eyes.

She pulled her daughter into a tight hug, but Eleanor wriggled free, fearful of getting overcome by emotion again. "Goodnight, mum," she said, and made her way tipsily up the creaking wooden stairway to the open door of her moonlit bedroom. As she approached the heavy wooden doorway, Eleanor stopped dead in her tracks. There was a pale figure floating by the window. Eleanor's heart leapt in her chest, but a split second later she was laughing hysterically to herself. It was only her wedding dress, carefully hung next to the window by her mother. Eleanor was still giggling when she climbed into bed.

She drifted into sleep easily, but was awake and restless less than an hour later. The more she tried to calm her overactive mind, the more fretful she became. What if she overslept and missed her 8am beauty appointment? What if she didn't sleep at all and no amount of time in the salon could cover the signs of exhaustion?

No sooner had she finally fallen into a deep sleep than her alarm was rudely jolting her back to life. She reached groggily for the snooze button. After the third snooze, she pulled herself up and out of bed. She couldn't believe how rough she was feeling on the most important day of her life.

After much-needed coffee, Eleanor and her parents drove to the hotel to pick up the bridesmaids for the beauty appointment. But it seemed the party had continued after she left, and the other women were not for rousing.

Eleanor wished she could go back to bed, too, and silently cursed the wedding planner for booking such an early visit to the salon.

"Good morning, beautiful bride!" Her grandmother's cheery voice announced her arrival, and she was in the less-cheerful company of Eleanor's bleary-eyed sister-in-law Bridget. At least a couple of them had bothered to get up, thought Eleanor.

"Yeh'd meant tae ha' nine wimmen, an' naw yeh're down tae jus' four!" The beauty salon manager was barking at Eleanor in an accent so thick that Eleanor was struggling to understand a word of it. "Pardon?" She blinked at the furious looking woman brandishing a blusher brush like a weapon.

"Yeh'd meant tae ha' nine wimmen, an' naw yeh're down tae jus' four," the woman repeated, more slowly. She seemed impatient.

Eleanor realised she was referring to the number of people who had turned up.

"It's totally absurd that the wedding planner booked us in at this time!" Eleanor rebuffed, although she knew the manager was unlikely to understand her southern accent. "Nobody wanted to get up at the crack of dawn after a party last night, and the wedding isn't even until three!" She was tired, stressed, and mildly hungover. The beautician backed off with her blusher brush, mumbling under her breath as she retreated behind a pink curtain. She emerged a minute later, in the company of a woman Eleanor recognised.

She had sprayed Eleanor a bright orange two days before, and had seemed to understand the reference when Eleanor asked if she looked like she'd been Tangoed. ("Not even Irn Bru'd!" the Scotswoman had joked.).

"I told you earlier this week that it was unlikely I'd have all the bridesmaids here for this time," Eleanor said, hoping this would be translated for the beauty boss.

Eleanor heard the spray-tanner say something that sounded like "I out nee gonna be nee near nought," which she assumed was a translation of her words. But the manager looked even more affronted, turning to the increasingly-annoyed bride to say what sounded to Eleanor like, "here yeh are booked in the three beautify aims this mornin' fittin' you all in 'afore the next weddin', and now they have naught to do. Yeh's nowt compared wi' the ned weddin'."

Eleanor inferred that the manager was angry that she had brought staff in to make up the missing bridesmaids. But was it her fault the sleeping beauties couldn't be bothered? "It's ridiculous that we had such an early appointment," she repeated. "I mean, my wedding isn't until three for God's sake! Half the makeup will have come off by then!" She was on an angry roll. "And why couldn't the beauticians go to the castle and do it there? That's how it's normally done! Even in the Highlands!"

The lady gave her a blank stare. As neither woman could fully understand the other, they just glowered at each other. Eventually, the brush-wielding beauty boss gave an angry sigh and gestured for the women to sit down. As two other beauticians emerged sheepishly from behind the pink curtain, the manager set to work tugging Eleanor's hair - none-too-gently - into the complicated up-do Eleanor had requested via the wedding planner.

The three women emerged two hours later, admiring each other's hair and makeup, but scared to sleep or eat for fear of ruining the effect. Eleanor sat quietly through the car ride back, and then bolt upright back at the castle - she was terrified of falling asleep and ruining the up-do. The other bridesmaids arrived full of apologies but each looking gorgeous - they'd done a pretty decent job of each other's makeup, and looked fresher than Eleanor felt: maybe beauty sleep was more important than a beauty salon. They were all clutching hair-of-the-dog drinks, and when her sister-in-law offered a glass of champagne half an hour before they set off for the chapel on the castle grounds, Eleanor accepted it gratefully. She was desperate to steady her nerves.

Walking down the aisle with her father, Eleanor was glad she'd had the champagne to slow her racing heart. She could barely believe this was happening, and felt she needed to cling to her father's solid arm to stop herself from stumbling with nerves and anticipation. Ryan was standing stiff as a board at the altar, looking every bit the dream husband in his three-piece suit, with his hair cut shorter than she'd ever seen it.

Eleanor met his eyes, and he smiled at her, but his steady gaze showed little by way of emotion. He delivered his vows with one hand in his breast pocket, speaking so calmly and confidently he could have been talking shop to a work colleague. When it came to Eleanor's turn, her voice cracked, and her "I do" came out almost as a whisper.

She clutched his hand as they walked past the applauding guests, posing for endless photos and clasping glasses of champagne in their free hands.

The weather was on their side, the speeches brought tears and laughter in the right measures, and the dinner and dancing were just the right side of raucous. But even as she danced to their hired ceilidh band and accepted everybody's congratulations, Eleanor couldn't shake off the sensation of something missing. Had she just imagined the distant look in Ryan's eyes at the altar? He had seemed so devoid of emotion.

She silenced her fears with glass after glass of expensive wine - joking that she was doing her bit to justify the five bottles per head that Ryan had ordered. And when the newlyweds fell tipsily onto their hotel bed, it seemed her fears were unwarranted. Ryan lifted her layers of silk and voile - no easy task, she couldn't help noting - and made love to her in her wedding dress. If he had looked passionless at the altar, he made up for it on their wedding bed. Spent, he fell instantly into a deep sleep, while Eleanor lay awake in the antique bed, looking at her husband. "My husband," she kept thinking to herself. As she lay in her white dress, it seemed like a fairytale. Eventually, she slipped out of the dress and off to sleep, the Scottish moonlight peeping through the curtains, and casting a mysterious glow over the dark room.

# Chapter 19

# *Three's a Crowd*

Eleanor is tired of Praia do Forte, tired of repair work on her apartment, and most of all, she's tired of Edilson. He's become really clingy since they had sex, and she's uncomfortable with him appearing on her doorstep all the time. She needs to get away.

She gets to work with Google, looking for places that seem worth a few days' visit. It needs to be far enough to put some distance between herself and Edilson, but close enough that she can take a bus rather than having to stump up for a flight. The first place that catches her attention is Chapada Diamantina National Park. The photos - all sweeping sand dunes and underground pools in the most incredible hues of turquoise and blue - are enough to convince her, and she's chatted to enough backpackers to know it's easy to find cheap accommodation not too far from the bus station at the town of Lençóis. Like so many places in Brazil, the national park is absolutely huge - larger than some European countries - so she doesn't want to risk rocking up without knowing she'll have a place to sleep.

"Yeah, no worries," an Aussie member of staff named Izzy reassures her. "Just ask for the hostel when you arrive and they'll sort you out. Sure, you can leave your stuff here until you get back." Eleanor's planning to get the first bus out of there, so she settles her bill with Izzy and tells her she'll be back in a week or so.

Eleanor's up before anyone else, and leaves the hostel at dawn, double checking Edilson isn't loitering anywhere nearby before she jumps in her pre-booked cab to the bus station. She has no idea when she'll be back, so asks for a one-way ticket. The six-hour journey is cheaper than she expected, and she sinks into a relaxed sleep as the bus trundles along dusty highways.

The green palms and cattle-filled fields gradually give way to dusty brown plains and dried-up trees. It looks a lot less spectacular than the images she's seen, but Eleanor's sure there will be treasures to uncover. The bus pulls into a small, unassuming town, where new breeze block houses sit side-by-side with colonial buildings in fading pastels.

Watching bony horses pulling carts up the cobbled streets, Eleanor's oblivious to the fact that she's the only passenger left on the bus. *This can't be Lençóis, can it?* Apparently it can, as the driver is gesturing impatiently for her to get her things and leave.

She clambers down, and asks the first pedestrian she sees where the local hostel is. He points to a white concrete building at the end of the street. Eleanor walks up to the open reception area with its patched-up wooden roof and backpackers lazing on sofas in the lobby.

"This is Lençóis?" Eleanor asks the girl at the desk, embarrassed that she's not even sure she got off in the right town. In perfect English, the girl replies, "That's the one!"

They have beds available for as long as Eleanor wants to stay, and the receptionist talks her through the tours they run to nearby attractions. Eleanor flips through a wad of fliers and asks the receptionist which she would recommend.

"My favourite is the *Poço Encantado,* or 'Enchanted Pool.' It's a 45 minute cave tour with a hike on the way there. We have a trip going this afternoon in an hour."

Eleanor books a bed and signs up for the tour, stopping only to freshen up from the bus journey and sling her bag onto the one spare bed in a mixed dorm.

A group of sweaty-browed backpackers and a cooler-looking group of Brazilian guys has already gathered at the hostel, ready to make the descent into the vast, water-filled caverns.

They pile into a hot minibus, and Eleanor watches from the window as Chapada Diamantina unfurls in front of her window seat. It gets more impressive with every passing mile, and Eleanor realises it reminds her of Yosemite, in California. There are huge canyons cutting through arid, red-brown rock faces, and the tour guide tells the group that this is the best part of the country for hiking.

"The name Chapada Diamantina comes from the diamond exploration that once took place here," the guide continues, "today the hidden diamonds are underground pools and hidden waterfalls." It's clear the guide has delivered the same speech countless times, but he still looks upbeat and enthusiastic as he addresses the mini-bus full of tourists.

He hands over head torches to each of the passengers as they descend the bus, with a white-toothed smile and the words: "you'll need it!"

Eleanor occasionally struggles with claustrophobia, and feels slightly edgy at the thought of this descent into the darkness. As she picks her way down a rocky path to the caves, struggling slightly in her Havaianas flip-flops, Eleanor hears a man's voice behind her. She lets out an audible gasp of fear as she feels an arm on her shoulder.

"Sorry! I didn't mean to frighten you - I was just asking if you wanted me to take your photo."

Eleanor feels a rush of relief as she squints into the sunlight to see who's talking to her. A ridiculously handsome guy is standing inches away, beaming at her with a smile that's almost as dazzling as the Bahian sunshine.

She had feared she was about to be mugged, but instead, a gorgeous young Brazilian is offering to take her photo.

She might not be looking for romance, but attention from a good looking man always feels good: her self-confidence had taken a dive when her husband repeatedly spurned her advances.

She reaches out her camera to the smiling stranger and lets her hand brush against his as she passes it over. "Thanks very much," She says, and makes her best attempt at the type of breezily confident pose that seems to come so naturally to Brazilian females.

Holding a leg-and-bum-flattering stance on a slippery rock at the entrance to a cave is harder than it looks. Still, she flashes a smile and sucks in her waist as the hottie snaps her picture.

"Are you from England?" he asks her in a Brazilian accent that has a distinctly British tinge to it.

Before she can get a word in, he says: "I used to live in England, I liked it very much. My name is João."

"Nice to meet you, João," Eleanor says with a smile. "Yes, I'm from London, but I'm staying in Brazil for a while."

João steps next to her onto the rock, and they make their way through a series of dark tunnels into a wide cave. Eleanor's a little scared, as she doesn't like confined spaces, but she finds João's presence strangely reassuring. It's unusual for her to feel so at ease with somebody she's just met.

There's no light in the cave, but Eleanor can hear voices and the sound of feet shuffling around in the shadows. The tour guide's voice echoes in the darkness, advising everybody to switch on their headlamps. Eleanor does so, but the weak shaft of light does little to illuminate the situation. She can barely see what's around her, but senses João by her side. Feeling a sudden rush of fear, she's surprised to hear her own voice imploring him to hold her hand. "I don't like the dark," she whispers.

A sweet male voice replies, "Don't worry, I am here for you."

As they make their way further into the depths of the cave, the rocky ground gives way to into cool water. After a blissfully cool swim through the near-darkness of the cave, shafts of light begin to light the way. Stepping onto dry land, Eleanor takes a long look at João. He looks a few years younger than her, and has the kind of flawless looks that wouldn't look out of place on the cover of a men's fashion magazine. But there's no arrogance to him, and his eyes have a kindness about them. His hands had felt disarmingly soft and gentle when she'd held them. She realises she's staring, and shifts her gaze to the beams of sunshine that are now streaming into the cave, lighting their way towards the exit.

As the group emerges, blinking, from the cave, everyone starts talking at once. It's almost as if they had all been keeping a respectful silence in a library or church.

João introduces her to the group of Brazilian guys, who are all from São Paulo, and they seem excited that Eleanor is from London. He calls over his friend Alex, and Eleanor finds herself looking at two of the best-looking travel buddies she has ever seen. Eleanor is relishing the attention and does her best to answer the barrage of questions about life in London.

Their wet clothes drying on their bodies in the sun, everybody makes their way back to the hostel, the staff seem preoccupied with setting up a barbecue on the terrace. Eleanor barely has time to throw her backpack onto her bunk before João is pressing a caipirinha into her hand.

The lazy late-afternoon vibes and free-flowing caipirinhas set everybody at ease, and Eleanor shamelessly flirts with João well into the night. Before she heads off to bed, painfully aware that she's supposed to be up early for a 15km hike, he asks her if she'd like to join him and Alex at Salvador carnival. She mumbles something about her hiking schedule, but says she'll think about it.

When she wakes up at dawn with a dry mouth, a lingering taste of cheap sugar cane rum, and a blinding headache, Eleanor quickly decides against a day's hiking in the blistering heat. João and Alex are already booked on an early bus for Salvador, but she tells them she'll join them the following day, and João scribbles down a list of carnival parties to buy tickets for. She waves them off and goes back to sleep, clutching the list in her hand.

When she wakes up, she's excited but increasingly apprehensive. She's never been to a carnival in Brazil before, and the parties in Salvador are famously hedonistic.

The hostel staff don't hold back on sharing carnival horror stories with her - some of them pretty hair-raising. "But don't worry, you'll have great fun!" beams the 20-something Australian girl on reception, after recounting a particularly graphic tale of violent carnival muggings.

Not for the first time, Eleanor starts to wonder what she's let herself in for. But she reassures herself that she'll be with two strapping Brazilian guys, so what's the worst that can happen? She tries to silence the nagging internal voice that says she's only going because she wants to see João again.

After the calm and relative quiet of the Chapada, Salvador bus terminal feels overwhelming. Taxi drivers and tour operators loudly compete for custom, yelling at the top of their voices as families and groups of friends dart around in a frenzy of pre-carnival chaos. She's landed slap bang in the middle of the build up to one of the biggest parties on the planet.

She pulls out João's list of carnival events - he's neatly underlined the name of the mall, and the ticket shop that she needs to go to. Wincing at the steep prices, Eleanor takes a cab to the mall, taking advantage of the opportunity to pick up new heels, makeup, and a couple of suitably tiny tops. She wants to look as glam as possible for her week of partying.

As she hands over her credit card to the ticket seller, Eleanor realises that her new sexy, strappy tops were probably a waste of money. The 'tickets' come in the form of t-shirts with the name of each event on them, and are so extortionately priced that Eleanor suspects she's being taken for a *burra gringa* - 'stupid foreigner.' After furiously demanding to talk to an English-speaking sales assistant, Eleanor sheepishly realises that everybody else in the queue is paying the same price, for the same t-shirts.

She's uncomfortably aware that her credit card is close to being maxed out, and finds herself glancing nervously at the machine as she inputs her PIN. After a drawn-out wait for the machine to successfully get a signal, the payment goes through. Clutching the t-shirts to her chest, she jumps in another cab - this one thankfully cheaper - and texts João to say she's on the way to the bar where they had agreed to meet.

She steps out into the baking hot early evening sun, and spots João winding his way toward her through the crowd. Alex is trailing behind him, stumbling and crashing into visibly annoyed party people.

Saying "we need to take him home! You can drop your stuff off," João hails the same cab that Eleanor just got out of. When they get in, João peels off Alex's sweat-soaked t-shirt and hands it to Eleanor. "You can have his ticket," he says with a grin, "you didn't buy a ticket to this party."

With a sweaty t-shirt on her back and a vodka and Coke in her hand, Eleanor steps out into the still-hot night with João. "This is going to be fun," She assures herself, as João grabs her hand and pulls her headlong into the biggest crowd she has ever seen.

Eleanor had been expecting samba, but the revellers are all following a giant truck pumping out cheesy pop. Somehow João manages to look both cool and hot while drunk dancing to Shakira. Eleanor's heart is racing as he pulls her towards him and jams his leg between hers, doing his best to guide her into some northeastern dance floor moves.

After repeatedly sampling the wares of the many strolling vendors selling frozen caipirinha ice pops from styrofoam boxes, they eventually stumble home, still hand in hand. She thinks he might kiss her when they get home, and leans in close in the doorway as he struggles to turn the key. She lurches towards him, but the door unlocks at the same time, and the two of them stumble giggling into the living room. With an exaggerated 'shhhhhh,' João manages to inflate a blow-up mattress, fetches her some water and sheets, and switches on the overhead fan. It's still stiflingly hot.

Eleanor's drunk but happy, thinking what a gentleman João is, as she sinks into a deep sleep on her inflatable mattress.

The next morning, João is up early, bringing Eleanor a sugary coffee, and announcing that he's making her scrambled eggs on toast. As she blinks herself awake, taking in the alien surroundings of this Airbnb apartment, she smiles a weak smile. As much as she appreciates the effort, she can't help thinking the whole thing seems too good to be true. After all, how many hot guys are total gentlemen about sleeping arrangements, and then cook breakfast in the morning without even being asked?

Misgivings aside, the eggs, toast and caffeine work like magic in getting rid of her hangover. "So what are we doing today?" She asks, as she finishes the last bite and carries her plate through to João and Alex in the kitchen. "Beach day?" they reply, almost in unison.

As soon as they arrive at the city beach, a man rushes over and pours cold water on their feet, which is pure heaven after their hot walk. He then holds out his hand, and Eleanor passes him a few reais from her pocket. He's the first of many, many vendors they meet on the beach. Alex, surprisingly upbeat after his wasted state the night before ("Hey, I got an early night, it was strategic!" he insists) stumps up the stiff rental price for beach chairs and sun umbrellas, which they haul down the beach. Once they're pitched up, it's a never-ending procession of vendors selling every type of food you could imagine, as well as others hawking fake designer shades, tiny bikinis, sarongs, and ice cold beers. Embracing the novelty, Eleanor sips near-frozen cans of Skol ("How come this stuff is so popular here?" she asks, incredulously), and nibbles on salted quail's eggs, skewers of grilled shrimp, ice cream, and energy-boosting açaí.

The parade of bodies is incredible. Everybody - regardless of age, gender, size, or shape - is dressed in the smallest swimwear imaginable. Every walk of life is here, enjoying the priceless pleasures of soft sands, hot sun, and cooling water. Against the noisy backdrop of beach vendors shouting their wares and Alex and João having some kind of heated discussion in Portuguese, Eleanor closes her eyes and drifts off into sleep.

After a blissful beach nap, Eleanor blinks into the sun to see João and Alex gathering their belongings together, ready to head back and get ready for the night ahead. The previous night was only a warm-up for the 'real' carnival parties, and Eleanor is both excited and apprehensive about the chaos that's sure to ensue.

Back at the flat, João mixes caipirinhas in the kitchen while they get themselves ready. "You won't need those" says Alex, pointing to the heels and short skirt Eleanor was pulling out of her bag. "Just wear shorts and trainers or things will get messy." Eleanor reluctantly puts her glam clothes to one side as she pulls on the carnival t-shirt over her bikini top. She slips into denim cutoffs in the bathroom, carefully applying her makeup, even though she knows it's only going to slide down her face in the sticky heat.

With her money hidden inside her bra and her shoes, as advised by her handsome companions, Eleanor heads into the night with João and Alex. She has no idea what to expect.

Their Airbnb is close to the main carnival action, and they join the tipsy hordes heading towards the sound of repetitive, rhythmic drumming, They reach a security check, and the stony-faced police on duty give a cursory glance at their t-shirt 'tickets' before letting them pass into the biggest crowd Eleanor has ever seen. They are among very few white faces in the mainly local crowd, and Eleanor's well aware that they look very obviously like tourists. But Alex and João look totally at ease in the crowd, dancing away as they suck on one frozen caipirinhas. Eleanor is holding on to João's hand for dear life as the crowd surges around her. She feels him slip something into her free hand - a pill.

She's already tipsy, and puts it into her mouth with only a second's hesitation. Before she knows it, she's fully immersed in the frenzy of dancing, feeling like this is the best night of her life.

Her reverie is interrupted when João abruptly slips off to the side, barely holding himself upright. He lurches through the crowd towards the human shield of heavily-armed police, and to Eleanor's horror, releases a stream of urine in the direction of their feet.

*Jesus Christ.*

A cop steps forward and grabs him, beginning to beat him around the ears and shoulders with his meaty fists. Alex is nowhere to be seen, so Eleanor grabs João's shirt and yanks him back into the comparative safety of the crowd. But as João lurches into one pissed-off looking partier after another, she realises they need to get out of there. Somehow, she manages to manoeuvre the two of them out of the fenced-off carnival area, and onto the street. João falls onto the floor among discarded beer bottles, cigarette butts and plastic cups. He's laughing so hard he can barely speak. Eleanor wonders how many of the pills he's swallowed, because he's in a far worse state than she is.

She'd expected him to look after her, but here she is trying to keep him safe. She helps him to his feet, and he lurches towards her for a kiss. She responds, feeling the rush of chemicals and alcohol sweep her away.

Suddenly there's a hand on her shoulder, and a furious-looking Alex is standing over them, yelling in Portuguese. João is on the defensive, and suddenly the blindingly obvious becomes clear.

"You two you're a couple?" She's the one with the giggles now. And when João nods, she tries to mask her disappointment with bravado.

"Does this mean I get to kiss Alex too?" She's a lot less sober than she had thought, and suddenly the three of them are taking it in turns to kiss each other, oblivious to the crowds around them.

But then the pair of them pull away from her and cling on to each other, in rapture as the superstar Brazilian singer Ivete Sangalo takes to the stage in the distance, belting out her biggest hit and sending the crowd into a frenzy. Alex and João look at each other with love, lust, and happiness in their eyes, and she suddenly feels very alone. She's just a tourist onlooker to their intimacy, and it's suddenly obvious that three's a crowd.

# Chapter 20

# *Honeymoon On Hot Coals*

The honeymoon was not panning out the way Eleanor had hoped. As she lay staring at the canopy of the four poster bed, she could barely believe that Ryan had made passionate love to her in her wedding dress the night before. Now it was as though he couldn't even bear to touch her. If he'd put any more distance between them in this giant bed, he would have fallen off the edge.

Snoring gently, he was lying with one arm flung over the side of the carved wooden frame. The wrapper from the chocolate love heart that staff had left on his pillow was unceremoniously screwed up and dropped on the floor.

He was even wearing his pyjamas, as though he wanted to make sure any possible spark of passion was extinguished from the get-go.

Eleanor envied his escape into sleep. Her own racing mind kept mulling over their giant row that morning. It could hardly have been a worse start to married life.

Although they'd woken up still wrapped in each others' arms and enjoyed a long, lazy breakfast in bed, tempers had started fraying as soon they went back to the chapel to settle up their bills. There were over 300 bottles of wine left over, and Eleanor felt her hackles rise. What a ridiculous waste of money. She bit her tongue, but couldn't help thinking *I bloody told you so.* She knew they had a couple of crates of Champagne left too, which she was less annoyed about, because it was good stuff, and not too hard to store. But the crates were missing, and

Cecil denied any knowledge of their whereabouts. When he presented them with a bill full of mysterious extra charges, Ryan glowered.

"Your own family are trying to rip us off," he hissed at Eleanor under his breath.

"We've already paid a ridiculous amount for this bloody wedding. I bet that Champagne has gone straight into his cellar."

Eleanor saw red. "How the hell is the missing Champagne my fault? Or the 300 bottles of leftover wine? I told you not to order so much! Where will we even put it all?

Cecil had begun trying to justify the extra charges - they'd used a lot of electricity, he said, and they'd need to contract cleaners to deal with the mess.

Ryan seemed to be more annoyed with her than with Cecil, and Eleanor's own temper got the better of her.

"We're not paying a penny more than we agreed, Cecil. Why don't you go and jump into the loch?" She felt like a petulant teenager even as the words left her mouth.

Cecil looked more amused than offended, but Ryan was in full mansplaining mode, telling Eleanor she needed to calm down and let them figure out the sums.

Eleanor wasn't sure who she was most irritated with - Ryan or Cecil. The red mist descended, and she spat out a few choice insults at both men, before yelling "just sort it out between you, I've had enough of this crap!" and storming off to the car.

Looking in the rear view mirror, she saw a woman flushed with anger, beads of sweat on her knitted brow. She barely recognised her own reflection, and wasn't sure why she was quite so furious. She just wanted to be out of there and enjoying her honeymoon, not dealing with all this mess and two men's fragile egos.

She sat stewing in her own anger for what seemed like hours, but her watch told her it was about 15 minutes. When Ryan didn't emerge, she returned to the chapel to find him slapping Cecil on the back good-naturedly. The two men were laughing and joking like old pals.

Apparently Cecil had agreed to take 30 of the bottles of wine and write off the extra charges. There was still no mention of the missing Champagne, which she found deeply irritating, even though she knew they would have struggled to transport itt.

As petty as she knew it was, Eleanor was damned if she was going to help Ryan fit 270 bottles of leftover wine into the car. She said nothing, but knew that her expression said "I told you so," so clearly that it was almost audible.

Ryan packed the boot, the back seat and the footwells with as much wine as he could jam in alongside their luggage. There were still 170 bottles left on the roadside, taunting him in their Majestic packing crates.

"I'll ask my parents to pick them up later," he said defensively: Eleanor's stony silence was speaking volumes.

Wine bottles clinking ominously with each of the many bumps in the road, they waved goodbye to Cecil, and to the hungover-looking party guests who had emerged to see them off. They were finally on their way to the Fontel - the five-star spa hotel that they were booked into for the next three nights. Eleanor tried to lighten the mood in the car, but Ryan's tense grip on the steering wheel told her he wasn't interested in her small talk. It felt less like the start of a honeymoon and more like the end stages of a relationship grown bitter and resentful.

Swallowing her pride to try and save the situation, Eleanor apologised for losing her temperature. "It's fine," Ryan snapped in a voice that told her it definitely wasn't fine at all. Eleanor stuck the radio on to fill the silence for the hour-long drive.

Ryan was still looking churlish when they arrived at the hotel, but Eleanor felt her spirits lift in spite of the tense atmosphere. The place was gorgeous. The morning mist had cleared, leaving a cloudless blue sky, and the sweeping driveway led them to a restored 18th century manor house, sitting elegantly among manicured lawns and fragrant flower gardens. A bellboy in top hat and tails strode over to greet them, and Eleanor put on her brightest smile. They were a honeymooning couple, after all.

Ryan was brisk but polite with the receptionists, and shoved a note into the bellboy's hand when he brought their luggage to the enormous room. By the look on the bellboy's face, she suspected he was probably accustomed to getting more than a fiver from the wealthy guests, but she didn't want to dwell on it.

The honeymoon suite was enormous, with floor to ceiling windows taking in the full splendour of the grounds outside - the hotel even had its own small lake. The enormous four-poster bed was strewn with rose petals, and a huge claw foot bath sat in the middle of the room. "Good thing we're not overlooked!" Eleanor said, throwing herself onto the huge bed.

"True," said Ryan distractedly, before he announced he was going outside to have a cigarette. He seemed calmer, but oddly distant.

Eleanor unpacked, and carefully applied her makeup before going downstairs to look for her husband. *Husband.* The word still sounded somehow magical to her.

"Have you seen my husband?" she asked the smiling woman at reception, trying the word out for size. The receptionist pointed her in the direction of the driveway, where Eleanor found Ryan stubbing out a cigarette.

"Shall we make reservations for dinner?" She asked, trying her best to sound upbeat.

"Why not?" He replied, and smiled at his wife for the first time since they'd left their wedding bed.

There were only a handful of other guests in the hotel ("not surprising it's nearly empty, at these prices," Ryan had said as he scanned the empty parking spaces) and reception staff were anxious to please the honeymooning couple. They were given a full breakdown of all the big names who had stayed there - apparently Clint Eastwood regularly stayed in their room, which was an odd thought. "I never thought I'd be sleeping in Clint Eastwood's bed!" Eleanor's joke drew a half smile from her husband. They were booked into the hotel's fine dining restaurant for dinner, and were enthusiastically informed that they were entitled to a complimentary champagne cruise around Loch Lomond.

Ryan had lost some of his earlier gruffness, but Eleanor felt he was still distracted and guarded. She knew she had really lost her temper that morning, and that Ryan struggled to handle her fiery side. But her fits of temper usually burned out as quickly as they started - she wasn't one to give people the silent treatment.

They walked arm in arm around the grounds, and Eleanor even rolled down a hill in an effort to get Ryan to laugh, but he merely rolled his eyes, leaving her feeling more than a little foolish. But Eleanor was quickly distracted from her worrying by the buzz of a helicopter overhead. She'd noticed the landing pad, but hadn't expected to see anybody actually using it. "Ooh maybe it's somebody famous!" she said excitedly, pulling Ryan by the hand to a spot with a good view of the landing pad.

Ryan looked nonchalant about the whole thing, but Eleanor was excited when she actually recognised the man stepping down from the helicopter, followed by a stunning, immaculately-dressed woman. It was Anthony Robbins - the famous self-help guru known for literally walking on hot coals. Some of her friends had even tried the technique for themselves at wellness retreats, and lived to tell the tale. Eleanor had several of his books at home, and felt a real buzz at seeing him in the flesh.

Ryan didn't recognise him, and seemed unmoved by Eleanor's excitement. When she approached Robbins and his wife later that day, asking for a photograph, Ryan looked like he wanted the ground to open up and swallow him.

Robbins was warmly polite, and after enthusing about his books, Eleanor turned to ask Ryan to take her picture with the star. But thought better of it when she clocked the embarrassed look on his face. Instead, she wished Robbins and his wife a pleasant stay, reaching out her arm for a slightly awkward handshake.

"For God's sake, Eleanor," said Ryan as soon as the glamorous couple were out of earshot. "Couldn't you just have left those poor people alone?"

"Poor people?" she was taken aback at the real vitriol in his voice. "He makes his money by getting the public on his side, I'm sure he doesn't mind being recognised."

But Ryan looked both furious and mortified. She'd never seen him so embarrassed by her behaviour, and felt a stab of something like claustrophobia.

Was she never going to be allowed to be herself around her husband? They were walking towards the restaurant, and he swapped his scowl for a forced-looking grin when the porter held the door open for them.

They browsed the extortionately-priced menu in silence, and Eleanor could sense his silent disapproval. She didn't want to attract the attention of the other diners by crying, but had to fight to hold back tears. Why was he so angry all the time? This was supposed to be the happiest time of their lives. Spotting Robbins and his wife seated at the other end of the restaurant, Eleanor felt she didn't need to walk on hot coals - the first day of her married life was already filling her with burning pain.

After paying a fortune for a meal eaten in uncomfortable near-silence, they returned to their hotel room. Eleanor opened a bottle of wine from the mini-bar, but Ryan just disappeared into the bathroom and reappeared in his pyjamas. "I'm going to try and get a proper sleep. It's been a long day," he said, climbing into bed. He was snoring within minutes, leaving Eleanor wide awake and beginning to ask herself just how well she knew the man she married.

He was already up when she woke the next day, and Eleanor decided that the best thing she could do in the situation was to go on a charm offensive. She just wouldn't buy into Ryan's bad mood, she told herself.

Her new husband already seemed a little less churlish than the previous day, accepting her offer of a cup of coffee from the machine. It took her several attempts to get the thing to work, but eventually she was able to bring him a strong espresso as he flicked through the TV news channels. She felt genuine relief that she had got this small thing right, at least.

She enthused about everything throughout the day: the perfectly poached eggs at breakfast; the sunset view on the cruise; the effervescent Champagne. She even mustered up enthusiasm for the golf course, even though she found golf tedious beyond belief. "Isn't this wonderful?" she asked, although the words sounded hollow to her own ears. It sounded as though she was trying to convince herself.

Back in their hotel room after the afternoon's cruise, she took a bath as Ryan lay on the bed watching TV. The setting sun was bathing the suite in a golden glow, and she knew it would cast her body in a good light. Standing, dripping wet, with sun rays playing across her body, she reached for a towel and hoped to elicit some kind of physical response from Ryan. But instead of the burning desire she had hoped for, she saw something like panic flash across his face.

She wrapped herself in the soft hotel robe and lay down next to him, but Ryan merely continued flicking through TV channels. *So much for the honeymoon period.* Staring at the whirring ceiling fan, she wondered how it had all gone so wrong so fast. Less than three days into her marriage, and already it seemed her husband didn't even want to touch her.

After lying awake for most of the night, Eleanor found herself incapable of getting out of bed the following day. Her head pounded, her throat burned, her limbs ached. Ryan looked at her with genuine concern, putting a hand to her forehead. She felt oddly like a little girl, imploring her mother for a day off school. "You do feel hot, actually," Ryan said. "Maybe see if you're well enough for a spa treatment later." He shuffled around for a while, brought her a cup of tea, then disappeared out the door, saying he'd check in later.

It felt as though her immune system had given up on her. After the stress of planning the wedding and the excesses of the hen night, the arguments and tension were more than she could take. It was as though the emotional impact of the past couple of days was manifesting itself physically. She was wiped out.

Tossing and turning in sweaty sheets, Eleanor realised that, quite apart from feeling physically burned out, she felt desperately lonely. She had no idea where Ryan had gone, and doubted he would offer much comfort when he returned. What had happened to the man she fell in love with? So far Project Husband was failing and Project Procreation was non-existent.

She lay there, between consciousness and anxious fever dreams, for the whole day. When Ryan eventually returned, smelling of whisky and cigarettes, he brought her some water, asked if she needed anything else, then climbed into his side of the bed and fell fast asleep.

She woke to glorious sunshine streaming through the windows, feeling weak but less feverish than the previous day. Ryan was already up and about - he told her he had ordered breakfast in bed and booked her in for a heated body wrap treatment at the spa. It seemed almost sweet and attentive, until he added that he'd be spending the day on the golf course with some American guests he'd met in the bar the night before.

But at least his attitude towards her seemed to have softened a little, and after she had managed to stomach a breakfast of cereal, juice and coffee, he made the effort to walk across the grounds with her to the spa. When they arrived, Eleanor noticed a large sign offering couples' massages, but Ryan didn't even glance at it.

Eleanor felt both physically and emotionally exhausted. There was a deep, almost physical, sadness in her heart. This was not how she had imagined her honeymoon.

After a polite checkout that afternoon, they made the journey home in near-silence, eased only by the mundane chatter on the radio. Ryan occasionally asked how she was feeling, but she could barely muster a reply. She drifted in and out of sleep as the miles ticked by, grateful for the release from worrying about why Ryan was acting so cold.

When they arrived home, he headed to bed almost immediately. She was all-too-aware that this was Ryan's home and not her own, and often felt slightly ill-at-ease - as though she were intruding on somebody else's space. She curled up with a book on the sofa and a cup of tea, trying to relax. She was asleep before she had even reached the end of the first page, waking up stiff and uncomfortable in the middle of the night. She climbed the stairs and into bed next to her sleeping husband.

He was awake before she was the next day, grabbing his coat as she drank her coffee. Before he could disappear out of the door, Eleanor cautiously mentioned that it might be better for their relationship if they were living somewhere they'd chosen together.

He rolled his eyes and said, as though he were talking to an impatient child, "Eleanor, we haven't found the right place to live yet, and that is the end of it."

She sipped her coffee in silence and watched Ryan's front door close behind him.

Eleanor was actually relieved to be back in the office the next day. Her backlog of work was a welcome distraction from worrying about her marriage, and even her dreaded boss Belinda seemed warm and friendly in comparison to the way Ryan had been acting since their wedding.

The difficult part was feigning enthusiasm about the honeymoon and married life. The photos from her glamorous wedding day were enough to impress her co-workers with, but it already felt like a lifetime ago. She plastered a smile on her face and pretended she was loving married life - she could hardly tell her colleagues that her husband hadn't touched her since their wedding night.

The truth was, Eleanor had never felt so alone as she felt in the weeks following her marriage. And the loneliness was made even worse by the stifling claustrophobia of feeling like an unwelcome guest in somebody else's home.

She couldn't tell her workmates that Ryan spent much of his time out of the house, and even when he was physically present, he seemed emotionally absent. How could she admit that he never cuddled up with Eleanor in front of a movie like he used to, or that he brushed her off whenever she suggested going out for dinner, or for a walk, or anything else? Or that he didn't like any of the meals she cooked, so she had given up trying. Eleanor was too embarrassed to tell anyone that she frequently found herself eating a takeaway or a ready meal by herself in front of the TV.

Female friends rarely called, assuming she would be too loved-up with her new husband to fancy a girls' night out. And when she did speak to friends and family, Eleanor put on her cheeriest voice and told them everything was fine. In truth, she couldn't remember the last time he had displayed any sign of warmth or affection towards her. When she asked him what was wrong, he would just blame tiredness or work stress.

Before the wedding, she and Ryan had agreed that Eleanor would take two weeks' annual leave in August, which they would use for a 'real' honeymoon abroad. They had talked of going to Italy or even the Caribbean, but Ryan had been reluctant to book anything. Three weeks after the wedding, Ryan bluntly told Eleanor he was too busy to go away.

She was browsing booking websites for hotels in St Lucia at the time, and almost spilled her coffee over the laptop. She had been counting on this time away to bring some romance back into their lives.

"I just really need to help my parents with the estate. But you should go with some girlfriends instead, don't waste your time off," said Ryan, and he put his hand on her shoulder. It was the first time he had touched her in what seemed like forever.

A couple of Eleanor's friends were planning a trip to Sicily, and were surprised when she asked to tag along. Wasn't she planning a romantic getaway?

Eleanor made excuses about Ryan's workload, and booked her flights to Sicily.

Two weeks in the sun with her friends brought Eleanor almost back to her old self, but she couldn't bring herself to open up about her marital problems. She didn't tell them that he never called her during the whole two weeks they were away.

She'd emailed Ryan with her flight details, and half-hoped he would be waiting at the airport. But there was nobody there to meet her, so she took a cab home and let herself in, to find Ryan sitting drinking in front of the television as though she'd never been away.

It was more than she could take. Hadn't he missed her at all? Eleanor burst into tears, and demanded that he explain what was going on.

Ryan refilled his whisky glass and blurted out: "I didn't even enjoy my own wedding."

Eleanor stood in stunned silence, suitcase still at her feet.

Ryan looked her in the eye and said: "Not one person at the wedding told me I was lucky to have you."

She blinked at him in confusion.

"Why do you need someone else to tell you that you are lucky to have me?" She asked, floored. "I didn't need anyone to tell me that. I just knew it. No one at the wedding told me I was lucky to have you, either!"

It was such a childish, hurtful comment that she didn't even know how to respond. Half of her wanted to pack her things and just leave, but the other half of her wasn't willing to call time on their marriage already.

He was looking at her, balefully, as though she had done him some great wrong. But what had she done? She couldn't understand it.

He sipped his whisky and said, "I don't understand why you thought it was a good idea to go swanning off to Italy when we were supposed to be looking at houses."

*Wait, what?* "You told me I should go!" Eleanor was baffled. "You never said anything about looking at houses. We can do that at weekends, and in the evenings. What are you talking about?"

She looked at Ryan. Really looked at him. For the first time, she didn't see a handsome man looking back at her. She saw a petulant child.

"You never mentioned looking at houses," Eleanor repeated, exasperated. "If you had said that before I left I would have stayed. You know I would. But all you said was that you were too busy to go away and have our honeymoon. We can look at houses any time, this was supposed to be our time together."

He huffed and stood up. There was clearly more on his mind. "I want someone that looks after me. I want someone to iron my shirts and cook for me. All my friends' wives do that for them."

For a second, she thought he must be joking. But then she saw the deadly serious expression on his face.

She could hardly believe what she was hearing.

"Ryan, you work two days a week for your multi-millionaire parents. I have a two-hour commute and a 10-hour day. You really think I should be doing your cleaning and ironing?"

He opened his mouth to interrupt her, but Eleanor was furious. "This is why we have a cleaner! Because you don't want to do this stuff, and I don't have the time."

She was too tired for a fight, but her blood was boiling.

"I don't want a stranger to do it, I want you to do it." Ryan was staring at her, unblinking.

Eleanor knew if she said what was on her mind - *that this wasn't the fucking 18th century and he could iron his own fucking clothes* - they would get into a nasty fight. Instead, she said, "I'm too tired for this right now, Ryan," and dragged her suitcases up to their bedroom. His dirty clothes and wet towels were strewn all over the floor.

She had been hopeful that the time apart might have reignited a spark in Ryan, but it seemed he'd just spent the past fortnight thinking up reasons to resent her.

Eleanor took a shower, washing away specks of Sicilian sand and traces of salt water from the sea. Scrubbing at her tanned skin - she had hoped Ryan would at least compliment her on her golden colour - Eleanor felt her optimism washing away with the warm water.

She towelled herself dry, pulled on her pyjamas, and stood staring at the grey London sky and the raindrops on the window. She wanted to be anywhere else but there.

# Chapter 21

# *Amazonian Adventures*

It takes one glance at the half-finished repairs and dusty building equipment for Eleanor to realise no progress has been made on the apartment in her absence. She gives a sigh of resignation. She was aware the whole of Brazil would come to a grinding halt during the four days of carnival partying, but she'd half-hoped something might have happened in the days beforehand. Oh well, the workers were there now, hauling heavy bags of cement around dressed in nothing but Bermuda shorts and flip-flops. Carnival already seemed like a hazy dream.

After her initial embarrassment at realising João was very much spoken for - and that she wasn't even his gender of choice - Eleanor had thrown herself into the carnival spirit, embracing the 'anything goes' approach to dancing and flirting with any shirtless young partier that caught her eye. She lost track of the number of guys she shared sweaty, caipirinha-fuelled kisses with - no words exchanged.

The workmen are in good spirits, showing no signs of a carnival hangover, but instead setting about their tasks against the tinny sound of Brazilian funk music blasting from dusty radios. They seem so laid back that Eleanor wishes some of their no-stress spirit would rub off on her - she's back to worrying about her apartment, her broken marriage, and the fact that her tourist visa is set to expire within weeks. She doesn't even know where to go once her visa is up, and she doesn't want to spend her last weeks in Brazil staring at her building site of an apartment.

She's always wanted to visit the Amazon, and a boat trip to Manaus - the famous capital of Amazonia - seems the perfect way to round off her Brazilian adventure - and take her mind off the fact that Ryan still hasn't sent so much as a text or an email.

She heads back to the hostel, sinks into one of the hammocks with a cold beer, and starts browsing Amazon cruises online. "How much? Bloody hell! Why are these Amazon cruises so expensive?" Eleanor's talking as much to herself as to the lounging backpackers on the hostel terrace, but it turns out several of them have done Amazon tours on the cheap. "It's not posh, like, but we saw pink dolphins!" enthuses a young student whose accent immediately identifies him as being from northeastern England. Several others join in the conversation - apparently there's a local, no-frills boat that sails twice a week from the nearby city of Belem to Manaus. Eleanor swings back and forth in the hammock, laptop on her knees, reading online reviews of the trips. It sounds like an adventure, but not one that she should be embarking on alone, and with limited Portuguese. She's idly wondering whether any of the other backpackers would join her, when a familiar face appears at the hostel gate. Edilson. She'd almost forgotten about him - is it just her, or has he got better looking in her absence?

"You left without saying goodbye." He's staring at her as she sways in the hammock.

"I went to enjoy Carnival." She says bluntly. "I didn't want to take anybody else along." He doesn't reply, but nods his head as if he understands. After a while he says: "I would love to take you around Brazil, if I had more money." The look on his face says he's serious. "Actually, I have an idea…" she begins. "Ever been to the Amazon?"

He grins a dazzling white grin, and before she can talk herself out of it, Eleanor's booking them both on a flight to Belem. They agree that they'll each pay their own boat ticket, and Eleanor reasons that having a Brazilian in tow will save her getting ripped off with 'gringo prices.' And maybe she'll actually enjoy having some male company on the trip.

As soon as they arrive at the boat terminal, she's questioning her own judgement. Edilson insists that they need to pay extra for the 'first class cabin,' but he doesn't even have enough for the basic fare. He idly smokes a cigarette as she stumps up for the pair of them.

'First class' is a bit of a stretch, she thinks, taking in the poky room with its rusted shower unit sitting inches away from the tired-looking bunk beds. Oh well, she thinks... It's only for three days.

Edilson throws his backpack on the top bunk and announces he's going to the bar. "I'll get you a beer," he adds, and heads out the door.

There's one small white plastic chair on the deck outside their room. Eleanor sits down and watches the waters churn beneath the boat as it chugs out of the harbour, leaving the city's tower blocks behind. She sits, mesmerised, as the urban cityscape gives way to dense Atlantic rainforest hugging the water's edge. They pass small wooden houses on stilts, and small fishing boats whose occupants barely glance up at the larger vessel chugging past.

The boat is moving slowly enough for Eleanor to catch a glimpse inside the waterfront houses along the river. She sees shirtless male figures smoking cigarettes, and women in vests and shorts brushing small children's hair. Some of the homes have docks for canoes, and some have satellite dishes clinging perilously to their wood-and-tin walls. She wonders what it must be like, this life on the water.

The river widens, and begins to take on a golden glow - the fiery sun is sinking in the cloudless sky.

"It's beautiful, isn't it?" Edilson's voice yanks Eleanor back from her daydreaming. She realises she has no idea how long she's been staring at the river.

He passes her an ice-cold beer, and cracks one open for himself. They sip them in silence, Edilson standing behind Eleanor's chair with one hand on her shoulder. It's the first attempt at physical contact he's made since before she left for carnival, and Eleanor feels a frisson of tingly lust running down her spine. He leans in to kiss her, and she's about to kiss him back when the captain appears on the deck beside them. He's gesturing at the river, showing them a spot on the horizon where the water parts ways. Eleanor can barely make out a word of his Portuguese. Clocking her blank expression, Edilson steps in to translate: "He's just telling you that we'll reach that fork in the river around midnight, and will be stopping for more passengers before we get there."

Gesturing at his empty beer bottle, Edilson departs with the captain - presumably in the direction of the bar. As tempted as she is to follow him, Eleanor finds it hard to move from her seat on the deck. There's something hypnotic about the ever-changing view, and the scenes unfolding slowly in front of her. Darkness falls, but lights twinkling on the water alert them to riverside settlements and they stop at each one for passengers to offload gigantic fish on ice, and enormous cardboard boxes whose contents are anybody's guess. Passengers climb on board - mainly tough-looking characters with sinewy arms wrapped around plastic cases and cardboard boxes. Eleanor thinks she spots poultry flapping around in some of the containers.

Biting insects send her indoors not long after the boat forks to the right, and Eleanor falls asleep, alone, on the bottom deck of the bed. She's awoken by the sound of Edilson hauling himself onto the top bunk, and realises there's water dripping from his bed onto hers. "Turn the air conditioning off for God's sake," she says groggily, realising she's soaked. It's so hot, she's not sure what's sweat, and what's water dripping from the noisy old air conditioner.

When she blinks her eyes open, it's daylight, and cargo is being loudly hefted onto the boat. Edilson emerges from the deck, looking bright-eyed and bushy-tailed.

"Let's go to breakfast?" he asks. Eleanor has yet to explore the rest of the boat, and wonders what delights are in store.

Their cabin might not be Eleanor's idea of luxury, but when she sees the accommodation on the lower deck, she's glad she stumped up for a private cabin. Jam-packed hammocks barely have an inch of swinging room, and the whole place smells of a mix of sweat, fish, and poultry. They have to physically push aside sleeping passengers' hammocks in order to reach the canteen in the hull of the boat.

"I'm so glad you convinced me to go first class," Eleanor says over strong coffee and a plate of bread and scrambled egg. "Imagine what the shared toilets are like!" Edilson shakes his head with a grimace, and stirs a third sugar into his coffee.

After breakfast, Eleanor settles back into the white chair on the top deck. "I'm going to the bar, do you want to come?" asks Edilson, but she's happy just to sit and watch the river drift by. Occasionally, small children in kayaks paddle up to the side of the boat, offering food and drink for sale. Eleanor's curious, but too high up to see what they're selling. "I'll get you a beer," says Edilson as he heads in the direction of *pagode* music blaring out across the water.

Eleanor grabs a book and settles down to reading and watching life on the Amazon drift by. She's only mildly irritated that Edilson hasn't returned with her beer hours later.

Her stomach's starting to grumble when he wobbles through the door at around 2pm. "Here's your beer. Do you want lunch?"

He hands her a room temperature beer - and the temperature of the room is cloyingly hot. "Wow, thanks Edilson," she says with a laugh. "Have you been drinking all morning?" He tries to mumble an apology but she bats it off: "It's ok, I get it - it's pretty boring on this boat, right?"

He grins, and his near-perfect English breaks a little. "Well at first the river is beautiful and you think oh wow, the river is so beautiful. And then you think 'oh wow the river is so beautiful', but after a day I think it's all looking the same."

"Ha, you're not wrong. Sleep it off for a bit, I'll go and get our lunch."

Edilson collapses onto the bottom bunk, and Eleanor steels herself to brave the canteen alone.

She spots the gringo couple as soon as she enters the canteen, and immediately engages them in conversation over the vats of rice, chicken and black beans.

In perfect English, they introduce themselves as Kirsten and Tomas, from Germany. Kirsten's blonde hair is wrapped up in a tie-dye scarf, but a few damp spirals spill out down her back. They both looked flushed and freckled in the midday heat.

"How are you enjoying the Amazon?" Eleanor asks, sitting down to join them at a table by the window. "I might like it better if I could actually sleep," Kristen says through a mouthful of rice and beans, "we're in the hammocks in the middle and we have to slide on our bellies to get to the toilet." Eleanor suddenly realises that the girl is probably a lot younger than the dark circles under her eyes suggest. "And it stinks," Tomas chips in, "and have you heard all the weird animal noises?"

"You're more hardcore than me, I went crazy and treated myself to a first class cabin," says Eleanor with a laugh, "but it's not exactly luxurious."

Eleanor hadn't realised just how much she'd missed speaking to other travellers.

They've been swapping tales for an hour before she remembers she'd promised to bring lunch back for Edilson. She loads up a plate for him and weaves her way back upstairs, but he's still dead to the world, so she slides it under the bunk and hopes it won't attract an army of bugs or beasts. She realises she could murder a drink herself, but doesn't fancy braving the bar alone. She takes her seat on the deck again, but the view has lost some of its magic.

She climbs onto the top bunk not long after sunset, briefly blinking awake to see Edilson slipping through the door in the direction of the bar. Too sleepy to follow him, she drifts back to sleep.

She's awake at sunrise, and Edilson is passed out asleep on the bottom bunk again. She can't help wondering how he seems to have enough money to get blind drunk all day. When she returns from breakfast to find an empty bunk, she decides to seek out this mysterious bar for herself.

Nudging aside hammocks and stepping over loose chickens, she pushes her way to the front of the bottom deck, in the direction of the blaring music and rowdy voices.

Edilson is propping up one end of the bar, having an animated conversation with two rough-looking characters.

One of them, who appears to have lost most of his teeth, looks up in surprise as she approaches. When she addresses Edilson in English, his surprise turns to something like curiosity and lust, mixed with disdain. "Oiii gringinha," he slurs. She ignores him, and addresses an amused-looking Edilson. "What are you drinking?" He raises his grubby glass. "Cuba Libre," he says.

She smiles and says: "get me one, too."

If she can't beat him she might as well join him.

But it seems Edilson doesn't want her to join him. He pushes the drink in her direction and carries on talking to his friends as though she wasn't there. She sips it in silence, then says "I'm going now," but he doesn't hear her. She's genuinely excited to spot the German couple shouldering their way through the hammocks in the direction of the canteen. "Mind if I join you for lunch?"

They're vegetarian, and the three of them sit painstakingly pushing lumps of chicken to the side of their plates, eyeing the rice and beans with suspicion. "Is that meat gristle? I think my standards have slipped," Kirsten deadpans.

"I'm definitely ready to get off this boat now," says Eleanor, and Tomas raises his eyes heavenwards. "Yes...we can't wait to get to Santarém tonight just so we can sleep

Eleanor almost chokes on her rice. "Where?"

"Santarém. That's the city we stop at tonight."

"I thought it was Manaus?"

"No, Manaus is four more days from here."

"But when I asked the ticket guy he said three days to Manaus." Eleanor is seriously worried.

Kristen looks at her with something like pity. "No, it's three days from Manaus to Belem. But the other way around takes seven days because of the current."

Eleanor suddenly realises the scale of her fuck up. Why didn't Edilson say anything when she bought the tickets? He knew she really wanted to get to Manaus. "We're flying to Manaus tomorrow," Tomas is saying, "but the other way to get there is just to stay there another four days."

"Is there anything to see in Santarém? Should I just go there instead of Manaus?" Eleanor is clutching at straws.

"Apparently it's pretty industrial, says Kristen, handing a battered *Rough Guide to Brazil* over to Eleanor, "but it's supposed to have a really amazing beach nearby. And it's famous for the meeting of the Amazon with the Tapajós River.""

"God, Thanks for your help, I really need to buy a guide book instead of just winging it!" Eleanor excuses herself and goes back to the bar.

"Edilson, we have to talk about our schedule!" She shouts above the music. His companions eye her with amusement.

"Why?"

"Please just come with me. I can't talk here." Eleanor shouts above the music. She's trying to nudge him towards the exit when she sees a baby, barely a year old by the looks of things, sitting crying on the floor. A young woman lies passed out in a hammock nearby, long limbs and bare feet trailing onto the floor.

Instinctively, Eleanor picks up the baby. He feels wet, and is screaming at the top of his lungs. She nudges the woman she assumes to be the mother. She stirs but doesn't move. Eleanor tries to catch somebody's attention, but nobody looks concerned. She waves at Edilson and takes the least crowded route through the hammocks back to the top deck. She's never changed a nappy before, but the child looks desperate.

Sure enough, when she takes the nappy off, the baby boy is wet and dirty. He's still screaming when she rinses him carefully under the warm shower, his sobs subsiding when she pats him down with a towel. It's not soft, but at least it's clean.

Eleanor's almost on auto-pilot. She hopes nobody's going to accuse her of kidnapping the baby - Edilson knows where she is, after all. She wraps his little brown bottom in one of her old t-shirts, and sits on the deck, baby on her lap.

"Hi baby," she says softly, and gives him the tip of her finger to suck. He's clawing at her breasts in desperation, and she's not sure if he's looking for food, comfort, or both. "Sorry, little guy, those are just false advertising."

The baby's deep brown eyes gaze calmly into her own, and Eleanor feels a rush of emotion so intense, it's overwhelming. She kisses the damp brown ringlets on the back of his head, and watches his eyes gently close. His mouth relaxes its grip on her finger.

"Why are you crying?" Edilson is standing in the doorway, clutching a carrier bag. Embarrassed, Eleanor wipes tears from her cheeks.

"I don't know."

"Is it because you want a baby also?"

Edilson is looking at her with gentle, non-judgemental, eyes. Her feelings towards him soften. "Don't worry, I can give you a baby," he says with a wink. She laughs in response, but knows he's not entirely joking.

"That girl, the mother, these baby things were next to her hammock. I told the guys in the bar to tell her where her baby is when she wakes up."

Edilson hands Eleanor the bag, and she peeks at the bottles, jars, wipes and nappies inside. She doesn't know what to do with any of it, but at least she can feed him when he wakes up at least.

She relaxes into her chair and pulls a sarong over the sleeping baby. She soaks up the feeling of his soft new skin on hers. She looks at her hands holding him, their lines and spots, showing her age compared to his unblemished youth.

When other passengers come onto the deck, they shoot warm looks in her direction. *They think I'm a mother.* She smiles back, kissing the baby's warm head. Edilson is adding warm water to baby formula, and Eleanor's struck once again by the softer side to his personality.

But there's the small issue of their next destination to address. "I know," he shrugs when she tells him it takes four more days to reach Manaus. "I thought you did too?"

He's totally nonplussed when she tells him she'll have to pay for flights to Manaus. "We just sleep on the boat. Why do we need to get a plane?"

"That's easy for you to say, drinking all day with your friends. I need to get off the boat! Please, I can't be stuck here for another four days."

He leans in close and strokes the baby's head. "Ok…I think it gets in after midnight so we'll need to stay on the boat tonight, it's not safe to walk around looking for somewhere to stay." Eleanor looks at the sleeping baby in her lap. "Just one more night, and we're off." She says with a sigh.

Edilson disappears to the bar "to check if the mother's awake." Eleanor suspects he's looking for another drink. She watches the city lights appear on the horizon for what seems like hours, and retreats indoors when the baby wakes up, she watches him suck hungrily at the bottle.

Eventually, Edilson reappears at the doorway, the baby's mother standing groggily at his side. She barely says a word, but scoops up her son from Eleanor's lap. Edilson grabs the bag of baby things and helps her make her way through the hammocks back to the bar.

Once again, Eleanor feels tears stinging her eyes as she climbs into bed and tries her best to go to sleep. They can't leave the door open here in the port, and the AC unit clunks noisily overhead.

"What's wrong, baby?" Edilson is back, and climbing into bed beside her. The warmth of another human is soothing, and she lets herself melt into the moment. He licks the tears from her lips and climbs on top of her, scrabbling around for a condom in the dark. He makes love to her with tenderness and she responds with passion, then they sink into a deep sleep, oblivious to the drips of water falling onto their bedclothes.

# Chapter 22

# Red Room

Eleanor often tells people that she only puts up with her job because of the press invites to super-exclusive events. She's not even joking. And if there's one perk that really makes all the tense deadlines and tedious editorial meetings seem worth the hassle, it's the annual Monaco Private Equity Conference. When the gilded press invite drops onto her desk one overcast Tuesday morning, she feels her spirits instantly soar.

The reception is always in a glitzy waterside venue, and the delegates are the biggest names in finance. Eleanor once saw the conference as an opportunity to add some billionaire contacts to her little black book, but right now she's just looking forward to enjoying a few days of real luxury on work time, and with her work credit card snug in her Gucci purse.

In the mood to enjoy Monaco's sunny surroundings before she needs to start talking shop, she suggests that her three best London friends join her the weekend before the conference starts. To her surprise, they all say yes. Turns out they all have annual leave to take, and vacation savings burning a hole in their pockets.

They're all party people, and say they're willing to bunk down in one room if it helps the budget stretch to a hotel right by the beach, so Eleanor suggests the super trendy HI Life Hotel. It always has big name DJs, the breakfast is served late enough to allow them to sleep off their hangovers, and it has direct access to the beach.

It's known as a place where the rich and fabulous go to let their hair down, and Eleanor's been in the rooftop lounge bar before, sinking fancy cocktails on some internet rich kid's account. She never made it into one of the bedrooms though.

When she looks at the rooms online, she can only imagine what kind of parties take place behind closed doors. There's a room available that sleeps four, but it's clearly not aimed at families (in fact, the small print points out that the entire complex is strictly off-limits to under 18s).

The 'White Room' features a four poster bed set on a lower level with glass windows around it and another four-poster set slightly back on a kind of raised stage. Both are draped with brilliant white curtains. Even the floor is bright white.

The shower stands in the dead centre of the room with a see-through linen curtain around it. *Clearly not for shy types…*Eleanor thinks to herself. She texts the link to her friends: "Are we up for this, ladies? Whoever designed it clearly had orgies in mind. Or was off their face on drugs. Probably both."

The suggested depravity doesn't put them off, so Eleanor goes ahead and makes the reservation. It's only a week away.

They head for the airport all giddy. There's a superstar hip hop DJ playing at the hotel on the night they arrive, and the girls seem hugely excited about the event Eleanor hasn't even heard of him, but gets caught up in the buzz all the same. They fork out for champagne at the airport and on the plane and arrive in high spirits.

The weather is warm, it's spring and everyone is ready to party. They walk around the nicest parts of town until night falls on the main square. The open marble entryways are packed with restaurants and bars full of tourists and residents enjoying their evening. The friends wait in line to have dinner at a hip no-reservations balcony restaurant overlooking the square.

"It doesn't get better than this does it girls?" Vanessa giggles. She lifts her glass so they can all toast each other and to Eleanor it feels like an episode out of Sex in the City. Just the four of them, mature ladies, up for some adult fun.

"I can't wait to score some coke tonight." Vanessa says. "And did you see that DJ in the hotel lounge? OH MY God, was he hot or what?"

They all laugh, and she knows they must look like successful, sexy women: a redhead, a brunette and two blondes, dressed to kill in designer labels and towering heels. Man-eaters looking for prey. Well, all except Eleanor, who's still clinging on to her status as a married woman.

As the girls eat their beautifully plated French food and laugh about their hopes for that night's conquests, she lifts her hand and looks at her diamond ring sparkling bright in the candlelight. It really is beautiful. And even though Ryan has refused to sleep with her for over a year now, she still loves him despite herself. She's not prepared to give up and break her marriage vows with a silly one-night stand, knowing it would destroy any chance of saving their marriage.

Her thoughts are abruptly interrupted. She realises she feels hot and wet between her legs. In horror, she looks down to see red streaks running along her calves.

She kicks Vanessa under the table. "Jesus, look at my legs, they're covered in blood. I'm not even due my period, Jesus, Vanessa, help me!"

Vanessa glances down and registers no shock at all. She whispers: "Eleanor, that does look bad, but don't freak out. It's probably the travel messing up your cycle. It's a good job you've got a black skirt on and it's dark up here. Nobody will even notice!" She squeezes Eleanor's hand reassuringly.

"Just go to the toilets in the back and wash the blood off. I'll come to check on you in ten minutes, ok? This happens all the time."

The restaurant is indeed dark, with only candlelight exposing the diners' uniformly photogenic faces.

Eleanor feels wobbly, winding between tables until she reaches the toilets tucked away in a separate corner at the back. There's a white sink in the middle, with the ladies' toilet on the left and the men's on the right. She makes a lunge for the ladies, but it's locked. She then clamps down hard on the men's toilet door directly opposite, thinking *desperate times call for desperate measures*. It too is locked. She stands there waiting in the bright neon light glaring out from over the sink. To her absolute horror, pools of blood have formed around each of her ankles on the white floor.

A bloke comes out of the men's and goes to wash his hands. She sighs with relief as he checks his bright white teeth and leaves, barely giving her a second glance. She knocks again on the ladies.

"One minute!" yells a voice from behind the door. She thinks about going into the men's but there's another stupidly handsome man walking towards the door. She stays still hoping that, like the last guy, he won't notice the horror scene on the white tiles. He comes from the darkness into the light and sees the red all over the floor.

"Oh my god, are you ok?"

"Yes I'm ok. Look, I just need to use the toilet."

"Please just use the men's," he says, opening the door for her. She slips inside, feeling faint. She unravels the toilet roll into thick wads and starts padding down her thighs. She sticks at least a hundred sheets between her legs to stop the bleeding.

Even after everything is wiped off, there are blotchy red patches on her legs, and her short black skirt isn't hiding anything. And she's wadded so much toilet roll into her knickers, she feels like she's wearing a nappy. She's also paranoid that a flimsy thong isn't going to contain her makeshift sanitary protection.

She's relieved to hear Vanessa calling her name, knocking on the women's toilet door. Eleanor opens the men's door and shoves her a pile of toilet tissue.

"Thank God, Vanessa, can you wet that in the sink so I can wash my legs properly? And I don't suppose you have any sanitary towels on you?"

"I don't babe, but here you go." Vanessa hands over the dampened paper.

As she leaves the men's loo with Vanessa beside her, Eleanor notices another man approach the toilet, recoiling in horror when he sees the bloody mess outside. They make their way through the fabulous people and back to the table, but by now Eleanor feels less like she's in an episode of Sex and the City, and more like she's in CSI Miami.

"Ladies, I've got my period really badly and can't stay here any longer. I really need to go back to the hotel and get changed. Please just let me know what I owe you and I'll pay you back later." Before anyone can change her mind, Eleanor is off and making her way back to their room.

She passes through the lobby, and feels a sharp stab of FOMO. The DJ is already behind the decks, and a crowd of fashionable young things are already making moves towards the dance floor. But she's never felt less like dancing. She checks her appearance in the thankfully empty lift, and is startled by the whiteness of her own face: she looks like she's about to pass out. But she makes it as far as the door, swiping the keycard and stumbling inside. She audibly groans as she enters the bright white room. It's going to be impossible to keep it clean. She still has no sanitary towels and really doesn't want to make this place look like a crime scene.

Eleanor folds a large thick white towel and wraps it between her legs like a turban. She lies down and closes her eyes in the hope that staying horizontal will stem the bleeding.

The girls come back around an hour later, full of concern. They know something must be wrong if Eleanor's missing the party. She insists they must go without her, saying she'll be fine, the party is only downstairs. They have brought an extra bottle of champagne from the restaurant, and she sips a tiny bit, watching them touch up their makeup and slip into even shorter dresses than they were already wearing.

It pains Eleanor to watch them head out and listen to the music thumping from downstairs. But she's also grateful for the solitude, she needs to calm her nerves and try to figure out what's going on. She's pretty sure her last period was only two weeks ago.

The next morning, she wakes to bright sunlight streaming through the white curtains. Vanessa, who should be sharing her bed, hasn't come back. Sonya and Maria are face-down, passed out on their bed in crab-like positions, dead to the world.

Eleanor sits up and slowly unwraps the towel to find the entire thing drenched in blood. She drags herself to the shower in the middle of the room, and watches in dismay as blood continues to splatter down onto the white tiles. She puts on a bathrobe to dry off and get dressed as fast as she can. Then she shoves the bloodied red towel into a bag so housekeeping can't find it.

She knows this is way more serious than her period coming early. She slips out before the others have woken and asks the receptionist where the nearest hospital is.

"Oh *Madame*. It's a few miles away on the hill, but you can just take bus number C from directly outside here and it will drop you right there." The bleary-eyed lady explains in broken English.

"What about a cab?"

"It can be hard to get cabs at this time on Sunday morning Madame, but I'll try to call one." The receptionist dials one number after another, shooting apologetic glances towards Eleanor. After a couple of minutes, she says: "It looks like all our drivers are either busy or still sleeping. You should take the bus, they are quite frequent."

Eleanor hopes the towel between her legs will last the journey, and is relieved when the bus comes right away. She asks the driver to let her know where to get off for the hospital. They drive up a winding road until they reach a fork.

"There." The bus driver points. "Go to the top of the hill straight up that road. The hospital is on the other side."

"It looks really far away. Is there another bus going that way?"

"No. It's not that far, maybe 20 minutes." It's clear that he wants Eleanor to get off.

She steps down into muggy heat. It had been cool earlier, but now the sun is starting to beat down. She marches up the steep hill, feeling like she might pass out. The hotel towel is rubbing and she wonders if the blood has gone through it.

Sweat is pouring down her forehead and she's dying of thirst. Google Maps is sending her round in circles, and what was meant to be a 20-minute walk has turned into 40. When she finally reaches the hospital, she asks for Emergency in bad French, and gets shuffled around various departments. At last, she spots a nurse entering another hallway and manages to get her attention.

*"Madame, s'il vous plaît, pouvez-vous m'aider j'ai eu un accident."*

Eleanor pulls up her skirt to expose the blood that is now smeared all over her inner thighs.

*"Mon dieu, mon dieu. Cette femme a fait une fausse couche, aidez-moi,"* she cries to another nurse and grabs Eleanor's hand, running with her to an inner office. She knocks with a sense of urgency and to Eleanor's annoyance a handsome male emerges: the kind you really don't want looking down there.

"Madame, this nurse tells me you have had a miscarriage and that you are British." Eleanor doesn't know whether to laugh or cry. Is he telling her that being British is on a par with having miscarried?

"Doctor, yes, I am bleeding. It's not a miscarriage but the bleeding is intense," she explains. He brings her right away to the bed in his inner room and asks her to remove her underwear.

"There's usually some foreplay," she jokes to hide her mounting panic.

"It's definitely a miscarriage," he says with deadpan certainty.

"Sorry, doctor, that just isn't possible." He looks at her big bright wedding ring.

"But you are married and with so much blood I don't see what else this can be, unless you are not telling me of some accident perhaps?" He looks at her quizzically.

Eleanor is ashamed to tell him her husband won't touch her.

"It's simply not possible, we use protection." She feels her cheeks burning.

"Ok, well, I am going to give you a scan immediately. Protection does not always work." A female nurse arrives, and swiftly helps him perform the ultrasound. They then tell her to wait in the seating area outside. She checks her mobile. There's a text from Vanessa.

"Hey, where are you? Just got back to the hotel and no one is here. Had a great night last night, met some fit bloke. When are you coming back?"

"I will be back in an hour or two. Meet you at the hotel." Eleanor replies, not wanting to alarm her.

The handsome doctor reemerges.

"Mrs. Rankton, you have a tumour in your womb. And some other complications. It's not life threatening so I am going to let you sort this out when you are back in the UK, as you say you are only here a few more days. I am prescribing a very strong drug to stop the bleeding. In no circumstances should you take more than the prescribed amount. I recommend you take this for the next three days. I will write you a full prescription, and will also write your report in English right now so you can present it to your doctor at home."

"Thank you, doctor, thank you so much." Eleanor is nearly crying.

He looks at her big diamond ring and pauses. "And Mrs Rankton, have you had heavy bleeding before this? Sex would trigger bleeding, considering the size of the tumour."

*Did he just wink?* Maybe he knows she fancies him. Or maybe it's obvious she hasn't had sex in a long time, she thinks. She always struggles to control her inner flirt, even when she's literally a bloody mess. Maybe she should tell him she has a very unaffectionate English husband, and ask him to be her lover? After all, that's the French way, isn't it?

Instead, she skulks off, walking slowly out of the concrete hallway to hail a taxi outside to get back to town. She has to rush to a pharmacy before it closes, since it's Sunday.

Eleanor gets there to find the pharmacist locking up, and pleads with him to give her the prescription. The damsel in distress act clearly works, and he steps back inside and shuffles around behind the counter. He eventually hands her three little glass bottles of liquids, telling her to take one each day. She drinks the first immediately and heads back to the hotel. When she sticks her head into their room, all three girls are chatting. Vanessa launches into a long story about her guy from the night before, and the other two start showing Eleanor their shopping purchases. Not one of them seems to remember Eleanor was in a critical condition last night. While they've been having fun, she's spent the day in hospital, alone.

She gives them an angry frown and Vanessa catches the look.

"How's the bleeding?" She asks.

"Oh, it's nothing, I was just in the emergency unit at the hospital and have a tumour in my womb." Eleanor waits for the shock factor to take effect. Everyone just sits quietly looking at her.

"Oh hun, at least you know what it is now." Vanessa hugs her, and the others begin to shoot her a barrage of questions about what it means and what she needs to do now. "Apparently I can sort it out when I get back to the UK. And I have some meds to stop me bleeding everywhere in the meantime."

The silence hangs heavy.

"So, are we all going out tonight?" Eleanor tries to lighten the mood, but really doesn't feel up to partying. Luckily, everybody looks too hungover to go out again.

"No one wants to admit they can't do two nights in a row. Well, let's just have dinner and an early night then?" Eleanor laughs.

"Sounds good," Vanessa says.

Her friends leave the following afternoon, repeatedly asking her if she's really OK to go to the conference. She feels physically OK, but emotionally shaken, and also sad that their trip is over and she didn't get to relax with her friends. The bleeding still hasn't stopped completely. She calls Ryan a few times, and he seems uncharacteristically concerned. It's not like he's dying to have children with her, so why would her tumour matter to him?

She gets to the conference, but finds she barely wants to talk to delegates. She usually enjoys networking over a steady supply of top quality wine, but she's not sure if it's even safe to drink. And for the first time in her professional life, she finds she couldn't care less about getting a big story.

She's worried the tumour means she will never have a baby, and leaves early to go to bed, feeling like a slacker for not putting in the hard graft and late night networking. She wonders if she should use her illness as a reason to go home early, but she checks online, and the air ticket change fee is enormous. So she sticks it out, gets a few less-than-stellar story leads, and gladly makes her way home at the end of it. She figures she's done enough for the company finances by sticking to her scheduled flight, so decides not to get a taxi back to the airport. She hands over her work expense account credit card to take the helicopter that flies from Monaco to Nice. The prospect of the long, swerving car ride just makes her feel too nauseous.

As serendipity would have it, she sits next to two CEOs in the helicopter, and when they find out Eleanor is a journalist they seem delighted to have an audience, practically force feeding her industry gossip all the way to the British Airways Executive lounge. Eleanor knows her editor will be delighted with her exclusive stories.

She sleeps all the way from Nice to Gatwick, feeling physically and emotionally spent. The queue for passport control in the UK seems a slog, and she's pleased to find a black cab straight away. It's been such a trying few days she wants to just sit and hug Ryan when she gets home. But when she walks into the living room, he barely asks her anything about her trip, her health or her work.

Sensing he's not interested in conversation, she makes herself a sandwich and retreats to the spare room, where, like most nights, she spends the night. It feels like a stab to the heart that the 'spare' room is essentially her bedroom.

The next morning, Ryan is a little more conversational and attempts to show interest in her physical condition. He drives her to the private health clinic her work pays for, and she feels pathetically grateful that at least she doesn't have to go alone. They tell her she must get the tumour removed as quickly as possible and the procedure is booked for the following week. She feels oddly numb. "I just want the thing out," she tells Ryan as he drives home. He merely nods, eyes fixed on the road ahead.

When she checks into the hospital six days later for a two-night stay, Eleanor feels something approaching happiness. She realises she's grateful for the sense that somebody is looking after her. The place looks and feels more like a high-end hotel, and after the operation staff wait on her hand and foot for two days. She gets food in bed, good TV, flowers and visits from her friends, and finds herself reluctant to leave and return to her lonely room at home. When Ryan comes to pick her up, she's still talking with the consultant signing her out. "You shouldn't have any problem conceiving," the consultant is addressing Eleanor, but shoots a glance at Ryan. "This isn't likely to affect your current fertility, but I would advise you to start trying soon if you are planning a family."

Eleanor attempts to squeeze Ryan's hand in relief, but he whisks it away and shakes the consultant's hand. "Many thanks for your assistance, doctor."

Back home, Ryan plays the devoted husband. He cooks for Eleanor and her friends, drives her around, and buys her wine, bath oils, and stacks of magazines. But he still won't kiss or touch her.

One night after a couple of glasses of Merlot, she tries to relax but the ticking of her biological clock has become so loud that she can no longer ignore it. Eleanor finds Ryan in his usual spot in front of the TV, and bites the bullet. "Do you still want a baby, Ryan? You looked so horrified when I asked the doctor if I could have children." He barely looks up from Top Gear.

"And you never try to sleep with me. Please tell me what's wrong. We really need to fix this. I'm running out of time. I'm nearly 38. You heard the doctor, we need to start trying."

The silence is deafening. She starts crying, and he lets out a long sigh.

"We need to find a home," he says finally. "We aren't settled enough to have a baby. And I don't know why I don't have a sex drive. Maybe I have male menopause." He continues staring at the TV.

"Well, it's been over a year now that you have just ignored me. Let's go to the doctor together and sort this thing out. It's not fair on me. What did I do to deserve this?"

"I won't go to the doctor with you. Just give it more time." He shrugs.

"You said we would try for a baby right after the wedding. You made me wait two years before we married and now another year? These are my last years to have a baby and you are wasting them." Eleanor feels almost hysterical with frustration and panic.

She flings herself onto the single bed in the spare room, sobbing into the pillow. *Why has everything gone so wrong, why doesn't he love me anymore?* She never expected perfection, but has always believed marriage is something that needs to be worked at. He just doesn't seem prepared to do any work at all. She can't believe Project Husband is failing so badly that Project Procreation hasn't even started.

Ryan stays on the sofa, and Eleanor hears the closing credits of Top Gear before the opening credits of some bad movie rerun. Not for the first time, Eleanor resentfully muses on the fact that, for somebody who watches so much TV, he's surprisingly reluctant to let her pay for cable.

# Chapter 23

# *Jacaré*

The long, lazy days in Alter do Chão feel to Eleanor as though they are filled with a kind of low-key magic. The heat and humidity make for a slow pace of life, and the insects, butterflies and birds flitting through the air make everything feel tantalisingly tropical.

Even Edilson seems to have taken on an alluring, man-of-the-earth, appeal, and she's finding him increasingly hard to resist.

Their hotel isn't luxurious, but it's cosy and clean, and their mornings begin with the kind of incredible breakfast spread that Eleanor has come to love about unpretentious Brazilian guest houses. Outdoor tables groan under the weight of cakes, bread rolls, salty white cheeses, cold cuts of meat, fresh mango and papaya, and metal flasks full of sweet, strong coffee.

The town has a relaxed, hippy-ish vibe to it, and there's very little pressure to do anything other than relax and take things easy. She spends long, sweat-soaked days with Edilson, drinking beer at bars where the legs of the plastic chairs are submerged in the river so that guests can keep their own feet cool.

Eleanor wonders if the heat has got to her head, because she finds herself repeatedly getting so swept up in the moment that she doesn't ask Edilson to use protection. Their sweat-slicked bodies are drawn together like slippery magnets.

Eleanor finds herself almost hoping that she gets pregnant, and Edilson doesn't even ask if she's on the pill. It strikes her, not for the first time, that the Brazilian men she has been with have been unconcerned about birth control - a fact she imagines is related to the fact that the lion's share of the parenting seems to be unquestioningly allocated to the mother. She sees a lot of men out drinking, and a lot of exhausted-looking women scrubbing front porches surrounded by kids and toddlers.

One afternoon. Eleanor and Edilson are sitting outside at a simple local restaurant, eating the set lunch of rice, black beans, and freshly-caught fish. Edilson picks up the owner's guitar and is strumming away when suddenly the sky turns black. Eleanor's eyes widen in astonishment when she realises that it's not a tropical storm but a swarm of huge, flying insects. Like the biblical plagues of locusts. Eleanor's both terrified and amazed, batting locusts away from her face and feeling them crawl all over her hair. She's never witnessed anything so wild and so raw.

Laughing hysterically and swatting away the giant insects that land on their table and in their food, she's amazed that the waitress remains totally calm, picking locusts off her bare arms.

Soon the buzzing black cloud moves on, and diners casually sweep up the locusts that are injured or dead and kick them into the sand. Edilson stops strumming the guitar to pick insects out of the guitar strings, his drink and hair.

"That was amazing! Like the scene out of the Bible when God sent the locusts as a plague to Egypt!

Edilson looks blank

"You know, when Moses warned the Pharaoh that God would send so many locusts that they will cover each and every tree of the land and eat all that is there to be eaten. Do you know this story, Edilson?" He professes to be a Catholic, but Eleanor's never seen him pick up a bible or known him go to church.

She watches him distractedly pick a locust from the long dark hair that frames his handsome face

Edilson shakes his head in amusement. Eleanor always assumed the stories she heard in Sunday school were totally made up, so she's amazed to have witnessed an actual plague of locusts first hand. She stares in awe at the enormous hopping creatures left behind by the swarm. Something about this brush with wild nature - combined with the blissful haziness of a hot Amazonian afternoon sipping ice cold beers - sparks her appetite for adventure.

"We should do a tour deeper into the Amazon, I love it here but I want to see more! What do you think?"

Edilson shrugs, apparently unmoved by the insect invasion. But Eleanor is inspired. "I saw a poster advertising a boat tour into the Amazon, it was on the door of one of the houses next to our hotel. What do you think?" She refills her tiny beer glass from the large bottle in its plastic cooling sheaf.

The sticky heat means Brazilians never drink pints of beer - it's all about small glasses served *'estupidamente gelada'* - 'stupidly cold.'

Edilson drains his glass, nodding his head as he does so. "Sounds good." He clinks his glass onto the plastic table. Handing over a crumpled wad of notes as his contribution to the bill, he stands up to leave. "Where's this house? Shall we go there now?" He seems genuinely enthusiastic, but Eleanor's not sure if this is largely because he assumes she'll be paying for the trip.

Flip-flops in their hands, they walk barefoot on the sandy river bank until they reach the door of a small, modest-looking whitewashed house. The faded floral curtains in the window suggest the house is inhabited by one of the town's senior ladies, so Eleanor's taken by surprise when a tall, well-built black man with wide muscular shoulders appears in the small doorway. His biceps are almost grazing the doorframe.

Edilson exchanges a few animated words in Portuguese with this man, the two of them speaking so fast that she only manages to pick up a couple of slang words and something about scuba. Edilson turns to her and explains in English that it's 600 *reais* for a two-day boat trip into the jungle, accommodation and scuba equipment included. The man occupying the doorway says something in an enthusiastic tone, looking in Eleanor's direction even though she can't understand a word he says.

"He says you might see pink dolphins," Edilson explains.

"Ok, I'm sold!" Eleanor says with a grin. She's already picturing herself running naked with the tribes of the Amazon, drinking water from leaves, meeting a shaman and taking some Ayahuasca. She's heard of the psychoactive brew through a British friend who once fought depression and said it was like "having years of mental therapy in one session."

But she's also wary of what might lie in the depths of the Amazon river.

"Can you ask him if he's a certified diving instructor? And what about piranhas? There are piranhas in the Amazon, right?" Over the man's broad shoulder, Eleanor makes out a petite, long-haired woman attending to a whistling pressure cooker in the kitchen.

Edilson says something, and the man laughs. He points to a PADI diving instructor certificate on the wall. "Manuel da Silva, that's me," he tells Eleanor in English. He has an honest face, so Eleanor decides to bite the bullet.

"We can leave tomorrow if you want to," Edilson says. "It's just us, with Manuel, but we have to leave at four am," He explains. Eleanor flinches at the thought of such an early start, but nevertheless she agrees, and heads off to the town's one and only cashpoint, hoping it actually has money in it for once. She's in luck, and when she returns the two men are still casually chatting in the street, the way Brazilians seem to do for hours. *Tranquilo,* says Manuel, taking the cash. "I see you here at four."

A few hours later, they are strapping up their life jackets in the darkness as Manuel steers them out of the small harbour with wooden boat. The small lady who was in the kitchen is in the boat, handing out juice packets, sweet bread, and coffee.

"Why did we have to leave so early?," Eleanor complains, barely awake.

"It gets too hot later on, and this is the best time to see the pink dolphins. If we are lucky," Edilson explains. His big brown eyes turn from her to the horizon. The rising sun captures his tan skin, and dark hair, making him look literally radiant.

Eleanor slides her hand onto his knee and he clasps it with his own. The sun is casting an orange glow on the river, and Eleanor's annoyance is melting away.

There's a sudden flash of movement, and a school of dolphins burst out of the water, swimming past them towards the rising sun. There are at least 15 of them. "Pink dolphins! They really are pink!" Eleanor stands up to get a better look at these magical creatures, rocking the boat. The dolphins disappear beneath the water as fast as they had appeared, leaving Eleanor's nerves tingling with excitement.

But when the thrill of the moment dissipates, Eleanor feels her energy levels flagging in the stifling heat. The early start and muggy humidity take their toll, and the tin roof of the boat only seems to ramp up the heat even more. Eleanor's hair is soaked through with sweat, strands clinging to her forehead and beads of perspiration rolling down her back. She's wearing just shorts and a bikini top, and the sight of rivulets of sweat running along her arms and legs make her feel like she's in a sauna. Except in a sauna you can step out of the heat when you've had enough.

None of the Brazilians have even broken a sweat.

Manuel pulls the boat over onto a sand bar so they can all take a dip in the water and stretch their legs on the white sand. Edilson seems totally comfortable in the heat, running along the beach in his bermuda shorts. Eleanor's envious of this ability to keep cool in extreme heat, but reasons that growing up in London doesn't really prepare you for life in the tropics. Edilson has lived in this climate all his life. There's not even a whisper of shade on the sandbar, so Eleanor retreats back to the boat to drink her juice and eat her sandwiches under the little tin roof.

She stares out at the Amazon river - so wide it looks like an ocean, dark waters contrasting with the spits of pristine white sand that run along its edges. They're well away from the beaten tourist track, and not another soul is there.

The midday sun is losing a little of its fiery power by the time Manuel pulls up his boat at a shady mangrove swamp. The four of them climb over enormous tree roots to get to shore. He says something in Portuguese, and Edilson explains to Eleanor that they have a 'short walk' to the home stay. She hopes it really is short. Eleanor baulks slightly at the sight of Manuel's tiny wife carrying a huge plastic barrel of water on her slim shoulders, while her husband hauls the rest of the supplies onto his own broad back. Edilson carries a large rucksack, and Eleanor feels a little guilty about the fact that she only has her own small backpack to carry. But with the heat, and the long, sun-baked path, she can't muster the energy to offer any more help.

"How much further is it?" Eleanor winces at the sound of her own voice, hoping she doesn't sound like a petulant child. It's just so hot. "I don't think we need to walk much further," says Edilson. Sure enough, the path clears into a yard filled with roaming chickens.

Hammocks hang under the shade of enormous trees, in a makeshift plastic tent that provides at least a little protection from the elements. A couple of small white huts nearby look like they might contain toilets and showers, but they have no doors. Manuel and his wife, who has said little, but now introduces herself as Tatiana, start to unpack the supplies in the little mud cottage next to the hammock area. He speaks briefly to Edilson while getting his little gas burner set up.

"This is our place for tonight," Edilson translates, pointing to the hammocks. "Manuel says we can take a short rest and then we will go to see the village."

Eleanor's far too exhausted to complain about the extremely rough and ready nature of their accommodation. She slumps into one of the hammocks, grateful for the shade and plastic shelter that offer some respite from the sun. Swinging back and forth, she almost drops off to sleep, thinking to herself that she finds hammocks more comfortable than most beds.

She rouses herself to walk with Edilson to the local village, which turns out to be little more than a small concrete evangelical church and a couple of small houses on a dirt track. There isn't even a bar or restaurant, and after a short wander around the place they decide to walk back to their "accommodation" for dinner. Eleanor's been putting off paying a visit to the dubious-looking toilet huts, but having failed to find a bar with a loo in the village, she knows she needs to brave it.

There's no door, and no flush, just a plank with a hole onto a long drop. She's grateful for the fact that the toilet is at least out of view of hammocks and the cooking area. Manuel has prepared grilled chicken, but it's tough and hard to chew. Eleanor wonders if they're eating one of the skinny chickens that was running around beneath their hammocks earlier on. Being vegetarian most of the time, she is upset to be eating chicken again since nothing else is available.

Later that night Manuel lights a fire, and Edilson somehow produces a *pandeiro* - the small tambourine that crops up in so much

Brazilian music - from the depths of his backpack. He also produces a plastic, grenade-shaped bottle of rough cachaça, and Eleanor sips it gingerly from a plastic cup. It tastes like a hangover waiting to happen. Tatiana has already gone to sleep in one of the hammocks, so Eleanor climbs into another, leaving Edilson and Manuel to bond by the fire with their firewater. She finds their presence reassuring - is it even safe to sleep out here in the middle of the jungle with no solid walls around them? Eleanor's mind flashes back to the horrible events of Mexico, but she bats the thoughts away. She still doesn't know what happened to her, and isn't sure she wants to.

She drifts off to sleep with the sound of Edilson shaking his pandeiro, and the two men singing *pagode* tunes in soft voices. The smoke is irritating her eyes, but she feels safe and protected with the two men close by, and sleepiness wraps around her like a blanket.

She's brought abruptly back to the land of the living by the loud crows of a rooster. A glance at her watch tells her it's only 4am. Her legs and arms are filled with a fiery itching - it seems they're been sharing their accommodation with most of the local mosquito population. Eleanor swings herself out of the hammock and shuffles to the mud hut long drop before anyone else wakes up

Manuel makes coffee and scrambled eggs on his gas burner, and Eleanor begins to feel excited for the day of diving that lies ahead. She just hopes Manuel really is a qualified instructor like he claims, and that piranhas can't bite them through a scuba diving suit.

The rough track back to the boat feels somehow shorter than it had the day before, and the sticky heat is a fraction more bearable at this early hour. Edilson helps Eleanor scramble over more of those thick tree roots and back onto the boat. She sits with one hand trailing in the water, until she remembers the piranha presence and whips it back onto her lap.

The boat drifts along through narrow tributaries of the Amazon river, clear waters teeming with colourful fish and dotted with lily pads the size of satellite dishes. To Eleanor, it all feels somehow unreal. She can't wait to dive into those clear waters - piranhas or not.

Manuel has promised diving after lunch, and heats up some rice and beans on his trusty gas stove. Eleanor can only stomach a few forkfuls of the heavy meal in the hot midday sun, and she's itching to get into the water.

Her impatience must be visible, because Edilson makes short work of his own lunch and chivvies Manuel into action. The two men carry worn-out looking scuba suits over their shoulders, and Manuel leads the way towards an opening into the river. A group of boys swing from mangrove trees and splash into the water, noisily climbing back out and repeating the same process over and over.

Eleanor stares in dismay. The water is sludgy and brown, not like the clear, transparent waters they had sailed through earlier. If Edilson is surprised, he doesn't show it, but wriggles into his scuba suit for a quick diving lesson from their guide. Eleanor has dived quite a few times before, but the water was never like this. She descends into the brown water, unable to make out anything other than vague forms in the dark waters. She and Edilson swim aimlessly around in circles a few times, before clambering back onto the scorching white sands.

"Why didn't we go further out? It's terrible visibility here," Eleanor asks, deflated. Edilson shrugs his shoulders. "Oh Manuel tells me it's because of the jacaré. "

"What's jacaré?"

"Crocodiles. The crocodiles don't like it here because it's low visibility and there are villagers around. Manuel said we should stay in the low visibility area near the other villagers so the crocodiles don't see us.

"Why didn't you explain that to me before? I would never have gone. This is just pure insanity to scuba dive here in the first place."

This is not the Amazonian diving adventure Eleanor had dreamed of. She looks at the teenagers playing on the shore.

"Is that why those boys don't stay long in the water? Even though it's boiling hot, they are just jumping in and out."

"I guess so," Edilson shrugs. Eleanor feels mildly irritated at his lack of local knowledge, but is more annoyed with herself. She should have known that 'real' scuba diving wouldn't be possible in the waters of the Amazon.

She turns down the promised second dive of the package, but looks on as Edilson earnestly takes another "diving lesson" from Manuel.

Watching him flounder around emptying his mask and dropping just below the water with his oxygen tank barely attached, she feels a pang of pity for Edilson. This is his only chance to really learn diving, and he's having to take instruction in this haphazard way, on the banks of a muddy river. He emerges from the water reluctantly some time later, professing to have enjoyed himself.

Back at the hammock area, Tatiana has cooked up more chicken. Eleanor does a silent headcount of the chickens pecking around their encampment - their numbers don't seem to have diminished, so she can only assume Tatiana has sourced their dinner in the village rather than slaughtering one of the birds with her own two hands.

After a day on the river, the chicken, rice and beans taste good. The campers eat around the fire, swatting away mosquitoes and taking sips of rough booze while Edilson entertains everybody with his singing and pandeiro-shaking.

Eleanor climbs back into her hammock but struggles to sleep through the high-pitched whine of a million mosquitoes, but she stares at the stars, so bright in this black, black sky, and slaps at the mosquitoes each time they land on her.

Just as she's almost drifting into unconsciousness, Edilson arrives at the side of her hammock. "Manuel says we must take a larger boat back that leaves for Alter do Chão early tomorrow morning, because he and Tatiana will stay here longer. He will pay our tickets with the other captain."

Eleanor's surprised but not unhappy. "I'll be glad to get out of here, so absolutely no problem to leave earlier. I'm just glad we chose the three day trip and not the longer one."

She's determined to keep a sense of humour about the situation, even though her dreams of bonding with tribes, taking part in Ayahuasca ceremonies, and diving in clear waters have proved to be laughably optimistic.

The next morning, a long wooden boat arrives, already loaded with locals from a town further along the coast. Eleanor climbs in happily - this boat seems more secure than the one they arrived in, and it seems to move faster, too. Eleanor and Edilson squeeze in alongside a local family accompanied by what appears to be a large pet carrier filled with chickens. Once again, a tin roof provides the only shade from the boiling sun, so Eleanor's pleased that the captain seems keen to get back to Alter do Chão as speedily as possible. He says something to the passengers in Portuguese, and then looks at Eleanor. "I want to move quickly before the tides change."

Eleanor's so surprised by the perfect English from this salty seafarer that she doesn't even ask herself what that means. After moving at a good clip for a few hours, the captain pulls into a wooden pier at another small river town. A handful of people clamber aboard, jostling for space on the wooden seats with their bulky luggage. It's cramped and clammily hot, so Eleanor's hugely relieved when the captain makes a pit stop at a sandbar to allow the stiff-limbed passengers to stretch their legs. She immerses her hot, mosquito-bitten legs in the water, looking for some relief from the torturous itching.

When they get back in, there's a gentle breeze blowing over the river. It's cooling, but the captain frowns at the increasingly choppy waters. Every time Eleanor looks at him she thinks of the Hemingway story of *The Old Man and the Sea*.

The boat ploughs directly into the waves, and the captain turns to the passengers. As he speaks, he strokes his long grey beard, which has knotted itself into thick dreadlocks. Eleanor makes out that he is apologising for being unable to go faster. The slow progress doesn't really worry Eleanor. She's enjoying watching the sunset with Edilson, accompanied by chilled cans of Skol that the captain sells from a cool-box at his feet.

But when night falls and the boat is still struggling against the tide, Eleanor becomes concerned. The boat isn't far from the shore, and she sees parts of the forest glowing orange. There's a smell of burning wood, and Eleanor feels uncomfortably like she's floating through a scene from a horror film.

In a mix of Portuguese and English, the captain explains that some dishonest farmers deliberately set fires in the forest, claiming that the destruction was caused by natural forest fires, and legally using the land for cattle farming.

The moonlight and orange glow over the waves of the river are eerily beautiful, but it's past midnight and the boat still seems to be a long way from home.

To Eleanor's dismay, the captain announces that they're going to have to dock the boat and spend the night on the sands. For security, he suggests they all sleep in a circle a few feet away from the water. None of the passengers looks happy, and Eleanor hears the word "jacare" several times. The captain starts swinging a gun around and Eleanor feels a rush of terror. "He says he's ready to shoot any crocodiles or animals that come close," whispers Edilson, nonchalantly. Eleanor doesn't feel hugely reassured.

"Come on, I already paid for the hotel tonight and it's crazy to sleep here, it's not safe even on the beach," she says to Edilson. He explains to the captain that they'll walk along the coast to their hotel.

"You're a crazy gringa! It's two hours' walk to the town!" The captain shouts.

She can't help thinking that a two-hour walk through the jungle seems less insane than sleeping with a boatful of strangers by crocodile-infested waters while a gnarly boat captain swings a gun around.

"Edilson, is it walkable? We won't get lost?"

"We just have to follow the river. I think we'll be fine."

It seems the least insane option, so Eleanor grabs her backpack and Edilson hoists his own onto his shoulders.

They begin to walk towards the moonlit track running along the riverfront, leaving the group shouting after them in disapproval.

"Don't worry I will protect you from any jaguar or snake or crocodile. I will protect you," Edilson says, picking up a long stick. The two walk for an hour and a half along the shore in near silence. It's oddly pleasurable, walking in the moonlight against the backdrop of jungle sounds. Eleanor giggles to herself, wondering what her friends - or Ryan - would think if they could see her now, walking in the Amazon jungle in the middle of the night, with Edilson, who definitely has a bit of a Tarzan look about him.

Eventually, a golden glow of light tells them they are close to the city, and she feels a sense of accomplishment, as well as a real pull of affection towards Edilson, strong and silent at her side. Here, finally, is the sense of adventure and excitement she had hoped to find in the jungle.

They reach their hotel and much to Eleanor's relief, the apparently-tireless receptionist is still awake and manning the desk.

They go straight to the room, and Eleanor jumps into the shower. She emerges naked and dripping wet, turns the air con on full blast and immediately collapses on the bed, slipping into a blissful sleep.

When she wakes the next day, her whole body seems like it's on fire. She feels nauseous and hot and every joint in her body hurts like hell.

"Please get me a doctor," she says, weakly, and Edilson looks at her with concern. He tells her he'll be right back and returns with a serious-looking woman that Eleanor recognises from the pharmacy.

The young woman takes one look at Eleanor and diagnoses dengue fever. "It's spread by mosquitoes and it's common here," she explains. "It would be more dangerous if you were very young or very old, but you will feel ill for a while."

Eleanor winces with pain.

"There's nothing much you can do except take paracetamol and stay in bed," the pharmacist sympathises.

Eleanor lies in a sweaty bed for three days, cursing the mosquitos that took such a liking to her blood. Apparently, crocodiles and piranhas were the least of her worries.

Edilson drifts in and out, usually coming in late at night smelling strongly of beer. Eleanor barely moves from her bed. As comfy as it is, she's beginning to get sick of channel-hopping, napping, and staring at the same four walls.

"Oh Edilson, this is useless, staying here in an expensive hotel when I'm too sick to enjoy anything. Let's go back to Praia do Forte and I will stay at your place." Eleanor has never been to his place before, but he has often told her how nice it is.

It takes a couple of days before she's well enough to board the flight back to Salvador and then brave the bumpy bus to Praia do Forte. When they get to Edilson's place, it turns out to be even hotter and full of mosquitoes than their Amazon accommodation had been.

The noisy plastic fan by her bedside does little to alleviate the sticky heat, and Eleanor feels the haze of fever setting in once again. She struggles to find the energy to even keep awake for more than an hour at a time. Edilson appears at regular intervals with coconut water, paracetamol, and sugary fruit juices 'for energy,' but she can barely keep any of it down. By day three, he calls a cab to take them to the hospital. Eleanor's reluctant to leave her bed, and dreads the thought of hours in a hot sticky waiting room. But she summons the energy to change her clothes, slips her feet into flip flops and accompanies Edilson to the cab.

Sure enough, when they get to the hospital, there's a queue of less-than-healthy-looking folk snaking out the door. Inside, a mixed bag of characters in various states of ill-health sit on white plastic chairs or on the floor, fanning themselves with government-issued health cards.

Edilson has a word with the receptionist, and Eleanor picks up the word '*dengue*' several times. She's bracing herself for a long wait, so it's a pleasant surprise when she's waved through to see a doctor straight away.

It's a less pleasant surprise when the young and disconcertingly handsome doctor sticks a giant needle in her backside with barely a word of explanation. "This is the best way to get the antibiotics into your system," he explains in English while she pulls her shorts back up.

"Just to let you know this is the same stuff they use to cure syphilis, so it's strong. It might knock you out for a couple of days."

Weak, fever-addled, and with an increasingly sore bum, Eleanor struggles to make sense of the situation. "Well I suppose if you gave me syphilis I'd be cured of that too," she says to Edilson. It's an attempt at a joke, but neither Edilson nor the doctor laughs. She picks up her bag, reaches for Edilson's arm and slinks out of the room in embarrassment. She's expecting to have to settle a bill somewhere, but it turns out that, even as a foreigner not registered in the healthcare system, her treatment was free. It might have been a bit rough and ready, but she feels grateful to have been taken care of so quickly.

Edilson takes her back to his house, leaving her propped up on the sofa watching a noisy Brazilian gameshow while he goes to the supermarket for supplies. She feels a pang of real affection for Edilson - he's really come through for her in her hour of need.

Her romantic musings are abruptly interrupted by a loud banging on the front door. She drags herself off the sunken sofa to open it, wearing only a T- shirt and Havaianas. Pulse racing, she opens the door to see a large woman waving a baseball bat in her direction and yelling in Portuguese.

Eleanor must have looked blank, because the woman switches to broken English. "You have take my man! I want my husband back!"

Her bosom prominent in a brightly-coloured stretch mini-dress, the woman leans in towards Eleanor, baseball bat pointing to the heavens and her brown eyes alight with fury. Despite the bizarre situation, Eleanor can't help thinking the woman would be very attractive if she didn't look so furiously insane.

"I don't know what you are talking about..." Eleanor stares at this rage-filled stranger waving a baseball bat in her direction. She just wants to go back to sleep.

"You are living with my husband here. We are not divorced. If you want him to get a divorce you have to pay!"

Eleanor's too exhausted to be shocked.

"I didn't even know Edilson was married and I certainly don't want to marry him..." she begins to close the door but the woman pushes it open again with the baseball bat.

"You are a *burra gringa*! Edilson wants your money. He wants to divorce me for free. You tell him if he wants divorce then you, the gringa must pay."

She stares at Eleanor, apparently waiting for a reaction.

Eleanor's head is pounding. "Ok. I will give him the message, but we're not planning to get married."

The woman begins to shout but Eleanor interjects.

"I'm really ill, I need to go back to sleep now. OK?"

The woman turns to leave, shouting "He is just using you. You think he loves you? He has many gringa women. How do you think he knows English? So many gringas. He always comes back to me."

Shaken, Eleanor slams the door and locks it. She never intended to marry Edilson, but she has real feelings for him, and thought he did for her, too.

She slumps down on his bed, wondering why he told her he was already divorced from his crazy wife.

The woman's words have cut too close to home. Eleanor has been paying for everything. Edilson has told her almost nothing about his past, and it's true that he speaks extremely good English for somebody with no formal education, and who's never lived abroad. Apart from speaking English with his German ex, he had told her he just "watched a lot of English movies.

He has the kind of rugged good looks that middle-class foreign women go wild for, and there's always a steady stream of attractive, wealthy *gringas* passing through. It all feels painfully true. She is just a meal ticket.

With Edilson still out shopping - on her credit card - Eleanor realises that she needs to walk away as soon as she's physically better. She's already dealing with the aftermath of one messy relationship, she doesn't need to get into another. And her own divorce proceedings are difficult enough, without getting involved with anybody else's. And she doesn't want to waste any more of her own savings on him - God knows, she's going to need them for her divorce proceedings. Mind made up, she mentally chastises herself for being naive, and drifts back into a feverish sleep.

# Chapter 24

# *Make It Right*

Swirling the ice in her afternoon gin and tonic, Jane looked at her husband across the table. He appeared engrossed in something he was reading. "I'm so worried about Eleanor and Ryan. You know, I really want to help make things right between them." She paused for a beat to check that Ted was listening, then continued. "I decided that for Ryan's birthday, I would treat them both to a weekend in the countryside. It might help get them back on a positive footing. We all know he can be so difficult to live with, and she's had a tough time of it. I feel so sorry for the poor girl having had the tumour and then little or no family around for her." Ted made a non-committal grunt by way of reply, looking up briefly from behind the pages of the FT.

"Ryan has never been one to spend money on the ladies, and I want to make sure he and Eleanor have some romantic time together. How else will they get back on track?" Jane continued, speaking more to herself than her husband. Ted nodded distractedly, which was enough encouragement for her to continue. She had always been the talkative one of the pair.

"I mean, I remember when we were just married, we used to go away for romantic weekends all the time, especially before Ryan was born. But Ryan has never seemed interested in pampering Eleanor, or anybody else for that matter. I already approached him and offered him the weekend away but he told me it wasn't necessary to do anything special for Eleanor, that her recovery was going well. I said

I would book it anyway and he almost seemed angry. I really wonder why he can't just accept our generosity and be happy?" Ted shrugged and said: "That boy doesn't know a good thing when he sees it."

"You know, I thought it would be a lovely treat for them if I booked the Cliveden. But when I told him, he demanded to know the price, and then he was annoyed that I had spent so much.

"I told him that it would be a nice surprise for Eleanor, and she could do with a treat after being so poorly. Do you know what he said?"

Ted shook his head. "What did he say, dear?"

"He said, and I quote, 'It's not necessary to have a posh hotel in order to have a good time.' And then he ticked me off for booking dinner at the hotel restaurant, so I told him that was a treat for his birthday. Well! He said he wasn't even fond of fine dining. Talk about ungrateful!"

Jane finished her drink and for once second it looked like she might slam the delicate crystal gin glass onto the patio table, but instead she placed it delicately on the lace coaster.

"Do you know what he said next? He said Eleanor can pay her own way! He said she's always trying to make him go on trips away and he's already sick of it without me nagging as well. He says he's happy to have his birthday at the pub and wished I would just stay out of it. I mean! I'm only trying to do something nice."

Looking sadly out over their garden to the River Thames, she said:

"Honestly Ted, I marvel at his trite attitude. How much longer can she put up with him?"

Ted nodded in agreement, face still buried in the Financial Times.

"I tried to get Ryan to see he was being unreasonable. I told him she's just had surgery, has he no sympathy for his own wife? As far as I'm aware, he's never taken Eleanor away anywhere nice at all."

Her voice dropped to a whisper, as though she was ashamed of what she was about to say. "You know, I think she even paid for most of their honeymoon. You have always known how to be romantic and make me feel special, Ted, why is he so against the idea? Can't you have a word, man to man?" Ted looked up, and firmly folded the newspaper closed.

"Of course, darling. If you think it will help, I will have a word with him about making a bit more effort in the romance department."

"Thanks darling. Gosh he's been so contrary, from the minute he decided to come out sideways and make it such a difficult birth! But maybe it was a mistake to send him to boarding school at five years old. You remember how he would scream and cry every time it came to packing his things up? Everybody told us it would give him a great start in life, but you know I've always wondered if it didn't do him more harm than good."

Ted nodded. "All those school fees to pay. But he just mucked about! I lost track of the amount of times we got dragged to see the headmaster. And those pitiable exam results!" Ted shook his head in frustration. "All that money spent, and he was never going to get anywhere near Oxbridge!" A self-made millionaire, Ted had always assumed that his son would achieve great things and he felt bitterly disappointed that things weren't playing out that way.

"For heaven's sake, Jane, we still treat him like an errant kid and he's going to be 40 soon. I'd like to think my entrepreneurial spirit had just skipped a generation, but he can't even find the get up and go to produce grandchildren!"

Jane's tone softened. "I told him, 'you know, darling, you don't have to act like you have no money all the time. We have lots of money and who are we going to leave it to, the dogs? So please just ask me anytime you need anything.' But he just said he didn't want pity."

"Mr Dennings said he saw him the other day in his ripped up shirt walking around near here and he thought he was a homeless man before he realised who it was. Imagine, Ted! I feel quite embarrassed."

Ted shifted uneasily in his chair.

"What do I care what Mr Dennings says about his clothing? Perhaps it's the fashion now." Ted picked up the paper again, as though drawing the conversation to a close.

Jane would not drop it so easily.

"He seemed to be floundering so much in his 20s, you know I'm sure he was taking drugs when he fell in with that bad crowd in Rotterdam. I heard all sorts of horrible rumours. I was so relieved when we got him onto the straight and narrow and focused on training to be a trader. I thought he was going to make something of himself! But then he just got the doctor to sign him off with stress and never took it up again. Oh, when will he make something of himself?

"He's so clever and charming, but he never sees things through, and I wonder where we went wrong? Maybe we should have doted on him less and spoiled him too much? As an only child he never had to share, and he knows we will always rescue him? Or maybe we didn't do enough, I don't know…I'm just upset to still be dealing with his problems when we ought to be enjoying our retirement."

"Well Jane, I am sure Eleanor knew what he was like before she married him," Ted retorted.

"I don't think Eleanor is aware of any of these things… because she told me the other day that I must be proud that Ryan had already paid his mortgage off. She clearly didn't know we gave Ryan the money to buy his home in cash. I suppose he was trying to impress her. It concerns me, though, that he stretches the truth to make himself look more successful than he truly is. What else is he lying to her about?"

Ted was still trying to close the conversation. "I don't think the past matters so much, Jane," he muttered. "Let it go."

"I do hope the past doesn't matter. I mean Eleanor seems like a good match for him. She is a self-starter, she's motivated and inspired. She's clever, pretty and responsible, and I really can't see a reason why she shouldn't be a good match for Ryan. She likes to travel a bit too much and could certainly do more on the domestic side, but I know how hard it is balancing work and home life. Remember Ted, how I used to go modelling in the early days and still make you your dinner after a whole day at a photo shoot?"

"Oh yes how can I have forgotten that, darling?" Ted's face brightened. He dropped his drooping broadsheet newspaper and reached for Jane's hand. "And you are still a beauty." He touched her face tenderly.

"Most importantly, I can see that she loves Ryan and that her positive energy somehow balances his negativity at times."

In a hushed, conspiratorial tone, she says: "But Ted, she recently came to me complaining that Ryan isn't performing his marital duties. This wasn't a conversation I wished to have with him, but I did talk to him and now something needs to be said to Eleanor. I do like her ever so much. But Ryan says she's spoken to him very aggressively and I need to raise this with her somehow. He never responds well to a raised voice."

"Well, that's for sure, because we know how he reacts to any kind of telling off or to anybody that even disagrees with him."

"Don't worry darling it will all work out. And, you know he doesn't inherit his lack of libido from me, my darling," Ted laughs, leaning in to kiss his wife.

Later that afternoon, Jane was wrapped in her silk dressing gown and feeling a warm, post-coital sense of calm. It seemed a good time to respond to Eleanor's latest email.

*Dear Eleanor,*

*So sorry to hear that you are still sore after the operation. I hope that you are taking it easy and not rushing things.*

*I hope the weekend away might help you and Ryan to fix your relationship, but it seems he is still unhappy about things. He doesn't seem especially keen to go. I must say this situation you are in at present is not helping either of you. He has been very stressed, and his blood pressure has rocketed to a worrying level. I do so hope you can both sort out the issues, and some time apart might be good for your relationship.*

*I think some of the problems have been caused by some of the things you have said to him when in a temper. You have probably forgotten them, but he has not, and has been wounded by them. He won't talk much to me about his feelings, and I am loathe to cause more stress by pushing the issue. He does not know that you and I email as we do, so please don't mention our correspondence to him. I think you are a wonderful woman, and given enough patience things will work out.*

*Please come here to visit us at the weekend. Ryan has agreed to come. You will get away from London for a few hours and Ted and I would love to see you. I will book the pub for Sunday lunch.*

*The doggie boys are looking terrific, they spent yesterday at their hairdresser. Looking forward to seeing you."*

*Love, Jane.*

After sending the email, Jane closed her laptop, telling herself she couldn't afford to dwell on it another moment. She needed to dash to the delicatessen as they were having their friends the Struttons round for dinner, and the Struttons always put on a grand affair. She had ordered a full guinea fowl, four bottles of chilled champagne, a beautiful handmade tart, and black chocolate roulade.

Jane sought out her perky Slovakian home help, who was washing dishes in the kitchen. "Eva, please can you set out the best china once you're done here? The Struttons are coming tonight, and I still have to walk the dogs. And before you leave for the day, can you bake some of that delicious fresh bread for tonight?"

She walked over the bridge that Ted had constructed, linking their private island to the banks of the Thames. The sun was setting, and Jane walked quickly around the thick undergrowth by the river, to go through the apple orchard. One of the dogs skimmed by the edge of the swimming pool and ran all the way to the boat house. Jane came to the second clearing, where she kept her greenhouse and rose gardens. Some of the tomatoes looked very dry so she noted she must remind Derrick, the gardener, to water them.

She cut some roses for Ryan to take back to Eleanor, who always seemed to appreciate the gesture. Holding the roses, Jane turned from the garden and walked along the river's edge, back past the Roman statue and swimming pool to the bridge. She paused on the top to watch the Thames sliding beneath. There was a golden hue to the sunset. Jane took a last look at the slivers of pink in the sky before heading in to finish her dinner preparations.

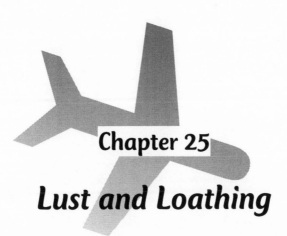

# Chapter 25

# *Lust and Loathing*

Exhausted from her adventures but with many a colourful story to add to her collection of traveller's tales, Eleanor returns to Bahia from São Paulo to oversee the repairs to her apartment. She's cautiously optimistic that she'll get the job finished within the next couple of months. Then it's just a matter of finding some long term tenants to make sure the pigeons don't move back in.

And then there's the small issue of resolving the drawn-out drama of the property paperwork. She tells herself that once she's finished sorting everything out, she's done with Brazil for a good long time. As much as she loves the place, the red tape and the lack of organisation is fraying her nerves. And she's feeling the need to cut ties with Edilson, too.

Having spent some more time hanging out with João and Andre, Edilson seems dull and unsophisticated in comparison. Great sex aside, they really have nothing in common. It's more a meeting of bodies than a meeting of minds. At the other end of the compatibility scale, João loves the same music as her, has great conversation, and the man can really dance. Shame there's no sex - great or otherwise.

Eleanor cringes inwardly at the fact that she's basically in love with a gay man. Recently, João has seemed like the only thing getting her through this divorce period. She finds herself thinking about him constantly. She flirts shamelessly, and he seems to love the attention. It's a shame he's in São Paulo and she's miles away in Bahia, and then there's the small matter of him preferring men. And being in a relationship with a man.

She's had bigger hurdles to get over in her life. Maybe he's bi?

On the morning of her second day back in Bahia, someone knocks on her hostel door.

"Eleanor, you have a visitor, your friend is here to see you."

Eleanor is half asleep and totally confused.

"What friend?"

"Your gentleman friend – the tall one with the curly hair," says Lene, the friendly receptionist. Her voice gives nothing away, but Eleanor suspects the whole hostel knows he's Eleanor's lover.

"Oh Lene, please can you tell him I'm feeling sick today? I really don't feel well." It's pretty weak, she knows, but Eleanor can't think of a better excuse right now. Wasn't their bust up cos of his crazy ex wife, or wife (whatever she is) enough for him not to try to keep seeing her?

"No problem! Hope you feel better soon!" Lene pulls the door closed behind her and heads back to reception.

When she left Alter do Chão, Edilson had asked Eleanor to pay for his flight to come with her. Although she did pay it, she had to complain about paying everything for him, and he didn't take it well. She had tried to explain to him that being a *gringa* didn't mean she had a magical money tree in the backyard.

She had pointed out that her own funds were stretched tight, particularly with the legal costs of the looming divorce. Edilson had accused her of thinking only with her head, never with her heart, and stormed off into the night.

She hasn't seen him since the day he had taken her card to go shopping and his crazy ex wife had come over. Even though she still felt sick she had headed from Praia do Forte straight to São Paulo, where João had put her name alongside his on guest lists at several of the city's nightclubs and gallery openings. "Come and party with me!" he had said, and she didn't need to be asked twice.

And it was a relief not to have to pay for somebody else all the time - João seemed to have a money tree of his own, and was happy to foot the bill when he wasn't getting a freebie. She had barely given Edilson a thought - she just assumed he had been spending time in Bahia with his pals on the boat and forgotten about her.

Now, lying in a hammock, wading through a backlog of emails, Eleanor is startled to see Lena hovering over her.

"The gentleman is back at reception, asking to see you," Lene is poker faced again, peering down at Eleanor in the purple nylon hammock.

"Which one?" Eleanor tries to feign ignorance.

"The same one as yesterday."

"Oh sorry…" Eleanor bites her lip. "Please can you tell him I'm still sick?"

She feels pathetic – Lene knows full well Eleanor is not ill. But she duly heads back to reception to pass on the message, and Eleanor wonders what it's going to take to shake him off for good.

Her attempt at getting over one man by getting under another hasn't panned out. Perhaps she had just chosen the wrong man for a rebound romance: Edilson seemed to think of himself as an artist, but from what she had seen - and heard on the rumour mill - his lifestyle involved a lot of sponging off foreign women.

Eleanor's still ruminating on the state of her love life when two young Italian girls from her dorm room pitch up in sun loungers next to her hammock. She's glad of the female company, and the three strike up an easy conversation, grabbing their sarongs and heading to the beach together. By mid-afternoon, they're ready for a drink, and decide to 'bar-hop' their way along the sands, moving from one feet-in-the-water beachfront shack to another. When they see a fisherman hauling an enormous red snapper from a boat to one of the beachfront restaurants, Eleanor suggests it's time for lunch.

Sure enough, the restaurant staff are happy to cook the huge fish for them on their outdoor grill, and the three sit down to enjoy their super-fresh catch with ice-cold beers. Eleanor's two new friends - Silvia and Marina - speak to her in perfect English, and to each other in Italian.

They sit in plastic chairs half in the water as is the Brazilian way in the hotter parts of the country. Eleanor starts to talk to the two girls about her marriage problems but Silvia cuts her short, and abruptly changes the subject to a surf competition beginning the following week.

Perhaps it was good not to think about her alternate life, the one she was meant to be living. And these young girls have better things than to be listening to a stranger talk about her heart ache, Eleanor realises. She drinks another beer and then heads back to the hostel for a nap in one of the hammocks.

"Eleanor...Eleanor?" She wakes Lene calling her name and looking at her questioningly. Eleanor had clearly been completely lost in her snooze.

"Sorry, Lene, I was miles away! Dreaming about good things. Is something up?"

"Yes, your gentleman friend is outside again."

This time, Lene seems annoyed, and Eleanor doesn't blame her. It's annoying the hell out of her, too.

"Oh gosh," she says, thinking fast. "I'm so sorry for all this trouble. Please can you tell him I'm busy today?"

Eleanor doesn't know why she can't tell Edilson straight to his face that she doesn't want to see him anymore. Perhaps she's afraid of his reaction, or perhaps she knows all too well how it feels to be unwanted.

She opens her ipad to check her emails, trying to concentrate.

Lene sighs and heads back to reception. She's back a minute later. "Edilson says he gets the message now."

Eleanor feels a nagging sense of guilt, tempered by self-justification. She knows, deep down, that she just used him just to prove to herself that she is still desirable, but was it actually wrong of her?

He got nice dinners out of it, and sex too, and Eleanor suspects Edilson makes a living mooching off gullible, lonely female tourists.

They hadn't made long term commitments. As far as she is concerned, it was just sex, and to Edilson she was presumably a fleeting meal ticket. So why does she feel guilty?

It's late afternoon by the time she drags herself out of her hammock and calls her regular moto taxi man. He doesn't speak any English and her Portuguese is still limited, but they understand each other perfectly. She just calls on her local mobile and says, "Faulty Villas," and he picks her up at the hostel, usually within 10 minutes. Eleanor always finds the arrangement funny - it's unlikely he gets the reference to Faulty Towers, but she certainly wouldn't get the same level of service in London.

Today they zip along the busy streets, and his driving is even crazier than usual: overtaking lorries and playing fast and loose with both their lives. Eleanor feels almost drunk with fear. Climbing down on wobbly legs, she gives him the usual 20 reais and smiles groggily at the guard letting her into the complex.

To Eleanor's surprise and relief, it looks like some real progress has been made. The piles of plaster are gone, and the collapsed roof has been replaced with temporary plastic sheeting. The workmen have left random beams of wood around the place but otherwise it feels like it's almost finished. Eleanor starts cleaning and emptying. The work makes her feel like she is part of the project. After so many years of sitting at a desk, slaving over the deals of rich, bored bankers, it feels oddly satisfying to do some physical labour.

She's about to walk downstairs when she sees a figure silhouetted in the frosted glass front door of her apartment.

"Hello?" Eleanor says, her heart lurching in her chest. She has heard too many horror stories about violent robberies in the area.

"It's Edilson, sorry to scare you, I just walked here from the town."

He looks a little skinnier than she had remembered, and Eleanor's startled that he managed to get past the super-strict Sunny Villas security guards. She opens the door, almost automatically. "Edilson, what on earth…?"

He slides past her into the living room and starts speaking softly.

"You just left that day I went shopping. I came home and you were gone without explanation? I found out my wife had stopped by so I figured she had told you lies and scared you away."

Eleanor opens her mouth to speak but he holds up his hand and continues his apparently pre-prepared monologue.

"But then you have refused to talk to me since getting back to the hostel. I have no idea why. Or where have you been? I thought we were important to each other. I feel hurt by what you did."

Eleanor throws her head back in bitter laughter. "You don't understand why? You never told me you were still married!"

"I don't love my wife…' he begins, but this time Eleanor cuts him off.

"And yes, your wife said some pretty horrible things about you. I am not supposed to be upset?

"But why should you believe the things she says? Couldn't you see she's totally crazy? I wanted to divorce her a long time ago but she won't let me."

Edilson looks more hurt than angry. He shrugs and says: "At least instead of running off you could have asked me what was going on."

"I went to São Paulo to clear my mind. I've heard rumours that you use gringas for their money, and she basically confirmed that."

Eleanor looks him straight in the eyes. Despite herself, she feels the familiar stirring of lust that she always gets in his presence.

"If I was using you then why am I always so hard around you?" He meets her gaze and puts her hand on his groin. He motions her to follow him to the back room. Against her better judgement, she does as he says. As soon as they get there, he has his hands on her breast and crotch. She leans in and kisses him, head spinning with the familiar scent of slightly bitter sweat on his lean body.

Her hands are sliding down his flat stomach towards his crotch when a crashing sound brings Eleanor abruptly back to the moment. One of the workmen is clapping his hands loudly for attention (Eleanor has come to realise that this is standard practice in a land of faulty doorbells) and shouting from outside that he needs to pick up his things. Eleanor pushes Edilson away.

"Edilson this is wrong, you have to go," she insists, marching him to the door.

"Ok, ok I see you tomorrow," he says, passing the workman in the doorway. She watches as he walks off down to the front gate. Eleanor smooths down her hair and gets herself a glass of water, asking herself what the hell just happened. She can't still be attracted to Edilson can she? Dialling her regular 'suicide by moto-taxi' man again, she's not sure her nerves can handle another bumpy ride, but gets herself back to town.

The next day passes without any visits from Edilson. And the next, until a week has passed without contact. Eleanor feels a stab of rejection, but tells herself this is very much a good thing - she's less on edge without constantly fretting about him popping up at any minute.

There's real progress happening at the apartment, and Eleanor's feeling almost relaxed for the first time in as long as she can remember. Swinging in her customary hostel hammock and planning her next move, an email pings in from Sonya, her travel editor friend in London.

"Darling, I have another amazing assignment and I can bring a plus one. Fancy showing people how to party hard in Miami and Key West next month?"

The start date for the trip is only two weeks away, but it's a press freebie with all manner of luxuries thrown into the mix. And then there's Sonya's fabulous company, of course. Eleanor replies immediately.

"Yes, yes and yes! I'm already booking my flight."

Animated at the prospect of her impromptu press trip with one of her most glamorous friends, Eleanor throws herself into the logistics of packing, planning, and chivvying along the laid-back labourers working at Sunny Villas. She's been so busy, she's almost forgotten to stress about her divorce. Then, as she's sweeping her apartment floors the day before her departure, Edilson strolls in uninvited.

"I have come to get you for lunch on the beach." He announces. Once again, Eleanor wonders how he got past security. But she's learned to expect the unexpected in Brazil. Besides, she's pretty hungry and there's nothing to eat in the fridge. Eleanor feels emboldened by the fact she's going to be out of there in a day's time.

They stroll down a dirt path parallel to the sea, leading away from the beach alongside an estuary. He stops at a small, straw-roofed restaurant on a pretty spot where the estuary opens up to a river beach. It's not a place Eleanor's been to before, and she's relieved to be anonymous - she doesn't really want to be seen socialising with Edilson now she knows he's still married.

A quick scan of the place sets her mind at ease - there's nobody she knows inside. Edilson orders a beer for himself and a caipirinha for Eleanor, while they wait for their lunch to arrive: there's no menu, just a set dish of rice, beans, and grilled fish. Eleanor sips her drink, hoping the strong alcohol will help diffuse the tense silence. She gives him a nervous smile and asks: "What are you looking at?"

"You. You are a beautiful woman and I would like to start again with us."

He doesn't crack a smile, but turns his gaze away when a young boy brings their plates to the table.

"You want to start again now?" Despite the calming effect of the caipirinha, she's feeling too tense to eat much. She knows she ought to resist him, but the sexual tension is almost crackling in the air. His new found confidence and assertiveness seem to be some kind of peculiar aphrodisiac. Or maybe she's just horny.

Edilson usually quietly wanders off while she pays, but this time he gets up and settles the bill, and they walk back to her place. He follows her, and she finds herself walking to the back bedroom.

"You could be my girlfriend," he says looking at her with lust.

She stares at the newly repaired ceiling and finds herself thinking about the things she needs to finish before leaving. A relationship with Edilson is out of the question, isn't it? Apart from anything else, he's married.

"Edilson, we have had great times together but it's better that you leave now," she says. "The guards in this block pay attention to everything. Surely they might tell your wife you saw me again?"

He shrugs, and gets up to leave.

"Ok. But she means nothing to me, I tried to explain that to you. How many times do I need to say it? Anyway, I will see you tomorrow." He shrugs and leans in for a kiss.

She doesn't tell him she's leaving the next day, and no sooner is he out the door than she emails her flight arrival details to Sonya, flips her laptop shut, and starts packing.

# Chapter 26

## *Six reasons*

"I'm pretty sure I know the best course of action for my own life," Ryan is emailing his lawyer, taking occasional sips from a glass of Scotch next to his computer. "After all, I very rarely make unwise decisions."

He takes another sip of the whisky, screws up his nose slightly at the strong taste, and glances up at the paper aeroplane dangling above his head. He's set up his Macbook in his childhood bedroom, where his extensive collection of Beano comic books occupies a large portion of the shelving space.

"I always know what's best for me, from the relationships I create to the work I take on, to the food I eat." He's warming to his theme, confident that his lawyer will realise he has every right to divorce the woman who has spent the last few months "flitting around South America like an overgrown gap year student," as Ryan describes it to everybody who will listen.

Jabbing the keyboard with self-righteous indignation, Ryan becomes increasingly confident that he does indeed make solid life choices, marriage aside. So what if some people might question his decision to move back into his childhood bedroom at the age of 40? His parents can't manage the estate by themselves - and it's only on weeknights. He's just doing his bit to be a good son.

But despite his indignation, he is struggling to come up with the 'six good reasons for divorce' that his lawyer has asked him to provide.

Eleanor would have never cooked him a yummy steak like his mother made earlier that evening, because she's largely vegetarian, which Ryan has always found problematic. But could one use "bad cook," or "vegetarian" as a reason for divorce? He takes another sip as he muses on the subject. Maybe the divorce judge is vegetarian, or female, or both? In that case she might see "bad cook" as a somewhat sexist reason for divorce. Bloody feminists. He bites his nails as he racks his brain for something more politically correct..

He doesn't know if Eleanor has been unfaithful, so he can't really use that as a reason.

He could cite "incompatible views on travel" as a reason, as she's obsessed with heading off to godforsaken parts of the world, and he hates travel. But what else?

Ryan tries to recall all the times Eleanor did things that displeased him, in the hope that her annoying habits could somehow be classed as grounds for divorce.

The time she complained that it was too cold when they were watching Formula One races at Silverstone, that was unpleasant and unacceptable. And she never once asked him about his own past experiences as a race car driver. Surely her lack of interest in, or knowledge of, car racing was a strong reason for divorce? He adds it to the list. It's late and he knows he ought to be getting to sleep, but he needs to find four more reasons.

He decides to play the 'pity me' card. "Eleanor made me feel drained," he types, feeling sorry for himself as he does so. "She did nothing but complain about not starting a family, crying all the time and doing nothing to pull herself out of her black hole. It was exhausting."

He continues his email rant: "I have no idea why she didn't try to be happy around me, to cook for me and contribute to a happy home life, even without children. Therefore I can rightly say that our outlooks on life were different."

So now he had three irreconcilable differences - travel, car racing, and life goals. He was a go-getter, no time for somebody else's pity party. Now he just needs three more.

His lawyer has advised him not to mention the biggest reason of all - that he is about to come into a large sum of money, and doesn't want her to get her hands on any of it. It's for the best that she never knows about it, he thinks, giving himself a mental pat on the back for keeping his financial records, and news of his upcoming inheritance, so well-hidden.

Suddenly, another painfully annoying memory comes to mind. Ryan cringes as he recalls Eleanor spreading The Guardian newspaper across the breakfast table every morning, its annoyingly-large sheets of paper intruding into his space as he attempts to eat his toast in peace.

He had been irritated from the very first time he approached his own front door to find that leftwing twaddle jamming the letterbox. How dare she have it delivered to his house? He had no patience for the paper's middle-class bleatings about taxes and the like. There was a reason he didn't socialise outside his own upper-class bubble, and nursed his trust fund like a baby. He'd proudly avoided paying taxes for most of his adult life.

He had always been frustrated with Eleanor, asking her every day how she could read such leftist crap. But now her choice of reading material brought a smile to his face. Bingo - a fourth reason to leave her. Political incompatibility. He was a staunch capitalist, she had socialist tendencies. How could it ever have worked? He tapped this into his email with glee, taking a self-satisfied swig from his glass.

As he wracked his brain for a fifth reason, Ryan kept recalling his wife's unrelenting misery. Could it have been depression? And would that seem an insensitive reason to leave somebody?

Perhaps he could claim sexual incompatibility. After all, they hadn't been physical since their wedding night. He just wasn't attracted to her sexually any more.

Not because he was gay, he reassured himself. He might have had male lovers in the past, but that was just companionship and convenience more than anything else. No, he wasn't gay, even if she used to throw that accusation at him ever since she had found out about Frank, his lover of a few months. They had really just been roommates with benefits, she needn't have made such a fuss about it. That sort of thing had been perfectly normal at his boarding school, and weren't all his former classmates strong, straight, married men now? Well, most of them.

No, it wasn't that he was drawn to men. It was Eleanor's self-sabotage. She had destroyed any attraction he felt for her by crying all the time and abandoning a perfectly good job. And then running away to South America? He shook his head in distaste, before adding 'sexual incompatibility' to his email list. He left a question mark next to it as he knew the lawyer would question whether they had been quite compatible early on. Indeed they had, but Eleanor had destroyed that by being so miserable, and accusing him of being gay when he didn't want to sleep with her.

Ryan's eyes are drooping, and his Scotch glass is empty. He needs one more reason, then he can get to sleep for the night. He casts his mind back over their five years together, recalling the worst things Eleanor has done. There was the time she went out for a work party and the police had to drop her off at his house because she was so drunk that she couldn't find her way home.

That was a bad night. But most of his friends liked a good binge drinking session, and he wasn't averse to the occasional over-indulgence himself on occasion. He reasoned that he shouldn't use her drinking against her, in case it came back to haunt him. And then it comes to him. That time they went to the horse racing.

They went to Ascot together, and Eleanor spent so long getting dressed up, she made them late for the first race of the season. She had even fussed with her makeup all day, and was in the toilet for the second race. She took no interest in his race ballot or which horses had the best odds, or why. Ryan had found his final solid reason: her lack of interest in horse racing.

With his peace of mind restored, he added this insight to his list, signed off his email, and closed his laptop. Finally, he could go and brush his teeth and climb into his childhood single bed for a good night's sleep.

# Chapter 27

# *Meanwhile, Back in Blighty...*

Two elegantly dressed ladies are sipping tea and nibbling scones under a sun umbrella, sitting opposite each other at a table outside the Clarence Brasserie in Windsor. The elder of the pair clutches a brown Mulberry handbag on the lap of her fitted cream linen trouser suit. She touches the hand of her companion sitting across the table and says:

"No one seems to know where Eleanor is. I used to be able to talk to her or email her, but she says it's too painful to keep that up right now."

Her friend gives a sympathetic look and the lady continues: "I don't really understand why it would be painful for her to talk. After all, she was the one who took off. And according to Ryan, she gave him no idea of when she might return."

"Oh dear, Jane, that must be so very hard for you. How is Ryan coping with it all?"

"I just can't think why she would abandon Ryan just because she lost her job. It's so upsetting that they seem to be going different ways because I'm very fond of Eleanor. I wish she would stop this travelling lark…"

Jane shifts in her chair and trails off, looking distressed.

Refilling their cups from a white china teapot on the table, she says: "I used to look at that Facebook thing to see what part of the world she was in, but I can't even see her pictures anymore. Ted says she must have changed her privacy settings, whatever that means. He says I need to make a Facebook page for myself and ask her to be friends with me or something like that. I can't stand all this modern fuss. Give me a decent pen any day."

Her companion nods sympathetically and asks: "Would Ryan have her back if she turned up again now? I don't know how she could do this to him, and especially after the super wedding you gave her, how very ungrateful."

"You know, a month has passed now with no news. I really don't think I know the whole story. Everything was meant to be so wonderful – we thought they would enjoy the wedding in Scotland and then Ryan would finally be ready to start a family, I know Eleanor was keen."

"But apparently, he didn't enjoy his wedding at all, and now he wants Eleanor out. I had a letter from her parents, you know…"

The other lady leans in towards Jane. "Goodness, what does the letter say?"

"Oh Daphne, I wish I'd never received it. Do you mind if I read it to you? I just don't know how to reply, and Ted is never much good with this stuff."

"Go ahead," Daphne says, with clear enthusiasm.

Jane retrieves a Basildon Bond envelope from her Mulberry bag and pulls out two neatly folded pages.

*"Dear Jane and Ted,*

*We are writing to ask you if you think there is anything any of us can do to get Eleanor and Ryan back together.*

*Before their wedding, they talked about making a home and starting a family. Since then, it appears Ryan has changed his mind. We only hear Eleanor's side of the story, so we don't know what happened, but we know how much it has upset her, particularly since she is running out of time to start a family.*

*We wish that we lived closer so we could try to help them through whatever is causing these difficulties. We have tried from afar, to no avail. If you have any suggestions, we'd really appreciate hearing them.*

*Starting a family was very important to Eleanor and she said it was something that she and Ryan had agreed on before the wedding. He told us himself that he was going to find a suitable home for them to start a family.*

*We are hoping that it's not too late to find some way of bringing them back together.*

*If you have any ideas, please let us know.*

*With love and best wishes,*
*Mary and Jamie"*

Daphne's eyes have widened despite the glaring sun.

"Oh dear, the parents are clearly upset...I wonder why Ryan told Eleanor he was keen to start a family if that wasn't the case? You know, I have heard some really silly rumours, absolute nonsense of course..."

Jane raises an eyebrow. "What sort of rumours?"

"Oh, just silly tittle-tattle about Ryan being a 'gay bachelor', so to speak. I can't even remember who said it, but of course, I set them straight. No pun intended!"

"I should hope so! Goodness me, what a thing to say! Ryan has always had an eye for the ladies." Jane's hand is shaking as she raises her teacup to her lips.

"Well, quite. And you know I don't listen to gossip. But what now?"

Jane sighs. "I don't know...I faxed over the letter to Ryan, I suppose now I just wait and see what he says. I've suggested marriage counselling. But you know how stubborn he is. I hope he gives her another chance, it's ridiculous to be giving up on their marriage already."

Jane finishes her tea and motions to the waiter for the bill. "Thank you so much for your company, my dear. Hopefully that will cover it."

She places a 20-pound note next to the teapot and waves away her friend's protests.

"Let's catch up again soon, and keep me posted!" says Daphne, kissing her friend on her perfectly powdered cheek.

Jane walks over to her Porsche, parked nearby, and immediately calls Ryan. "So did you get my fax? You know everybody is gossiping about you and Eleanor now? I don't even know what to tell people!"

Ryan gives a wearied sigh. "Why does everybody care so much? I want a divorce, and it's my decision."

His mother inhales sharply at the mention of the D-word.

"Really son? You only just got married!"

"You don't know the full story. Besides, the divorce lawyer says that the longer I leave it, the more I will owe her. And I have that million in my account from your business interests – I want to spend some of it, maybe buy a new house. I want to move on in my life."

Jane dabs at her eyes with a handkerchief, putting her son on speakerphone. "But you have to share your life with someone at some point, you don't seem to realise how privileged you are! And we spent so much time and money on your wedding but you don't seem to care."

"You're getting hysterical, mother."

"And I don't have a good reason? I don't even know how to respond to this letter. Perhaps you would like to respond yourself? After all, you abandoned their daughter and then basically ignored her! Show some accountability for once."

Jane puts the key in the ignition with shaky hands.

"I've told you how I feel. I don't love Eleanor anymore and that's the end of it. Don't bother to reply to Eleanor's parents if you don't know what to say. I hate the way you always interfere in my private matters."

Ryan hangs up, leaving his mother sobbing with anger and frustration.

She's about to start driving when an email alert pings up on her phone. She's apparently been copied into an email to Ryan.

*Dear Ryan,*

*How are you? I hope you had a good Christmas? I have missed you in this time away. I know things weren't good when I left but I needed the time to go away and think about everything. I do really love you and I hope that you will give me another chance to show you that.*

*Please agree to try to work with me on this. Let me come back and see if we can work through it. I'm a different person now that I don't have the stress of working and have had the time to go and explore the world. I have had the opportunity to get in touch with myself. I've even lost some weight thanks to life on the road!. Honestly, Ryan, I'm a different woman.*

*Please remember the vows we made in the little church in Scotland: "To have and to hold." I have included your mother in this email as she seems to be as keen to resolve this as I am.*

*Big kisses.*
*Xx Eleanor*

Jane's sobs subside as she reads the email. Perhaps all is not lost.

She drives home, planning to speak to Ryan when he is a little calmer.

But as soon as she pulls into the driveway, another email notification pings in. This time, Ryan has evidently copied her into his reply to Eleanor.

*Dear Eleanor,*

*Regarding your email dated 15 January:*
*I confirm your possessions are safe at my house, and will remain so until you return or decide to remove them.*

*If you are not intending to come back immediately we may be able to arrange a meeting to discuss the next stages when we are closer to completing the divorce. I do not believe meeting before that date would be good for either of us. At the time of writing, I am waiting to hear back from the solicitor with his advice on how to proceed.*

*This situation is upsetting, but I want to move on with my life, as sadly we are not compatible. Also, copying my mother into these emails is awfully unfair, and you are making her very upset. I am copying her into this for clarity, but please refrain from doing so going forward.*

*Regards,*
*Ryan*

Despite Ryan's protestations on her behalf, Jane calls her son immediately and demands that he forwards Eleanor's reply as soon as it arrives. "For goodness sake, son, why are you being so cold to the poor girl? What has she done to deserve this treatment?"

Ryan gives another weary sigh. "Ok, mother, I'll send you her reply. I doubt it will even make sense."

Jane drives home and is busying herself in the garden when the forwarded message arrives.

*Dear Ryan,*

*Why the formal tone? You're talking to me as if I am a person that you don't know.*

*We were compatible once, and in love, otherwise, we wouldn't have got married, would we? We lived separate lives simply because you refused to do anything with me, not because I didn't try and involve you in my life. It seems, then, that everything is your choice, including your decision not to talk about the things that you believe make us incompatible.*

*You dragged me down and hurt me so much that I couldn't function, and I lost my job. And then you dropped this divorce bombshell on me while I was travelling alone, unemployed and without the security of my friends or family to help me through this.*

*I was always ready to come back if you asked me to. You have not even taken my calls, so I am at a loss to understand why you want this divorce in the first place.*

*You hurt me very much by not wanting a full relationship with me since our marriage. I am having a very hard time accepting that things have ended this way. It was also your choice to not sleep with me since our wedding night, so I wish you would start taking responsibility for your actions, instead of making out we just 'drifted apart'. We both know this is simply not true. I would have done anything to please you, but you wouldn't talk to me.*

*I found myself looking through some of our old emails, and you were so nice to me back when we first met. I don't understand what changed.*

*It's time for you to start telling people the truth, that you just aren't suited to marriage. It's fairly obvious to me. After all, you have destroyed ours before it even got started.*

*I have to accept that you don't love me anymore and you want to move on, but you never gave me a reason for all this, so it's hard to come to terms with. I included Jane in my emails to you because if I don't you just ignore them, and I need to talk to you. I just need to understand all this, otherwise, I can never get closure.*

*Eleanor*

Ryan has added a note to his mother beneath the forwarded email: "As you can see, Mother, she is quite hysterical. I can't reason with her."

Jane calls Ryan again. "Son, she is understandably upset and confused. Please stop accusing people of being hysterical whenever they show any emotion. She deserves an explanation. We all do."

In a curt tone, Ryan tells his mother that all future correspondence with Eleanor will be via his solicitor. "I can't handle hysterical women anymore!" He says and hangs up.

Jane sits in baffled silence, holding the phone in one hand and a trowel in the other.

# Chapter 28

# *Miami Vice*

Eleanor packs her bag, buzzing with excitement. She always enjoys being Sonya's 'plus one' on a press trip because she gets to revel in all the free pampering and luxury, without the stress of having to actually file any copy afterwards. And unlike Sonya, she's not there in a professional capacity, so doesn't have to swap pleasantries with PR people or feign interest in a tour of the hotel.

Bags packed, she leaves her almost-finished apartment and jumps in her cab to Salvador airport. It's an eight-hour flight, but she drops into a deep sleep for the first half of it, then grabs the attendant's attention as soon as she wakes up. A couple of gin and tonics and a few episodes of Seinfeld on the small screen in front of her are enough to keep her distracted for the rest of the journey.

There's barely any difference between the stifling South America heat at Salvador airport and the stifling North America heat at Miami airport. At least she was able to travel light - all she has in her case are skimpy summer clothes and a couple of pairs of heels. Sonya has told her the place they are staying at, Milano Beach Club, is a new celebrity hotspot, which is why Sonya has been tasked with checking the place out.

Eleanor books an Uber to take her to this celeb hot spot, painfully aware that her face is puffy from the plane ride and her hair has frizzed up with the humidity.

The building is a glistening white, with the kind of ostentatious gates that would immediately alert members of hoi polloi that this was not the place for them. Eleanor knows she could never afford it herself, and is thankful for a freebie in such a fancy place. She hauls her bag out of the cab, and is immediately greeted by a bellboy who looks like he just stepped off the pages of a high end fashion magazine. He flashes a blinding white smile and reaches out a manicured hand to take her bag. Eleanor immediately feels self conscious about how tattered it looks. This luggage has been dragged through jungles and over rivers. It's only now, in this fancy foyer, that Eleanor realises she looks like she's escaping a war zone. The bellboy drops her filthy luggage by a gold plated trolley and takes her to reception.

"Your name, Madame?" The six foot receptionist looks as though she stepped off the same fashion shoot as the bellboy. Everything from her gleaming hair to her high and mighty cheekbones is intimidating.

"Yes, thanks. I am here with Sonya Stein of Celebrity Week, the UK's top celebrity gossip magazine?" Eleanor feels an irrational need to defend her right to be there.

"Of course. Mrs Rankton, am I correct?"

The sound of her married name always makes Eleanor wince internally. "I am informed that Ms Stein is currently on her way from the airport. I will make sure someone shows you to your room immediately."

She gives Eleanor a condescending smile and hands the ridiculously handsome bellboy a key. Eleanor makes a grab for her shame-inducing bag, but the bellboy has it in both hands and is making his way to the elevator.

"I hope you enjoy your stay here," he says when they reach room 506. Eleanor feels so embarrassed she ushers him to open the door quickly, before she realises that he was probably only hanging around for a tip. She feels her embarrassment levels creeping up even higher.

She looks in the mirror at her crumpled, frizzy appearance. No wonder only movie stars come here. Anyone else would feel inferior, since the staff are so good looking.

The front lobby might be glamorous but the room seems tiny and stark. Sonya has told her that the Italian designer likes minimalist furnishings, but this is so minimal it takes the piss. There's not even a chair or a balcony, and the bathroom is separated from the bedroom by a clear glass panel. Eleanor immediately plans to take her toilet trips elsewhere.

The price list is set out in the hotel brochure laid out on the bed together with the room service menu: $650 a night for their room, which overlooks a back street. Sea view rooms are twice the price. Eleanor reminds herself that she's not paying, so can't really complain.

There's a bottle of champagne on ice on a side desk table to a bowl of perfect looking green apples. Eleanor wonders if the apples are for decoration, to offset the blinding white minimalism.

A handwritten note next to the Champagne reads: *Dear Ms Stein, we are delighted to welcome you as our honoured guest. Our PR representative wishes to take you and your friend to dinner tonight in our Delano poolside restaurant at 8pm. Have a great stay, and we hope you get to enjoy all our facilities. Please don't hesitate to contact the front desk and ask for me if you need anything. Roy Richardson, Hotel Manager."*

Eleanor collapses on the bed. It's been a long flight. Even after so many trips together she's always impressed by the celebrity treatment her friend Sonya receives in these fancy places. *Still, if they were that honoured to have her there, couldn't they have bumped her up to a suite or at least sea view room?,* Eleanor muses to herself as she falls asleep. An hour later she awakens with a jolt.

"Wake up, I am HERE!" Sonya shouts from behind the back of the same good looking bellboy, except this time he's carrying an immaculate Louis Vuitton weekend bag, and Sonya gives him a tip before he leaves. The two women give each other a huge hug.

"I hope you are ready to PARTYYYYY!" Sonya shouts, expertly cracking open the Champagne.

They toast their reunion and catch up on everything that has happened to them since they last saw each other. "I suppose we better go and meet this bloody PR woman," Sonya says, and Eleanor hurriedly rescues her hair, fixes her makeup, and slips into a floaty dress and heels.

With Sonya dressed in a little black dress and both of them slightly giddy from the bubbly, the two women head to the restaurant to meet Carolina, the public relations manager. She's another haughty looking blonde, who seems to take the world of celebrity extremely seriously.

She orders a bottle of sparkling water for the table, and nothing else. "Ms Stein, as you know, we get a lot of celebrities here, but we will not and cannot give you any information about which ones have visited recently. We cannot give you any background on what they did while at the resort either. We have total respect for our guest's privacy. I think it goes without saying that, while we are delighted that you want to highlight the Milano as a celebrity-friendly hotel, we request that you don't report back on who is staying here and what they are doing."

"Naturally!" says Sonya, with a forced grin.

To Eleanor's relief, Carolina drains her glass of Perrier and gets up to go. "It's been great meeting you, but I have to get home to my children. Please enjoy dinner on us tonight, and contact me if you want any other activities booked while you are in town." She hands them each a business card and retreats through the long, white curtains that drape around their secluded corner of the restaurant's interior.

"Thank goodness she's gone. She's as stiff as a plank." Eleanor giggles.

"Yeah, but it sucks if she won't tell me who has stayed here. How can I make this a celebrity feature? We don't run hotel reviews in the mag..."

Eleanor has flipped through the menu and landed on the cocktail list.

"Hey, you're with an investigative journalist. Don't worry, no problem. Who is the person in the hotel who always knows everything?"

"I dunno, that gorgeous bellboy?" Sonya grins.

"The bartender, of course. I'll get him to drop some names after dinner. I promise." Eleanor winks at her.

"Anyway, what are we having? Remember we're not footing the bill, so order what you want," Sonya is already waving the server over to order two margaritas.

They order the kind of ludicrously expensive tiny dishes that would infuriate Eleanor if she were actually paying. Everything comes served on crockery that wouldn't look out of place at a child's tea party, and while their dainty morsels of seafood and dainty quail eggs certainly taste delicious, they do very little to line the stomach. With a wine pairing to accompany every tiny 'course,' the pair are unsteady on their heels when they get up to leave the restaurant and head for the bathroom.

"I think they just want to get everybody so drunk they won't notice how expensive and small it all is!" Eleanor says, emerging from a fragrant stall. "At least the loos smell nice. Ooh look, posh hand cream."

"Make the most of it," says Sonya, "they're not footing the bill for anything else so we're fending for ourselves now."

Eleanor winces slightly as she makes her way through the crowd of tanned and toned bodies towards the poolside bar.

Not one of the bartenders appears to be over 25, and all of them are carved from the same ludicrously handsome cloth as the bellboy. As much as Eleanor appreciates a bit of eye candy, the youthful swagger and 'too cool for school' aloofness is beginning to grate. *Surely approachability is important in the hospitality trade?* She thinks to herself as the bartenders lean nonchalantly at either end of the bar, paying little attention to whether or not anybody wants to order. Eleanor manages to get one guy's attention for long enough to order two Long Island Ice Teas, and he acts like he's doing her a great favour. When she waves her credit card, he says: "That's 56 dollars please, madam."

Surely she misheard.

"Excuse me. How much?".

"That's 56 dollars."

"For two cocktails?"

"Yes, for two cocktails." He looks her straight in the eye. She hands over her credit card and carries the drinks back to Sonya.

"Bloody hell, we better not drink a lot here, it's almost thirty bucks a cocktail."

"Ok, let's have one more and then go somewhere cheaper," Sonya says calmly. She's used to these kinds of places.

Eleanor notices two conservatively dressed men standing nearby, engaged in an earnest-looking conversation that involves a lot of chin stroking and head nodding. They stand out like a pair of sore thumbs compared to the guys and girls in swimwear that are draped over sun loungers, bar stools, and each other.

When Sonya goes to get their next cocktail Eleanor passes by with her and starts up a conversation.

"You guys sound like you're talking business in this beautiful place."

Luckily, they start laughing.

"How did you know?" one of them asks.

"Oh, I have a sense of these things. So what line of work were you discussing so intently?"

A bit of humble bragging reveals they're big shot lawyers: "Oh, this property deal's only worth a couple of mil, we can take a break to talk to you lovely ladies!" says the tallest of the pair, while Eleanor and Sonya sip their stupidly expensive drinks.

"I hope you've paid for those yet?" Asks Cristopher, the younger-looking of the pair. "I put it on my room tab," says Sonya, acting as though she had money to burn. "Well let me go and switch it to mine, and I'll get you two more while I'm at the bar."

"Couple of show-offs," Sonya mutters to Eleanor, "it's probably all on expenses anyway."

All the same, they're happy to accept the drinks, and the two men - from Canada, it turns out - suggest they all go on somewhere else.

Everybody's a little the worse for wear when they fall into a cab to a hip hop club Sonya's heard about. There's a stiff entry fee, but once again Cristopher has whipped out his credit card before Sonya or Eleanor can even feign a protest.

The two women immediately make their way to the bathroom, wobbling on their heels.

"Sonya, do you think they wanna shag?" Eleanor slurs, reapplying her lipstick with what she optimistically hopes is precision.

"No, I don't get the feeling they're interested."

"Me neither. So why are they buying us drinks and being so nice to us?"

"Babes, I have no idea. Maybe they'll make a move later."

Sonya sways towards her.

Two cocktails later, they are barely able to stand and decide to make a runner before the guys return. But as they head to the exit, they materialise at the doorway.

"Ready to leave, ladies?" The tall one asks "Thanks, yes, we are ready to leave," she admits and he opens the cab door as Eleanor and Sonya stumble in.

Eleanor's questioning her own judgement as they drive past dark deserted warehouses and a suburban area before hitting familiar South Beach territory. As they get out of the cab and head for their rooms, they wait for the men to make their move.

"Well, goodnight, ladies, it was nice to meet you." Both of them move off toward their own rooms.

"How weird was that?" Eleanor laughs looking at Sonya.

"Hmmm, yeah, it's kind of sad it feels so rare. I usually get asked for a shag after a guy has bought me one drink, let alone paid for a whole night out."

The next morning, they drag themselves out of their beds nursing heavy hangovers. Sonya insists they swim in the Milano pool to clear their heads, but Eleanor only feels worse for being surrounded by fresh faced young lovelies clutching yoga mats, and stony-faced models swanning elegantly around the infinity pool. "You know, we're only about 90 miles from Cuba across the sea," says Sonya as they look out over the water. "I'd quite like to go, but I've heard the only celebrity they bang on about over there is Hemingway, and he's long gone, so I don't think I'd get a commission. Hemingway and voodoo priests are apparently both a big deal over there."

Eleanor laughs. "I'm fascinated by Hemingway!" she says, truthfully. And her hungover brain is telling her she could easily be fascinated by voodoo priests, too. In fact, she thinks she knows somebody who could do with a dose of bad juju.

Once they've drunk enough coffee to feel vaguely human again, they broach the subject of scuba diving. Eleanor has agreed to do an introductory dive with Sonya to help calm her nerves as it's her first experience underwater.

As they head for the door, Eleanor makes the mistake of glancing at her phone. She instantly clocks a message from her lawyer. She tells Sonya that she has to go to the bathroom, and retreats to face the message's contents in private.

Dear Eleanor, I know perhaps I should have told you but Ryan applied for decree absolute two weeks back. I didn't want to upset you while you are on a break. You had two weeks to contest the divorce but I could not see any argument why your marriage should not end. Since it went uncontested, you are now officially divorced. The court date for settlement however is not scheduled until a couple of months from now."

There are some attachments, which Eleanor assumes are court documents. She doesn't open them, and instead just leaves the toilet.

"Are you ok?" Sonya asks. "You look like you've seen a ghost."

Eleanor doesn't want to tell her about the email and she can't help seeing the irony that Ryan and Sonya never got along and now she is with her when the final notification comes. When Ryan stopped sleeping with her, Eleanor went on a lot of trips with Sonya. Ryan complained about it, but Eleanor had argued he had done nothing to improve their relationship, so she shouldn't have to give up time with a friend in order to please him. Now she wishes she had done anything to reverse this horrible situation and make her marriage work.

"I'm just tired," she lies. They have brunch, and head to the dive shop. Luckily Sonya is too nervous to notice Eleanor's lack of enthusiasm. Sonya tries on her scuba helmet but pulls it off seconds later. "I feel panicky," she tells Eleanor, "I feel like I can't breathe."

She grabs one of the instructors. "I am sorry. I just can't do this dive." She pleads. "My friend and I were meant to go together this morning. Can you give my friend another dive today and let me just go snorkelling?"

"The dive schedules are on that board over at the far end. Your friend can take her pick - it's on the house. We can take you snorkelling separately, no problem."

There is a dive scheduled later that day called "Shark feed," priced at $300.

Eleanor feels she can't pass up the opportunity to do this one for free.

"Can I do this shark feed instead? What does it involve?"

"We take you down twenty metres, then we bring in sharks by feeding them in front of you. Are you sure you want to do it? We have sharks up to seven or eight feet long. Are you sure you can hold your nerve?" The question sounds like a challenge.

"I don't give a toss about sharks. I'll do it."

"Good choice, we hardly get any shark attacks anyway." The instructor winks, and puts her name down.

Sonya goes off for her snorkelling while Eleanor prepares for her dive. Seven divers get on the boat and a gorgeous scuba instructor kits himself out in chain mail from head to toe. He's got a bucket of fish prepared to draw the sharks in. The group of divers on deck are deadly silent and the fear on the boat is palpable as they ride over the choppy waves. Once they get to their destination the boat slows, and they receive their instructions.

"Right, so listen up. I'm going to let your instructor John here to take you down 20 metres so you can sit yourself on the rocks before I bring the sharks to you."

*Bring on the big-toothed bastards,* Eleanor thinks.

"You must each find a rock in the circle we have created below and grip it tightly with your upper leg muscles and knees. You need to hold on and kneel, with your arms around you. Keep them around you at all times. Under no circumstances should you make ANY movements. These sharks are almost blind but their eyes are accustomed to motion. Any movement you make like circling an arm or hand, they will come and bite it off. If you get bitten, the rest of the sharks will see your blood and you will get eaten alive. The sharks might then turn on the other divers as blood in the water is the ultimate bait. So I am asking you to behave responsibly and not to move during the feeding. Don't leave the site until John indicates that you can. Then, when you get back to the boat, get out of the water as quickly as you can."

The rest of the group look terrified. Eleanor is the only woman there and she thinks it's quite funny that she probably looks indifferent. She realises she doesn't really care if she gets eaten. She already feels so dead inside. It's strange that although Ryan has been pushing this divorce forever now, somehow Eleanor still thought it would never really happen.

They reach the dive site and jump in. John leads them down and takes her by the hand to the rock underwater. She grips it between her knees and waits. Soon everybody is in place and ready for the incoming sharks. She sees the instructor swimming towards them with the large bucket of fish which he is throwing around him into the water. Soon huge sharks are circling the waters behind him, smashing their massive jaws down on the fish. Their instructor lands in the centre of their circle, throwing the fish while beating the sharks off with his right arm, heavy in its chain mail.

A large shark blunders into Eleanor's left side, knocking her to the right. She almost loses her balance but grips hard with her knees. She is so distracted by her inner thoughts she doesn't feel as terrified as she probably should. The cold eye of a second shark glares right into hers and she sees the depthless eternity of those black eyes: if the shark could see, it would have felt the black emptiness of her own eyes staring back.

This shark hits her too, but this time she falls forward to correct herself. Regaining her balance, she gazes in awe as the number of sharks around them grows larger. They are swarming around in a frenzy and she can see their wide jaws opening around them snapping up fish.

Feeling icy cold, she closes her eyes, emotionally exhausted. Suddenly the instructor starts swimming away, and the swarm of more than thirty sharks follows. He continues to feed them as he leads them off from the group.

The last fin sways its way into the deep blue and the other instructor, John, points to the surface. They all get out of the water with extreme speed. For the first time that day there's laughter as they strip off their equipment. The shark feeding instructor returns, flopping onto the back deck. He lies in the sun, his chain mail glistening, clutching his fish bucket. Eleanor can't help but be totally in awe of him.

"Are you alright?" She asks gazing down at him.

"Give me a hand up, missy." He lifts his leaden arm and she pulls him with all her strength.

"How can you not sink with all this metal on?" She asks gasping as he shuffles his way to standing.

"I just have enough air in my BCD to get me back." He laughs.

"And how can you feed those sharks and not be terrified?"

"Oh, it's nothing. They've only tried to bite me a few times." He lets out an anxious sounding laugh and then adds, "I would not want to do anything else for a living, this is a job I love. You can't get a better adrenalin rush than that."

He strips off his chain metal casually. Then he returns to the rest of the group. "I never feel so alive as when I'm down there with those sharks. Let's have a round of applause if you had a great dive." Everyone starts clapping.

When they get back to dry land, Sonya is already back from her snorkel trip and sipping a restorative gin and tonic.

"I'm so glad you're back ok, I was worried. You are so brave!" She hugs Eleanor.

Eleanor doesn't attempt to explain that it wasn't bravery, she just didn't feel fear the way she should have. She didn't care if the sharks got her. Surrounded by all this luxury, she still feels has hit rock bottom. She has sunk so low, she wonders if there will ever be a way back.

# Chapter 29

# *Voodoo Piss*

Although her trip with Sonya is coming to an end, Eleanor is not quite ready to head back to the UK just yet. After spending so long in the tropical heat, the thought of facing the British weather makes her heart sink. And it's not just the prospect of relentless drizzle and grey days that's filling her with a sense of dread.

It's the thought of returning to the domestic mess she ran away from. From the failed marriage. From facing up to the man she once thought loved her.

Ryan hasn't even attempted to get in contact with her, and she's still none the wiser about why he went so cold on her as soon as they tied the knot.

She feels totally conflicted - on the one hand, she still has warm memories of the first few months of their relationship. They had their difficulties, but she had truly believed he loved her. She had cherished that feeling of being loved and accepted, flaws and all. Some of her fondest memories were of the times they had spent with Ryan's family, and Eleanor had enjoyed the warm familiarity that his parents had extended towards her. With her own parents so far away, Eleanor sometimes felt she missed Ryan's parents almost as much as she missed him.

She wanted to hate him - after the wedding, he had been nothing but cruel to her. His constant sniping, put-downs and emotional absence had made her question her own sanity - especially as she tried to maintain a facade of domestic happiness to family and friends.

She'd never been one to take anybody's crap. But somehow, living in the constant shadow of his disapproval, she had found her own fiery personality starting to fade. She had wanted to make everything OK, somehow, to bring back the Ryan she had first met.

She still has some savings to draw on, and finds herself toying with the idea of a trip to Cuba, especially since Miami is so nearby. It seems like every traveller she meets bangs on and on about how important it is to go there "before it opens up and everything changes," and she's starting to think they might be right. The idea of visiting somewhere almost stuck in time seems oddly appealing. She's read enough Hemingway to be fascinated by the idea of visiting his old haunts, and the photographs she's seen of Havana look like stills from a movie. She knows she shouldn't really be digging into her fast-evaporating savings once again, but everybody tells her Cuba is cheap as long as she sticks with locals. Before she can talk herself out of it, she's booking a plane ticket. There's been very little progress on her apartment, and she's not sorry to see the back of that dusty building site. She knows she's going to miss Edilson, in spite of her many misgivings about him, and thinks it's better to put some distance between them to avoid getting tied up in another messy relationship.

Yes, Cuba is sounding more appealing by the minute. Without even telling Edilson her plans, she packs her bags, settles her hostel bill, and prepares herself for one last big adventure before she returns to the UK, and to real life.

Her flight touches down at the international airport, just outside Havana, in broad daylight. Passing through customs, Eleanor's first thought is how surprisingly modern it seems. She's not sure what she expected - maybe a 1950s airport full of people looking like Ernest Hemingway, Che Guevara and Fidel Castro, smoking huge cigars and drinking daiquiris.

Instead, it looks a lot like every other airport she's been to recently, except for the fact that this time her luggage isn't on the carousel. The other passengers from her flight grab theirs, and Eleanor's panic rises as the conveyor belt empties, and then stops.

She manages to get the attention of a bored-looking security guard, who makes a series of phone calls before telling her the bags have been found, but she needs to wait. He gestures to a row of chairs, where a woman is already sitting, looking even more fed up than Eleanor feels. In strongly-accented English, the woman tells Eleanor she's Cuban and returning from a trip to Italy. Almost as a casual afterthought, she adds that her bags have gone missing because of a curse. Eleanor's eyebrows shoot up in surprise. *Because of what, now?* The woman, who is dressed head to toe in Nike sportswear, tells Eleanor that she's had problems like this ever since she left her husband for a rich Italian man.

Eleanor's intrigued. With a look of weary resignation, the woman tells her that her husband is a follower of the Santeria religion and has been using its powers against her ever since she left him. When Eleanor looks blank, she says: "You've heard of Voodoo? It's similar. The religion isn't evil but some people use its power in a bad way. Like my husband." The security guard returns with Eleanor's wheeled suitcase. Eleanor's rudimentary Spanish is enough for her to decipher that he's telling the Cuban woman her bags have not been found. "You see?" she says to Eleanor with that same weary resignation. "It's a curse."

Eleanor's not quite sure how to respond, so she smiles sympathetically and wheels her own bag out of there. The seed of an idea has been planted in her mind.

She opens the case but it's intact, and a quick glance inside tells her nothing important is missing. Feeling thankful for the apparent lack of voodoo curses on her, she can't help thinking perhaps Ryan could do with some bad juju.

She doesn't have time to mull it over for long because as she wanders through Arrivals, five taxi drivers make animated gestures towards their vehicles, which all look exactly the same. For want of a better way to distinguish between them, she opts for the best-looking of the drivers. He's taller and younger than the other, with thick dark hair and smiling brown eyes.

It's an hour's drive to central Havana so she might as well spend it in good company, she reasons, handing her suitcase to the driver for him to put into the open boot of his cab.

He turns out to be good company, and a fluent English speaker. He tells her about his sister in Canada, his family in Cuba, and the best things to do in Havana. She tells him she's already booked onto a three day later that week, organised by her hotel. But when they reach the place and he helps her bring the luggage inside, the receptionist looks blank. "Your place on the tour is reserved, madam, but I'm afraid we have no record of a room booking. Did you make it through an agency?" Eleanor glances around the smart Art Deco lobby and wonders if this is good or bad juju kicking in. She hasn't actually paid for the room, and the driver had told her on the way that this place is overpriced.

"I know a place I can take you, it's a small family pension," the driver offers. "It's not a tourist place, but it's safe and it's cheap. Maria will take care of you."

As it's already beginning to get dark, Eleanor doesn't see that she has much choice. She tells the receptionist she'll be back in the morning for the tour, and follows the driver back out to his cab.

They wind through dark back streets, past crumbling mansions and tall, handsome townhouses in various states of decay. Shadowy characters lean against doorways and out of windows, and Eleanor's first thought is that she wouldn't want to wander these streets alone.

The cab pulls up at the doorway to a building with thick metal bars across all of its windows. "Here we are!" The driver sounds more enthusiastic than Eleanor feels, but she follows him and her bag indoors, past a scuffed statue of the Virgin Mary standing in the doorway. Is this the Maria who is supposed to look after her?

"Buenas noches, señorita, soy Maria." A very large, dark haired woman greets Eleanor in the hallway and immediately hauls her huge suitcase up the stairs.

"The price is 20 dollars a night for your room, is that okay?" the taxi driver asks. Considering that her case is already bouncing its way upstairs, he clearly doesn't seem to think she will object, and at least it's cheap. She tells herself it will be OK for one night.

"That's great, thanks so much." Eleanor says to him, handing him a wad of notes for the cab ride. "No problem. You can pay Maria directly when you leave." She presumes he means the woman who just greeted her, rather than the statue.

Before he can turn to go, she says: "can you suggest somewhere I should go tonight? Any place you like or recommend?"

The words come out of her mouth before she realises that this sounds like an invitation. Maybe she can *make* it an invitation...

"It's my first night out in Cuba, maybe you can join me?"

Neither the thought of venturing out alone or staying in this pension by herself seem appealing.

He looks at her for a minute, then smiles.

"I have the night off, it would be my pleasure to accompany you around the city tonight," he says. "I will be back at eight. I'm Pedro, by the way."

With that, he turns and heads back to his car, parked on the curb outside.

Relieved, Eleanor ventures up the stairs in search of her bag. Everything is spotlessly clean. The woman who hefted her bag upstairs is ushering her into one of the rooms. With a few abrupt sentences in Spanish, she gestures towards the bed, small TV screen, water jug and glasses, and the bathroom. Eleanor feels another wave of relief: she had half-expected to share a bathroom. She flops on the bed, thanking her lucky stars that she has Pedro taking her out later. Havana already seems an intimidating place to explore alone, and besides, everybody has told her that you need a local to see the best of the place and avoid the tourist prices.

A glance at her watch tells her she has just under two hours until Pedro comes back, so she takes a shower, changes into a slip dress suitable for the sticky heat outside, and pours herself a large rum from the bottle in her suitcase. Pedro arrives at eight on the dot. He's dressed in jeans, trainers and a plain white t-shirt, and greets her with a slightly nervous smile. Eleanor's not quite sure if this is a date or a paid taxi tour, or a bit of both. "I thought I would give you a city tour tonight, show you the highlights," he proposes. "If you can just pay for my petrol I won't ask anything more."

"That sounds great," Eleanor says, sliding into the front of his cab. The rum has given her an easy confidence, and she's excited to see Havana.

"First we go to meet Jesus," Pedro says, closing his cab door. He's smiling, but Eleanor feels suddenly freaked out. "Christ of Havana!"

he clarifies, possibly seeing the panic on her face. *Oh, yes.* She remembers seeing pictures of a big Christ statue on a hill.

It's dark, but the view from the foot of the statue is still impressive - a sweeping panorama of twinkling lights over city streets. They're surrounded by love-struck couples gazing at each other more than the views, so Eleanor snaps a few photos of the statue and the view, then indicates she's ready to move on. Preferably to somewhere with a bar.

They drive past the harbour and into the centre of town, which throngs with couples holding hands. Eleanor hadn't expected Cuba to be quite so loved up. One building they pass is lit with Chinese lanterns, and a huge line of young couples spills out of the door and halfway down the street. "What's going on in that Chinese place?" asks Eleanor, and Pedro replies that it's a restaurant. "It's Friday night." He adds, by way of explanation. "Is it that good?" asks Eleanor, "why is there such a huge queue? I've never seen people queue for a restaurant in London."

She catches herself sounding like an ignorant, spoiled tourist, and hurriedly adds: "It's different with clubs. You get huge queues for clubs."

It's too late - Pedro looks offended.

"This is the way it is in Cuba, if you want to go to a cheap place," he explains.

"You tourists can afford higher prices. I can take you to a tourist restaurant tonight, but I myself and most Cubans cannot afford to go there."

"No, please, I would love to go to the restaurant, but I insist — you are my guest, it's the least I can do, I will pay for you." She takes his hand. Eleanor wonders why it's so easy to be with him, how she can trust him so much even though she has only known him one afternoon.

They go to a spick-and-span restaurant overlooking the street, people and cars passing by. There's nothing too fancy about it and even the prices seem average, it's around $15 for a main dish. They have some rum cocktails and Eleanor feels increasingly relaxed.

Conversation with Pedro flows easily. He shows her photographs of his daughter, his mother and his ex-wife, and Eleanor opens up to him about her failing marriage and her fears about returning to the UK after Cuba. Despite the easy conversation, she can't tell if he's interested in her romantically, platonically, or as a paying customer. As the rum cocktails flow, she finds her mind repeatedly straying to the subject of Santerian curses, and whether Pedro can help her find somebody to work the dark arts on her twat of an ex-husband. She struggles for an easy way to drop the subject into casual conversation.

Mid-way through her fourth Cuba Libre, she says: "Pedro, I have a question," He's all ears. "It's quite a strange one. I'm researching and writing an article about different religions in Cuba, especially how Catholicism has mixed with African religions. Do you know if there are any ceremonies I could attend, or any Santerian priests I could talk to?" She tries to ask nonchalantly, like she is asking about the weather or where to make a hairdresser's appointment.

"I'm sorry – I don't know much about this." He looks a bit alarmed. "But I can certainly ask my friends if they know anyone," he offers, apologetically.

"Please do, it's really important."

Eleanor's never been religious, and has always thought of herself as a rational person. She's at a loss to explain, even to herself, how the idea of black magic has taken such a grip on her. She can't even attempt to explain it to anybody else, for fear of sounding mad, or evil, or both. She just knows she's terrified of facing up to her husband in the divorce courts, and she strongly suspects that she's going to walk away with nothing while he laughs all the way to the bank with his trust funds and property portfolio and inheritance from his uncle. She's sure that he's hiding something, and wants the court to see how unfairly he has treated her. But she doesn't know what it is that he's been keeping from her, and feels like she has no fight left.

When Pedro goes to the toilet, she ruminates on the subject. She's gone from being a fiery, feisty and fun career woman to the type of person that wakes up face down in a sand dune after a mugging and just dusts herself down, blaming herself above anybody else. She wants her fighting spirit back, and if she needs to get some voodoo spirits on board to help her beat Ryan, so be it. He's due a dose of bad luck.

Pedro returns, and tells her he's already settled the bill. It doesn't seem fair, as she's had five strong drinks on top of her meal, but he insists. "I'll pay next time," she says, grabbing her bag. Dropping her at the guest house, he leans in and kisses her gently. "Until next time," he says, smiling. "I can pick you up at nine tomorrow morning and show you more of Havana." She gets out of the cab feeling like a giddy school girl after a chaste date with a nice boy.

She sneaks upstairs as quietly as possible and falls asleep thinking of his soft lips and gentle eyes.

All thoughts of Pedro's dreamy eyes vanish the next morning, when Eleanor arrives at the breakfast table to find three tall, muscular German men sitting chatting over the spread of fruit, bread, eggs and coffee. They seem happy enough to talk to her in English, and she automatically slips into flirt mode. Maria arrives to refill the coffee, and addresses Eleanor with a somewhat stern look.

"Your special friend is coming to pick you up at nine thirty," she says, through pursed lips.

"My special friend?" Eleanor is momentarily baffled.

"Your friend, the taxi driver, called me this morning to say he will be a little bit late to meet you."

Eleanor suddenly realises that very little goes unnoticed in Maria's guest house. Maria might already have told Pedro that Eleanor has spent the best part of an hour flirting with these boys.

Her eyes travel to the big, plastic Madonna in the hallway and for a moment Eleanor thinks the holy lady is looking at her funny. As though Mary's beady plastic eyes have already cast Eleanor as a sinner.

Smiling to herself, Eleanor takes a swig of coffee and stands up. "Thanks, I'll get ready then."

She waves goodbye to the Germans and heads upstairs, feeling like she's been sent to the naughty step.

When he arrives, Pedro looks happy to see her. It's hot, and she's dressed for the weather in a flimsy summer dress, realising too late that it clings in the sticky heat. She keeps catching Pedro taking sideways glances at her while he points out the sights. "As you're a writer, I thought you would be interested in Hemingway, right?" Right. He shows her Hemingway's house on the coast, and then they drive to La Floridita, famously one of the writer's favourite hangouts. "It would be rude not to drink a daiquiri in his honour!" she says, ordering two.

Half an hour later, Pedro takes her to another bar that Hemingway apparently used to love, and Eleanor swiftly realises that raising a toast in every bar that claimed Hemingway as a patron would leave her both drunk and skint.

"Ernest Hemingway loved Cuba so much he lived many years here," says Pedro. "Look at this picture, he even met Castro."

They have an easy familiarity with each other, but Eleanor's still a little conflicted about what exactly is going on: she's still paying for his services as a cab driver, but half the time it feels as though they're out on a romantic date. She's leaving the next day for the organised trip she had booked before she arrived in Cuba, and even feels conflicted about that. She's looking forward to seeing more of the country, but has enjoyed being shown around by a local rather than as part of a tourist group. The hotel receptionist has contacted her to apologise for the mix up and tell her that her room is ready for her: the group tour leaves early in the morning. Eleanor has her suitcase ready and Pedro drops her in his cab at the fancy hotel in town where her group tour starts.

"Can I see you tonight?" he asks as he drops her bags.

"I'm sorry, Pedro," She says, genuinely a little sad. "Tonight we're having a group meet-up at the hotel and then going out for dinner." He smiles, but it feels like a chasm has suddenly opened between them.

"I'll have five days in Havana after the trip ends, so I can see you when I get back?"

"I'll be here," he tells her. "I work out of this hotel a lot so I will be around."

She takes her case to reception and up to her room. In the grandeur of the hotel lobby it seems inappropriate to kiss him goodbye, but awkward to leave so casually after the time they've spent together.

He waves her off as though she were a casual acquaintance, and gets back into his cab. Later that evening, she's sitting drinking in the lobby with the 10 other European travellers on the tour when she sees Pedro hauling a large suitcase behind a wealthy-looking couple who are about to check in. Their eyes meet for a split second but he says nothing, and Eleanor feels an odd mixture of disappointment and relief.

Eleanor appears to be the eldest in the group by at least a decade - a running theme on her group tours - but she enjoys the party spirit that comes with hanging out with people too young for real ties and responsibilities. She sparks up a friendship with two Norwegian boys in their early 20s, feeling almost maternal towards them. But if she's going to feel like a mama, she wants to feel like a cool mama - and so she embraces the constant rum-drinking and the puffing on giant Cuban cigars.

They tour Cuba's west coast, staying in grande dame hotels that have begun to fall into disrepair. Eleanor eats more lobster in three days than she had eaten in her whole life up to that point. She has always thought of it as a luxury, but after her initial excitement at being served freshly-caught lobster with rice and beans, her enthusiasm wanes with each successive serving. Every hotel dinner and set lunch menu seems to involve lobster. One morning, she goes for a swim in clear, clean water only to find several huge lobsters swimming with her in the shallows. She swims away, quickly, avoiding their snapping claws.

One night at dinner, the conversation turns to Santerian priests and ceremonies, and Eleanor's ears prick up. One of the other guests is reading about the subject in her guidebook and stops to ask their Cuban tour guide, Lorenzo, if the religion is widespread in Cuba. Lorenzo replies that yes, many people follow the religion - "It's common to see them dressed all in white," he affirms.

Sitting by Lorenzo's side, Eleanor seizes her opportunity. She asks him in a low voice whether he knows anybody who dabbles in the dark arts.

"Eleanor, I know of these people, but I will never help you with such a thing. Some of these people are evil."

He looks horrified, so she spares no detail in telling him about her husband's horrible behaviour - they're a couple of drinks in, so the oversharing comes quite naturally.

"No. This is not something to mess with. It will harm you more than your husband. I won't help you!"

"What won't Lorenzo help you with?" asks the English girl sitting on the other side of Lorenzo. His raised voice has cut through the dinner table chatter. "He won't help me get a voodoo curse put on my ex-husband," Eleanor says loudly, and the whole table turns to stare at her. The silence is deafening. In the split second before anybody talks, she thinks she sees judgement, fear, and even pity in the eyes of the others at the dinner table. She feels more annoyed than embarrassed.

"My God, It's not like I'm proposing killing a kitten or anything!" she blurts out. "I just want to teach my bastard husband a lesson! Trust me, he deserves it."

"Hear that? You better not step out of line here in Cuba," says the English girl to her boyfriend. The laughter relieves the awkwardness, but Eleanor still feels pissed off.

The next day, the whole group is taking a trip into a cave, but the very last thing Eleanor feels like is being crammed into a confined dark space with a load of people who think her private life is weird, funny or pitiful. She doesn't know which of those is the worst. She's feeling claustrophobic enough as it is, with shared hotel rooms and group meals, and every minute planned out.

Eleanor boards the tour bus with the others but when they reach the entrance to the park that houses the cave, feigns that she's forgotten her walking trainers and couldn't possibly go into a dark cave in her slippy rubber flip-flops. She catches some of the others sharing dubious glances, but doesn't care. She says she'll just wait in the van and wander around a little.

"Well, if you're sure?" Lorenzo says, gathering the group together. She nods. As soon as the group is safely out of sight, Eleanor bursts into tears. Streams and streams of tears and snot running down her face, like a dam has broken on all the emotions she has been holding back for the last year or more.

She feels lonely, but above all, she feels hopeless. Like nothing is going to have a happy ending. The memory of that terrible morning on the beach in Mexico comes crashing back into her mind like an unwelcome guest, mingling with anger at her husband and a deep fear that the court case is going to go entirely his way. Whoever attacked and robbed her has got away with it, and Ryan is getting away with treating her like dirt and making her out to be the guilty party.

Deep down, she knows that even the darkest voodoo magic isn't going to help her get the happy ending she wants.

Eventually, her sobs subside. She cleans her face with the wet wipes she carries in her backpack, and dabs concealer under her swollen eyes. She reapplies her smudged mascara. She feels like a hollowed out shell of her usual self, but is ready to pretend again. Ready to make out everything's fine. She climbs down from the bus for some fresh air, and hides her face behind her giant sunglasses, plastering a smile on her face when the group returns. Nobody needs to know that the girl who drinks Cuba Libre every night, dances to salsa and laughs all the time is broken inside.

When it's time to return to Havana, she finds she's looking forward to seeing Pedro again. For some reason, she feels she can let her mask slip a little with him. She has one night at the more upscale hotel, but there's no sign of Pedro in the lobby, or at the taxi rank when they walk past on their way out for drinks.

The next day the hotel calls her a cab back to Maria's guesthouse, but the driver is nobody she knows. Maria greets her warmly, and it feels reassuring that at least somebody is pleased to see her.

Trying to ignore the aching loneliness, Eleanor visits museums, parks and local beauty spots with Eloise, a young French woman from the tour group. They'd instantly hit it off as they were both travelling alone, but Eloise is due to leave early the next morning, and Eleanor's not looking forward to sightseeing alone again. Not for the first time, she wonders where Pedro is. The two women splash out on a meal at one of Havana's better tourist restaurants, then bid each other farewell on a street clogged with traffic fumes.

Eleanor realises that she frequently finds it hard to breathe in Havana. Walking back to the guesthouse through narrow streets lined with semi-derelict buildings, windows lit to reveal family scenes inside, she wonders what locals must think of her, this woman travelling alone. She hurries back to the guest house, feeling the stab of loneliness once again.

She finally reaches her doorway and lets herself into the dark hall. The huge Madonna statue staring as she enters. She falls on her bed, happy to be back somewhere that already feels familiar. She's still got Pedro's number in her phone and contemplates calling him, but can't bring herself to do it. She'd hoped to just casually bump into him, but now she's wondering if he resents her for not calling as she had promised. She's craving his company but thinks it's probably just loneliness - it's not like they could have a future together, after all. She knows she's crazy for even considering it - his family, his life, is all here in Havana.

Unable to sleep, she can't stop her mind drifting back to Ryan and the way he treated her.

She feels like a piece of bread, tossed out to sea, waiting to be picked over by seagulls. Ryan had been her anchor, and now what did she have? She was at sea, adrift.

She hates the thought of returning to the UK. She can't imagine patching up her life again without Ryan.

The despair threatens to consume her and she decides that she has to do something. She has to move, she can't just stay wide awake in bed. Although it's past 1am, she decides to walk back to the upmarket hotel, as it's the only place she knows of in Havana with the internet. She knows the lobby staff won't object to her using it, even at this late hour.

Her justification for the late-night internet session was that she needed to plan the remainder of her trip, but as soon as she's online she starts Googling 'Voodoo in Havana'. She comes across a Havana museum dedicated to Santerian 'orishas', or deities, and decides she must go there in the morning. It might be her best chance of finding somebody who can make Ryan's luck run out.

As she's leaving the hotel lobby, she's surprised to see Jensen and Hugo, the young Norwegians from her trip, slumped on sofas by the door.

"What on earth are you guys doing here?" She asks, changing direction mid-step.

"We still couldn't get money from the ATM machines so we couldn't get to the airport for our flight to Tobago," Jensen explains. "We don't even have money for a hotel so we came here to sleep until we can figure out what to do."

Without even thinking, Eleanor suggests they stay in her room. "There's plenty of space - I have two double beds! You can't sleep in a hotel lobby."

Eleanor's pretty sure she's not allowed guests, and knows there are some pretty tight government regulations, but it doesn't seem right to leave them on an uncomfy sofa. The boys readily accept, so she warns them they'll have to be super careful not to get spotted. She's not sure who would be in the most trouble - herself, the boys, or the guest house owner.

They pick up their bags and walk back to the guest house, and Eleanor is grateful for the company walking dark alleys at such a late hour.

In the darkness, she almost steps on a dead chicken, lying in a pool of blood outside an unlit window. Jensen shouts at her to walk around it rather than in front.

"Don't cross that chicken!" It makes her jump and she stares at him.

"What on Earth is wrong?"

"Look, it's Voodoo, girl! Don't you know it's bad luck to cross a dead black chicken? Look, there are two outside this house."

They stop to look at the birds lying in a pool of its own blood.

Someone had positioned them equally on each corner of the entrance to the house. It gives Eleanor the shivers, but also further conviction to find somebody who can help her deal out some bad luck of her own.

The three of them sneak through the guest house door as silently as possible, creeping up the stairs without turning on the lights.

In the morning, she gets them up at 6 am and does a reccy mission downstairs before leading them through the house to the front door. Nobody is watching them except the huge Madonna in the hallway.

They arrange to meet later in the afternoon to take a trip to the beach, but first Eleanor wants to make a solo trip to what she's dubbed 'the Voodoo museum.'

She emerges with an increased knowledge of the Santerian spirit world, but absolutely none the wiser about how to arrange a Voodoo curse.

When she does meet the Norwegians, they've got company - two young local men are keen to tag along for the ride.

"They said they can show us the cheap, non-touristy places," Jensen enthuses. The taller of the two, who looks to be in his mid-20s, hails a cab, and Eleanor is struck by how much cheaper it is when there are locals in tow.

They jump out at a beach that stretches for miles, liberally sprinkled with straw shacks serving drinks and snacks. The cocktails are a fraction of the price she's been paying, so Eleanor's more than happy to shout everybody a round of margaritas.

One of the Cuban boys sits down next to her on the sand, and tells her his name is Maceo. "You know, I have tried to swim out of here three times," he tells her.

He gazes forlornly over the ocean, sipping his drink. "The Cuban government won't let me leave the country. Will you be my official sponsor to come to England?" he asks.

She's had a few too many drinks. "Sure, why not?" she says, without thinking it through.

He pulls out a travel guide to the UK, that looks like it was written in the 1970s, and starts firing questions. How easy is it to get a job? A house? Does everybody eat fish and chips?

Sensing she might be giving him false hopes, Eleanor excuses herself and slips into the water for a swim. Maceo follows her into the water, reaching for her hand and trying to lean in for a kiss.

"This is not going anywhere, Maceo, I am still sad about my husband. Sorry."

It's the best reason she can give, and it's true.

"I can help you get over your husband," he tells her, suggestively.

His lean, muscled body is gleaming with water droplets in the sunshine. Still, she knows no good can come of kissing this eager young man.

"Please Maceo, don't ruin the day, we're having such a nice time." She pushes him away. "It's just not where my mind is." She wades towards the safe haven of the public beach and runs over to Jensen.

"You gotta help me," she tells him, "Maceo is getting kind of fresh."

Jensen just laughs, already drunk.

Maceo comes onto the beach, shaking himself off. "Sorry," he apologises. "I just think you are beautiful."

She ignores his comment. She knows she's probably just another tourist that looks to him like an escape route off the island. When the sun goes down, Jensen the travelling Norwegian is persistent and manages to flag down a huge, black, cloud-producing, 1950s Chevy. It grinds noisily to a halt the minute they enter a huge, busy tunnel.

Sitting in the dark, cars swerving around their car at the last minute, Eleanor is petrified. "This is really not how I want to die."

"Don't worry lady, this happens all the time. You boys have to get out and push!" the driver insists.

Without a second thought, all four of them leap out of the car and start pushing. Thankfully, the engine revs up and they jump back in. She is amazed that the amazing big beast of a car has been brought back to life.

"In Cuba, the cars always break down," the taxi driver grumbles. "We can't buy new parts for these cars, or get new ones. That's why there are cranes at each end of the tunnel, because they break down so often." Eleanor emerges shakily from the cab once they arrive safely back in Havana, and steps into the nearest shop to grab some rum and Coke - they're going to take the party back to Maceo's. "I am very lucky I have a very big apartment all to myself," he explains. "My mother left it to me when she went to Trinidad."

They enter a graffiti-strewn hallway, where strip light flickers overhead. There's no lift, so they climb the four flights of stairs in the near-dark. The small, grey apartment has no sink, no bathroom door, and no furniture.

"Thieves stole everything," he looks at her, reading Eleanor's expression. "But in Havana I am a rich man – many girls want me for my apartment."

"It's great," Eleanor lies.

She's opening the rum and pouring it into tiny, cracked mugs. Soon Maceo has his little radio on and they are dancing around his empty living room. But the more she looks around at her new friends, the more out of place she feels. Soon, she wants to leave. What's the point of getting drunk with boys half her age?

"I can't stay Maceo, I have things to do tomorrow."

"But the party just got started," he protests. "What's so important tomorrow? You are on holiday, girl!"

"I have to interview the woman in my guesthouse about Voodoo," Eleanor's making it up as she goes along. "I'm doing an article on Voodoo. I'm looking for witch doctors."

Maceo laughs.

"No way! I am a witch doctor!" He looks her straight in the eye and something in his gaze stops her in her tracks.

"No way, dude!" Jensen says, voicing her thoughts. "How are you a witch doctor? You can't be old enough!"

"I am 25," Macio cries. "I learnt everything from my father, who is a witchdoctor in Trinidad. Why does a witchdoctor have to be old?"

He reaches into a concealed hole in the wall and brings out a covered stone vase.

"What do you want to know?"

He strips his shirt off right there and then, and hangs chains of tiny skulls around his neck. The atmosphere changes dramatically.

He sits facing the wall in the corner of the room, shaking the stone vase and chanting.

Jensen and Hugo look on in shock, almost hypnotised. Eleanor is the most shocked of all. She had been wondering all afternoon how she was ever going to find a witchdoctor without knowing she had been sitting next to one.

"I want to put a curse on my husband," she says, bluntly.

"Why you want to do that?" Macio asks.

"He's divorcing me. The court case is coming up."

"You still love him, right?" Maceo says, still shaking the vase.

"Yes." She answers automatically and it surprises her that this is still the truth.

"So what you need is not a curse," he tells me. "You need to change his mind. Sit down with me."

He motions to her to sit next to him. She's in shock, but does as he asks.

He throws the contents of the vase against the wall and as they fall she sees bits of shell, animal bone, beans, some small skulls, a dried out grasshopper and other items she can't begin to identify.

Maceo shuffles through the objects with his eyes closed.

"You loved each other, but you didn't live together well," Macio tells her. His voice is different now and it scares her a little. "He's decided you are no longer meant to be together, it's unclear the reasons because he didn't give you much chance to be in his life."

She wonders how this man can possibly understand their relationship so well, so far from her home.

"Will we get back together?" She asks. It sounds desperate even to her.

"He will come to you, wanting to talk but you will turn him away."

"Can you tell me anything more, Maceo?" She is practically begging him.

"He will die before you do," he says, with a very pained look on his face.

She doesn't ask if this is going to happen naturally, or if this is Maceo's offering to 'help her.

"Here, take this."

He puts some small items in a brown bottle and hands it to her.

"You must urinate into this bottle within two hours once you land back home. Then you must take it to the courtroom for the divorce trial. It will bring the forces onto your side," he instructs her.

She raises a sceptical eyebrow, but everything he has told her so far about her past has seemed accurate, and she feels in awe of him.

"Please can I have your email address and number so I can call you after the court case. To let you know how it goes?"

She grabs onto him like a lifeline. Maceo gives her the number to the only phone in the building, it's a pay phone on the bottom floor.

"Just call and ask for me," he tells me. "They all know me here. Everything will be alright, you will see."

He hugs her. She leaves the derelict block, head swimming with rum and giddiness at the strange turn the day has taken. She crawls into bed, happier than she has been in days.

Now she has the hope of a miracle.

The next morning she has breakfast with the guest house owner, still light-headed from the previous night's rum. It's her last full day in Cuba and the thought of returning to the UK the next day is making her feel edgy.

"Your boyfriend called this morning. He's coming at 10," Maria says matter-of-factly. Eleanor presumes she's talking about Pedro, and her stomach flips a little, in spite of herself. "Yes thanks, I'd better get ready then."

Pedro arrives at the door looking a bit put out.

"Where have you been the last couple of days?" he asks. "I heard you came back on Thursday."

"Sorry Pedro, I had some friends in to see. I looked for you at the hotel taxi rank and you weren't there."

His face brightens excitedly. "Anyway, I have the day off today and a surprise for you."

They get in his car and he drives along the coast.

"I found a witchdoctor for you to interview," he tells me, his eyes on the road. "A friend of mine gave me the address. The only thing is that he doesn't speak English so I will have to translate."

She feigns real excitement, but inside is concerned that seeing another witch doctor might negate the spell of the first one. She can't bring herself to tell Pedro that she saw one yesterday, and she doesn't want him to know her real story. "You should pay him a ten peso fee, it's a token of respect for his time." Pedro adds.

They arrive at a block of flats that looks and smells a lot like Maceo's place. Like the worst type of council block you might find in the UK, graffiti and resident urine stench included.

Pedro takes her to the top floor and knocks at a dingy looking door. An elderly lady answers, and takes them to wait in the living room. She sits side by side with Pedro, in uncomfortable silence. Eventually the witch doctor comes out, wearing a bandana and, like Maceo the night before, no shirt. She wonders if this is a kind of witch doctor uniform – a sign that he is in touch with the spirits. He's decades older than Maceo, with kind, smiling eyes. He leads them into a small side-room.

Pedro asks her to explain to him why she is there, so he can translate. She briefly considers pretending to be interviewing him, but decides to bite the bullet and tell the truth.

"I am here because I have a court case with my husband. He wants to end our marriage in two weeks and I want to put a curse on him and to win the case."

Pedro looks shocked, but he translates for her anyway. The witch doctor speaks and Pedro says, "He doesn't do curses, but he can make a spell that can help you win the case."

She is a little disappointed that no one seems willing to use the dark arts to curse the scheming cold bastard, but is glad for any help.

Like Maceo before him, the man shakes some items in a vase and throws them on the floor. He picks through them and tells Pedro a bunch of things about Eleanor that don't ring true at all.

"About your ex," Pedro translates. "You used to do everything for him, but he never did anything for you. He made you do too much work in the home. Everything was just for him. He never did anything for you. He's not a nice man."

She almost bursts out laughing. She had insisted on bringing in a cleaner once a week and had cooked maybe four times that year.

The last part might be true enough, but Eleanor thought it was fairly obvious she didn't consider her ex a nice man if she wanted to put a curse on him.

"He always wanted sex, with no thought to pleasure you," Pedro continues his translation, blushing and looking awkward.

This is so untrue Eleanor almost bursts out laughing. She knows a con man when she sees one.

She pays lip service to the rest of the guy's questions, gives him his 10 pesos and gets out of there. She bursts out laughing as soon as they leave.

"What's so funny?" Pedro asks.

"Nothing, I am just happy the witchdoctor is going to work some magic on my court case," she tells him. "Thank you so much for helping me to find him." It's not Pedro's fault the guy's a fraud, after all.

Pedro seems pleased.

"I will always help you whenever I can. I already told people you are my girlfriend. You can move here and write from my apartment."

Perhaps Eleanor's surprise at this suggestion is written on her face. He takes her hand and says, with a serious face: "Like Ernest Hemingway. Let me take you there to where he lived."

For the third time that morning she has to fight to stop herself bursting out laughing. Pedro looks so sincere, she doesn't have the heart to laugh at his pipe dreams.

Even if the idea does hold a certain charm, things could never work out. Eleanor decides to find a way to let him down gently.

Pedro drives them to a spot where Hemingway apparently wrote some of his books. It's a bar with a wide view of the sea, and a

Hemingway quote above the row of spirits: *I drink to make other people interesting.*

Eleanor smiles, thinking that she does the same thing.

Sipping a drink and taking in the view in the afternoon heat, she starts to wonder if there isn't actually something to Pedro's idea. Spending her days writing and drinking in the sun, Hemingway style, doesn't seem a bad way to live.

"Do you know, I like your idea about me being a writer," she tells Pedro. "And I love it here – the people are so warm and friendly."

"Shall I show you my apartment before I go?" he asks. Eleanor doesn't feel excited at the prospect, but smiles in agreement.

They drive along the coast, back towards the centre of the city.

Eleanor's bracing herself for another down-at-heel building, but Pedro pulls up in front of a smart block of flats in a refurbished colonial building. There's a large balcony overlooking the water, a spick and span bedroom, and another smaller a room covered in princess motifs. "My daughter's room," he says with a proud smile. Eleanor suddenly remembers reading that taxi drivers earn more than doctors in Cuba because of the topsy turvy economy. She had assumed it was an urban myth. "You see, I'm rich in Cuba," Pedro tells her, almost visibly puffing out his chest. "I took the taxi job to provide for my wife and daughter. My wife, she's still my friend even though we divorced. She lives next door."

He leads Eleanor by the hand to his balcony and the two of them stand looking out over the Caribbean - it glimmers like silk shot through with emeralds. He kisses her, softly and gently. "I want a girl like you, Eleanor," he tells her, earnestly.

"Someone who is honest, a good woman, not fake like so many girls here are. This ex of yours, you have to let him go and find yourself a new boyfriend. I didn't tell you, but the witchdoctor said you will find a new boyfriend," he continues, and the hope in his voice is heartbreaking. "He won't be rich by Western standards, but he will be good. And good for you."

She knows he's probably just trying his luck, but enjoys the moment, holding Pedro's hands and kissing. She doesn't feel like ripping his clothes off. She just can't see herself living here, dreams of Ernest Hemingway or not. It would be wrong to pretend otherwise.

"I need to pack for my flight tomorrow, Pedro, we better go," she tells him gently. "I will come back here when I can." She can't quite abandon his fantasy just yet. A new, kind boyfriend, a warm, sunny country; a new step-daughter; everything new.

She smiles at him, half wishing that she could stay. "I can't commit to anything yet. Not until the court case is over, but you are a kind and wonderful person, and I am glad to have met you."

He looks disappointed, but accepts her words. She kisses him again, thinking *this is the best I can offer.*

# Chapter 30

## Drug Smuggler

Eleanor has been in summer travel mode for months now, leather jacket, mini skirt, blonde streaks in her hair and a great tan. She feels confident and beautiful when Pedro bids her a tearful goodbye at the airport.

Then her mood changes. At the airline check-in a security guard comes up and leads her away. This surely isn't regular procedure. He takes her to a back room, all metal and concrete, with a wooden table and one chair.

"Sit down," he instructs, lifting her bag onto the table and inspecting the contents. "Why have you been to Cuba?" he asks, somewhat aggressively.

"I have a love of different cultures." She can't think of a better answer than the truth.

She maintains eye contact with the security guard while he roots through her dirty laundry bag.

Then she begins to get annoyed.

"When are you coming back?" he grunts, starting to close the bag up. She doesn't think this is part of the usual line of questioning.

"As soon as possible, I hope." She flashes him a smile and hopes it's over.

"Fine, you can go." He ushers her towards the metal grey door of the investigation room.

The flight is long and uncomfortable, reminding Eleanor why she hates long-haul travel. Finally, she reaches Lisbon for a two hour layover. The morning is dim, with grey clouds and she misses Cuba already.

She's grateful when she can just collapse onto the next plane and fall asleep on the way to Gatwick. She assumes that, since she just came from Lisbon, she can use the EU exit, and she heads towards it.

A big bloke comes striding over.

"Excuse me, madam, where did you just come from?"

"Lisbon."

"Then why does your bag tag say Cuba?"

"I came from Cuba via Lisbon."

"Right, well come over here – I need to search your bag."

Eleanor groans. It seems strange that this is happening to her twice on the same trip. Hopefully it's not a curse.

This guy is even more brusque than the officer in Cuba, and Eleanor's too tired to be patient. She audibly sighs in frustration when he begins searching through her bags, even opening boxes of chocolate bought as gifts.

"So, how long have you been travelling?" he asks.

"Eight months." It hits her that in two weeks, when she has her court case, she will have been separated from Ryan for almost exactly the amount of time it takes to make a baby. Nine months. And the lack of a baby, or even hope of one, is the whole reason she left in the first place. The irony is not lost on her.

"Give me your passport."

He glances through the pages, but all Eleanor can think about is the baby she will never have.

"How did you get the money to go travelling for this long?" he demands.

"I got made redundant." She doesn't feel like elaborating.

"By whom?"

"The Times, you know, the newspaper?" She replies in a deliberately condescending tone.

"The Times isn't making redundancies," he says with conviction. Eleanor wonders how on earth an airport security guy would know about hirings and firings within the media.

"I don't know why you think that," she tells him bitterly. "Call my bloody boss, I'm sure she'd love to hear from you."

"Everyone knows the Times is in high demand," he repeats.

"I wasn't wanted anymore, what else do you need to know?" she snaps.

"What are these documents?" He lifts up her envelope of divorce papers.

"Divorce documents. My court case is coming up."

She expects him to soften up and start feeling sorry for her at this point but it has the opposite effect.

"I didn't ask about your personal life!"

Now he's really crossed the line. Eleanor raises her voice, angry.

"You asked me what they were and I am telling you! I really don't see the need for you to be questioning me like this. And I got the same treatment when I left Cuba. What's going on here?"

"We've had a lot of drugs coming in through Cuba, Brazil, from Columbia and Peru. I can see from your passport you have been into Brazil on three separate occasions, and to all of these countries."

"Right." She realises they've pegged her as a potential drug trafficker. The overweight bulbous eyed man then starts digging into her bag of sanitary towels. Then he spots her iPad bag.

"You have to pay customs on this," he states matter-of-factly. "How much did you pay for it?" He opens the packaging and her heart sinks. She only bought it because it was cheaper in the US.

"Three hundred and fifty nine dollars."

Customs dude now looks really pissed off.

"That's under the tax threshold," he tells her gruffly. "Right, well, get a move on then."

She reminds herself to hold her temper. She has to get out of the airport before she can say anything stupid.

*At least it's a sunny day* she thinks, staring out the window of the black cab speeding her home. She feels a buzz of anticipation, thinking about the friends she can call up for terrace cocktails somewhere in the city.

But as soon as she's showered and changed she crashes onto the bed and drops into a deep sleep. Sure enough, the next day it's raining and her excitement at getting back and seeing her friends plummets.

Returning to London without Ryan feels unexpectedly awful; everywhere she goes she thinks about him. Illogically, she wants to see him, to go for lunch on the Thames with his mother, or to visit a quiet country pub with his family.

Instead, She writes him an email telling him that she has arranged for her removal man, Ed, to collect her things on Saturday and that Ryan should pay him £300 for clearing space in his apartment. Ryan emails immediately, in return, copying his lawyer into the correspondence.

"The removal of your things must be done in a certain manner. I have informed your lawyer of this and you will follow my procedures."

Well, fuck. His cold, controlling, dismissive tone sends Eleanor straight into rage. How dare he try to control this?

She closes her laptop with a snap and drops her face into her hands. Tears drop through her fingers, much to her surprise. She hadn't even realised she was crying.

She is still on Brazilian time, and filled with frustrated sadness. Ryan's refusal will incur further legal costs. She emails him back, resisting the urge to write the whole thing in caps.

"My lawyer has been on holiday and I was not informed of this delay in getting my things. I was expecting my stuff and I have no idea what you are doing. For all I know, you won't let me have it at all. I gave you the collection date ages ago and you didn't object then, why should you object now? Not everything has to go through our lawyers."

This time, there's no reply.

As she's back home and determined to confront her demons head on, the next day Eleanor manages to get a last minute appointment at her doctor's - she wants to get some answers about some extra bleeding she has been having between periods. It's one of the many things she's been pushing to the back of her mind for months.

The doctor pulls up her file.

"I see you had endometriosis two years ago and it was operated on," he says slowly.

"Yes. It's the same symptoms as before."

"Well, it's very common for it to come back. I'll give you some medicine to stop the bleeding. It's progesterone, which will shrink your ovaries so that you can't produce blood anymore."

"How long will I have to take the medication? Can I get it operated on again? Is this stress related?" Eleanor feels bewildered.

"You will have to take this every day until you reach menopause. They don't recommend operating on your condition as it can just return again."

"But that could be at least a decade away! And why can't I have a baby?"

"I am afraid it's very hard to get pregnant when you have this condition. And impossible if you're taking progesterone. What made you wait so long if you wanted a baby?"

Eleanor wants to scream at this guy that he might have a medical degree but he certainly has no PhD in communication. But she doesn't. Instead, she bursts into tears. a

"I've wanted a baby for a long time but my husband wouldn't give me one. I put some pressure on and then he didn't want to be married anymore. He's divorcing me now, so please don't ask me why I waited." The tears continue to stream down her face, and the doctor doesn't seem to know where to look.

He smiles curtly and says "I'll give you a prescription for some antidepressants also. And I'll schedule you in for a cervical smear test just in case the cells from your endometriosis are cancerous," he adds, as if it's just an afterthought.

Two days later, Eleanor emails Ryan again about her things. Eventually, he says he'll compromise on an earlier date for her stuff, but she is not to come to the house or be seen on his street.

It's as if he's ashamed of her. And she wonders whether he has rifled through her belongings. Is he intending to keep some of her stuff? The thought raises her temperature again.

Determined that she should at least be allowed to supervise the removal of her own things, she tells him so by email. She calls her trusted removal guy, feeling embarrassed.

"Ed, yes, how are you? Good..." She goes through the usual pleasantries, wondering how to admit that Ryan is once again controlling every part of this whole, excruciating process. "Yes. Unfortunately I'm not allowed to pick things up, so can you do the removal without me?" As usual, Ed is agreeable and to her relief, doesn't ask too many questions.

Ed is at Ryan's house at the appointed time, and appears at Eleanor's flat in Brick Lane with all her things. As she helps him carry the boxes in, she's retreating into the cupboard to cry so that Ed can't see her. All those weekend trips where Ryan and she slowly moved her stuff to his place loom up in her mind. They both seemed so excited about their future together.

Ed sees her red eyes and tries to cheer her up.

"You know, I really think Ryan is crazy," he jokes, "you should have seen his eyes! He kept bringing one thing out at a time and then closing the front door so I couldn't get inside. He poked his head out as if you might appear any minute with a machine gun!"

Ed cracks up laughing. Eleanor has to admit she feels a thousand times better and even laughs a bit. Then Ed's face grows more serious and he looks at her with more sympathy than she expects.

"Seriously, though, how much longer are you going to let this go on?" he asks. Eleanor lets out a long, exhausted sigh.

"I have no idea how long it will take," I tell him. "My family spent a lot of money on our wedding. Ryan let them waste it knowing that he didn't want to be with me. He knew I wanted a child and let me spend my last fertile years waiting for him to tell me it was time."

"What do you mean?" Ed asks, sympathetic.

"You won't tell him about this conversation, will you?"

"No, of course not."

"Well, two years ago I went to a fertility consultant," she tells him, and every word is painful. "They said I had enough eggs to do artificial insemination. I decided to have a child on my own. I went through all the tests and was going to do the treatment, but then they asked if I was married. I told them I was and they gave me a form releasing Ryan from the responsibility and legal obligation of being a father."

Ed looks shocked.

"Ryan wouldn't sign it. He said I was trying to trick him into having a baby and he refused to love the child once it was born. He would not sign the papers, even though they released him from all obligations. The clinic refused to go ahead. I didn't have a baby, I lost my job, and now I have a condition that makes it much harder to conceive. Instead of feeling bad and at least compensating me in some way, he's making me fight for crumbs. Even though his family are millionaires, he made me pay for our honeymoon."

She falters for a moment and pauses to compose herself.

"He took everything from me."

She knows she must look a mess, standing there with tears streaming down her face. She can't look at Ed and it's obvious that he doesn't know what to say. He gives her an awkward sort of half hug and brings in the rest of the boxes.

When he's finished and she is on her own again, she runs through the boxes of clothes and shoes and starts unpacking. As she unpacks, she realises that the bastard has kept all their wedding presents.

She sits among the boxes, feeling alone and overwhelmed.

*Why can't Ryan see he's treated her appallingly? Why does he think that he deserves to keep everything? Any woman in their right mind would have left him the way he treated her in their marriage. She stares at her sad collection of things and wonders how she ever let herself get taken in by him. Did he ever love her at all?*

# Chapter 31

# *Brick Lane Bagels*

Eleanor walks briskly down the street, collar up against what seems like a constant drizzle. She's been back in the UK for three days, and has just reached the end of a stressful day of financial paperwork for her impending court case.

Ryan has demanded to see her up-to-date tax records before he will disclose his own financial situation, so Eleanor has been wading through reams of paperwork with her accountant, making sure all her tax returns are in order. Eleanor hates this sort of thing with a passion but it seems like a necessary evil if she wants to fight for a decent divorce settlement from Ryan. She knows she'd been putting it off too long anyway, so maybe his ultimatum was the kick up the backside she needed.

But it was a slog, and right now she wants to get drunk. She's arranged to meet Vanessa at Coq D'Argent, a bar that tends to be packed with bankers and city workers. Vanessa's already found a sheltered spot on the roof terrace, and has a bottle of wine sitting in a cooler of ice. "I got vino!" Vanessa smiles her endearingly crooked smile and gestures at the two glasses. Eleanor doesn't need to be asked twice.

"God, this feels weird," says Eleanor, half way through her second glass. "All our adventures in crazy places, and we're back here again, like nothing's changed."

Eleanor has lost count of the number of times she's sat in this place after work, often with Vanessa, and very often eyeing up the rich men hanging out at the bar. That was back in the days when she was fully invested in Project Husband. If only she'd known what she was letting herself in for.

It seems ironic that, after so many after-work sessions plotting how to find the ideal husband, she's now drowning her sorrows about divorce papers and her soon-to-be-ex's courtroom demands.

"He did you a favour, if you really think about it," Vanessa reasons. "You needed to do your tax returns anyway, you can't keep ignoring that stuff."

Eleanor knows her friend is talking sense, and feels a rush of gratitude for Vanessa's straight-talking support. The bitter-sweet tang of the wine feels familiar and comforting, after so many months drinking whatever South American firewater happened to be available.

The two women drain their glasses and Vanessa gestures to the waiter to bring another bottle. "I know you're right, it's just that this is not how I wanted this to end. Court is so expensive, and you know what? I looked online today and my old apartment, one that Ryan advised me to sell when we first got together, is now worth £150,000 more. Why did I listen to him? Why did I let my parents waste so much money on our wedding? Why did I waste my last fertile years on him?"

Eleanor's not really expecting Vanessa to answer, she's just in desperate need of a rant.

"I wish so much I'd never met him."

"Love is blind," says Vanessa, patting her arm. "Just remember how cheap he was, how he had so much stashed away but was always penny-pinching. You've been through a lot, and you'll get through this." Vanessa gives Eleanor a hug. "Let's just get pissed and you'll forget all about it. Maybe find a guy to go home with tonight, a rebound lover might be exactly what you need!"."

The booze is rushing straight to Eleanor's head. She realises that she's badly out of practice when it comes to drinking wine, but tries to keep pace with Vanessa. In the past, the pair could easily put away a bottle each before getting started on the spirits. True to form, Vanessa returns from the bar with a tray of sambucas as soon as the second bottle is finished. Another tray follows, this time brought over by a group of City-types who had evidently been eyeing them from a distance. Eleanor drinks a shot of some kind of Polish vodka, and the room begins to swim. "Ness, I'm just going to the loo, be right back. Can you look after my things?"

Eleanor wakes up with a pounding headache. Her mouth tastes like something crawled inside there and died. For a second she can't remember where she is, but gradually makes out the familiar shape of her own bedroom furnishings in the semi-darkness. But why is she so warm? What's that noise? Eleanor rolls to the other side of the bed, and comes face to face with a snoring, undeniably handsome, dark-haired man. He's stark naked. Eleanor's consciousness is slow to make sense of anything, but she's pretty sure she's naked too amid her tell-tale tangle of sheets.

She gropes for her handbag and phone at the side of the bed, where she always leaves them.

The man beside her begins to stir and she stares at him through a lingering fog of alcohol.

"Umm, who are you?" she's startled at the way her voice croaks into the silence. "What – how did I meet you? Where's my handbag?"

He grins blearily.

"I'm Joe. I met you outside zer Bagel Shop last night in Brick Lane. You asked me to break in because your bag and keys it was stolen."

She's trying to place his accent... Eastern Europe somewhere...

*Wait, did he say her bag was stolen? Fuck!*

"My bag was stolen?" She repeats. Her brain is numb and it feels like someone is playing the timpani drums just behind her right eyeball.

He shakes his head and says yes, which confuses the hell out of her.

"You vere drunk and couldn't get into your house," he explains in his thick accent. "A damsel in distress. I helped you break in and zen you... repaid the favour."

"Did we use protection?" She asks, a knot of fear in her stomach.

"Yes," he says, shaking his head again. Eleanor wonders if she's somehow so hungover that she's forgotten the way 'yes' and 'no' gestures are supposed to work. "You had condoms in ze house." He looks pleased with himself, but Eleanor's nagging sense of fear doesn't subside. Those condoms were years out of date.

It's not the most pressing issue right now, though. Her bag, with three years of tax return receipts in it as well as her iPad, mobile, and purse, is missing.

"Joe, can I borrow your phone, please? I need to make a call…"

He hands it over and she calls her own mobile number. After two rings, a familiar voice answers, and Eleanor nearly passes out with relief.

"Oh my God! Thank God it's you, Vanessa. You have my phone! What happened last night?"

"Yes, you nutter," the weak voice on the other line suggests Vanessa is almost as hungover as Eleanor. "What the hell happened to you last night? I sat in that bar for ages, waiting for you to come back from the toilet. In the end I gave up and took your stuff home with me; some blokes were with us at the bar wondering where you went, too."

"Bloody hell…you're my hero, Vanessa! Do you have my other stuff? My iPad, and the tax papers in the brown bag? Oh my God, I absolutely love you."

"No worries, come around later. I'll be here all day, nursing my mother of a hangover."

Vanessa hangs up and Eleanor wonders if she's gone straight back to sleep. The idea of a slump back into unconsciousness is appealing right now, but there's the small matter of a handsome stranger in her bed to attend to.

"So sorry," Eleanor begins, "please remind me how we got in here? I have the first half of the story figured out but now I need the rest."

"I risk my neck and climb into window. Crazy, I never do a thing like this if I'm not drunk!" He laughs, and looks even more ridiculously handsome. Eleanor's eyes are groggily taking in the brown, muscled limbs, tousled brown hair and green eyes. No matter how hard she tries, she can't remember a thing.

She must have realised she had no keys after she left the bar and started to walk to Vanessa's – it's the only reason for her to pass the Bagel Shop on Brick Lane. Or maybe she was getting a post-pub bagel to try and sober up.

A vague memory of asking her neighbours to let Joe climb from their balcony to hers surfaces. She feels as though she ought to be embarrassed, but can't muster up the energy. Nothing much phases her neighbours, anyway.

"Oh," She says feebly, and Joe laughs again. "Where are you from, Joe?"

"Bulgaria."

Bulgaria.

Eleanor gets up to have a shower, self-conscious at having to walk out naked in front of the stranger in her bedroom. At least her tan will show off her curves in the best light. Her new short crop has given her a confidence boost, too. She knows it draws attention to her eyes, and they're her best feature.

Brushing her teeth after taking a shower, Eleanor looks in the mirror and lets out an audible yelp. Her right eye is completely black.

"Joe..." She calls from the bathroom. "What the fuck happened to my eye?"

Joe's still draped on top of the bed covers when she sticks her head around the door.

"You are falling into the ladder when you hold it for me," he says, "but you don't have black eyes last night."

She slides back into bed with him, her head still swimming. Joe starts kissing her - wet hair, black eye, and all.

After several rounds of the most spectacular sex she can remember, Eleanor starts to wonder if she asked Joe to help her because he was there, or because she has particularly good taste in men when she's drunk. By late afternoon, the need for food and water drives them out of bed.

Joe gets her a bagel and coffee, and pays for the tube to Vanessa's since she has no cards or cash. She's surprised that he wants to come with her, but appreciates his company in her wobbly state. He holds her hand like they have been dating forever, which strikes her as a little odd, but she clings on all the same. When they reach Vanessa's flat, Joe abruptly stops and kisses her, stroking her hair behind her ears. She loves it when men stroke her hair. She feels her heart leap in her chest. What is happening to me? She asks herself.

"Can you feel this?" he asks, softly. "This special connection?" She doesn't answer, but knocks on Vanessa's door by way of distraction.

Vanessa answers the door in her pyjamas, and her jaw drops. She takes in first the black eye, then the handsome stranger on her doorstep. "It's a long story," Eleanor says, touching her sore eye. She clocks her friend's eyes widening as Joe introduces himself. Eleanor can't help feeling a little smug - Vanessa's usually the one pulling the hot guys. Eleanor gives her the biggest hug possible for rescuing her belongings, and Joe carries the bags through the door with a polite wave. Vanessa flips Eleanor a thumbs up behind his back, and winks.

Eleanor's too hungover to face the tube again, so she's more than happy to pay for a cab now she has her money back. "Hey, baby, how about we stop and get some beer or wine?" Joe says in a low voice, leaning close to her in the back of the taxi.

Eleanor finds herself agreeing. It's only early afternoon, but maybe a few hair of the dog drinks will make her feel less groggy and shake off the lingering sense of doom that seems to have accompanied every hangover since she entered her late 30s. She asks the cab driver to stop at the next off-licence. "Oh baby, sorry, I have to go to a bank, can you pay? I pay you back later."

Already the 'baby' is starting to grate, it sounds too familiar for somebody she's known less than 24 hours, but she lets it go.

"Sure, no problem," She says pressing a 20 pound note into the checkout operator's hand.

It's just a few minutes' walk from the off licence back to Eleanor's place, and they open a chilled bottle of white as soon as they get in. They stick the stereo on and chat about anything and everything. Eleanor feels her headache and anxiety dissipating, and she's grateful for the distraction from fretting about her life.

Eleanor wakes up with Joe's arm flung across her chest, and with a worse hangover than the day before. Aside from the pounding headache, there's a crushing sense of anxiety. It's Sunday morning, she's been drunk or hungover since Friday, and she's lying in bed with a man she knows next to nothing about. Her body's aching from all the sex, and she's not sure they used protection. To make matters worse, Joe is sitting up in bed and making noises about getting more wine.

She pulls a disgusted face, and he raises an eyebrow. "How about something else?

"You like cocaine?" He's so matter of fact, it sounds like he's asking if she would prefer almond milk to cow's milk.

She hasn't touched anything illegal since Colombia, but right now it starts to sound tempting. Anything to keep her mind from drifting back to the court case and dwelling on what Ryan might be doing at that very moment. At least she can tell herself she's having more fun than he is. "Sure," she says, "how much do you need?" Once again, she reaches for her purse.

He returns with vodka and mixers as well as the coke, and the day goes by in a giddy blur. By 10pm, Joe's phone is beeping incessantly with texts from friends asking him to go out. He tells Eleanor that everybody's meeting at the Bull and Crown. Does she want to come too? She does not, she's seen the rough-looking types that spill out of there.

Suddenly Eleanor just wants to be alone, and to take a break from the drinking and snorting. Everything hurts, and she's exhausted. Joe puts up a half-hearted resistance when she says he should go out, but eventually agrees to meet his friends and come back in a few hours. Eleanor flings herself onto the bed, wiped out. She's still not even fully over her jet lag.

She wakes at 4am to an empty bed. She has no idea if Joe arrived and couldn't get in, so she dials his number in case he's locked out. He answers after a few rings, and there's electronic dance music bleeping in the background. "Elaine! Come to the party!"

*Elaine?* Eleanor's self-esteem takes another body blow. He tells her he'll be back soon, but doesn't sound very convincing. Eleanor lets sleep take her away again, and wakes to an empty bed and no missed calls. The whole episode feels grubby in the harsh light of sobriety, and she's hit with a wave of longing for the wholesome Sundays she used to spend with Ryan - all cooked breakfasts, lingering over the paper, and bracing walks to country pubs. Suddenly, more than anything, she wants her old life back. She wonders what he'd think if he could see her now - black eye, hungover, on a coke comedown and lying in sheets stained by sex with a stranger. Not fully trusting herself not to drunk dial him at some point, Eleanor deletes Joe's number from her contacts.

A knock at the door. *Oh god, not him?* Eleanor just wants to be left alone to cope with her hangover and her misery by herself. She peers through the spy-hole and sees Darren, her upstairs neighbour. His usually-calm face has anger written all over it. She opens the door sheepishly, and Darren does a double take when he spots her black eye. But if he feels any concern, he doesn't show it. Without mincing his words, Darren tells her he doesn't appreciate "Some random guy on my balcony in the middle of the night."

Just when she thinks her mood can't get worse, Darren adds: "And nobody wants to see and hear you having a shag in the communal garden, either, Jesus Christ."

Eleanor feels a punch of self-disgust in the pit of her stomach. An unwelcome memory comes creeping back.

"Oh my God, I am so sorry, Darren. I don't know what I was thinking, obviously it won't happen again…"

"It better bloody not," says Darren, and he turns on his heel and walks off. She feels sick, she'd always had a polite relationship with her neighbours.

Eleanor picks up her phone and texts the one person she can trust not to judge her.

"Ohhh my God, Vanessa. Apparently I had noisy sex in the communal garden. It's coming back to me. I was trying to get Joe to climb over my backyard fence but ended up going myself. I vaguely remember falling off the wooden ledge and onto the grass. I suppose that explains the black eye. And once I was down there I think I just went for it with Joe. Oh my God, Ness, I am dying of shame here."

Her phone flashes: Vanessa's response comes via the medium of emoji - shocked face emoji, crying laughing emoji, and the see-no-evil, hear-no-evil monkeys.

Eleanor slumps on her bed, weighed down by a crushing self-loathing so heavy it feels almost physical. Just a year ago she was married, with a good job, expecting to start a family. How did it come to this?

She scrolls through Facebook for distraction, but finds herself looking through her own wedding photos, somehow envious of her own former life. Who is that beautiful bride with a fabulous ceremony and a handsome groom? It no longer even feels real.

She wonders what Ryan is doing. Certainly not crawling back into bed at midday on a Monday morning, she thinks. It's hard for her to believe that he's probably sitting in their marital home, just a couple of miles away.

Maybe he's talking business on the phone, or walking the dogs and having a post-lunch cigarette. Maybe he's lunching with his retired friends at the Clivedon Hotel, sitting on deck chairs in front of the perfect manicured lawns. She can picture him, shifting around in his deckchair in that anxious, constantly-fidgeting way of his.

She wonders, just as she does every day, how the person she once considered her best friend could have become her greatest enemy. She wonders why she constantly feels like she's treading water at best, drowning at worst. She feels like she's submerged in water, and wonders just how far under she will have to get, before she can finally break to the surface and get over everything.

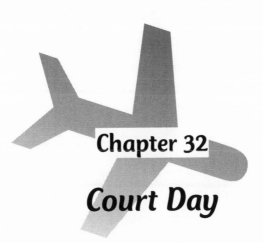

# Chapter 32

# Court Day

It's Eleanor and Ryan's big day, part two. This time there are no smiling relatives, and no makeup artists waiting in the wings. The bride and groom will not be exchanging rings and pledging undying love.

The divorce hearing is the painful sequel to the fairytale wedding. And just like on that first fateful day, Eleanor has barely slept a wink. She's filled with heartbreak and confusion, and rage. She's just about able to face the harsh reality that Ryan never truly loved her, and that she wasted the last of her childbearing years with him, but she needs something to make the bitter pill easier to swallow. Ryan's a rich man, and Eleanor's damned if she's going to let him leave her broke as well as broken.

She doesn't feel she's asking too much of the man who once professed to love her. All she wants is to claw back the money her parents spent on the wedding, and receive some compensation for the loss of her job, her emotional pain and suffering, and her rapidly fading years of fertility. She spent the entire night lying awake and consumed with frustration that Ryan was making her beg for crumbs from his millionaires' table.

Eleanor arrives at the court an hour ahead of time, and heads straight to the nearby Starbucks, where her stoic aunt Catherine has agreed to meet her for moral support. Not for the first time, Eleanor feels a pang of resentment that her parents haven't come over from America to help her through the hardest day of her life. After three strong coffees in quick succession, Eleanor feels less like she's sleepwalking, but the caffeine does little to help her frayed nerves.

She's returning from her fifth anxiety-induced bathroom trip when aunt Catherine steps through the door.

Eleanor's relieved to see her, and grateful for the quiet, unquestioning support. "Well, who would have imagined that we would have ended up here?" Catherine says, pulling out a chair. "Nothing for me, thanks, dear. If I have tea or coffee now I'll be needing to nip to the loo all afternoon."

She looks as sad as Eleanor feels. "We all thought Ryan was a gentleman, who would have thought he would treat you like this?"

Eleanor sighs with weary resignation. "Certainly not me, and I thought I was a good judge of personality."

She grabs her coat. "Shall we go before I chicken out?"

The two women head towards the courtroom arm in arm, Eleanor feeling so weak from anxiety and lack of sleep that she finds herself almost relying on her dainty, elderly aunt to keep her upright.

They approach the court house together, and Aunt Catherine doesn't attract a second glance from bored-looking staff at the entrance security check. Her small handbag passes through the metal detector with no problems.

Her aunt looks cool, calm and collected, but Eleanor feels her own pulse racing. She hadn't thought about court house security when she packed the Cuban witchdoctor's bottle of voodoo piss into her bag for good luck. She doesn't fancy having to explain *that* to the civil court.

Her panic lessens when she sees there's no airport-style clampdown on liquids, and sure enough, her smart black Chanel tote bag passes through the scanner without setting off any alarms.

Eleanor's long red hair extensions are back and looking immaculate, and she's taken the time to painstakingly apply her 'natural' makeup and dress in the tailored Miu Miu pencil skirt, Joseph blouse and L.K. Bennett heels that she usually saves for boardroom meetings.

She almost giggles at the fact that she probably couldn't look less likely to be smuggling contraband South American urine into the courtroom.

Her slick look is also very much at odds with the court house ambience. The place looks like something from a dark British TV crime drama, with its scuffed '70s decor and small, square courtrooms opening off from dark, tunnel-like halls with stained grey carpets.

Eleanor whispers to Aunt Catherine that if the look the architect was aiming for was 'claustrophobic and oppressive,' then they succeeded. She's trying to make light of it, but the atmosphere feels truly suffocating, and she can feel her pulse starting to race again.

She's beginning to feel lightheaded, and is about to take a seat on one of the hard metal benches when she catches sight of her barrister, Edward, striding confidently down the corridor towards her. His presence feels akin to taking a strong sedative, and Eleanor feels immediately reassured by his no-nonsense approach and his dapper Italian suit.

True to form, she can't help finding him disconcertingly attractive, with big, blue eyes that look directly into her own.

She finds his educated, upper class tone of voice both soothing and confidence-boosting, and manages to greet him calmly, even though she feels on the verge of tears.

Edward leads her into a small side room whose peeling, yellowed paint suggests it was last decorated way before the indoor smoking ban came into force. "So give me the general details of your case. I've read the information your lawyer Alicia sent over, but it's always a good idea to hear it first hand."

Eleanor paints a picture of her five years with Ryan in broad brush strokes, trying to keep her emotions out of her voice and her description of events.

"I need to know, did you contribute to home bills while you lived together?"

Eleanor was not prepared for the question.

"No, Ryan wouldn't let me, he insisted on paying the bills."

She pauses for a second then adds, "But I paid for almost all activities that we did outside the home. It seemed a fair contribution, as Ryan doesn't have a mortgage."

Edward raises an eyebrow and lets out a kind of lawyerly huffing noise. Eleanor's heart drops - she suspects that this is not good.

"That's not good." He confirms her fear. "Any household bills in your name would prove that you contributed. Without that, there's a chance that the judge might not rule in your favour. You might come out of this with nothing. Are you aware Ryan is even denying you ever lived with him?"

"I paid for a cleaner, you can see it in my bank statements," she offers, "although he was reluctant to agree even to that. And I wanted to pay for cable TV but he refused to have it installed." She trails off mid-sentence, *wait, what? Denying she lived with him?*

Eleanor begins to feel a wave of nausea. It's like the blinkers have come off and she's seeing Ryan's true nature for the first time. *He didn't want a trace of me living with him.*

Suddenly, it all makes sense. Ryan's refusal to let her install Sky TV in his home, his reluctance to let her hire a cleaner. Her mind flashes back to the time when her father was driving Ryan's car and got a parking ticket, and Ryan had written a strange letter about how he and Eleanor lived separately but he would foot the parking ticket bill all the same. She'd been confused at the time but put it down to him just trying to make a false show of generosity.

Now the truth hits her like a punch in the gut. *He had been planning for this divorce right from the start.*

The realisation floors her and she can't focus on a thing the barrister is saying. She can see his mouth moving but he might as well be speaking Russian for all the sense she can make of it.

"Eleanor, are you ok?"

Edward's gentle hand on her shoulder brings her back to reality. He's still talking about worst and best case scenarios.

"If all goes well, based on your case I would say you could be awarded anything up to £50,000. Have you seen his trust fund details?"

"Yes £1.8 million, divided between five people."

"Yes, well that's from 1998," the barrister tells her. "The portfolio of properties in his personal fund will be worth significantly more now, closer to £15 million."

Eleanor shrugs. She has resigned herself that little, if any, of this money will come to her.

"I believe Alicia has uncovered some documents pertinent to the case," Edward is still talking, but Eleanor feels so sick with nerves and bitterness that she can barely pay attention.

"Apparently it's something to do with his godfather's will."

Eleanor winces at the memory of Ryan's shady behaviour at the time his godfather became ill. She wonders how any documents related to the will could possibly impact on the court case.

Her thoughts are interrupted when a young woman with poker-straight chestnut hair peers around the door. "The judge is ready to see you."

Through the open doorway, Eleanor can see Ryan sitting rigid in one of the uncomfortable chairs.

He looks straight towards her. His eyes look almost manic. Like he's taken a whole packet of Pro-Plus or a gram of Peruvian marching powder. It's the first time Eleanor has seen him in several months, but he seems to have aged several years. His hair is more salt than pepper, and his hair is receding at the front to meet the bald spot at the back.

She glowers back at him, willing him to hear her thoughts:

*"Make my day, you fuck. I am ready to take you on."*

He looks away and gets up, following his barrister. Eleanor has to follow behind with her own lawyer, watching Ryan's bald patch bob up and down as they all shuffle along the corridor.

They all file into a small room. It's not what she expected a courtroom to look like. It feels disconcertingly like a school exam room, with a bunch of chairs in front of what could be a headmistress's desk. The judge presiding does indeed have an imposing, schoolmarmly air. She looks so stern that Eleanor feels like she's been caught smoking behind the bike sheds.

But she realises she is no longer afraid. Her racing heart begins to slow down and she feels a strange sense of calm settle over her. Whatever happens, even if she doesn't get a penny from Ryan, she knows she will be free of him once she leaves the courtroom. She can walk away from him and never look back. A clean slate.

Ryan's barrister addresses the judge.

"Your honour, we have proposed to strike this out as a waste of court time. This woman has no case for claim and shouldn't be allowed to further take up my client's time."

Eleanor shoots her barrister a worried look. This is the first either of them have heard about a move to dismiss the case.

The judge looks Eleanor up and down, before turning her attention to the paperwork in front of her. The court room is so silent that the rifling of paper sounds painfully loud to Eleanor's ears.

The judge turns to Eleanor's barrister.

"What do you say to this?" the judge asks.

"Your honour, we were not aware until now ago that a motion to dismiss this case would be filed, so I am afraid we haven't had time to prepare a counter argument."

Edward's poise and calm demeanour gives Eleanor hope. At this point she could not bear to hear "case dismissed," and to be shrugged off as a waste of everybody's time.

"We believe that our client has a needs based case." Edward addresses the judge, who nods encouragingly. Eleanor's heart is in her throat.

"From the facts in front of me, Eleanor Nosworthy has a maintenance case and your motion, Mr Rankton, to throw out the case is dismissed."

The judge spreads out the papers in front of her.

"What I can see here is two people who have spent an awful lot of money on lawyers. I am demanding that you take this case right through to completion today. I see no reason this case should continue after today. Please leave my chambers to think about numbers and come back in half an hour."

If she didn't think it would be used against her as proof of insanity, Eleanor would have jumped up and kissed her.

The judge slams the gavel on the table and they all get up and shuffle back through the ridiculously long hallway to their respective meeting rooms.

"That went well," Eleanors barrister assures her. "It looks like she's going to vote in your favour, hopefully it's just a case of determining how much she awards you."

They sit and wait. The time seems to be speeding up and slowing down by turns, as if someone has a magnet to the hands on the clock on the wall, pushing and pulling it backwards and forwards. Eventually they are summoned by the poker-haired lady once again.

Like a herd of cattle, everybody moves slowly back to the courtroom.

The judge peers up as they enter the room.

"Mr Rankton, what kind of settlement have you come up with?"

"Your honour, my client is willing to pay £10,000 to Ms Nosworthy," Ryan's barrister says.

"On what basis has he come up with that number?" the judge asks. Her voice is emotionless, but her eyes have narrowed slightly.

Eleanor's fingers close around the arm of her chair. This 'offer' wouldn't even come close to covering her legal fees. "He feels it is what he can afford, your honour." The judge raises an eyebrow.

"I have your client's financial details in front of me and he can afford a lot more than that," she deadpans.

She turns her steely gaze towards Eleanor.

"How long will it take you, Ms Nosworthy, to get another job?"

"At least six months, your honour," says Eleanor's barrister. Eleanor finds it frustrating that she can't answer the judge's questions herself.

"And it says here you were previously paid in the region of £65,000 a year, is that correct?"

"Indeed, your honour. We propose Mr Rankton pays her six months of living expenses."

"Noted," the judge accepts, briskly. "You say that your client has been ill?" she is speaking to Eleanor's barrister now.

"Yes your honour," Edward says. "She's been very ill. We have a letter from her doctor.

She needs an operation, but has been waiting many months for this as she no longer has the funds to pay for private health care."

The judge inspects her paperwork before turning her penetrating gaze onto Eleanor who tries not to squirm. It isn't easy to hear her medical details discussed like this. "How much will this operation cost her?"

"Your honour. She had this same operation on her womb two years ago when she was hoping to conceive, and it cost £6,000. We don't know how much it will cost this time, but the condition has returned."

The judge nods, as though inviting him to elaborate. "And she was unable to conceive?"

"Your honour, for many years, my client has wanted nothing more than to be a mother. She longed to raise a family with Mr Rankton. But despite assuring her during their courtship that he wanted to start a family as soon as they were married, Mr Rankton did not honour those promises. He refused to help my client to deal with her fertility issues, either financially or emotionally. He point blank refused to discuss starting a family from the moment they were married, and did not even maintain a physical relationship with my client."

Eleanor squirms in her seat.

The judge looks at her paperwork and announces: "I award Miss Nosworthy £30,000 pounds." Eleanor lets out the breath she has been holding. It's not nearly enough to make up for what she has been through, but at least it's something. "You can now leave the room to negotiate, but based on her need for an income for the next six months and £10,000 for her operation I feel the settlement should come to this amount. We can reconvene in half an hour in my chambers."

She pauses and looks at the four of them. "May I remind you it's in both your interests to settle this today?"

The judge bangs her gavel again. It sounds like a full stop.

They walk in single file down the hall. Eleanor feels oddly numb.

"We had a good result today," Edward assures her. "We don't want this case to come back to court where a different judge might see things differently."

Eleanor's numbness recedes, as she does a quick bit of mental arithmetic. After the court costs and the operation, she won't be left with much to live off while she looks for work.

She's trying not to feel sorry for herself, but can't help thinking that perhaps the judge should have taken into account the fact that she lost her last natural childbearing years to a loveless marriage. And there seems to have been no consideration for the emotional distress caused.

Half an hour later, they go back to the court room yet again.

Eleanor looks at Ryan, now sitting bolt upright in his chair on the other side of the room. He has put on weight and his belly is poking through his wrinkled, blue striped shirt. He looks like an overgrown kid trying to play teacher's pet, she thinks. Like he's about to say 'Miss, miss, it wasn't my fault!'

Ryan keeps his head straight ahead and averts his eyes from hers, but she's sure he can feel her eyes on him. He has that tell-tale clenched jaw he gets when he's angry.

"Excuse me your honour," Ryan's barrister pipes up. "My client does not see why he should be responsible for his former wife's medical bills when they have been separated for a year."

"Your honour, Ms Nosworthy was not even forced to take the redundancy," the barrister continues. "She didn't need to leave her last job."

Eleanor feels a surge of rage. She tries to keep a lid on her anger, but knows the entire courtroom must be able to see the dark flush of it on her pale cheeks.

The judge looks, "Mr Rankton, you have purposefully allowed this to go on for far too long. You have the means to settle, now leave this courtroom again and don't come back until a reasonable offer is made."

The judge bangs her gavel, a little more forcefully than before, and once more they all leave the room.

It's past 5pm, and members of courtroom staff are emerging from other rooms, coats slung over their arms. Eleanor can see her aunt outside waiting for her.

"We've got to wrap this up - tell him I will take £26,000," she says, suddenly just wanting the day to be over. Wanting the whole thing to be over.

"You don't have to settle on that," Edward says.

"I hope you realise that you are signing away your rights to everything Ryan has by signing this."

He's filling in some paperwork that evidently needs Eleanor's signature. "Just one moment, I'm going to put your offer to him."

Edward leaves the door ajar, and Eleanor watches him enter a small room where Ryan is sitting with his own lawyer. Then she sees an insufferably smug expression spread across Ryan's sweaty face.

"Golly, well done!" his lawyer claps him on the back.

Ryan gives a loud laugh and Eleanor feels her blood boil.

"Do you still want to take the settlement?" Edward asks, returning to the room.

She is tired. She is tired of this whole thing. She just wants it to end. She looks down at the paper in her hands.

"Another day is another £4000 in fees for your services, right?"

There's a chance she won't get any more, and there's a chance that she will end up with nothing, but watching Ryan gloat is too much for her. She tears up the agreement.

"I think you're making the right decision, Eleanor," Edward says.

Eleanor is shocked to see her lawyer, Alicia, rushing down the corridor towards them.

"The judge has agreed to see us one last time," she says, and Eleanor is astonished. "I have some important information. Quickly, come on."

Ryan and his legal team are already inside the courtroom— his barrister is screeching at the judge that this is all highly irregular. The judge sharply advises her to sit down. Her voice is sharp and Alicia pats Eleanor's hand.

"Mr. Rankton," the judge addresses Ryan. "I have been reviewing the paperwork associated with this case, and I would like to give you one last chance to make a sensible decision."

"My client has offered a settlement of £25,000 and Ms Nosworthy has accepted it," Ryan's barrister snaps.

"Have you accepted it, Ms Nosworthy?"

"No, my client does not accept the offer." Alicia interjects. "I have found information which I think indicates Ryan did not have Eleanor's best interests at heart when he asked her to marry him."

"Is that so?" the judge raises an eyebrow sharply.

"When investigating Ryan's financial situation, I found a payment for £1.5million that went into Ryan's account just days before he applied for a divorce." Alicia begins, and the judge nods for her to continue. "I demanded under the financial disclosure act to get more information on this transaction. It turns out it was money from his godfather's will, held in escrow. The money was dependent on Ryan marrying a woman." Eleanor's heart lurches.

The barrister hands the judge a copy of William's will, with the terms and conditions.

Eleanor struggles to breathe. Her heart is racing so hard and so fast she's scared that it's going to literally break. She feels dizzy and sick and short of breath. She feels like she's been hit by a two-tonne car.

*Ryan needed to marry a woman – any woman – in order to satisfy
the terms of his godfather's will. Ryan had often mentioned his godfather's
rather 'old-fashioned' views. Reading between the lines, Eleanor had long
suspected he harboured some rather nasty and bigoted opinions. Had he
heard the rumours that Ryan might be gay?*

*And Susan knew Ryan's godfather well. She must have known the
terms and conditions of the will. Was this why they broke up?*

Eleanor's mind is racing, trying to make sense of this new
information.

She feels sick. Here it is, in black and white, confirmation that
her husband never felt a thing for her at all. Eleanor was convenient,
nothing more.

She can see Ryan struggling to look composed.

"Mr Rankton, the documents I have in front of me suggest that
you have not engaged in marital life in an appropriate manner," she
says.

Once again Eleanor feels as if she is going to faint – she is relieved
she is sitting down. "As far as I am concerned, you have not fulfilled
your duty as a husband, in any shape or form. You appear to have
prevented Ms Nosworthy from contributing to the household and your
refusal to start a family or maintain physical relations had a significant
negative impact on her mental and emotional wellbeing."

"I don't think you have been honest with her, or with me. This,
Mr Rankton, is a mistake."

She pauses and everyone in the courtroom freezes. Eleanor has
now held her breath long enough that she's afraid her lungs might
actually pop out of her chest.

"I have here a document, provided by you, in your own financial
disclosure, that suggests that if you had not married Ms Nosworthy,
you would not have been entitled to any part of the substantial
inheritance you have just received," the judge holds up a copy of Ryan's
godfather's will.

"Now, hang on –" Ryan protests, but the judge silences him with
a look.

"It would not be wise to interrupt me again, Mr Rankton," she
informs him, coldly. "You received this information a week before
you proposed to your spouse, and based on the behaviour you have

displayed throughout your marriage and the contempt you have shown both your wife and this court, I strongly suspect that this is the only reason you married her in the first place.

"The emotional turmoil you have wilfully caused this young woman is not only cruel and uncalled for, it is also indefensible," says the judge, and for a moment Eleanor imagines her towering above them, dispensing justice like some ancient God. "With this in mind, I am awarding Ms Nosworthy half the inheritance you received for the total of £750,000. I believe she has earned it."

Eleanor is in total shock. She can't possibly have heard what she thinks she's heard. She is dimly aware that Ryan has lost all his composure, and is now yelling at the top of his voice.

Eleanor stares, open-mouthed, at her barrister and lawyer.

"What did she just say?" She asks.

Ryan is being manhandled out of the courtroom by two burly looking security men who wouldn't have been out of place on a rugby pitch. He's still shouting hoarsely. Eleanor risks a glance behind her and catches a glimpse of her tiny aunt kicking him in the shins as they hustle him past her.

She laughs – a high, slightly crazy laugh.

Edward is grinning widely and trying to talk to Eleanor, but she has literally no idea what he's saying. The judge smiles at her from her table.

"That is the will of this court," she says, and bangs her gavel.

"Eleanor – do you know what this means?" Alicia asks her as she looks dumbfounded and confused. "Eleanor?"

"What does it mean?"

"It means he can't contest it!" she beams. "You've won! He has to pay up in two weeks or he'll be prosecuted."

"I won?" She asks incredulously.

"Yes!" Alicia laughs.

"I won," Eleanor says, aloud, savouring the words. "I won..."

She turns to her aunt, who is peering into the courtroom, curious.

"I won!" Eleanor shouts, louder than she intends to.

Her aunt squeals and runs over, hugging her tighter than she has ever been hugged. Her phone rings and she squirms out of her grasp. It's Ryan's mother. Eleanor's heart almost stops.

She doesn't want to deal with her right now – so she lets the call ring out.

She gets to the bottom of the steps, feeling truly free for the first time in five years. She can start over – can find a new job, find a new place…she can even start Project Baby on her own. She knows there are ways to do it, now she has the money.

This is the fresh start she needed.

Her phone buzzes again and she checks the screen. Ryan's mother has texted her. She takes a breath and opens the message.

*Eleanor – Ryan called. Congratulations. You deserve every penny. I cannot apologise enough for my son's behaviour. Keep in touch!*

A giggle escapes Eleanor's mouth.

*I won.*

# About The Author

Emerging novelist Rachel Rigby has worked as a financial journalist for over 20 years, writing for publications including the Financial Times, Mergermarket, DealReporter, Media Week, Sunday Business, and Breaking Views.

She is a regular guest speaker at corporate events, and has appeared on live television on CNBC and CNN.

She has a BA degree in History and Government from Smith College, Massachusetts, USA.

A true international citizen, Rachel was born in Scotland to a Scottish father and American mother. She spent her early years in Kenya, where her parents were stationed as charity workers. She returned to London in year 2000.

She has also lived in the USA, Brazil, Hong Kong, and Portugal, and currently lives in London with her British-Brazilian daughter.

Rachel loves to explore the world, and her aim is to visit 100 countries before the age of 60. At the time of writing, she has already ticks 85 countries off the list! She is currently debating which 15 countries she should see in the next 9 years.

When she's not busy working, writing, and parenting, Rachel loves to scuba dive, and has completed over 500 dives at locations around the world. She also loves to paint, and to discover new countries and cultures through food, culture, and art.

Under and Over is Rachel's first novel.

If you want to read more about Rachel, please visit https://rachel-rigby.com/

9781664118300